PRAISE FOR DOUGLAS NILES'S
Watershed Trilogy:

"Douglas Niles and I worked on *Dragonlance* together. This book captures all the adventure and romance of *Dragonlance*."

—Margaret Weis

"The landscapes are sweeping and complete, and the various races are believable ... new and exciting. The detailed pantheon of gods gives the readers a deeper and richer understanding and appreciation of the motivations of the characters. Any reader will come away from this book fully satisfied."

—R. A. Salvatore, bestselling author of
The Demon Awakens

"Douglas Niles ... writes so well that his characters come to life after only a few lines. ... This middle book ... keeps the trilogy moving."

—*Starlog*

*Don't miss the exciting second novel of the
Seven Circles Trilogy*

Worldfall

CIRCLE AT CENTER

Book One of the Seven Circles Trilogy

Douglas Niles

ACE BOOKS, NEW YORK

This is a work of fiction. Names, characters, places, and incidents either are the product of the author's imagination or are used fictitiously, and any resemblance to actual persons, living or dead, business establishments, events, or locales is entirely coincidental.

CIRCLE AT CENTER

An Ace Book / published by arrangement with the author

PRINTING HISTORY
Ace trade edition / June 2000
Ace mass-market edition / July 2002

Copyright © 2000 by Douglas Niles.
Cover art by Jean Pierre Targete.

Visit our website at
www.penguinputnam.com
Check out the ACE Science Fiction & Fantasy newsletter!

ISBN: 0-441-00960-3

ACE®
Ace Books are published by The Berkley Publishing Group,
a division of Penguin Putnam Inc.,
375 Hudson Street, New York, New York 10014.
ACE and the "A" design are trademarks
belonging to Penguin Putnam Inc.

PRINTED IN THE UNITED STATES OF AMERICA

10 9 8 7 6 5 4 3 2

This book is dedicated to Tim Brown, Jeff Grubb, Rob King, Troy Denning, Steve Winter, Lester Smith, Don Perrin, Dave Gross, and SDS. My fellow Alliterates: teachers, critics, and friends.

In the perfection of the warrior
does the Seventh Circle
achieve her ultimate ideal.
But perfection is honed
to a double edge,
for the shiny blade of humankind
reflects the specter
of apocalypse.

From the Tapestry of the Worldweaver
Chronicles of a Circle Called Earth

Prologue

Dawn swelled on the horizon beyond the volcano, and Natac was glad that he would see this place once before he died. The celestial unveiling was utterly serene, lavender merging into rose and pale turquoise, all advancing with a majesty that tightened his throat and brought tears to his eyes. The swath of soft blue expanded skyward from the conical mountain, and he dared to imagine that the eternally smoldering summit gave birth to this day. Scarcely breathing, he wondered at the perfection of the dark cloud that twisted upward from the massif to hang like a serpentine banner over the Valley of the Mexica.

It seemed fitting that his life would end here, today—that Natac, who had provided so much blood, so many lives, to the hungry gods, would at last offer his own heart on an occasion of high honor to the fearsome immortals who ruled over every aspect of the world. He would give his life on the altar of his enemies, the Aztecs—or Mexica, as they arrogantly styled themselves. Yet Natac was content to know that his heart would sustain the gods and allow life here and in his own homeland of Tlaxcala to continue to flourish.

On this day Tlaloc and Tonatiuh, voracious gods of rain and sun, would be feted with many hearts. Deities of wind and nightfall, of motherhood and spring, of *maíz* and catfish and herons, would gain strength from grand ritual. And of course, here in the city of the Mexica the Aztec god of war, Huitzilopochtli, would be offered the greatest number of hearts—Natac had been told that a river of blood would flow from his temple during the ritual.

For a moment he felt a small glimmer of regret, knowing that Tezcatlipoca, the Smoking Mirror, would receive little acknowledgment from the Mexicans, who were far more concerned with the needs of their insatiable war god. Silently, Natac extended a prayer into the cloudless dawn. He thanked Tezcatlipoca, who was also called the Enemy on Every Side, for his warrior's life, and for the many enemies he had been allowed to take in battle. Every one of them had been sanctified to the glory of the gods, had died knowing that his lifeblood would sustain the world, and Natac had no doubt but that the immortals had been mightily pleased by these blood offerings. As he prayed, preparing for his journey to black Mictlan, the realm of death, he realized that never in his life had he seen a finer sunrise.

And he knew that there was no better way to die.

A guard, a respectful young stripling apprenticed to an Aztec Eagle Knight, stood uneasily several paces away. He was a big fellow bearing an obsidian-tipped spear, garbed in practical armor of padded quilting that protected him from groin to shoulders. Still, he had certainly heard of Natac's reputation—doubtless he believed that the prisoner could have broken his neck at any moment.

But perhaps he perceived another truth as well: The Tlaxcalan Natac had no thoughts of escape. Since the moment he had been fairly captured in war, he had known that his life was ended. He was satisfied to be playing his final part in tasks laid out by godly scheme.

By the time the eastern sky was blue, people moved around the temples, pyramids, and other ritual sites that came into Natac's view. Priests lit torches and beacon fires, while slaves swept the flagstone surface that would soon be the host of a great gathering. A servant approached with a copper plate, offering *maíz* and beans to the honored captive. Natac, his eyes still fixed to the brightening eastern sky, made no acknowledgment of the offer—he had purged his body over the previous days, and would leave no unseemly waste on the sacrificial altar.

Soon Mexicans by tens, and then by hundreds, began to filter through the constricting entries into the plaza. Some were richly dressed nobles trailed by courtiers and slaves as they sought good vantages for the day's rites. Others were families, fathers bearing little girls on their shoulders, boys playing warrior, darting about with make-believe bows, spears, and maquahuitls. Already the square grew crowded as people filled the broad swaths of space between palaces and pyramids.

Finally bright light flamed along the western ridge crest, a swath of brilliance creeping slowly downward, driving back the lingering shadows of night. The great pyramid, whitewashed stone steps flanked by bright, serpentine images painted red, blue, and green, gleamed with supernatural brightness. Atop the steep structure stood two altars, sacred sites dedicated to the rain god, Tlaloc, and martial Huitzilopochtli. Viewing the lofty temples, rising so far above the great city of the Mexica, Natac couldn't help but feel awe.

Closer by he saw the flat simplicity of the Warstone, a circular platform only a few paces in diameter. Four stairways, perfectly oriented to the earthly directions, led to the top of the ceremonial stage, which was just over a tall man's height above the ground. On that stone surface, later this morning, Natac would die.

Like countless others today, his blood and heart would be given to sustain the fierce and immortal gods. But of all those who would perish, only Natac was being granted the high honor of sacrifice by combat. As any priest could affirm, this ritual killing of a well-known and esteemed war leader of Tlaxcala would be highly pleasing to the god of war.

By the time the line of sunlight had marched well down the western ridges, the great plaza of the Aztecs teemed with people. Intrigued by his first peaceful encounter with his lifelong enemies, Natac unabashedly looked around. He easily identified the nobles, each trailed by a slave who bore aloft an ornately decorative banner proclaiming his master's exalted status. The feathery pennants floated like kites over the crowd, in colors of yellow and sapphire, crimson and violet, brighter than any hues Natac had ever seen.

In fact, *everything* was more colorful, here—from the plumage of heraldry and headdress to the splendid mantles worn by so many, and the twisting mosaics of bright paint that framed the ceremonial centers and palaces in this vast square. For the first time Natac's warrior's mind perceived how the Aztecs, by controlling all the realms around intransigent Tlaxcala, had strangled his homeland, blocking trade for the brilliant plumage of the Maya country, or the pure, vivid dyes from the coast.

The young guard blinked in surprise, but made no objection when Natac walked toward the Warstone and, with measured paces, ascended to the raised platform. From here he could see over the heads of the gathered throng of Mexica commoners, and even above the feathered heraldry of the nobles. A hundred paces away the great skull rack, with its many thousands of fleshless, bony heads, was a shadow-encased trophy of Aztec might. Other structures rose above the people, too—every one of them grand and imperial, many with ornate façades or columned porticos, pristine whitewash accented by brightly colored paint.

He found himself facing the Smoking Mirror, the temple of Tezcatlipoca atop its own angular, terraced pyramid, of a size eclipsed only by the great pyramid itself. From this great edifice the jaguar image of the Enemy on Every Side looked from his temple over this corner of the world. Natac shivered, touched by an uncanny sense that he looked into that Smoking Mirror and saw his own death reflected in all of the men he had killed.

Turning his gaze to the purpled slopes, he admired the distant borders of the valley. Closer, the ridges surrounding the great island city and its lake were green with forests, verdant woodlands now brightening in spreading day. To the southeast, the warrior beheld the lofty magnificence of that great volcano. North, and still farther east of the conical summit lay Tlaxcala.

For a moment he let himself remember his wife and sons. His devoted bride had, somehow and almost unnoticed by him, become an old woman, but he knew that her comfort would be assured by his estate. He was also confident that his boys, young men now, would prosper, and he was content that his people would be free of Aztec domination for a long time.

And they would know that he died well.

As to the gods, Natac suspected that they cared little whether the hearts were offered in Tlaxcala or here in the city of the Mexica. Regardless, they should continue to favor the peoples of the world with good fortune, plentiful sustenance, and benign climate.

His mind summoned another memory, the image of a pretty little girl. Her name was Yellow Hummingbird, and she had been the only sister in a house of rambunctious boys. She was his daughter, and she had been gone for many years now—she had been given to the rain god as a virginal twelve-year old. Now he wondered if he would see her in Mictlan. The thought gave him a pang of anticipation, a sense of hope for a mysterious future.

There was a ripple of excitement and murmuring as black-clad priests—hair, garments and skin matted with crusted blood and other filth—moved ostentatiously through the crowd. People shrank back, frightened by the fierce aspect and profound stench of these holy men, many of whom carried smoking braziers, while others trilled upon flutes or brayed loud prayers. Some made their way with deliberate haste up the steps of the great pyramid, and soon colored smoke billowed into view from before those lofty altars. Conch horns blared exultantly from all corners and heights of the plaza, while the music of the flutes swelled into a shrill cacophony.

Huitzilopochtli, naturally, would receive the first sacrificial victims in this place that was by its very existence a testament to the Aztec war god's might. A file of men, dressed like Natac in plain, clean loincloths, began ascending the steep steps of the great pyramid. Those who would die today, the *xochimilche*, were mostly captives taken by the Aztecs in their battle with Tlaxcala. Additional victims were slaves, purchased and then given for sacrifice by a master who had reasons to seek the favor of this god or that.

Natac knew that the *xochimilche* leading the serpentine queue were Aztec warriors who had been crippled, maimed, blinded, or otherwise injured in the recent battle. Their days of combat ended, they offered themselves willingly to the ravenous god of war. The sight of their struggles moved Natac as he watched the first, a man whose left leg had been cruelly split by an obsidian-bladed maquahuitl. A priest climbed to his side, but the warrior brusquely waved away any suggestion of assistance. Instead he bore his weight on the good leg, using his hands to lift himself higher in a series of careful hops.

Finally the crippled Aztec stood at the top of the pyramid. Now more horns moaned, long and deep and quavering, as a ring of priests closed in. Though he couldn't see inside the alcove of the temple, Natac knew that the fanged and bestial image of Huitzilopochtli, maw gaping hungrily, crouched beside the flat altar where the *xochimilche* would be stretched backward.

With startling brilliance, the rays of the rising sun struck the roof of the temple, and a patina of gold shimmered downward, creeping toward the sanctified altar. Suddenly the priests stepped back and the crowd buzzed with excitement as a blaze of viridescent color flashed amid the dark clerics. The brilliant plumage cloaked a man, a regal figure in a rich mantle of aquamarine hummingbird feathers, head crowned by the emerald-green tail feathers of the quetzal bird. With sudden recognition and awe, Natac knew this was Moctezuma himself, the Eloquent One—ruler of the Aztec empire.

The noble figure raised a hand and sunlight flickered momentarily off a blade of sharpened, fire-orange jade. The knife dropped, and in another moment Moctezuma's other hand came up. At the same time the advancing sunlight engulfed the company before the temple, dazzlingly bright and magical. In the clutching fingers, tiny with distance but crimson and bright as a ruby, a human heart pulsed in the first rays of the sun.

The golden sheen continued down the face of the pyramid as, one by one, more *xochimilche* advanced into the temple. Moctezuma himself performed several more sacrifices, then stepped back to allow the priests to assume the ritual butchery. Natac knew that each heart was placed into the maw of the god of war, no doubt reverently at first, although inevitably the grotesque jaws would soon overflow. Additional hearts would ultimately fall in a heap upon the floor while the gory work cast a layer of blood over the priests, the temple, and the entire top of the pyramid.

While the original file of *xochimilche* still marched forward, a second column now ascended the pyramid steps. This group was led by priests to the altar of Tlaloc, the other temple commanding a site on the city's most sacrosanct vantage. The neighboring altar, too, was soon drenched in blood as heart after heart was ripped forth, here in the name of the goggle-eyed deity of rain.

For a moment, Natac's eyes wandered to the farther pyramid, where the altar of Tezcatlipoca was currently unattended. His enemies would extend this ancient god a token feast of hearts, he was certain, but not in sufficiency deserved by the patron deity of Tlaxcala. He reminded himself that in his homeland many Aztec hearts would fill the jaguar-maw of the Enemy on Every Side, but he remained aggrieved by the sight of this Mexican temple's neglect.

Before the war god's temple on the great pyramid, the drained corpses were hauled away by burly priests and unceremoniously tumbled down the side of the blocky structure. A streak of bright red appeared at the lip of the sacred platform, quickly centering in the gutter beside the wide stairway. Oozing thickly, blood began to trickle down the chute, drawing a murmured reaction from the gathered throng. Natac watched the precious liquid intently, knowing that its appearance signaled the commencement of his own part in the festivities.

Several priests approached, magically parting the crowd that had closed around the Warstone, and Natac was pleased to see a familiar figure beside them. The Eagle Knight Takanatl was resplendent in his ceremonial costume, wooden helmet forming the beak of a great hunting bird—which was in turn an opening that framed the warrior's stern face. Takanatl's arms and calves were bare, but a rich mantle of white cotton and green parrot feathers framed the black and white of his eagle plumage and distinguished him as a man of great status. Now he came to stand at the base of the Warstone, gray eyes meeting those of the man he had captured.

"Greetings, Natac," said the Aztec, in the Nahuatl tongue that was a common link between their intractable nations. "I am pleased to anticipate your final battle."

"It is my honor to die before you—and to offer my heart to the gods," Natac replied. He felt a strong rush of affection for the proud Eagle Knight, his foe in countless battles over the last thirty years, and a momentary regret that he could not have the honor of slaying this man today, then journeying with him to Mictlan.

"Does your hand cause you pain?" asked Takanatl.

For a moment Natac was surprised. Then he looked down at the swollen purpled lump at the terminus of his left arm, remembered the rockslide ambush, crushing boulders trapping him, leading to his capture. The infection had become severe, swelling through his wrist and into his forearm.

"No—I have given it no thought," he replied truthfully.

"I am glad." Takanatl smiled broadly, relishing his memories. "It was my good fortune that you were coming through the pass as my men released the rockslide. The Eloquent One himself took notice!"

"Ah, but the pursuit that led me into that pass was a fine thing!" Natac declared. "To see tens of thousands of Aztecs fleeing the battle, leaving hundreds behind as offerings for Tlaxcalan temples. It was a victory worth dying for."

"Indeed." The Eagle Knight's expression became rueful. "Moctezuma was less than happy with the other details of the battle." Takanatl's eyes flickered to the great pyramid, and Natac was reminded that not all *xochimilche* went willingly to the realm of death.

Only then did the Tlaxcalan note a file of other warriors behind Takanatl, less grandly dressed than the Eagle Knight, but capable and sturdy-looking men nonetheless. There were a dozen or more, waiting impatiently for the ceremonies to be concluded, encircling the platform and congregating at the bases of the four stairways leading to the Warstone. Natac wondered which of them would kill him—and he hoped, for the honor of the Smoking Mirror and Tlaxcala, that it would not be the first man to try.

The closest, a hard-eyed young man of great size and scowling features, stared at Natac unblinkingly. He bore a sharp-edged maquahuitl and wore padded quilting to pro-

tect his chest, belly, and shoulders. Obviously this young
warrior would commence the battle with the Tlaxcalan
xochimilche, and as Natac admired the man's sinewy limbs
and the deadly weapon in his hand, he admitted to himself
that the Aztec had a good chance of winning.

Four priests climbed the stairways to the top of the Warstone. Three prayed loudly, wafting incense while the
fourth offered Natac his ritual weapons: a slender pole of
wood, which was merely a spear without the customary
head of sharp stone; and a parody of a lethal maquahuitl.
Instead of the razor-edged shards of obsidian characteristic
of the bladed club, the edges of this weapon were marked
only by colorful tufts of feathers.

Once again Natac was reminded of his useless left hand,
knowing that the injury rendered the pole an ineffective
tool.

"I choose only the ritual sword," he said, taking the blunt
maquahuitl from the priest's outstretched hand. Natac
watched impassively as the smelly, filth-encrusted cleric
hastily withdrew, apparently fearful even of this ludicrously
armed enemy.

The four holy men raised their voices in long, ululating
cries, a summons intended to draw the attention of the god
of war. The file of sacrificial victims on the great pyramid
came to a temporary halt as the eyes of seemingly all the
populace turned to the ceremony on the Warstone. Natac
was awed by a fresh appreciation of the crowd's size, which
must have numbered a hundred times a thousand and more.

The hard-eyed young Aztec bounded up the seven steps
on the east side of the platform, sharp-toothed weapon
held ready for a slash to right or left. Natac waited in the
middle of the circle, the feathered club held casually at
his side. The young man stood a hand-span taller than the
Tlaxcalan, and he all but sneered at the wounded, under-
armed *xochimilche*—a broken warrior who was apparently
resigned to a quick death.

It was in that arrogance that Natac foresaw the Mexican's doom. Predictably, the man charged with a sudden sprint, raising his maquahuitl high above his head. Those stony eyes never wavered from Natac's face as the weapon came down in a swooping rush, a blow deadly enough to cleave a man from crown to sternum—if the attack could but strike such a mortal target.

Calmly meeting his attacker's cold glare, Natac feinted to the right with a drop of his shoulder. The move turned the Aztec slightly in his onrush—and then the Tlaxcalan dodged left with whiplike quickness, bringing his club through a bone-crushing smash into the wrist of his enemy's weapon-hand. The lethal maquahuitl clattered to the stone as the man staggered to a stop at the far edge of the platform. With a quick rush Natac charged and kicked the Aztec in the chest, sending him toppling backward off the Warstone.

The stunned Mexican clutched his broken wrist and groaned weakly on the ground below as two priests closed in, but Natac didn't watch as the clerics hoisted the vanquished warrior to his feet and started him toward the great pyramid. Instead, the Tlaxcalan turned to the south stairway, where another determined warrior—a scarred and stocky veteran armed with a javelin as well as a maquahuitl—ascended to do glory for his god and his nation.

His predecessor's fate apparently gave this warrior little pause, for he, too, charged with headlong speed. Natac started to retreat, but then sprang forward to stab his club, head forward, between the careless guard of the Aztec's javelin and sword. The blow smashed into the padded quilt with enough force to crack the man's ribs, and he collapsed soundlessly. Looking at his enemy's lips, which were already blue, Natac knew he had died from a bruise to his heart.

The Tlaxcalan crossed to the other side of the platform while more priests dragged the warrior and his weapons away. Since the man was already dead, they wasted no time in slicing open his chest and raising that stilled heart toward the sun. The slick red muscle was then placed in a wicker basket and borne toward a nearby temple by a swiftly trotting apprentice.

Before the end of that brief ceremony, an Aztec warrior had climbed the west stairway to the Warstone. This man bore only a maquahuitl, and he moved with feline grace, balancing on the balls of his feet and weaving back and forth unpredictably. He might have the quickness to become a Jaguar Knight someday, Natac suspected—if he had tenacity and strength, as well.

It was at that moment that the Tlaxcalan was struck by an odd thought: His own death at the hands of one of these young Mexicans would greatly exalt that aspiring warrior's status. The victor might be granted command of a hundred warriors, or even that exalted knighthood in the orders of the Jaguars or Eagles. The notion gave rise to a strangely calming sense of tranquillity.

The graceful Aztec approached with caution, circling warily. Natac allowed him to hold a respectful distance as the two combatants faced each other like dancers, slowly pivoting around the stage. They sparred with quick slashes, the clash of their weapons harsh in the still plaza until, as if by mutual plan, they separated.

Over three sharp exchanges the young man revealed quick reflexes in defense, but also displayed a predilection for a high, slashing attack. The fourth time that catlike swipe whipped past his face, Natac was ready with his own counter. He ducked into a full squat and struck from his crouch, a vicious sideswipe that shattered the Aztec's knee. Sobbing in disbelief, the promising young warrior was borne toward the temple of the war god as a fourth fighter, this one climbing up the north stairway, took up the challenge.

And he was followed by a fifth, and then a sixth.

When the seventh man fell, knocked senseless by a blow to the head, several heartbeats passed without the next challenger appearing. A freshening breeze cooled the sheen of sweat that glistened on Natac's nearly hairless skin. He was vaguely aware of a stillness, a sense of awe that had quieted the once boisterous crowd.

When he looked around curiously, he saw the reason: Sternly upright amid the framing plumage of slave-borne fans, Moctezuma himself had come to observe the duel.

The Eloquent One, most powerful ruler in the known world, was resplendent in his bright feathered mantle and the brilliant headdress of long, emerald-colored plumes lofting half again above his own height. A large plug of turquoise and gold graced his lower lip, which was now curled downward in a pout of displeasure. In Moctezuma's wake crowded a retinue of nobles anxious for a look at the Tlaxcalan *xochimilche*. Yet all left space around the Eloquent One, and hastened to back away from the ruler's every gesture or move.

The next warrior climbed to the Warstone, no doubt deeply honored by the exalted observer, and charged at the waiting Natac. A heartbeat later, larynx crushed by the wooden club that had long since lost its feathered totems, the Aztec tumbled away to a slow death by strangulation.

"Enough!"

The cry came from the Eagle Knight, Takanatl. The veteran stared at the purple-faced corpse, then looked to Natac, his expression tortured. Finally the helmed warrior turned toward Moctezuma, kneeling and bending his face to the ground with a graceful sweep of plumage.

"My lord—I beg leave to battle this captive myself! I offer his blood, and my own, in the name of Huitzilopochtli!"

"This is the man Natac, captured by you in the recent battle?" Moctezuma, still scowling, regarded the Tlaxcalan. As Natac returned the Aztec ruler's gaze, he realized that he was the only person in the plaza who was looking upon that face—the tens and tens of thousands of Mexicans in view all had their eyes turned respectfully downward or away.

"Aye, lord." Takanatl spoke from the depths of his bow, addressing the ground at his feet.

"And he has been your foe, and ours, for these last three tens of years?"

"Aye, lord. Always Natac was at the forefront of the attack. He has killed and captured many of our warriors. In the battle of seven days past, it was he who led the pursuit that turned our withdrawal into a disgraceful rout."

"A shameful outcome," Moctezuma declared, addressing Takanatl sternly. "This Tlaxcalan's capture was the only moment of good news in a valley full of disasters. I should hate to have it be the cause of your own loss, as well."

"My lord—I beg you! He is the greatest foe I have ever known. Behold today: Even in capture, in defeat, he decimates my company and slays my best men!"

"Very well." Moctezuma turned to Natac. "You have heard my Eagle Knight. I shall grant his request, an honor I bestow graciously. But know, Tlaxcalan, that he shall be your last opponent. If the gods so decree, he will give your heart to the gods—but should you defeat him, the honor of the Mexica will compel me to set you free.

"Now"—the Eloquent One turned to Takanatl again—"commence the fight."

The Eagle Knight leapt up the steep stairway in three giant strides. His dark eyes, warm with relief, pride and martial fervor, met Natac's, and the Tlaxcalan felt a profound wave of joy.

"I regret the rules of the ritual—it would be better if you had a real weapon," the Eagle Knight said.

"I know. But the club serves well enough." Natac allowed himself a tight smile, seeing his dark humor reflected as chagrin in the Aztec's eyes.

Natac met Takanatl warily, deflecting a dazzling series of slashing blows—attacks that steadily whittled away at the battered stick that was the Tlaxcalan's only weapon. Yet despite the onslaught, his wounds, and the strain of the previous duels, he had no sensation of fatigue. Indeed, he felt as if he was only now gaining true understanding of his deepest skills. He ducked and weaved and dodged, supple as a gust of wind swirling around a great bird of prey in flight.

The Eagle Knight's shield deflected each smashing blow. Several times the obsidian teeth of his maquahuitl sliced Natac's skin and flesh, and for the first time that day Tlaxcalan blood spattered onto the Warstone. Quickly following each advantage, the Aztec veteran pressed his enemy hard, and now Natac was forced to evade the whistling slashes with ever-increasing desperation.

He lunged right, desperately skipped left as the jagged sword slashed. Only then did he see that the attack had been a feint—now Takanatl used his shield as a weapon, smashing the hardened wood against Natac's injured, swollen hand. Pain shrieked through the warrior's nerves, staggering him, dropping him for a brief instant onto one knee. For the first time he saw defeat, certain death, awaiting him at the end of this fight.

But not yet. His mind still clouded by agony, Natac lunged to the side, dodging a nearly fatal swipe. Forcing his thoughts into focus, the Tlaxcalan groaned and slumped in apparent weakness.

And then Takanatl made his mistake. A vicious blow curled past Natac, gouging the Tlaxcalan's bicep, but this time the *xochimilche* dived past the shield of his lifelong foe. Springing to his feet in a lightning attack, Natac swung the wooden club past the bottom of the Aztec's wooden helmet, smashing the Eagle Knight where his neck merged with his shoulders.

Bone snapped as Takanatl grunted in surprise, then collapsed onto his face. He lay motionless, making a strangled, choking sound.

Quickly Natac knelt and turned the Eagle Knight over. The Aztec's eyes were open and focused, shaded by an intense fear that was very disturbing to see in this battle-hardened veteran. His head lolled to the side, drool trickling from his mouth until the Tlaxcalan wiped his lips and gently turned him to face toward the sky.

"I am already dying ... my body is gone from me ... my legs ... my arms ... like smoke. ..." Takanatl's words were weak, forced out by lungs that strained just to sustain his life.

"I am grateful that we journey to Mictlan together, my enemy," declared Natac sincerely. He took one of the Aztec's hands, surprised at the utter flaccidity of the limp fingers.

"Yes, my life-enemy. It seems that the gods have conspired to keep us ... together ... even beyond. ..."

Takanatl coughed again, a violent spasm that flecked his lips with foam, and then the Eagle Knight was still. His eyes, sightless to views in this world, stared in the direction of that pure blue sky.

"Enough of killing my warriors!" cried Moctezuma, his rage a scythe that shivered through the Mexican crowd. "Go back to Tlaxcala and be done with my city!"

For a moment Natac blinked, startled, even tempted, by the prospect of walking away from this place. But then he remembered the peace he had made with his gods, the destiny that had stood before him with this dawn, and he was disappointed in his own momentary weakness.

"My lord, you do me high honor ... as I have intended high honor to the gods. Please allow me to bestow that honor with my heart and my life." Only then did a pragmatic and decisive thought occur to Natac. He held up the swollen hand, and the black lines of blood poisoning were clearly visible to the ruler of the Aztecs.

"And in any event, it seems that the wound inflicted by Takanatl's ambush will see to the end of my life. My time as a warrior is finished."

The Eloquent One, no doubt considering the recent toll upon his own fighting men, looked skeptical at Natac's words. Yet he continued to listen as the Tlaxcalan pointed to a nearby temple, the lone edifice atop its pyramid. The site was conspicuously silent, empty of activity amid the panoply of festivities.

"I ask that my heart be offered to the Smoking Mirror. Doubtless you know that Tezcatlipoca is the patron god of my people. It is in his honor that I have waged a lifetime of war, and to his honor that I would dedicate my death."

Moctezuma laughed a sharp, bitter bark of sound. "You choose sacrifice on the altar of the Enemy on Every Side? Somehow, that seems a fitting end to this ceremony."

Priests flanked Natac as he descended from the Warstone to continue his journey toward the realm of death. The crowd parted, allowing the *xochimilche* and his clerical escort to cross the plaza, circling the great pyramid close enough to see the blood pooling at the base of the stairs. Finally they approached the pyramid of Tezcatlipoca. A surge of anticipation filled Natac as he thought of the black mountains of Mictlan and the dangerous and exciting journey he would soon undertake. So it was with firm steps that he started up the steep stairway of stone.

Atop the pyramid, Natac could at last see the dazzling lakes that surrounded the island city of the Mexica. Sunlight sparkled in broad swaths, liquid silver shimmering to the verdant horizon. Closer, he saw the vast plaza and surrounding streets, all thronged by crowds, while the canals beyond were thick with canoes. Banners floated and lofty headdresses danced above the people like magically enchanted snakes and birds. It was a wondrous scene, a perfect vision of man's crowning achievement as allowed by the benevolence of the gods.

Finally the priests closed in and Natac laid himself across the altar without any assistance. Now his eyes turned upward, to the sky of that perfect blue. He felt a fleeting moment of sadness as he beheld the surreal hue, knowing that in the blackness of Mictlan he would miss such beauty.

He smelled shit on the nearest priest, and that made him sad, too.

Then the knife was there, blocking his view of the sky, plunging, cutting his chest with a shocking rip of pain. In a brief moment the agony was gone, and Natac felt only numbness as he stared into the grime-smeared face of the leering holy man. A filthy hand came forward, and he was vaguely aware of fingers penetrating, pushing into his flesh.

He strained for breath, but there was no air.

Blackness fringed his vision, a circle swiftly drawing tight. Then Natac saw his own heart, red and bright and dripping, pulsing with the last vestiges of vitality.

Finally, the darkness was everywhere.

And in the black infinity he sensed a woman. Her musk surrounded him, a tangible spoor that teased and cajoled, moving him with a raw and sexual summons. The feeling intoxicated Natac, drew him with a promise of unprecedented delight.

Even so, he was rather startled to find himself utterly, tumescently, aroused.

PART ONE

1

A Sage-Ambassador

Know that it is carved in the *Tablets of Inception:*

The Seven Circles remain, and in their balance stands the hope of all futures.

The First Circle, called Underworld, is the realm of rock; it lies below.

The Second Circle, called Dissona, is the realm of metal; it lies across the Worldsea, in the direction of metal.

The Third Circle, called Lignia, is the realm of wood; it lies across the Worldsea, in the direction of wood.

The Fourth Circle is Nayve, sacred realm of flesh. It is the center of the Worldsea, the center of all.

The Fifth Circle is Loamar, realm of dirt; it lies beyond the Worldsea, in the direction that is neither metal nor wood.

The Sixth Circle is Overworld, and it is the realm of air; it lies above.

The Seventh Circle is the universe called Earth, realm of water; it lies in the directions of everywhere and nowhere.

Belynda read the words again. She knew them by heart, but there was always comfort to be gained from the calm repetition, the silent mouthing of text reciting the fundamental order of the cosmos. Yet, for some reason, today even the massive, gold-bound tome—her personal copy of the *Tablets of Inception*—was not enough to calm a vague sense of disquiet. An edge of tension thrummed in the back of her mind, a sensation she was unable to banish.

She found her eyes drifting, seeking the cloudy globe that rested so snugly in its alcove. There was no glimmer of light in the milky glass, nothing to suggest the powerful magic she had worked only a few minutes before. But the memory of her failure lingered like a sour taste, casting a pall over the rest of the day.

Decisively she rose and crossed to the magical sphere perched on a marble pedestal of classic simplicity. Belynda placed her hands on the smooth surface, already cool.

"Caranor . . . hear me. Please heed my call," she whispered, using the pressure of her hands to squeeze the words into the glass, vaulting her magical message into the distant wilds of Nayve. She placed extra force behind the summons, a nudge that should awaken the enchantress if she were sleeping—though it was unthinkable that any dignified and proper elf would be asleep this long after the Lighten Hour.

And the sage-enchantress Caranor was a particularly industrious elf. She lived alone, as did all the most powerful spell casters, but she was ever laboring to help the less fortunate members of her race. Yet even at her busiest, Caranor should have heard, and replied to, the magical call of the sage-ambassador.

The knock on Belynda's door was like a sudden crash of thunder and she gasped, sitting upright with a start that put a crick in her neck.

"What?" she demanded crossly, and then immediately regretted her harsh tone. "Please, come in," she said in a more inviting voice.

For a moment there was only silence beyond the solid

oak door to her apartments and meditation chambers. Finally, she heard one soft word:

"No."

She sighed, smiling in spite of herself as she recognized the speaker. She addressed the door politely.

"I'm sorry, Nistel. I promise that I'm not mad at you— or anybody, really. Now, won't you *please* come in?"

"You won't yell?" The voice was injured pride tempered by a tremolo of worry.

"I promise."

The door opened to reveal a person who was reaching upward to turn the knob. His face was masked by a bush of white whiskers, a beard that hung straight down to a point just below his belly. He continued to cling to the brass doorknob while he scrutinzed Belynda, clearly ready to flee at the first sign of displeasure.

"See. I'm not yelling." Belynda forced herself to smile, coaxing the gnome forward with a gesture. "Now, was there something you wanted to tell me?"

"What? Oh yes," Nistel admitted. "The delegates . . . you know, the elves from Argentian? They're here. They've come to the College to see you. They said you knew they were coming."

"Yes, I knew," Belynda replied, her sigh this time reflecting deep exasperation. The elves were her own people, but even so she had to admit that they spent overmuch time complaining. Of course, in her role as sage-ambassador she was compelled to listen to those complaints, soothing worries as much as possible. No doubt that was why she had begun to find them so irritating.

"Should I send them away?" asked Nistel, concerned.

"No, no. Of course I'll see them. Have them wait for me in the Metal Garden, beside the Golden Fountains."

"Very well, my lady." The gnome bowed stiffly, his rigid formality telling Belynda that he would just as soon have sent the elven delegation hastening back to their homeland.

He hesitated for a moment, and the elfwoman sensed that something else concerned Nistel. "What is it, my friend?"

"Just . . . well . . ." The gnome fidgeted in a great display of reluctance, but Belynda knew that he wanted to speak. Finally he could contain himself no longer. "A giant came. To Thickwhistle. I just heard."

The news was startling. "What would a giant want in a big nest of gnomes?" wondered the sage-ambassador, thinking aloud.

"No one knows," declared the gnome. "But it's pretty strange, and that's for sure." The little fellow shivered nervously—strangeness was an unfamiliar occurrence in Nayve, and experience had shown him that it generally presaged trouble and disruption.

Nevertheless, the ever-dutiful assistant withdrew to carry Belynda's message to the elven delegation.

Listlessly she returned to her reading table, but left the massive volume of the *Tablets* open to the pages of the Cosmic Order. It would be comforting, she hoped, to see those verses before her when she returned at the end of what promised to be a trying day.

She took her time getting ready, for a while merely wandering through the sumptuous chambers of her ambassadorial residence, eventually pausing long enough to drape a shawl of white silk over her slender shoulders. A word of command whisked a door closed across the entry to the messaging globe's alcove. The panel matched the deep wood grain of the wall, and was virtually undetectable. Slipping tiny feet into diamond-studded slippers of silver foil, she examined herself in one of the full-length crystal mirrors lining the wall of her reception room. The shimmering gold of her ambassador's robe rippled over her skin, outlining a figure that might have looked frail to one who did not know her: slender limbs, breasts small and firmly pointed, a belly that was flat and framed by narrow hips. Her blond hair—the color maintained by a mixture of herbal dyes—was swept back from a high, unlined forehead. Belynda's ears were typically small, delicately pointed at the lobe. It was the chin that distinguished her elven face as one of unusual strength and character. Square and stern, it lacked the narrowness common in her race, and many had remarked that it was this straightforward visage that had allowed her to progress to a position of such high honor.

Examining the serene expression, seeing her cool blue eyes reflected in the flawless glass, Belynda sighed again. She wished that she could actually feel the calm dignity embodied by the image in the mirror.

Her preparations were concluded as she donned a circlet of silver wire, a control for her long, golden mane. Still, she was in no hurry; instead of taking the direct route through the College halls she decided to take the outer paths to the garden. The glass doors opened soundlessly as she murmured the word of command, and she stepped into the private refuge of her small, walled garden—another mark of the status awarded to a sage-ambassador.

Trilling songbirds leapt into the air as she came outside. The canaries and bluebirds flew in cheery circles, a fluttering escort ready to herald her crossing of the grounds. Today, however, Belynda decided that she didn't want the ostentation, and curtly shooed the birds back to their perches in her rose trees. Sulking, they settled to the branches, and she felt even worse than she had before.

Passing under the arched gateway that gave egress from her garden, she faced the Center of Everything, and here, at last, her mood lifted—at least slightly. The Silver Loom dominated the view, rising toward the sky from the center of the circular, verdant valley. Mounted in a broad dome of crystal that was surmounted by a higher dome of gold, the argent spire lofted every bit as tall as the summit of a great mountain, and symbolized the unchanging purity of the Fourth Circle.

For a few moments Belynda was content to know that within those domes the Goddess Worldweaver was busy at her weaving, and that her labors would assure the continuity of halcyon Nayve. Hearing a deep thrumming, a sound of power that she felt in the pit of her stomach, the elven sage knew that she had emerged just in time to witness the casting of the threads. She held her breath, as awestruck now as she had been the first time she beheld this daily ritual.

The songbirds grew still and it seemed that the very wind held its breath as a bright glow came into view at the base of the spire. The illumination flared into a ring of fiery intensity nearly equal to the brightness of the sun. Then, slowly at first, the glow began to ascend the lofty spike of silver. Faster and faster it climbed and, as always, Belynda found that she was holding her breath as the casting approached its climax.

Racing to the top of the spire, the bright glow reached the end and exploded into the air, sending balls of sparking fire crackling and weaving upward. A hundred or more of these fiery globes hissed into the air, each trailing smoke, spiraling upward and gradually vanishing into the corona of the sun. Only the smoky trails remained, and even those swiftly dissipated in the light breeze.

Belynda inevitably felt cleaner, knowing that a few more of the wild impulses, the untamed forces of the chaotic world, had been spun away from Nayve by the casting of the Goddess Worldweaver. Those threads would form the lives of a different place, affecting only an outer realm that held little importance for the halcyon Fourth Circle.

Only with reluctance did the elfwoman's eyes lower from the majestic spire to behold the worldly manifestation of the Circle's perfection: Three great institutions formed a broad ring around the dome of the Worldweaver's Loom. The palatial edifices of the College, Senate, and Grove occupied the ridge of hills surrounding the bowl-shaped val-

ley at the Center of Everything. Each of the three great
structures was a teeming center of living, learning, and debate, and each, too, formed a portion of a ring, between
them encircling the great Loom. Broad avenues, one oriented to each of the three directions, passed between the
edifices, cutting through a trio of notches in the surrounding
hills. The College, Senate, and Grove, in turn, all looked
inward toward the shallow valley, in the center of which
rose the Worldweaver's Loom. The entire valley was more
than a mile in diameter, well-watered and beautifully verdant. And with that spike of silvered steel pointed straight
toward the sun, the scene possessed a magical symmetry
that could soothe one's spirit even when nothing else
availed.

But Belynda could only reflect on this grandeur for so
long. Slowly she started along the bark-paved pathway meandering through stands of flowering trees, past gardens,
and over arched bridges. She paused on one of these—it
seemed that she could never tire of watching the rippling
streams flow toward the myriad pools in the valley. Starting
off again, she wandered vaguely in the direction of metal,
comfortable in the knowledge that the delegation from Argentian would be awed and intrigued by the wonders of
Circle at Center. Surely they wouldn't mind waiting a few
extra minutes.

All too soon, however, she passed beneath a bower of
blooming dogwood to find eight of the sylvan folk, her
people, clustered in a small knot in the Metal Garden. The
delegates included a mix of male and female, ranging in
age from soft-skinned adults to elders, hair dyed a metallic
gold in the fashion of Belynda's. The visitors wore silk
ceremonial robes, and she was glad to see that they had
taken time to bathe and rest after the long journey from
Argentian—not because of any offense to her genteel sen-
sibilities, but since this was an indication that their

complaints lacked any real urgency. Probably just the usual litany, Belynda reflected glumly.

The visiting elves stared in awe at the fluted spires of the Golden Fountain, which pointed straight at the sun and reflected the light in dazzling prisms. As if in honor of Belynda's arrival, these gilded pipes suddenly spumed with a spray of sparkling water. Soft noise washed over the on-lookers as the arcing froth first outlined the image of a swan with wings spread wide, then gradually settled, furling the wings into a steadily maintained simulacrum of a stately bird resting upon the water. The sound of the splashing fountain muted to a gentle shower in the background.

"It's the sage-ambassador!" cried one of the elves, sud-denly catching sight of her. The delegation hurried forward as one, reminding Belynda of chicks scurrying toward the shelter of a mother hen.

"Greetings, Tamarwind," she offered, recognizing an elf, taller than the others, who wore the green mantle of scout. "It has been many years."

"Indeed, my lady Sage-Ambassador." The lean, wiry del-egate from the forested uplands of Argentian looked at Be-lynda closely, and she was surprised to feel herself blushing. Her time with this male had been so long ago, and for such a brief interval in her centuries of life, that she'd assumed any such frivolous responses would have been long out of her system.

He continued: "You look very well. I trust your life is unchanging?"

"As unchanging as peace. And yours as well, I hope?"

"Certainly, my lady Sage-Amb—"

"Please, you remember that my name is Belynda. You should call me that."

"Of course, my—that is, Belynda." Tamarwind smiled, and an element of tension seemed to flow from his body as he relaxed. "Lady Belynda Wysterian, as I recall."

Again she blushed, unconsciously responding to ancient

memories: After all, this was the elf who had joined her in the conception of her two offspring. Of course, that fact was of little consequence to their continuing lives—but still she felt uniquely, surprisingly, awkward.

"This is Wiytstar Sharand," Tamarwind said smoothly as a mature male, head crowned by a stiff mane of metallic hair, stepped forward. The elf wore the gold mantle of leadership. "He is the spokesman for the delegates."

"My lady Sage-Ambassador." Wiytstar bowed gracefully. "I trust your life is unchanging?"

She replied with the ritual words, but as soon as the formalities of introduction were concluded the elder frowned. Belynda knew that the complaints were about to begin.

"We seek constancy, the elven ideal, and the perfect stasis of the Circle—but in truth, there have been some changes at Argentian—disturbing developments, to be sure."

"Yes?" Even though Belynda was fairly certain she knew what was coming, she added: "Please elaborate."

"Most significant, the rains of the past three intervals have left us nearly an inch short of our quota!"

"Yes . . . there was a report of this in the Senate. Sage-Astrologer Domarkian spoke to the issue, declaring that the reduction in water has occurred throughout Nayve. But he has learned that there is no danger."

"But—will this continue through the next intervals? Will it always be different?"

"Domarkian could not say for sure, though he indicated that the chances are good. However, as I said, the effect has been noticed in many parts of the Circle. The same reduction has apparently been experienced everywhere."

"It's the same? *Everywhere*?" Wiytstar seemed to find this news comforting.

"Yes. And there is no perceived harm in the effect. Now, were there other matters that brought you here as well?"

"There is something of a mystery we thought we should bring to your attention," Tamarwind reported. "At least, I did."

"And?" Belynda was curious—mysteries were altogether unusual in her serene, sedate world.

"Over the past years, ten or twenty or more, an increasing number of young elves have departed Argentian. They are mostly male—individuals who reportedly have been quite normal throughout their upbringing. The pattern is the same: The elf makes no announcement to kin or companion; he merely boards a riverboat in the city and rides to some point down the Sweetwater. They debark at any of a hundred villages and towns along the water, and then simply disappear."

"Of course, the fact that they make no announcement doesn't mean much—we all know how private our people can be. Still, to disappear, with no word, no sign?" The sage-ambassador frowned. "How many of them have gone?"

"There is really no way to tell, of course. But it would seem to be upward of twoscore, just in the last year alone."

"I will take this up with the other ambassadors," Belynda decided. "First we will try and determine if this is a matter affecting just Argentian, or the other realms as well."

"Has it happened here, in Circle at Center?" Tam wondered.

Belynda could only shrug. "It has not been reported. Of course, there are so many elves here—something like twelve ten-thousands' worth—that it would be difficult to notice a small change in numbers."

Tamarwind nodded, apparently satisfied. Belynda noticed that the other elves had been fidgeting nervously, waiting for this seemingly trivial matter to be resolved before they continued with the litany. "And what is the next matter?" she inquired politely.

"It's the children!" declared another delegate, a wiry

woman nearly as petite as Belynda. Her hair was short, but spiked stiffly outward in a series of golden spurs. "I have joined this delegation, made this arduous journey only after a series of events so outrageous that I was left with no alternative but to seek ambassadorial intervention."

"I understand." Belynda was not surprised by the complaint, though she knew that the route between Argentian and Circle at Center consisted of good roads and a placid river ride. "Though of course you realize that the sage-ambassador's role is to provide wise counsel, not action. But please, outline your complaints."

"These young elves today—they're . . . they've gone beyond any reach of control. They lack all semblance of respect!" The elfwoman shook her head in exasperation.

"It has been noted, without rebuttal, that they universally lack the discipline necessary for serious study!" claimed Wiytstar. "Why, there's a painting class that is supposed to meet in the village hall every day at the Lighten Hour— and they have never visited their classroom!"

"It's taught by that young firebrand, Deltan Columbine," another elf maintained. "He says that walls aren't conducive to art!"

"He takes those youngsters all over the place!" clucked the still-exasperated female. "Sometimes to the shore, or to the aspen groves. Wherever it is, they can be counted on to be loud and disruptive."

"I see," Belynda murmured calmly.

"And they have no manners." Wiytstar resumed the litany, and Belynda assumed that he had expanded the topic to include elven youth as a whole. "They tease and laugh, and can be counted on to make noise even on the most solemn of occasions! Why, we had to have a funeral last year when Kime Fallyerae faded—and everyone there could hear children rustling the curtains behind the choir!"

"The offspring today are much worse-behaved than when we had our own children," sniffed a third elf, a stout female with a hint of silver in the combed wave of her hair. "They have no respect, no appreciation for the greatness of our race—and their parents have no notion of proper control!"

Belynda did her best to look concerned as, inwardly, she sighed once again. Children, weather, or dogs: It was almost always one of these, and often two or all three, that brought complaints to the sage-ambassador of the Senate from the various elven homelands. It had been so ever since she had held her post, and no doubt before, as well.

Unfortunately, the topic of children made her rather squeamish. Of course, as a dutiful elf, she had given birth precisely twice in her early life: once, when she had reached nine hundred years of age, and then again fifty years later. Both of her offspring had matured and reached independence before her thousandth birthday, freeing her to spend her time on more important and interesting duties.

Such as listening to the complaints of these elves, she thought, forcing her mind to return to the present.

"—digging up the gardens with impunity!" the silver-maned Wiytstar was saying.

"And—and they're breeding in the woods!" declared the matronly elf indignantly, speaking up for the second time.

"The children?" gasped Belynda, shocked into emotion by the unthinkable declaration.

"No! The dogs," Tamarwind declared solemnly, though the twinkle in his eye betrayed his amusement.

"Oh. Of course." Drawing a breath, Belynda tried to restore her dignity; clearly her mind had wandered as the recitation of complaints shifted topic. Yet she was shaken just the same, for she had allowed her mind to wander in neglect of her duties. Sternly she resolved to pay careful attention.

"Hah-woof." The polite, dignified bark came from another of the arched entries into the garden. A large dog regarded the elves from there, brown eyes warm and moist over a sharp and pointed muzzle. The dog was pure white, long-legged and slender of body, fluffy with a coat of cottony hair. That fur puffed into a crown atop the creature's head, while the ends of its long ears bore with regal dignity cascading tails of pure white. The animal stepped forward slowly, long tail wagging as the elves of the delegation looked askance.

"Hello, Ulfgang. Thank you for coming," Belynda said, secretly relishing the consternation among the delegates. She addressed the elves serenely. "I had an inkling about some of the problems we might be addressing today, and I have asked my friend Ulfgang if he would join us."

"A dog?" Tamarwind looked skeptical. Wiytstar, meanwhile, seemed stunned into speechlessness.

"He's very well-schooled, I assure you. And it could be that he has some insight into the current problem."

Still dubious, the elves of the delegation regarded the great canine. Ulfgang strolled up to them and sat on his haunches, turning chocolate eyes toward Belynda.

"You heard some of the concerns, about digging . . . and uncontrolled, er, procreation," the elven ambassador began. "Can you tell the delegation what you have learned?"

"Hmph . . . yes." The dog smacked his lips and passed a long tongue back and forth around his narrow snout. "It seems that there has been a . . . well, a discovery."

"You mean—something new?" demanded Wiytstar, his pale face blanching even whiter.

"Hmph, hmph . . . yes, in a sense." Ulfgang shook his head once, then looked at Belynda again. As gently as possible, she encouraged him to continue—though she herself was not keen on hearing him once more articulate his shocking revelation.

"It seems that the discovery—there's no easy or delicate way to say this—Some of the dogs have discerned an effect—my apologies, I hope you understand—of a certain ingredient found in the dung of some of the larger herbivores."

"Dung?" Wiytstar looked as if he was about to faint. Fortunately, the matronly elf took his arm and guided him to a nearby bench.

"Precisely. The effect seems to be, er, that a dog who rolls in the stuff becomes virtually irresistible to a prospective mate. At least, this is the case among the uneducated hounds of the countryside. Unfortunately, the discovery of such a powerful aphrodisiac, a discovery which has occurred in several parts of the Circle, has had an untoward effect on the population of my people."

"But—but this is awful!" the petite elfwoman spluttered. "Nothing like this has happened before!" The others gasped in sympathetic furor, exchanging worried looks.

"Do you have a suggestion for what we can do about it?"

Belynda gently prodded Ulfgang with the question. Unlike the other elves, she had been trained to search for solutions. The delegates, so unaccustomed to anything resembling a problem, would most likely only dither and cluck disapprovingly.

"I have a suggestion." The white dog smacked his jowls a few times, waiting until he had the attention of the elves. "I could go to Argentian, out to the pastures, and have a word with some of the shepherds. They're not educated, of course, but they're usually a pretty responsible sort of dog. With a little persuasion, they should be able to keep the riffraff out of the fields."

"Could you?" asked Wiytstar, momentarily enthused. As he recovered his dignity, his expression grew bland. "That is, please do so."

"It would be a pleasure," the dog replied, with a polite dip of that white-tufted head.

Belynda knew that Ulfgang wouldn't mind making the trip. For all his refinement, he enjoyed the company of the simple, uneducated dogs of Nayve—and there were very few of those to be found in Circle at Center.

"And when will he come to Argentian?" asked the wire-thin elfwoman, turning to the sage-ambassador.

"He will travel with your party, of course," Belynda snapped, allowing a hint of her true power to glare from her eyes. "Now, I assume you will stay for a few days before you commence the journey home?"

"Of course, Belynda—my lady Sage-Ambassador," declared Tamarwind smoothly.

"Ahem." Wiytstar spoke hesitantly. "There is the other matter . . ."

"Certainly." Belynda was terse now, tired of the complaining, seemingly helpless elves. "As to the problem of rambunctious children, I have counsel for you: The recent census shows that we have an unusually large number of offspring in their development just now. The condition is temporary, but will persist for several more decades. The solution, of course, is to wait."

"Wait. Yes, of course," echoed the elder male from his seat on the bench. This was a tactic that he, and every other elf, could understand.

"We thank you for your response," Tamarwind added. "It has been a pleasure to see you in the Center."

"And to have you visit, as well," Belynda replied. She wondered fleetingly about the children that she and Tamarwind had parented—he undoubtedly encountered them now and then in Argentian. Too, his company had been pleasant. In fact, she had considered herself fortunate to have mated with one she could also befriend. The elfwoman went to his side as the other elves turned their attention back to the fountain, which once more blossomed into a wide-winged imitation of flight.

"Perhaps we could have a chance to visit more informally," he said politely.

"I'd like that. Why don't we meet for the evening meal?"

"I'm at your disposal." Tamarwind was clearly pleased

by the suggestion, though his features remained carefully cool.

"Meet me an hour before Darken at the Mercury Terrace—the one beside the lake."

"Very good, my lady." Tamarwind smiled and bowed. Belynda once more felt that flush creeping upward from her throat.

Accompanied by the regal dog, who went along to make some travel arrangements, the elven delegates withdrew from the garden. Finding that her irritation had only been increased by the meeting, Belynda turned up the hill, climbing toward the Senate.

She thought momentarily of teleporting back to her chambers and was surprised at her own impatience. Chiding herself, she resolved to take the long way, walking the whole distance. The rays of the sun, spilling from straight overhead, now seemed harsh and unrelenting. The white columns along the façade of the grand structure sometimes reminded her of ghostly trees, yet now they seemed more like the bars of a dungeon, or the wall formed by some kind of gigantic fence.

She hadn't taken a hundred steps when she saw Nistel coming down the path, and she forced herself to take a seat and smile in welcome as the gnome approached. Yet as he drew closer she quickly perceived that the friendly overtures passed unseen by her frowning, preoccupied assistant.

"Blinker—what's wrong?" she asked, using the gnome's nickname as he halted before her.

Stammering, he shifted his weight from one curl-toed boot to another. "My lady—it's trouble! Real trouble!" he blurted.

Belynda's stomach churned as she tried without success to imagine what could be causing his agitation.

"They're talking about it in the Senate already, and I came to find you as soon as I heard! It's Caranor—she was found by a centaur!"

"She's fine, isn't she? What was her news?" Belynda stammered the questions, dreading to hear what Nistel would say next. She remembered her sense of unease when she had been unable to reach the sage-enchantress earlier that day.

"She's not fine," the gnome said, with a grim shake of his head. "She's not even alive anymore! And the centaur said she was killed by fire!"

Natac was acutely conscious of his erection, but only gradually did he realize that, somehow, his loincloth had been removed. Perhaps he wouldn't need the garment in Mictlan. But, except for the pervasive darkness, this was nothing like the realm of death he had always imagined—or that the priests had invariably described.

Primarily, there was that female aura, a scent that seeped into his pores, that had brought him to this profound arousal. He tried to reach out, sought the touch of womanly flesh, but he felt no motion in his arms or legs—Indeed, it was hard to recall the reality of limbs, of sight or sound or other sensation.

There was only the compelling smell and a massive, pulsing desire.

"Warrior Natac . . ."

The words were a whisper through the darkness, a sound of pure beauty in a womanly voice that drew a groan of desire from his lips. And with the utterance he began to feel a measure of control over the muscles of his mouth and throat.

At the same time, he realized that she had spoken to him in a language that he had never heard—yet the words burned with clear meaning in his mind. To compound his wonder, he replied in the same tongue:

"Woman . . . I hear you . . . but where are you? Where am I?"

"Shhh . . . you must listen, warrior."

"Speak—tell me!" Natac demanded, struggling again to move, to feel his arms and legs.

Gradually he perceived that he was standing, with his feet planted firmly on a smooth, hard floor. His fingers clenched in answer to his will, and then he could feel his arms. Immediately his hand went to his chest, where it seemed that only a moment ago the priest had ripped out his heart.

But his skin was whole. Too, he could feel the steady pumping of that vital muscle through the intact bones of his rib cage.

Only then did he begin to discern a faint illumination, a muted wash of light from several small clay lamps. He was surprised to see that, unlike the pottery found in even the most backward mountain village, these lamps were formed of simple curves, unadorned by the images of gods. They burned from niches in the stone walls, and the surfaces between the niches were lined with thick furs, the lush pelts of animals huger than any Natac had ever seen. He was looking at one side of a cozy chamber, and guessed that the woman must be behind him.

With that realization he tried to whirl around to seek her, but though his wish was clear in his mind, his flesh responded slowly. Almost as though mired in thick mud, his feet dragged across the floor, and even when he had turned, the woman came into view only gradually, an image emerging from a red, smoky haze.

First he saw her eyes: huge, wide, and so deep a purple that they might have been black. They stared at him with tenderness and affection—but in their depths lurked a haunting sadness that threatened to break the heart he had just rediscovered. Soft and liquid, her look drew him in until desire weakened his knees and brought another involuntary groan from his throat.

Very gradually he realized that those eyes were set into

a face of breathtaking beauty. The woman's skin of un-
blemished copper gleamed like gold in the soft lamplight,
highlighted by a small, upturned nose, and lips that were
full and wide, rouged to an exotic shade of bright crimson.
That lush mouth smiled, softly, and once again Natac had
an impression of a distant sadness, a shadow reflected in
those violet eyes hinting at something regretful within this
woman.

But he had no further thoughts about that.

Her hair was thick and black, straight and long enough
to spread in a fan over her shoulders and torso. A flower,
a bloodred poppy matching the shade of her lip rouge, was
set above her ear, blooming in perfect complement to the
triple petals of her high cheekbones and delicate chin.

"Who are you?" asked the Tlaxcalan, hesitantly giving
voice to the words—as if he feared that any further sound
might cause this exquisite apparition to disappear. Once
more that strange language came from his mouth, as flu-
ently as he had ever spoken Nahuatl.

"Call me Miradel, Warrior Natac." Again he heard that
deep, solid voice, and this time it seemed like a steadying
thing, a promise that she was real, that she would not vanish
in the blink of his eye.

"Miradel?" He had never heard a name like that, and it
was music when it flowed from his lips. "By the Smoking
Mirror—you're beautiful!"

"My beauty is a gift for you, now, and here."

He was stunned by her words, and desperate to have her.
But he forced a moment's hesitation with another question.

"Is this Mictlan . . . or what place?"

"There will be time, later, for that . . . for all of your
questions." She stood, and only then did Natac realize that
she had been kneeling on a fur-lined pallet that was itself
supported a short distance off the floor. A white mantle of
soft cotton was draped over her shoulders, and her unbound
breasts bounced slightly as she rose. When the garment

swirled to the side, he saw the bare skin of her hip, and ached with the knowledge that she was naked underneath the filmy gauze of cloth.

Somehow he had forgotten his own uncovered state, but even with sudden recollection he felt no discomfort, none of the modesty that should have inhibited him in the presence of this unknown woman.

"The time now is for us," Miradel concluded, coming to him, taking his hardness in her hand. "You need me, warrior—and you must make love to me with all your heart, all your being."

"Yes, my lady—I will!" he whispered, once again fearful that a strong breath of his voice might whisk her away.

Natac had enjoyed many women during his life. His beloved wife had been a splendid lover until age had dimmed her interest. And he had not infrequently availed himself of the young concubines who were always ready to serve the pleasure of honored warriors. But he had never felt desire, a consuming lust, such as now pounded in his chest.

Slowly, reverently, he reached to embrace her, then chilled as his arms moved through her with ghostly ease. He leaned into her, feeling the warmth of her flesh—but no other sensations, nothing in his own skin.

"You must let me touch you," she whispered. "At least in the beginning . . ."

Seeing the fire in her dark eyes, Natac guessed that Miradel's passion was as profound as his own. Her hand squeezed, and his lust surged beneath the pressure of her fingers. Then he felt her lips against his bare shoulder, smelled the cool fullness of her hair sweetened by the blossom.

They moved toward the pallet, she backward and he following like a shadow. Miradel sank down, curling her knees onto the soft fur. And then her mouth took him in, surrounding him with bliss. For timeless moments he knew only pleasure, and a building sense of imminent explosion.

Her hands reached around him, pulling him against her face, and he erupted with shuddering force. Natac still stood, swaying almost drunkenly as the pure onslaught of sensation melted into soft satisfaction.

But, surprisingly, he was still hard, still consumed with desire. His senses returned to the room and he watched as Miradel, once more raising that wistful smile, leaned backward across the soft bed of fur.

"The magic is strong . . . you can touch me, now," she said softly, invitingly.

He reached before she fully reclined, tugged away her mantle with a single pull. Finally she lay utterly naked before him, reaching upward, arching her back in sublime invitation. Hands alive with tingling feeling, Natac touched her slender foot, stroked the soft skin of her lower leg as he knelt.

The tiny tuft of black was a magnet, drawing his full attention. Reverently he knelt at the pallet, laid his smooth cheek against the silken skin of her leg. Her musk, that sensation that had been his first awareness of this strange existence, was like a powerful drug, drawing him inexorably. He kissed, and he relished the inhalation of her thick scent.

Finally he lifted his head and moved slowly upward, reluctant to break contact with any part of that glorious skin. His own flesh tingled as he stroked across her flat belly to the twin, coppery domes of her breasts. Miradel shivered as he nuzzled first one, then the other; finally she pulled him higher, so that their lips met, tongues intertwining like frantic serpents.

All the while he relished the new feeling in his skin. He touched the thick strands of her hair as he stroked downward from her neck, along her back, ultimately feeling the firm curve of her buttocks, cheeks clenching as his fingers slipped into the fleshy cleft. She sighed softly, pulling him against her as he stroked one of her breasts and felt the nipple harden in his gentle fingers.

Noticing new, soft sensations in his skin, he saw that the calluses that had hardened his fingertips and palms since his earliest days as a warrior were gone.

They gasped in unison. Engulfed by heat, he pressed as she strained against him. Her legs clamped his waist and for a moment he tried to tease her, to pull away. But inevitably he sank downward again and she shivered, moaned, clenched him with renewed desperation. Then for a long time they rose and fell in mutual rhythm, slowly at first, then faster, ultimately crying aloud in shared release.

It was with a sense of fulfillment that Natac drew long, ragged breaths, allowed Miradel to wriggle to the side. A languid contentment washed through him, though, surprisingly, he felt no inclination to sleep. Instead, he relished the tenderness and a momentary satiation, watching as she lifted her head to shake out the cascade of hair.

Her smile was coy, and the fire, barely banked, still smoldered in her eyes. "Once more, my warrior . . . you must take me again. It is the law of the goddess and the spell: three times before the Lighten Hour."

Natac had no desire to argue, and when a round breast poked out from the curtain of black hair he was once more awed by her allure. By Teztcatlipoca, he wanted her again—now!

She looked at him, and he saw an almost desperate hunger in those dark eyes. He reached, moaning in protest when she slipped farther away from him, but it was only to roll onto her belly. He was still erect as he watched her rise to her knees, that glossy black hair a gleaming shroud over her back, fanning outward across the pallet.

He pounced on her like a jaguar taking a deer. Again she took him, crying out her own delight as ecstasy overwhelmed him. They mated like wild animals, she squirming and bucking, he clenching, thrusting, entering her so deeply that he felt he must be reaching all the way to her heart. The intensity of their lovemaking expanded to gather in his entire consciousness, building toward utter, complete release. Miradel matched his passion, lifting herself wildly, crying out with inarticulate expressions of need, of joy.

Finally he seized her hips, squeezed her against him, and once again his world focused into a shuddering convulsion. For long moments they remained clenched, muscles locked as they strained together, covered with sweat, shivering with tremors of remembered passion.

And only then did he sleep, drained and sated by his welcome into the afterlife.

2

Masters of the Underworld

Dwarves of the First Circle: birthed in schism.
Delvers, blind in lightless warren;
Ever did they hate,
poison tainting unmirrored soul.
Seers, dwarves of light;
Fleeing darkness and claws of steel,
seeking hope, finding life
under a canopy of coolfyre.

From the Tapestry of the Worldweaver
Lore of the Underworld

It was Karkald's job to see that the watchlights kept burning. Ten times each cycle he inspected the wicks of coolfyre, measured the flamestone, ensuring that the six beacons of his station blazed through the sunless Underworld in proud, bright testament of the Seer Dwarves realm.

And now he was ready, even eager to start on that routine . . . but first he would savor one more look. He struck a spark to the wick of a lamp and held the soft flame above the bed. The sight of Darann's soft curls, so light in color they seemed almost golden as they framed her sleep-gentled face, moved him almost to tears. He leaned over, touched her lips with a blunt finger, and then slowly kissed the soft down on the cheek so close beside her ear, glad that she would sleep.

As to himself, he was vibrant, eager to move, ready to work out the boisterous delight singing within him. Still holding the lamp, he clumped through the living chamber of their den, down the long, curving entry tunnel leading to the portico. Near the entrance, he stopped to strap on the tools stored neatly on a wall rack, murmuring softly as he dropped each of the eight items into its strap, belt loop, or sheath.

"Hammer, chisel, hatchet, file. Knife, pick, rope, spear."

Content and whole, he blew out the wick on the lamp and strode onto the portico, coming into the cool wash of illumination from the nearest of the watch-station beacons. That great lantern was posted a hundred feet over his head, while to the right and left he could see the swaths of light from the nearest of the additional lamps. He trusted that the three beacons on the other side of the island were burning as well, but he wouldn't take that for granted until he walked over there and saw for himself.

Looking across the inky waters of the Undersea, Karkald clearly saw the corona of light that marked Axial, the great center of dwarven culture. Some fifty miles away across the deep, eternally still waters, there were the smithies and forges, the alchemists and scholars, who had gathered all the knowledge of the last tens of thousands of intervals. There, too, were the inns and taverns, the schools and arenas of the greatest city in all the First Circle. In Axial, gold was jangling through countless transactions, while Seer Dwarf drums pulsed a steady cadence of vitality.

And Karkald couldn't help but chuckle as he realized that he didn't miss the place at all.

Indeed, there was no place in the Underworld that he would rather be than here—and it had been so since Darann had come to stay with him. The watch station was a pillar of rock that rose from the black, unplumbed depths of the sea. Above, far out of Karkald's sight, the stony column merged with the cavernous ceiling of the Underworld to form the lightless, solid sky of the First Circle. Far below the portico, extending like a rickety spur from the base of the pillar, a lone wharf jutted into the sea, nearly invisible in the thick shadows beneath the glare of the great lanterns. Two hundred steeply pitched stone stairs connected that dock to the portico and the den.

With an easy cadence of footsteps, Karkald marched steadily up the steep trail to the first beacon. At the lamp he climbed up the ladder from the trail, peering into the top of the great fyre-lens. He checked the level of powdered flamestone in the steel hopper, making sure that the automatic feeder would keep the beacon burning. As always, the coolfyre within the great globe of glass was fascinating, though too bright to look at directly. Yet he placed his hands against that lens, inevitably wondering that the surface was barely warm to his touch.

From the platform above the beacon he also looked out to sea, seeking any sign of movement on the still waters that lay within the broad cone of illumination. Not surprisingly, he saw nothing but darkness. Yet he never forgot that, far beyond the reach of his light, the Underworld teemed with savage Delvers, blind and utterly wicked killers who sought to capture, torture, and slay their seeing cousins.

The Blind Ones were the reason for this watch station, the threat that made life for the Seer Dwarves an ever-perilous undertaking in the First Circle. Cruel and ingenious, always eager to take prisoners for their vicious rites, the Delvers had waged merciless warfare against Seer Dwarves for thousands of cycles. It was only a dozen generations ago, after the Seers were trapped in a small corner of the First Circle and threatened with utter annihilation, that a Seer alchemist had made the discovery that changed the Underworld. He had mixed flamestone, water, and gold to make a fuel that burned for a long time, cast a pure white light, and didn't generate the searing heat that was the liability of most brilliant fires. With the development of coolfyre, Karkald's ancestors had been able to hold the Delvers at bay and, eventually, to prosper.

Even so, the threat remained, requiring constant vigilance on the part of the Seers. Karkald remembered a dwarven corpse that had floated up the dock three or four intervals ago. Half the hapless Seer's skin had been flayed away, and both eyes had been gouged out by Delver torture. Yet when Karkald pulled the body onto the shore, water ran out of the lungs. Even after all that punishment, the victim had lived long enough to suffer death by drowning!

For a moment he felt a wistful sadness, a melancholy awareness of the violent dangers that formed a threat to his world. He knew that far above them, through miles of solid bedrock—the foundation of worlds—was a land reputed to be a place of beauty and eternal peace. Elves and other peoples lived there, in the Fourth Circle called Nayve. Supposedly, they frolicked like happy children, unaware of danger, ignorant of violence. Dwarven explorers had visited that place, generations and generations ago. They had reported that Nayve was illuminated by a great "sun," and that all the peoples of that world had a plenitude of food and bountiful lands, free of deadly threats, on which to make their homes. The elves themselves had been described as capricious and trite people, with little grasp of the serious realities of life.

He wondered if that kind of place might not be a terrible land in which to live. Of course, in the Underworld there was never enough food. And even beyond Delvers, there were terrible beasts—fish and serpents in the Undersea, fierce and carnivorous wyslets that stalked the remote caves and even crawled about on the ceiling of the world. But the First Circle was a world that made its people strong, and strength was the attribute Karkald valued above all others.

Sauntering along the narrow trail, with the steep plunge to the sea on his right side, Karkald tried to banish memory of the gruesome corpse. He said the words again as his hands went to the tools fixed to different parts of his person.

"Hammer, chisel, hatchet, file. Knife, pick, rope, spear. Hammer chisel hatchet file. Knife pick rope spear." He matched the cadence of his words to the beat of his footsteps. As always, the litany brought a sense of comfort, reminded him that he was prepared to face any eventuality. With those eight tools, any one of which could be in his hand a fraction of a heartbeat after he wanted it, he knew there was no task, no challenge, that could possibly daunt him.

The high trail followed the curve around the steep cliffs of the precipitous outpost, the stone pillar that rose into the great, natural buttress so far overhead and eventually swept outward to merge into the cavern roof. The path was rugged, broken by many stretches of stairs and ladders, but Karkald didn't mind the steepness. And because of the beacons posted at six equal intervals around the pillar's circumference the whole route was well-lighted.

On the side of the pillar opposite the den he stopped for a very long time, looking out to sea, listening for some sound from that infinite darkness. He tried to picture the threat of Delver attack, which he had heard described but never seen. Their boats were fast and silent, he had been told, and they could be out there anywhere. He pictured the foe, imagined the terrifying thrill of imminent attack, and strained to observe any sign of danger. Only after he was certain that there was nothing to see did he move on.

Three-quarters of the way around the island Karkald reached his favorite vantage. From here he could again clearly see Axial glowing across the inky waters. Also, this was the battery platform, and he never ceased to admire the great weapon, to cherish this part of his inspection and maintenance chores.

A little sense of guilt tugged at him, for he was acutely conscious of the fact that his enthusiasm for the weapon was the one aspect of his life he didn't share with Darann. Discussion or even sight of the battery never failed to make her uneasy, and after several startlingly angry responses he had learned not to mention the thing. Of course, there had been a number of arguments over other matters in the last few intervals—sometimes it seemed as though Darann was fiercely resisting his best efforts to make her happy. Yet none of those spats had been as intense as the ones relating to his admiration for this great weapon.

Now he enthusiastically turned his attention toward the mass of gray stone and black metal. In time of war the battery would be manned by a full crew of dwarves, sixty sturdy gunners filling the breech and cranking back the mighty spring. The arc of fire crossed the approach to the distant city, and from here a lethal spray of shot could be cast over this part of the sea. Now, of course, the crew was absent, but the weapon was loaded and Karkald knew that should the Delvers appear, he would have the honor of taking the first shot.

The battery rested on a wide, flat platform, a shoulder of rock jutting from the side of the stone pillar from which the weapon had traverse over nearly half of the island's circumference. Squatting above the highest beacon of the watch station, the gun consisted of a vast chute of metal extending from a powerful granite frame. The spring that powered the weapon was bolted to that block of stone, and overhead stretched a framework of piping and storage bins that, under the guidance of many skilled hands, could be manipulated to reload the weapon. There was even a governor of Karkald's own design, a control to ensure that the lethal shot wasn't overly shaken during the loading process.

First he checked to see that the massive spring, a single

leaf nearly thirty feet long, was fully distended, poised to swiftly release its force following one precise hammer blow to the trigger. A small chock of stone held the powerful strip of metal in check, and the gunner had to strike that chip just perfectly to knock it instantaneously free. If he failed, the weapon would misfire, dumping the expensive shot onto the shore of the island—and the stuttering spring might catch his hammer or even his hand, with crushing force.

As Karkald looked out to sea, he suddenly stiffened with excitement, knowing that the cycles of waiting and watching had finally yielded results: A silver-hulled longboat sliced through the water near the periphery of the beacons' ring of brightness. Twenty oars propelled the low hull with impressive speed, and while the Delver crew was invisible at this range, Karkald knew that several dozen of the Unmirrored Dwarves no doubt crouched in the hull, probably hoping to raid Axial or attack one of the lumbering Seer barges that traversed the sea. Glimmering in the beacon's light was a white wake frothing behind the swiftly gliding boat.

It took a moment for his mind to process the truth: The Delvers were here! A tremor of nervousness shivered in Karkald's fingers, but he forced himself to breathe deeply and, in a moment, was calm.

"How many boats?"

He asked the question aloud, then sprinted to the edge of the battery platform. His eyes probed the darkness, sweeping the sea around the Delver craft, but he saw no indication of another metal hull or white, foaming wake.

Returning to the battery, he peered through the sight and followed the path of the longboat, which at its current speed and course would shortly be out of range. With quick, sure movements he turned the crank that raised the elevation of the long steel barrel. Next, he pushed hard on a stout capstan, slowly grinding the battery through a gradual traverse.

He dashed back to the sight, made a minute adjustment to elevation—taking into consideration the Delver vessel's movement—and then took up his hammer.

Instantly he tapped a sharp blow that sent the chockstone pinging across the platform. With a shuddering whine the spring whipped free, hurling the breech and its cargo of shot up the slightly inclined barrel. The breech slammed into the stop bar, but the shiny casings flew far out over the black water, reflecting and sparkling for a moment as they danced eerily in the light of the beacon. With stately majesty the spheres finally tumbled downward, falling away from the light to scatter with a series of splashes into the sea—though Karkald was satisfied to hear a loud clang as at least one of the metallic globes found the target.

He rushed to the edge of the battery platform, anxious to see what would happen next. He knew that within each ball a glass vial had shattered, mingling caustic acid with a powder of phosphorus. Several of the metal spheres became visible as they slowly bobbed to the surface. First they glowed red, then white, finally bursting into clouds of froth and steam as the casings cracked and melted from the pressure of contained fire.

More significantly, Karkald saw a crimson glow rising from within the hull of the Delver boat, near the bow. In that steadily brightening illumination he saw the frantic Blind Ones scrambling about as they heard and felt and smelled the sensations of doom. The hissing sphere finally melted, spilling hot, liquid fire into the midst of the vessel. The hull, unable to withstand such heat, was quickly holed.

After that, the ship and its Delver crew vanished in the space of a few heartbeats, leaving the white glow of burning phosphorus to linger on the eerily still sea. Karkald allowed himself a moment of satisfaction, though he remained watchful. Squinting, he stared across the expanse of water, and saw no sign of another Delver craft. As far as the light extended, the vast sweep of sea was utterly black, still, and lifeless.

Until he looked toward his own shore in the shadows below. Then his stomach lurched to the sight of boats, more than he could count, clustering in the darkness at the base of the watch station pillar. The closest of the vessels teemed with metal-clad Delvers and was just drawing up to the dock. Another craft was already beached beside the small wharf.

That silver hull was empty, and Karkald nearly sobbed aloud as he saw movement on the steeply pitched stairway above the dock.

There were the Unmirrored, a column of deadly warriors moving stealthily upward. They climbed toward the portico, toward the den . . .

Toward Darann.

She lay with her eyes closed, too tired—or too bored—to move. She knew what awaited when she finally crawled out of bed: the dark, empty den. Karkald would be busy on his rounds for hours, and until his return there would be nothing, absolutely *nothing*, for her to do.

So instead she stayed in bed, longing for Axial, remembering the life she had left behind in order to come to this forlorn outpost. Her family was there in the city, her parents and her sisters, and her elder brother and all his stalwart companions of the Royal Guard. She thought fondly of the great balls, the pounding of ritual drums, the frantic dancing that would last for the duration of a full interval or longer.

It was not that she didn't love Karkald—she did, very much. Hadn't she loved him enough to come here, to leave all that she knew to spend her cycles with this sturdy, quiet watchman? He was strong and wise, and tender in ways that she had never known. Of *course* she loved him.

But even so, it was quiet here, and so dark, and there

were times like this, when boredom and loneliness seemed to form a morass from which she could never escape. In the city she could have broken this mood in one of the huge libraries, reading the histories of the First Circle. Or perhaps she would have lost herself in some of the fantastic tales of the early dwarven explorers, those who had visited Nayve to return with tales of exotic elves, a bright "sun," and the Worldweaver's Loom rising at the Center of Everything.

It had been a long time since dwarves ventured so far from home, of course—since the discovery of coolfyre, Axial had offered anything that the Seers could desire. Now Darann wondered if perhaps it was the lights of the city that she missed the most. It was ironic to think of it, but here, on a watch station with six massive beacons of coolfyre, her life was spent in shadow and solitude. The great lamps cast their beams over the Darksea, but spilled little of their cheery illumination onto the shores of the island. In Axial, conversely, there were small lamps every two-score paces along the city streets, and more light would spill from the windows of inns and shops. Rivers of brightness marked the paths up the steep pillars that rose here and there in the city, the great columns that supported the roof of the Underworld. From those cliffs one could view great stretches of the fyre-brightened city. Dens carved into the walls of these pillars were considered prime real estate in Axial, and indeed, Darann's family lived in such a multi-room penthouse more than a quarter-mile above the city floor.

This must be what life was like for the elves of the Fourth Circle, she thought. No purpose, nothing to compel one out of bed on awakening. She felt a flash of sympathy for those simple people, but by the time she had drawn another sighing breath her attentions had become more localized. She was feeling sorrow only for herself.

She drew a deeper sigh and pulled the blanket up to her

chin. Opening her eyes, she blinked against the utter darkness of the sleeping chamber. She thought about firing the lamp, but didn't have the energy for that much work. Instead, she decided that she would get up and go out to the portico to wait for Karkald. While she was out there, she could at least look across the water at the lights of Axial—though she knew that might only make her more homesick.

Before she could kick her legs over the side of the bed she heard a sound from elsewhere in the den. She frowned, knowing it was too soon for Karkald to be returning. Or had she slept longer than she thought?

Again the sound was repeated, a long, snuffling inhalation of breath. Whoever breathed was trying to be quiet, Darann sensed. Still, there was an alertness, an urgency to that sniffing noise that suggested someone was trying to study his surroundings by smell.

Delver! The notion brought with it a sick sense of fear. Her eyes were wide open now, and she cursed herself for not lighting the lamp a few minutes earlier. As quietly as possible she lifted the covers off and slipped her feet onto the cold, stone floor. Soundlessly she sniffed the air, trying to smell anything different . . . Perhaps she was wrong, and it was only Karkald she'd heard, coming back. Maybe he had caught a cold, and his breathing was congested. . . .

Yet her hopes were dashed against the reality of a strange odor, a bitter scent of metal and sweat. She gulped and tried to still her trembling, certain now that a Delver Dwarf had somehow found his way into her home. And where there was one of the Unmirrored, there were bound to be others—the creatures could only reach this island by boat, and that meant at least a score of the wretched killers.

Her next thought was of Karkald, and it spiked her awareness with sheer terror. If Karkald had been surprised by the Blind Ones, then he was already dead. If not, he would be coming for her—but could he know of the menace that had already penetrated their very home?

Finally she moved to practical questions: What could she use as a weapon? Where should she go? She thought of the lantern and in the next instant the oil-filled jar was in her hand. She found a match and struck the tip, wincing as the harsh sound jarred the darkness. At the same time the smell of burning sulphur permeated the den—and there was a sharp intake of breath from the next room. She had been heard.

With the lantern aglow she looked across the chamber, to the main doorway. Dark shapes moved there, several Delvers charging toward the sound and smell of the lamp. To the side was the narrow passage that connected with the water room and, beyond, the corridor leading back to the kitchen. In that instant—she had no more time—Darann made her plan.

Two hideous figures rushed through the door into the bedchamber. In a single glance she took in the blank, eyeless face masks, the triple-bladed daggers clutched in each hand. Locating her by sound, one of the Delvers slashed his way toward her, crossing his lethal weapons with lightning quickness back and forth in front of his armored chest.

The Seer woman threw the lamp, hard, against the floor between the two attackers. Instantly the ceramic shattered and a splash of oil swept around the burning wick. Flames leapt onto the legs and bellies of the two Delvers, who screamed and dropped their blades as they desperately swiped at their fiery armor.

Darann was already running, into the water room with its stout door of sheet steel. She slammed the door shut and slapped the lock into place before running out the other side, to find herself in the kitchen. Immediately she stopped, listening, smelling, trying to see through the murky air of the den.

Some light spilled from the fire that had spread to engulf the bedchamber. The brightness was enhanced by the appearance of a burning Delver who stumbled from that

chamber to sprawl, flailing and crying out, across the floor
of the main room. Another Blind One, cursing the noise
and hysteria, slashed his daggers into the burning form of
his cohort. The injured dwarf cried out, then groaned as the
attacker, locating the neck, drove the blade in a thrust that
instantly silenced his shrieking companion.

Darann's arrival in the kitchen hadn't been heard or
smelled yet. She counted five or six Delvers poking through
the main room, grasping at her belongings, jabbing at the
walls, finding and breaking down the doors to the storage
room and the pantry.

"Silence!"

The command hissed through the room and immediately
the Delvers ceased all activity.

For the first time Darann's attention turned to the
speaker, an Unmirrored Dwarf who stood in shadowy darkness in the alcove leading from the portico. She heard a
gurgling breath, and knew this was the intruder she had
sensed initially. He came forward and in the dim illumination she saw that he did not wear the full-face masks of
his underlings. This Delver's moist red nostrils were exposed, and his jaws, while shiny and metallic, moved flex-
ibly when he spoke.

"There is one Seer here . . . a female," said the snuffling
Delver. "There!"

She knew that he had found her, was somehow indicating
her location to the other Delvers—though she didn't know
how. Two of the armored dwarves advanced toward the
wide arch leading into the kitchen. Her fear thrummed between her ears, and Darann knew that she was gasping for
breath, making more noise that she should. Yet even if she
could have willed herself completely silent, in these close
quarters the Blind Ones would be able to find her by scent
alone.

Not daring to take her eyes from the archway, but knowing the cooking surface well, she reached back and snatched

up a cleaver and a long-bladed knife. One of the blades clinked against the metal oven, however, and a Delver, weapons whirling, charged toward the sound. Darann screamed as she brought down the cleaver, gouging deep into the Blind One's wrist. The attacker grunted, but ignored the pain to slash the dagger in his other hand toward her face.

Some instinct of preservation had compelled her to raise her own knife, and the two blades clinked together. The strength of the Delver astonished her—the force of his blow knocked Darann backward two or three steps. The wounded dwarf charged after as she swung the cleaver again. This time the blade bit into the gap between the Delver's helmet and his shoulder plate. With a gasp he collapsed, dragging the weapon from Darann's hand.

The second attacker came on more slowly, feeling with his feet to avoid tripping over the body of his companion. All the while his triple-bladed daggers whirled before him, effectively blocking any attempt Darann could have made at stabbing him. Instead, she backed up another step, casting around for some avenue of escape.

She found herself staring into a face of unspeakable horror. Wide red nostrils flared wetly as the Delver reached out to pin her arms to her sides. Jaws of fleshless metal gaped into a grin, and he chortled between teeth that were sharpened steel points growing right out of the bloody bone of his gums.

Darann couldn't help herself—she screamed, a full-throated yell that exploded from her lungs and pierced the air of the den. Panic gave her strength, and she kicked and spat, trying to force herself out of that crushing grasp.

The grotesque Delver only threw back his head and laughed, a wet sound of cruel amusement. Like the others, he had a smooth face-plate over his forehead and the place where his eyes should be, but there the similarity ended. This Blind One revealed his wide nostrils, which flared obscenely as though seeking Darann's essence. And then there was that horrid mouth, as if a metallic coating had been melted over the creature's teeth and jaws, then forged into razor-edged fangs. The dwarfwoman sobbed and thrashed, knowing that those teeth could snap forward and tear out her throat at a momentary whim.

"Cease the attack—I, Zystyl, have claimed the prisoner!" cried the Delver captain.

Vaguely Darann was aware that she was still clutching the long-bladed knife. She squirmed, trying to raise her hand. As if he sensed the weapon, the Blind One reached down and twisted her wrist. With a gasp of pain she dropped the blade, then slumped against the counter as he pressed her back.

"Find the male—kill him, however you want!" hissed Zystyl. "This one is mine!"

A bright red tongue snaked from his mouth, licking along Darann's cheek, probing roughly against her eye. "Cry, wench!" he demanded. "I would taste your tears!"

Darann moaned and tried to turn away, but those hands were too strong. She was sobbing, and felt a fleeting impulse to hurl herself onto a weapon, to end her life before this monster could work his unspeakable tortures. But even if she'd made this choice, Zystyl's grasp was too firm.

And then coolfyre blazed through the den, sending all the rooms into brilliant relief. Karkald was there, charging in from the portico path. He had thrown a globe of the light onto the floor, and the glass had shattered with a light pop.

"The male!" shrieked Zystyl. "He has lighted us!"

Delvers rushed from the other rooms, but Karkald didn't wait for them to come to him. He lunged, holding his spear by the shaft and deftly plunging the weapon between the whirling daggers of a Blind One. That dwarf went down, but the Seer was already spinning away, bringing his hammer down on a black-armored skull, then throwing his hatchet through the air. The sharp-bladed weapon punctured the face-plate of another Delver, burying itself in the exposed flesh of his wide nose.

Darann's captor sniffed at the air, relaxing his grip on Darann as he tried to locate Karkald. She saw her chance and kicked him hard, in the knee. With an oath he stumbled away, and she snatched up the cleaver she had dropped and dashed across the room, hacking the blade into the neck of a Delver who was approaching Karkald from behind. That enemy fell and she stumbled over the body to lean against her husband's strong arm.

"Are you all right?" he gasped, his eyes wide with fear—for her, she realized. Even as he spoke he used his weapons with deft skill, chopping away another Delver, then sidling forward to stand before his wife.

But now more Delvers spilled through the passage Karkald himself had used—a dozen or more who had pursued him from the portico. Across the den Zystyl limped out of the kitchen. His nostrils sought, opening and closing, tasting the air until that gruesome face fixed itself upon Darann.

"She is there," the Blind One said quietly. "Bring her to me, and make sure that you spare her eyes until she has watched her mate die."

Karkald raised his weapons, but now he faced a full circle of Delvers. Grimly, with snorts of triumph, they closed in.

3

A Knight of the Temple

Proud Jerusalem!
Philistine, Roman,
Muslim Christian Jew;
All bleed red
beneath thy holy walls.

From the Tapestry of the Worldweaver
Chronicles of a Circle Called Earth

The witch lived at the top of the steepest crag in the Lodespikes, but Sir Christopher would go willingly, gladly, up the precipitous trail. Dismounting at the foot of a steep slope of boulders, he leaned his shield—upon which could still be seen the red cross of a Knight Templar—against a nearby stone. The symbol would ward against evil and the horse wait patiently, Christopher knew, while the man went about the work of God.

He started upward with his sword sheathed at his side, using a stout staff as support on the jagged, rocky mountainside. The rod was smooth and dark, higher than himself by a foot, and showed the gleam of meticulous oiling and no little polish.

In his other hand the knight carried a leather sack, holding the bag away from direct contact with his body. The serpent confined in the leathery prison twisted and writhed, hissing angrily, occasionally poking outward with a lethal fang. Sir Christopher was well satisfied with the vitality of the asp he had captured.

Surely the witch would do the rest.

Finally he came upon a trail that led him out of the boulders, then twisted up to a knifecrest of lofty ridge. A single step to either side would have sent him tumbling to his doom, but he marched forward resolutely.

Now his goal was in sight, a tiny hut of stone and thatch standing at the crest of the domed summit. It was simple and rude, but from what Sir Christopher knew of witches, the interior would be well-furnished and spacious.

She was waiting in the doorway, watching as he strode onto the broad cap of the mountaintop. Though he was winded, the knight betrayed no sign of fatigue as he walked up to the witch and stopped.

His first thought was that she looked old for an elf. Her gray hair was incongruous on one of these folk who so rarely showed any sign of age. In his experience, even elven witches were vain enough to slick their hair with gold as they grew older.

"You are human, but no druid," she said.

"I am a knight in service to Our Lord Jesus Christ," he declared. "And I come seeking a boon from a witch."

"I am the sage-enchantress Allevia . . . I am not a . . ."

The woman's voice trailed off as she stared, wide-eyed, at the white pearl that Sir Christopher drew into his hand. He extended his clenched fist, allowing the stone to swing on its chain of gold. A crimson shape, a mark in the shape of an X, blazed from the face of the stone.

"You bear the Stone of Command," she said, awestruck. "The talisman of Caranor, my sister—how came you to hold it?"

"She bestowed it upon me," Christopher replied. "And now you must perform the task I request, correct?"

"I will perform your task," the witch said without hesitation.

Sir Christopher seized the bottom of the sack, inverting it to dump the thrashing viper onto the ground. Instantly it coiled, then struck at the narrow shin of the elfwoman's leg. The witch snapped a single word, a sound unlike anything Christopher could have duplicated, and the snake halted in mid-strike. Jaws wide, fangs extended, it was frozen like an image carved in wood.

The knight tossed his staff to the ground beside the immobile reptile. "I want the snake to become the staff—and the staff, the snake. I desire a rod of righteousness, and you will give it to me."

"Of righteousness?" the witch said in wonder. "I do not know that word."

"It is not necessary that you do," Sir Christopher replied. "Righteousness is the Immutable Law of God, and that law is carried in my heart and my immortal soul."

The witch turned to her preparations as Sir Christopher followed her into the hut. As he had suspected, it was very large inside, at least as spacious as the knightly manor he had owned in England—before the calling of the Templars had carried him to Jerusalem so long, long ago.

He watched intently as the elfwoman prepared for her spell. She spoke a word of incantation and a blaze crackled into life, radiating fiercely from the hearth. Though Sir Christopher looked closely, he could see no sign of fuel within the fireplace. The witch then lifted a bucket of water above a sturdy table, pouring the liquid onto the tabletop as she croaked more guttural, arcane words. The knight was careful to conceal his astonishment as he watched the water turn to ice.

With deft movements the woman called Allevia used her hands to curl the ice, which was somehow pliable, into a long trough. She set the staff in that trough, then took up the snake. This time her spell-casting was like a reptile's hiss, and abruptly the serpent stretched, still rigid and now straight as the shaft. She placed the creature into the trough of ice, beside the rod of wood.

Finally she took up the long container, which had not yet begun to melt. She called a harsh sound and Christopher skipped backward with undignified haste as the fire advanced out of the fireplace to snap merrily in the middle of an ornate rug. He was not surprised to see that the carpet suffered not at all from the flames—even though he could feel the heat clearly warming the skin of his face.

The witch fed the trough of ice slowly into the fire, and the ice hissed into steam, obscuring the heart of the yellow brightness.

Christopher went to the far side of the blaze to take the object that came out of the flames. The wood was cool to his touch, and he could clearly feel the ripples of thin scales on the surface. It had an admirable heft, with a head that was wooden, but carved into the perfect visage of a striking snake, jaws gaping.

"You have your staff," Allevia said, staring at him with a directness that made him uneasy. "Now, are you righteous?"

"Aye," he replied without hesitation. "Aye, witch, I am righteous.

He smashed her in the left shoulder with the blunt end of his staff, hard enough to break the bone—though he was careful not to kill her. She flew against the wall and slumped to the floor, gasping, her good hand pressed to the awkwardly twisted shoulder.

Sir Christopher crossed to her and stepped down, hard, on her slender shin. Once again he heard a sharp snap, and—as always—he was startled by the brittleness of elder elven bone.

But, strangely, this elfwoman wasn't crying. Usually the folk of this corrupt and hedonistic race, so unused to pain or violence, would break down pathetically under the severity of their punishment. Angrily he tapped her broken shoulder, hard, with the end of the staff.

"Why do you attack me?" she asked, and those clear eyes pinned him with a fire that seared toward his soul.

"You are an abomination—a tool of Satan, cursed to eternal Hell." He spoke the words mostly for himself, knowing that she wouldn't understand. They never did, these witches that he punished.

"The stone!" she insisted, her voice surprisingly strong. "Give it to me!"

He laughed. "You are wise in the ways of witches, but overall a fool. The Stone of Command is mine, now."

"No!" For the first time he saw real fear in her green eyes. "You cannot—"

His next blow smashed her jaw so hard that, for a moment, he was afraid he had killed her. But no—once more those emerald eyes were watching him, albeit with a look that grew ever more dull and clouded. Still, she followed his movements as he pulled wooden shelves onto the floor, smashed furniture to kindling, and tore many of her books into shredded tinder. He was fortunate enough to find several jars of oil, and these he poured over the gathered wood, forming a ring around the witch.

A single spark from his tinderbox started the blaze, and he quickly retreated from the hut, backing away even farther as flames swiftly engulfed the structure. Soon the fire was high, and so hot that even the encircling cornice was hissing, lending a cloud of white vapor that swirled about the pyre of smoke.

"Good . . . snow boiling into steam. It is perfect."

Sir Christopher smiled as he started down the mountain, certain that God would enjoy the irony.

Natac was aware only of a consuming laziness. Even though he knew vaguely that it was light outside, he slept for long hours, luxuriously buried in the plush furs, sated by lingering memories of a night of impossible passion. There were screens across several windows, muting the bright daylight, and he allowed himself to languish in comfort, drowsy enough to avoid the questions that otherwise would have gnawed him to agitation.

Eventually it was the need to empty his bladder that compelled him to move. When he sat up in the bed he also became aware of fierce thirst, and hunger growled insistently in his belly. He stood at the side of the sleeping pallet, for the first time wondering where the woman had gone. He remembered her beauty, wondered for a fearful moment if it had all been a dream. But he touched his chest, found no wound there. His flesh was healed. And the pallet was the same . . . he saw the lamps in the niches on the wall. All the details of this place were the same.

Except for his companion.

He noticed a circle of golden dust upon the floor and realized that he had first appeared in the center of that ring. The dust had been scuffed away in one place, where he had walked toward the pallet. Next he recognized the exit from the room, which was a panel of wood not unlike a door that might be found in a splendid house of Tlaxcala. The hinges and latch were of a hard, cold material that was not familiar to him. Still, he had no difficulty lifting the latch and pushing open the door.

He found a short corridor extending away from his room, with a sunlit courtyard visible through an open archway at the opposite end. The faint smell of sweet pollen tickled his nostrils and he advanced with a quick, anticipatory step. He passed open, airy rooms to either side, but his eyes were fixed on the bright outdoors. From somewhere a tantalizing waft of grilling meat reached him, and his stomach rumbled at the prospect of hearty food.

Only then did he remember his nakedness. Quickly he returned to the room, where he found a white robe with sleeves and hem of perfect length for his sturdy, powerful body. The cloth was smooth and supple, almost liquid in its shimmering texture, gentle as the softest fawn's hide against his skin.

Returning to the hallway, he hastened to the courtyard beyond, and found himself standing before a wide, bowl-shaped pool of water. Plants, including familiar ferns, palms, and blossoms, as well as other, more exotic foliage, grew from numerous clay pots. The sky overhead was a rich blue, but as he walked through the garden and the view expanded his steps slowed. Finally he stopped, gawking at a vista that was like nothing in the world—at least, nothing in the world Natac had known all his life.

He stood on the paved veranda of a large, white-walled villa. The garden was forgotten as he looked across a sunlit expanse of blue water. Steep bluffs, such as the slope right before him, plunged to the shore of the lake, or perhaps it was a sea. From here the body of water looked fully as big as the entire valley of Mexico. In the center of the sparkling expanse was a large, hilly island, a place dotted with many tall buildings of white, gray, red, and black stone. From the center of that island a silver spire rose skyward, a structure as tall as a high mountain and, when viewed from here at least, as thin as a pole.

"The priests were wrong," he said aloud, remembering the tales of black Mictlan, with its sunless skies and midnight horizons. "The land of death is a wondrous place!"

He was stunned, elated, and confused. By rights, he should already be embarked upon an arduous and challenging journey, with only the comfort of his loyal friends, those who had died with him. But instead, he had found this paradise, with a beautiful woman to meet him, a splendid view of a sunlit horizon, and—judging by the aroma that wafted outside to him—at least one meal that promised to be very tasty.

And it was a place where his body seemed to work much

as it had during life. His broken hand was whole, and free of pain, healed as thoroughly as his chest. After he urinated off the edge of the veranda, he turned back to the house, determined to find the source of that wonderful aroma.

He was startled to see, amid the trees and flowering bushes in the garden, the figure of a youth or a small man— he couldn't be certain which. The fellow was slender, and his head was surrounded by a veil of hair the color of ripe straw.

"Hello. I'm Fallon," said the stranger, speaking in that same singsong language that Natac now comprehended so well.

"Hello, Fallon. I am called Natac." The warrior wondered if this might be a son or a brother to the woman called Miradel, but he quickly decided there could be no blood relation between them. Fallon was so fair in hair and skin, where she was coppery dark, and there was a fullness to Miradel's body that seemed utterly lacking in this young fellow—who was in fact so thin that he looked frail. He wore a green shirt with red leggings, and his ears were weirdly pointed and seemed too large for his narrow face. He carried a shiny pitcher in one hand.

"Is this your house?" Natac asked.

Fallon chuckled with easy humor. "It is Miradel's house . . . I help here with some of her tasks. That's all." With that explanation, the blond man reached into his pitcher and cupped some water in his hand. While Natac watched, he raised his hand, then breathed a puff of air across the drops of liquid.

The warrior blinked in astonishment as a cloud of mist billowed out of Fallon's hand. The fog swirled into the midst of the foliage, settling around the tops of the leaves and blossoms. And then it began to rain! For a minute or more the vaporous shape remained in place, and Natac heard the patter of drops, saw the moisture, as if a miniature rain cloud had been summoned upon Fallon's command.

Despite his surprise, the warrior suddenly realized that was exactly what had happened.

"Forgive me . . . I have to finish the watering . . . No doubt you will find something to eat inside."

Since that suggestion was utterly in keeping with Natac's desire, the warrior nodded, trying to conceal his astonishment as he went back into the large white house. He entered a room that was unmistakably a kitchen, and here he found a person. She was an elderly woman, her gray hair bound into a bun. She smiled shyly as he entered, and he saw that she wore a white robe similar to his own.

"Where is Miradel?" he asked, coming to look into the pot on the stove. That cooking vessel was of a hard black substance—similar to the hinges and latch on the door of his room. When he reached into the pot, he felt the heat radiating from the sizzling food, but snatched a piece of meat anyway. He was startled by the searing temperature, but too famished to stop himself from popping the tender morsel into his mouth

"You'll have to be careful," chided the woman. "This is iron . . . it can be heated much hotter than the stone bowls of your own land."

"A miracle of Mictlan?" Natac asked, amused, but willing to be patient.

The old woman shook her head. "This is not Mictlan. You are in a place called Nayve."

That brought him up short. "Do not play me for a fool, Grandmother . . . I know all about the land of death." He realized with a glimmer of unease that they were speaking that language he had come to know last night. That gave him another idea. "Or is Nayve simply your name for Mictlan?"

"Mictlan is a human fiction," replied the woman, with a hint of sternness in her tone. "You have been brought to Nayve."

"Where is Takanatl?" demanded Natac, unhappy with her

answer. "He died moments before me . . . I would find him, share food and a story with him."

"Takanatl is not here . . . there are very few humans of Earth here. You have been brought by magic." She hesitated, then looked at him frankly. "Miradel's magic."

"What is Earth? Do you speak of the world of Tlaxcala, of Mexico?"

The matron set down her spoon and pulled the iron pot off the heat. Then she crossed her arms over her chest and turned to face him. "You have much to learn, Warrior Natac."

He blinked, surprised as she addressed him in the same words Miradel had used the night before. She continued:

"Mexico and your homeland are a very small part of Earth. In truth, it is a doomed part of that world . . . The place you know, the existence of your people and your tribe, will be brought to a violent end only a few years after your own death."

"But the world is thriving!" he declared scornfully. "I myself have sanctified perhaps a hundred hearts to all the gods. And in the city of the Mexica on the day of my death I saw a thousand and more lives offered to ensure that the seasons bring rain, that the sun continues to rise into the sky."

"And those lives were claimed by fools!" snapped the woman harshly. "Not just fools—*evil* fools, who invented preposterous gods, who wallowed in their endless cruelties as a means of ensuring that their own class retains power and prestige!"

Natac was stunned by this accusation. He had never during his life heard anyone speak so critically of the priesthood. Surely this person was asking for some brutal retaliation from the gods she'd insulted through their priests. Half expectant, half curious, he waited and watched. The woman's angry gaze never left his face, and he found his convictions wilting in the glare of her furious violet eyes.

"Our priests are wise!" he retorted. "They know much, share their wisdom with the world! It is through them that we learn of the needs of the gods, that we may assure plentiful rain and good harvests each year!"

"Certainly they were wise." The woman's reedy voice was scornful. "They held you and your people in thrall. They did what they wanted, assured of food and treasure—and lives—through the labor of the people they fooled!"

It occurred to him, for the first time, that she might know a little more about the gods than he did—or than he thought he did. After all, judging from the evidence all around him, the priests had been more than a little misguided about Mictlan.

Only then did another idea occur to him, a horrifying thought that forced him to deny everything this female was telling him.

"You lie, old woman! My daughter . . . Yellow Hummingbird. She was a precious child, and beautiful. We gave her to the rain god while she was still a virgin! And for years afterward Tlaxcala was blessed with a plenitude of water from the heavens. You cannot tell me that her sacrifice was wasted."

"I can tell you that, and I will." This time the woman's face softened, and he sensed sadness in the lines around her eyes and mouth. There was something familiar about that melancholy, though he didn't make a connection. "It is tragic when a human life ends too soon—especially so when a child dies. But you will understand, Warrior Natac—I will *make* you understand—that the tragedy is only compounded when the life is taken capriciously, to satisfy the will of a cruel priest who refuses to acknowledge his own ignorance! Your land would have had the same rains had you allowed your child to grow into a woman, to bear you grandchildren and to brighten the world through her natural days."

"Hummingbird . . ." Natac's voice trailed into a whisper and he staggered out of the kitchen, pushing open doors to carry him onto another wide veranda. There were lofty mountains in the distance, but his eyes only vaguely registered the sight. Instead, his vision was focused inward, on memories of a black-haired innocent who had laughed upon his knee, who had garlanded her hair with flowers, who had, with heartbreaking solemnity that gradually grew into shrieking terror, been offered to the priests so that her family, her people, might be assured of steady rains.

He lifted his eyes finally, looking across a verdant valley, into a region of mountains higher than any in his experience. Great cornices of snow curled along the lofty ridges, and even the swales were bright with white snowfields. Of course, the great volcanoes of Mexico were massive summits, and had frequently been crowned by snow, but never had he seen sharp peaks, jagged and stony summits such as marked this skyline.

The mountains were dominated by a massif that must have challenged the very clouds. A huge block of gray-black stone, it was flat on the top and actually thinned to a narrow neck just below the peak. Farther down, the mountain broadened again, tumbling along steep slopes patched with snow, outcrops of rock, and verdant groves of pine trees.

He heard footsteps behind and whirled to face the gray-haired woman, knowing that rage was twisting his face into a snarl, wanting to lash out violently against the new knowledge that seemed destined only to torment him. "Every man I killed in battle—and there were a hundred or more—I killed to the greater glory of the gods. I took countless prisoners, and their hearts were torn forth, and offered to the gods! And my nation was strong—it prospered, even in the face of the mighty Aztecs!"

"Your nation was built on foolish cruelty and beliefs that were founded upon vile rot! Tlaxcala survived because the Aztec nation was just as foolish, and perhaps even more rotten at its core."

"No!" he shouted. Rage blurred his vision, flushed his mind with hatred and denial. Natac had never struck a woman, but now he came very close to attacking this aged female. His hands curled into trembling fists, and he forced himself to draw deep, calming breaths.

"Where is Miradel?" he demanded.

"There are more things you must learn before you find the answer to that question," the old woman said. Somehow, he found her tone soothing, and his anger slowly dissipated into a consuming wave of despair.

His focus gradually turned back to his surroundings. Again he noticed the blue lake, though now the valleys around the shore were cloaked in shadows. Indeed, the sky had paled, and twilight was creeping inward from the far horizon. Night was falling ... but it was a different night than he knew.

For one thing, his shadow, though pale, was still directly below him! Awestruck, he looked up, at a sun that was straight overhead, but seemed to be moving farther and farther away.

4

The Hour of Darken

Sadness spirals.
Lands unbalanced.
Seas flee,
in tangled sheets of storm.
The ocean floor is dry.

Swarm from Dissona,
from Lignia, from Loamar,
creatures of magic and fire
creatures of fang and claw.
Weeping, dying Nayve;
there came a darkness
drew a circle round the world.

From the First Tapestry
Tales of the Time Before

Even though it meant leaving the College an hour early, Belynda decided to make her way to the Mercury Terrace on foot rather than float through the air in her ambassador's chair. She hadn't gotten any work done all day—not since yesterday afternoon, as a matter of fact, when she had learned that Caranor was dead. Since then the sage-ambassador had been dazed and listless, numb even to any sensation of grief.

How long had it been since she had known anyone who died? A hundred years, perhaps . . . that had been Waynekar, an elder teacher. He had taught her the ways of elvenkind as a child—and had taught her parents nine centuries before! At the time of his passing, and still now, the memory of Waynekar brought only a sense of fulfillment, as the cycle of his life had been rich and, ultimately, complete.

But Caranor had died untimely, and by fire. Belynda could not imagine a more horrible circumstance. Why, then, was she not distraught by sorrow, tormented by grief and confusion?

Or perhaps she was. Certainly she was not herself, she realized, as she found herself walking aimlessly through a small market. How had she wandered off the Avenue of Metal, which would have taken her directly to her destination? Shaking her head, she consulted her small compass. The needle pointed unerringly in the direction of metal, and thus she knew she had not drifted far from her course. There was the great Gallery of Light, with its myriad crystals and prisms whirling gently under the brightness of the sun. And just beyond was the Museum of Black Rock, where the ubiquitous group of goblins slouched about on the long, shiny porch.

The road from the market curved around until it rejoined the main avenue, and she hurried along that wide street until she reached a hilltop from which she could see the Mercury Terrace and the dazzling waters of the lake beyond. A quick glance showed her that the sun had not yet begun to recede, so she paused for a moment to catch her breath.

It amazed her that after living in this city for centuries, she still found it possible to get lost. Yet when she looked across Circle at Center she understood how. Walking through this great metropolis, the sprawling city that surrounded the Center of Everything, was more like walking through a forest than a community of buildings. Most of the homes belonged to elves, and every elf surrounded his dwelling—be it mansion or cottage—with a surfeit of greenery and blossoms. Trees lined streets which, with the exception of the Avenues of Metal and Wood, tended to wind and curve. Furthermore, this was a hilly island, and clustered in many groves and vales were neighborhoods of faeries and gnomes that no self-respecting elf would ever visit.

The two causeways, of course, gave solid bearings. Too, the center of the island, a ring of hills higher than any others, was visible from any good vantage in the city. From here she could see the columned façade of the Senate, ringing nearly a third of the Center of Everything. And from beyond the great edifice jutted the long, silver spire of the Worldweaver's Loom. She had been too distracted to notice the casting of the threads today, but she took comfort as always in the lofty tower and its symbolic protection.

Conscious now of time passing, she made her way to the terrace. The streets were crowded, as they always were just before the Hour of Darken, but the crowds gave way readily at the sight of her sage's robe. She found Tamarwind waiting before the terrace, leaning on a railing above the lake with his back to her. Touching his arm as she joined him, Belynda suddenly felt comfort in the physical contact with another person. Her fingers lingered for a moment as he turned around and smiled broadly.

"No prettier sight in Nayve than twilight across the lake," he proclaimed, putting his own hand over hers.

"Indeed." Belynda tried to relish the beauty, saw the fringe of darkness cresting the mountainous horizon as the sun began to recede. Highest of all the summits was the Anvil, with its flat, gray-black top and the narrowed neck of cliff below the broad summit. Now the fading of daylight had rimmed that massif in purple and vermillion, a combination that should have been breathtaking.

Instead, she felt only that pervasive numbness.

"Shall we get a table?" the sage-ambassador asked, trying to sound bright.

"I've reserved one—though I think it was your name that got us the location," Tamarwind said with a smile.

She kept her hand on his arm, and he seemed to welcome the contact as the black-robed host—a tall elf with an expression of utmost serenity—glided across the plaza to give them a small table at the very edge of the terrace. The lake, now a brilliant lavender, sparkled and lapped below them.

Several officious gnomes brought glasses of iced water and presented each of them with a loaf of warm bread and dish of sweet butter. Tamarwind gawked at the splendor of the surroundings, permitting himself a smile of pleasure as he inhaled the aroma of the fresh bread. He took great pride in ordering an Argentian wine from an elven steward, and informed Belynda that it was a vintage regarded as one of the finest in Nayve. "Though of course each vineyard in the Fourth Circle has different strengths and weaknesses," he allowed.

"Hmm . . . I'm sorry." Belynda was embarrassed. "What did you say?"

"It's not important," Tam replied seriously. "But *something* is, I can see. What is it that's bothering you?"

She drew a breath, collecting her thoughts even as she tried to answer the question. "I learned that Caranor died . . . by fire."

"Caranor the sage-enchantress?" Tamarwind's eyes widened. "How could that happen?"

"No one knows . . . she was mistress of fire, of all the elements. And yet she and her house were burned to ashes." Even as she described the news, Belynda couldn't bring herself to believe that it was real.

Tamarwind thoughtfully chewed on a piece of bread. He turned to look at a nearby table as a ripple of laughter wafted through the soft air on the terrace. Belynda looked too. The eight diners there were dressed as elves, in robes of green and white, but there were distinctive differences: These people were slightly larger than elves, and had as many different hues of hair color as there were individuals at the table. A woman at the end had tresses of flowing red, while near her sat a stout maid with short brown hair. Two men and another woman had hair with various shades of lightness, but none approached the gilded blondness of elven locks. Another man and two women had hair that ranged from chocolate brown to the purest black but was tightly kinked, complemented by a rich dark skin color.

"Druids, aren't they?" Tamarwind said, politely averting his eyes from the strangers even as he asked the question.

"Yes . . . they live in the Grove, that great network of trees beyond the Senate."

"They're beautiful, in a rough sort of way."

"Most of them are," Belynda agreed. "Somehow humans seem more solid than do we elves . . . and many of our people, especially the males, find them appealing."

"A sight you won't see elsewhere in Nayve," Tam noted. "Eight humans together. It must be ten years since even a single druid visited Argentian."

"They rarely leave Circle at Center, or at least these lands around the lakeshore. They have everything they need here."

"Do you know any druids?"

Belynda nodded. "I have become friends with several—one, in particular, called Miradel. The Goddess brought her here perhaps two hundred years ago."

"From the Seventh Circle?" Tamarwind seemed very interested, and Belynda was relieved to have something to talk about, to take her mind off Caranor.

"Yes . . . the place they call Earth, where all humans come from."

"Are they all so beautiful, so tall and proud?"

Belynda shook her head ruefully. "Hardly. The druids are only the most splendid examples of the race . . . they are brought here by the Goddess only after they have lived many lives in their world, and through them demonstrate goodness and virtue. They are very tame and wise examples of humankind."

"Why do you say 'tame'?"

"Humans are a dangerous breed, for the most part," explained the sage-ambassador. "In many ways violent—not to mention prone to disease, and to incredibly rapid aging. Of course, here in Nayve they are not faced with those curses."

"It sounds like a good thing that the Goddess is selective . . . and that other humans stay on their own circle!" Tam declared with feeling.

Belynda felt she had to explain further. "There is another way that a human can come to Nayve . . . without the will of the Goddess. Fortunately, it is a costly procedure . . . very rarely used." Already she regretted opening this avenue of conversation. Though she herself had learned of the major druid spells during her centuries at the College, it was clearly not the sort of thing that ordinary elves needed to know, or should be encouraged to talk about.

"How?"

She felt herself blushing. She knew the particulars of the magic involved, but it was not anything she cared to discuss. "A druid can use her own power to summon a different kind of human . . . one who has made himself into a supreme warrior over the course of many lifetimes. These can be men of violence and impulse . . . If the druids are 'tame' humans, you might say that warriors are the opposite."

"Sounds frightening—but rare, you said?"

"Yes." Belynda felt uneasy. "The spell involved is costly . . . in a sense, it means doom for the druid who casts it." She hoped that Tamarwind wouldn't ask any more questions about that particular kind of magic.

Fortunately, at that moment the server approached with

the dinners they had ordered—a roasted lake trout for Tamarwind, and a pepper stuffed with cheese for Belynda. She was relieved at the good timing, and amused by the smile of frank anticipation that curled her companion's lips.

Abruptly Belynda felt a lurch that roiled her stomach and rocked her on her bench. The server stumbled, fish and stuffed pepper cascading across the table. Glasses shattered—not just here, but across the terrace. The sage-ambassador seized the edge of the table, wanting to hold onto something, and was shocked as the heavy slab twitched and tilted in her grasp. Tam's face had gone white, and she heard screams and sobs coming from across the plaza, cries of alarm from throughout the city. As she looked into the night, she saw pitching waves roil the surface of the lake. Still Belynda could not accept the truth, not until Tamarwind shouted the unthinkable words:

"The world is moving!"

The tremor rocked the floor beneath his feet, but Natac merely flexed his knees and waited for the earthquake to pass. It was not a violent temblor, though he knew that it might presage more significant jolts—perhaps in the very near future. He looked around the terrace, saw water splashing out of the bowl of the fountain, the leafy treetops swaying back and forth through the night air. In a sense the movement was almost a relief—it distracted him from the solitary brooding that had occupied him since twilight.

He heard a scream inside the villa. The sound was followed by a loud crash, and then the warrior was racing into the hall without further thought. The old woman screamed again, the sound coming from the kitchen, and he ran in to find her grasping the heavy wooden cooking bench, her eyes wide with horror.

Natac lifted her up in his arms and she clung to him, sobbing. Mindful of the chance of a subsequent tremor, he carried her carefully through the hall and under the open sky of the garden. There he found Fallon, who stared at them wide-eyed, trembling. "What's happening?" demanded the gardener.

"It was a small earthquake. Don't be frightened," Natac replied, wondering again at this childish display of fear.

He looked across the valley to see waves rippling and churning the lake, while from nearby ravines landslides tumbled down the steep slopes. He watched until the debris rattled and rumbled to rest at the bottom of the incline, much of it spilling into the lake.

Only then did he notice that the old woman was still crying, clinging to his arms and shoulders with her head buried against his chest.

"We're safe here," he said. "You only have to get out of the building—the real danger is having the roof fall on your head."

She drew a deep breath, and though her sobs softened, she still clutched him, obviously terrified.

"See," he said, trying to calm her—and mystified as to why she was acting like such a child. "It's gone now—and anyway, that wasn't even a bad one." He remembered at least a dozen earthquakes notably more violent, several of which had brought houses and temples crashing down in ruins.

"Nayve—the world moved!" said the woman with a moan.

"It hasn't happened before?"

She pulled her face back to stare into his eyes, still holding him by the shoulders. "Circle at Center is the foundation of *everything*. It *cannot* become unbalanced!"

"The foundation of everything—even Mexico and Mictlan?" Natac was still mystified, but her terror at the quake had served to restore much of his confidence. Oddly, he felt as though he now stood upon firmer ground, while her own beliefs had been shown to be somewhat tentative.

She looked at him sharply. "Of Mexico and all Earth, yes—in a way that you will come to understand. As to Mictlan, I told you—there is no such place!"

"And the world of Nayve cannot be shaken!" he retorted, with a sense of triumph that suddenly flashed into guilt when he saw the fear in her dark eyes—eyes that were alive, and so beautiful—such a deep and perfect violet.

The truth hit him like a blow, so much that he staggered back, gaping like a fool and then shaking his head, angry and disbelieving. But those eyes moistened, glistening with sadness, and he understood.

"Miradel?" The word came out like a croak, and that sound lingered alone in the air, for the old woman just nodded mutely in reply.

They sat in the garden while Nayve's night drew a curtain around them. In some back quarter of his mind, Natac remained alert for a subsequent earthquake, though the land had remained stable since that abrupt shock. Aside from this cautious awareness, his thoughts were chaotic, a jumble of questions, connections, and utter disbelief.

He looked at the old woman again—of *course* she was Miradel. How could it have taken him so long to recognize her? Her face had the same shape, a perfect oval with the three-petaled flower of cheeks and chin. Furthermore, those violet eyes were unique, he felt certain, in all the cosmos. True, the bronzed skin had darkened, and patterns of wrinkles webbed across her temples and her cheeks—and the musical voice had a harder edge to it, a sound that had been lacking in her soft, welcoming tones of the night before. Or had it been so recently, after all?

"How long was I asleep?" he asked, breaking the long silence. "Years? That you became an old woman in that time?"

"No—one night. Just one night."

"A night—" He leaned back, bracing himself with arms propped on the stone bench. Overhead was the night sky of Nayve—and the sight jarred him every time he'd looked up since sunset—that is, since the Hour of Darken.

The sun had receded to a bright point at the zenith of the heavens. Brighter than any star he had ever seen, even than the comet that had wandered across the skies of Mexico just before his death, it was still just a star, surrounded by the blackness of the beyond. On Nayve, as on Earth, the vault of the night was speckled with stars. But here the stars shifted position before his eyes, slowly evolving through a dance as chillingly unnatural as it was beautiful.

"How long is a night in Nayve? Will *I* be old with tomorrow's dawn?"

Miradel smiled wistfully and gently shook her head. "The Lighten Hour, we call it. And no, you will not. Our nights are much the same as nights in your own world. Just long enough for a thorough rest—though I sense, Warrior Natac, that you are not ready for sleep."

He stood up, feeling his confusion push as anguish into his limbs, his voice. "You said you brought me here with magic? What kind of magic—and which is the real Miradel? The maiden last night, or—you?"

She straightened, lifted her chin with pride as she glared at him again. "Both are really me—or the other *was* me, in precise truth. It is the cost of the spell . . . I aged from the casting." Her eyes flashed something—anger, or pride, he couldn't tell. "In the end, I will die."

Natac knelt before her, staring into her eyes. "We *all* die!"

Now Miradel smiled again, the sad smile that had changed not at all from the young woman to the old. "Not in Nayve . . . in the Fourth Circle humans—those lucky few who are called here—live forever. You will have centuries of youthful vigor before you—freedom from disease, or any infirmity."

"You—you would have had such a life, if not for the casting of this spell?"

"Yes."

"Why?" He stood and walked away from her, then whirled back. He was filled with awe, and a terrible sense of guilt. "Why did you do it?" he asked in a hoarse whisper.

"Because Nayve needs you—and because your world, your part of Earth, has so little time left."

"What's going to happen to my world?" he asked. He was surprised to find that, despite his resentment and suspicion, he believed her.

"Your warriors will meet warriors from a different land— invaders who, in a few short years, will destroy the nations, the places you have known."

"My sons—their children, their wives—killed?" Natac asked.

"I cannot say yet . . . the threads have not yet been woven into the Worldweaver's Tapestry. Still, the pattern is set— the result is inescapable as it applies to nations. When you ask about individuals, we cannot say until the pictures are before us."

"Who will invade Tlaxcala? Even the Aztecs have failed, every time they tried."

"These new enemies will destroy the Aztecs even more thoroughly than they will your own realm—again, it is inevitable."

"Are they gods?"

"No—they are humans from another part of Earth. People of white skin and hairy faces—larger than your own people, and bearers of deadly tools."

"Humans—of Earth. But where do they come from?"

"Perhaps it will help you to meet some of them—here, in Nayve."

"Other warriors—like me?"

Miradel nodded. "There are two of them near here, both brought years, in fact centuries, ago. They, like you, were summoned by druid magic, a spell cast by one who sacrificed her youth to weave the spell. I will take you to meet them some time after the Lighten Hour—they have developed the habit of sleeping very late."

Natac found that he didn't have that trait, at least not yet. He slept alone on the fur-lined bed, and awakened refreshed to feast on a breakfast of eggs, rice, and the beverage called "milk." The druid promised to describe to him the source of that nectar, but the explanation had been put off by other matters. Fallon was there, too. After the meal he took the dishes, cast a few droplets of water across them, and made the same puffing gesture with which he had watered the garden. This time water sprayed vigorously across the dirty plates, and moments later they were clean.

Miradel taught him more about Nayve during the morning, showing him the beautiful lake with its verdant island. She told him that the valley in the middle of the island, and specifically the silver spire rising high into the sky and visible even from the villa, was the exact center of all existence. This was a concept that remained unclear to him, but he nodded and let her keep speaking.

Late in the morning he had a chance to view a spectacle she called "the casting of the threads." Miradel directed Natac's attention to the distant silver tower. He watched in awe as a sparkling ring of brightness rose into view, apparently starting from the base of the tower—though that foundation was concealed from his view. The light rose higher and faster until it reached the summit of the spire. From there it crackled into the air in bolts of white brilliance, flashing like lightning upward into the sky until the bursts dissipated in the distance.

He had many questions, but the druid informed him that he would have to wait for those explanations. For now, Miradel prepared a midday meal that they enjoyed in the garden, dining on succulent meat and beans spiced with familiar peppers and other exotic flavors unlike any Natac had ever tasted. Only then did they start out from the villa, walking along a mountain trail that gradually curved around a tall summit and then descended toward a forested valley that sheltered a string of sparkling lakes.

"Our timing is chosen on purpose," she explained. "This way you'll be able to meet Fionn and Owen after they're awake—but, if we're lucky, they won't be drunk, yet."

"Drunk?" Natac knew the word, at least in the context of his native tongue, but he couldn't understand why it would be relevant here. Then he had a thought: "Is this some ritual day of celebration? A festival that they begin with the noon, perhaps?"

Miradel smiled sadly and shook her head. "For the most part, Owen and Fionn get drunk every day—they keep six or eight druids busy, just making wine for them."

"These warriors have druids serve them—are they slaves, like Fallon is for you?"

"No . . . they do so out of choice." She looked at him frankly. "And you should know that Fallon is no slave— he, too, does the work that he chooses to do. You will find no slaves in Nayve. Some druids, it seems, enjoy the . . . company of warriors. And these men have persuaded them to do their work."

By then they had come around the shoulder of the mountain. The pathway overlooked a green meadow, and in the center of the clearing was the strangest house Natac had ever seen. It was made of wooden timbers—he could see that much by the ends of logs jutting from the corners. But the walls had been overlaid with large animal pelts to make a large, apparently weatherproof enclosure. Smoke billowed from a wide stone chimney, and the yard nearby had been divided into sections by pole fences. Several bizarre animals grazed or lolled within these separate sections.

Natac was about to ask about those creatures, when he was startled by a booming voice emerging from the woods at the clearing's edge.

"Fionn! You sheep-buggering Irishman! Come out and defend yourself!"

"That's Owen—and it seems that we're too late." Miradel sighed. "Or else they're still drunk from the night before."

"That's a *human*?" asked Natac. The man who swaggered into view was huge, easily head and shoulders taller than the Tlaxcalan. His face was obscured by a thick, shaggy pelt of yellow hair, which darkened to brown as it extended across his torso and well down onto his legs. Some kind of armored shell covered the top of his head, an inverted bowl that was the same dark color as the iron Natac had seen in the villa. Owen bore a staff that was taller than himself, and as stout around as a man's wrist.

"I said come out, Fionn—you cow-loving son of a mare!"

"Owen?" The one called an Irishman emerged from the house. He was as big as the other warrior, and similarly shaggy—though his hair was like the red of tarnished copper. He wore a cap of leather, and carried a thick cudgel. "You faerie Viking! Why are you back—did you run out of little boys down at the fjord?"

Fionn was trailed by a pair of females who wore diaphanous gowns and clung to the big man's arms as if to hold him back. Natac saw that Owen, too, had brought women with him, a trio of maidens who now ran out to follow him across the field.

"Those are druids?" asked the Tlaxcalan.

"Yes—as I said, some of my Order enjoy warriors." Miradel looked at him through narrowed eyes. "No doubt you, too, will eventually have your pick."

He looked away, unwilling even to consider her words.

"We'd better wait here for a while," Miradel said. "But watch—you might find it interesting."

"Those are both men?" Natac pressed.

She nodded. "They are humans from a different part of

Earth than Mexico—but yes, they are of a people who are cousins to you and your own."

He shook his head in disbelief, half expecting to feel the ground shake as the two warriors approached each other. Owen had his staff raised, while Fionn swung his club back and forth, holding the narrow end in both hands.

"Liar!"

"Bastard!"

"Faggot!"

"Blackguard!"

The insults flew thick and loud, and Natac lost track of who was hurling the epithets. And in another moment it didn't matter as the pair flew at each other, wooden weapons whistling through the air. Fionn's club smashed Owen's iron hat with a loud clang, while the staff landed with stunning force on the Irishman's knee. A fist flew, bloodying a nose, and then came the loud crack of wood landing against a skull.

It was Fionn who went down, and Owen straddled him, ready to drive the staff into his foe's belly. But somehow the supine warrior found the leverage to flip the Viking over, and by the time Owen landed Fionn was on top of him, twisting the Viking's massive leg around. Natac winced as he imagined the pressure, the pain—and then there came a loud snap of bone. He gasped, knowing that such a break, even if it did not result in a fatal infection, must cripple a man for life.

The Viking, his leg jutting at an unnatural angle, shrieked as Fionn rolled off him and stood. "Do you yield?" he asked, snatching up his club and raising it.

"Yes, by Thor—I yield!" snarled Owen through clenched teeth.

Immediately the druidesses gathered around the injured man. One woman stood with her arms spread, spilling something like water over the wounded man. Two more knelt at each side, stroking the mangled limb. By the time

Natac and Miradel had reached the bottom of the slope, the Viking's leg had been straightened. The astonished Tlaxcalan watched as Owen lurched to his feet and stood on the limb with no apparent limp. "That was a good twist, there, at the end," he admitted grudgingly to Fionn, who beamed in triumph.

"What? Who's this?" asked the Irishman at the sight of the two new arrivals.

The druidesses gasped in unison, and one of them advanced hesitantly. She was staring at the old woman, and finally asked: "Miradel?"

"Yes, Nachol, it is I."

Immediately the woman called Nachol, who was a tall female with long hair the color of spun gold, blanched, then came forward and wrapped the older druid in a tearful embrace. Natac stood by awkwardly, conscious of the two warriors looking him over and at the same time wanting to ask Miradel a thousand questions.

"You went against the will of the council," Nachol was saying. "Why?"

"I had no choice," Miradel answered. "The threads of the Tapestry showed me that."

"When?" The golden-haired druidess relaxed her embrace and was joined by several other women who looked at Miradel with expressions mingling awe, pity, and sadness. A few cast appraising, accusing, or suspicious glances at Natac.

"Two nights past."

"And the spell worked," said a dark-haired, diminutive druidess, inspecting Natac archly. "You have brought Nayve another warrior?"

"Warrior?" The word was a hoot of amusement, uttered by Fionn. "More like a boy, I should say. Owen, maybe she brought him here for you!"

"Watch your tongue, you Celtic fool!"

Fionn threw his head back and laughed heartily. Owen's

burly fist flew, smashing the open mouth. Natac saw teeth
fly and watched the druidesses scamper out of the way as
the two men were at it again, crashing to the ground, rolling
back and forth with a barrage of smashing fists and jabbing
knees. Miradel sighed, the younger women stood around
wringing their hands, and blood spilled from both men.

"Druids brought them here, as well?" Natac asked. Miradel nodded. "For *this*?" he pressed.

"No—you will learn soon enough that we have no control over these men, once they are brought here. We tried
to reason with them, but they have learned to do as they
wish to." She looked at him strangely, and he knew she
was wondering if he would prove to be as intractable as
the two burly men still rolling around on the ground.

In that instant he was embarrassed for his race, for his
whole world. He would not give her cause for regret.

He picked up the staff that Owen had dropped in the first
bout. "Warriors of Earth!" he cried out as the two rolled
close. Plunging the end of the shaft between them, he used
his knee as a fulcrum and pulled, easily levering the men
apart. "Why are you fighting?" he asked.

"Why?" Owen blinked, speaking through puffed and
bleeding lips. "Because—because it's what we do! As well
ask why we breathe, why we eat!"

"We figh' 'cause his ances'ors s'ole the women of my
'ribe," growled Fionn, his words mushing through the
mouthful of broken teeth.

"Stole your women—and your land, too!" Owen retorted
with a laugh. "Not that you Irish would know what to do
with good land if you had it!"

'Women and land—my people have fought for those
things, as well," Natac said conversationally. "But here—
this place they call Nayve—it would seem that there are
women and land enough for all warriors."

Owen scowled, and squinted at Miradel. "She told you
that 'Nayve' poppycock, eh? Don't listen, boy—this is the

warrior's paradise, called Valhalla, and I've been here long enough to know that!" He turned to the short, dark-haired druidess. "Fetch us some wine, Fernie—I'm working up a thirst here."

The woman quickly ran into the house as Natac settled himself on the ground, squatting sociably with the two hairy men.

"I know it's Valhalla," Owen continued, "because it's what the priests told me to expect. I went straight from the battlefield, my blood and my guts running across the dirt, and into the arms of a beautiful woman. If that's not a warrior's reward, then I'm a Frenchman!"

"My priests had it wrong," Fionn said. "They spoke of a journey to a place of darkness, eternal chill."

"As I learned of Mictlan," Natac agreed. He looked at Owen. "So you must have had very wise priests?"

"Lucky, more than wise, I'd say," snorted the Viking. "They were wrong about plenty—my comrades and my enemies should have been here, but there was only me. And this red-haired Celt."

"I was here for two hundred years before Owen showed up," Fionn explained. Natac realized that one of the druids had done something to the Irishman's mouth—he no longer bled, and in fact had a full set of clean, whole teeth. "How long ago, now?"

"Last count we were five hundred years together," Owen said proudly. "And the sheep-buggering fool has still never learned to fight!"

"Why, you—"

"The pretty girls who greeted you here," Natac said quickly, interrupting the budding contest. "Where are they now?"

Both men shrugged and looked at each other, somewhat sheepishly.

"I don't know," the Viking admitted.

"The druid who was there to welcome me—I never saw her again," Fionn said.

"Do you know why?"

"Never asked," shrugged Owen. "There were plenty of others to take her place."

Natac sat back, thinking. His mind fixed on a picture of Yellow Hummingbird, of a young girl going to her death at the hands of false priests, to feed the will of nonexistent gods. Then he thought of another sacrifice, that made by Miradel when she had brought him here.

The two bearded warriors were busy sucking on the wineskins that Fernie had brought. Natac caught Miradel's eye, and asked her the question again.

"Why?" he wondered, trying to see the answer in her eyes.

"Because I think there are things you can teach us," she said, taking his young hand in her old fingers. "And these will be things that the people of Nayve have to learn."

5

A Crumbling Cornerstone

First Circle:
Foundation's footing,
bedrock to worlds.
Anchors present,
future's bastion.

From the Tapestry of the Worldweaver
Lore of the Underworld

Karkald's lungs strained for air and he could feel the weakness seeping into his legs and arms. The long, terrified run from the battery, the sight of Darann clutched by that hideous, silver-mawed Delver, now propelled him into a monstrous rage. Four of the Unmirrored already lay dead and bleeding on the floor.

But now he was nearly finished, and as more of the Dark Ones spilled into the den, he staggered backward, pulling Darann and himself against the wall. They faced a tight circle of attackers, and the sightless dwarves now stood shoulder to shoulder, presenting a solid front of whirling blades.

"I love you," Darann said, touching Karkald on the arm.

He looked at her miserably, saw scratches and smudges on her face, fear and despair in her eyes. He knew that she was here on the watch station because of him—and he saw how that devotion would, in mere moments, get her killed.

"I'm sorry!" he cried. The wall of the den was behind them now, blocking further retreat, and the Delvers continued to close in.

"No!" she retorted furiously. "Don't say that!" She picked up a coal poker from beside the burner and flailed the steel shaft at the nearest Delvers. "We're going to fight!" The blackened spike clattered against dagger blades while Karkald stabbed with his spear, once more driving the tip through enemy armor, then twisting and pulling back to wrench the weapon free.

"Kill him! Bring the wench to me!" The leader, the one called Zystyl, shrieked his orders, and the ring of Unmirrored pressed closer.

Frantically Karkald looked around the den. Flames smoldered in the direction of the bedchamber, and in any event he knew there was no escape that way. The steel-jawed captain still shouted from the kitchen, while the main room was full of Delvers blocking the passage out to the portico.

Still, the latter seemed like the only chance.

Momentarily he missed his hatchet, which was still buried in the skull of a dead Delver. But he still had his knife and his spear. He tapped Darann on the shoulder, nodded his head once toward the door, and then hurled himself against the front line of Delvers.

Leading with his spear, he stabbed one of the attackers through the throat. That Delver fell and Karkald rushed into the gap in the line, thrusting with his long knife, driving the blade into the next of the Unmirrored. At the same time he felt a burning pain in his back as another of the Blind Ones turned to slash at the space that had been created. Hearing the clash, the rest of the Delvers closed in.

Karkald gasped as another whirling knife ripped through his thigh. He flailed and stabbed at the enemy all around, until he felt a firm push against his back. Darann was there,

shoving hard, and then the two of them were through
the ring of Delvers. Limping, clenching his teeth against
the pain, the Seer now followed his wife into the entry
passageway. He remembered the dozens of boats at the base
of the pillar, knew that the island must be swarming with
the Unmirrored—yet all he wanted now was to get out of
the den.

Abruptly he smashed, face first, onto the floor. His initial
thought was that his wounded leg had collapsed—but then
the ground jolted under his feet with a violence that lifted
him into the air. Darann screamed and tumbled beside him,
and vaguely he understood that somehow the bedrock itself
was moving, shaking and rolling in supernatural convulsion.

A shrill cry emanated from the den, followed by a thunderous crash and a cloud of dust that billowed and rolled
across the two Seers lying on the floor of the tunnel. Darann
was crying, and Karkald felt numbed by shock. He could
see and feel the trembling of the ground, but his mind, all
his experience and his learning, told him that such an occurrence was impossible.

Yet there was no denying the reality of the violence, the
thunder of collapsing stone as rock spilled into the den,
choking and crushing. A rock thudded onto the floor beside
him, and a clatter of gravel spilled down the nearby wall.
Terror clutched Karkald's heart as he pictured them trapped
in this narrow passage, buried beneath a thousand tons of
rubble.

"Come on!" he urged, dropping his knife into the sheath
at his hip, reaching for Darann. Together they scrambled
toward the portico over the pitching, heaving floor. Twice,
large rocks smashed onto Karkald, one banging his skull
hard enough to stun him. But finally they tumbled from the
den's front door to sprawl on the flat portico jutting out
from the side of the island's cliff.

Even here rubble was scattered across the stones, and
Karkald was stunned to see great waves rising and surging
across the surface of the dark sea. Landslides spilled down
the sides of the watch station, and several of the great beacons had been destroyed. At least two of the beams still
swept across the dark water, highlighting the tortured expanse.

Karkald heard a crash from within the den. The sound
was followed by a groan, and then a very foul—and
lively—curse, proving that Delvers were still alive and ac-
tive inside. Silently the Seer tugged at Darann's hand,
placing a finger on his lips to caution her as they made
their way across the portico to the steep wall of the pillar.
Fortunately the stairway to the nearest beacon remained intact, and only a few steps were obstructed by rubble that
had fallen from above. He took care to step only upon solid
rock so as not to make a sound as he led his wife upward,
climbing toward the lantern that still blazed through the
darkness.

Finally they reached a perch nearly a hundred feet above
the portico. Here the two of them huddled on a narrow
ledge beside the beacon of coolfyre, still too numbed and
horrified to speak. Below them several Delvers were visible, crawling from the collapse within the den or gathering
on the portico from other parts of the island. More and
more emerged from various niches and ledges, until a hundred or more had gathered before the ruins of the Seers'
den.

The two Seers pressed back against the cliff, silent and
afraid. Karkald knew they could not be seen by the Blind
Ones, but even so he was reluctant to expose himself any
more than necessary. Beside him, Darann was watching the
lights of Axial, a bright swath across the sea. They could
even make out some of the great pillars, outlined by coolfyre, that rose from the city to merge with the stone sky of
the Underworld.

Neither of them was prepared for the next pulse of the earthquake, a jolt that rocked the pillar of the watch station harder than any of the previous shocks. They shouted in alarm and clung to each other, pitching perilously close to the precipice. Karkald snatched out his pick and curled the hook over the bar of the beacon's frame. Once more the bedrock shivered, and they tumbled and twisted over the hundred-foot drop. Only his grip on the tool, and the half-circle of metal curled over the rod, kept them from a fatal plummet.

Below, the Delvers were shrieking in terror, and Karkald hoped the sounds of their panic had drowned out the sharp cries he and his wife had made. He had good reason to believe this, for it seemed as though the whole of the First Circle reverberated with sound. Waves crashed on stony shores, or pitched against each other in chaotic surges. Massive pieces of the ceiling plunged downward, and great chunks of the watch station broke away to tumble into the sea.

"Look!" moaned Darann, rising to her knees and pointing through the vast dark of the First Circle. He looked to where she pointed and saw the lights of Axial pitching and lurching in the distance. A great swath of the city abruptly disappeared, as if ten thousand lights had been extinguished at once. The rest of Axial flared with a supernatural brightness, until another part was blinked out in the space of a few seconds. Still more of the city vanished next, blotted out in an instant.

More convulsions followed, and Karkald held his woman with all his strength, waiting for the boulder that at any instant would crush them or sweep them to their deaths. But instead, they somehow survived. Gradually this quake settled, and the rock beneath them ceased to move. Waves still pitched across the lake, and they could see many new islands, masses of rubble that jutted upward from the waves. The base of their own watch station had expanded because of falling debris, in places becoming a wide fan of loose rock that extended far out across the water.

Already there were Delvers making their way down this slope. It seemed to Karkald, in the light of the one beacon remaining, that quite a few of the Blind Ones had survived the quake. He heard words of harsh command, and recognized Zystyl's voice.

Darann uttered a strangled sob and at first Karkald thought she was reacting to that horrific dwarf's survival. But when he raised his eyes, he followed the direction of her horrified stare.

"No!" he whispered, as his wife clung to his arm and stared wordlessly through the darkness.

Across the sea, along the great swath where Axial had once brightened the First Circle, they saw only darkness.

Zystyl's nostrils were clogged by dust, his flesh bruised by the rocks that had dropped from overhead. Still, he was alive, and finally these unnatural quakes seemed to be over. Furthermore, he could tell by the clicks and shouts made by his warriors that many of them had survived, and were now fanning out to discern the layout of the new shoreline. He absorbed their senses as they moved, drawing a map in his mind as he heard the echoes return from Delver cries, sensed the presence of water and dust in the midst of new formations of ground.

He, meanwhile, stood on the slope high above the water, which had now settled to lap placidly against the multiple shores. Already he had discerned, by sound and echo, that there were many more obstacles on the water than there had been before. Rock jutted here and there, large islands pushed violently up from the sea. Furthermore, he had deduced that this was not necessarily a bad thing. After all, most if not all of his boats had undoubtedly been destroyed or sunk by falling debris, and it would be very useful to find a way that his warriors could get off this island by foot.

Or, even more tempting, what if they could get all the way to Axial by foot? Like all Delver arcanes, he knew that the Seer city had survived through the years for two reasons: One, the light of coolfyre gave the Seers a significant advantage over the Blind Ones, and second, their homeland was an island, reachable to the Unmirrored only by boat. As a result, the two great invasions his people had launched during Zystyl's lifetime had both been defeated in furious battle as soon as the Delvers tried to come ashore.

This last time, it should have been different. He, himself, had planned the attack, and it was to begin with the destruction of each of these watch stations posted on Axial's approaches. The greatest army ever assembled had departed Nightrock in more than a thousand boats, with the advance elements quickly, silently, landing on the isolated watch stations. That part of the operation, in fact, had been proceeding appropriately, until the utterly unprecedented rocking of their world had changed everything.

The Delver didn't know whether or not the Seer watchman and his woman had escaped the earthquake. He would have liked to take time to search for them—something about the woman, in particular, had touched him on a deep and visceral level. Not just her scent and her sound, but that *taste* of her cheek he had stolen, the tartness of sweat and fear, now tingled in his memory like a living thing.

"I seek you, lord." The words came from a dozen paces away, and he recognized the voice of his chief lieutenant.

"Porutt—what have you found?"

The other Delver made his way over the rough ground to Zystyl, where he could speak in a pale whisper, and only his listener could discern the sound.

"We have identified a ridge of rock extending a long way from the island, negotiable by foot. My dwarves advanced more than a mile, and echoed another similar distance."

"Very well. How many of our regiment survived?"

"More than two hundred here. There has been no word from any of the other regiments."

"Of course not—but we shall not assume they have perished. Use the horns, and we will commence the march."

"Yes, lord!"

"And Porutt, one more thing."

"Lord?"

"Let the men know I'm in the mood to toy with a captive . . . female, preferably. There will be a reward for anyone who can provide me with a little entertainment."

"Of course, my lord."

Zystyl heard the sly smile in Porutt's reply, and knew that his lieutenant would claim a portion of that reward. No matter . . . a good commander knew how to see to the morale of all his troops.

He started after Porutt, anxious to explore the dry route that would lead them away from here, and perhaps bring them closer to a successful attack against the Seers. At the same time, a part of his memory lingered above, remembering the taste and the terror of a victim who had escaped.

Karkald watched the Delvers march away, a long file snaking into the darkness of the Underworld. They followed the crest of a newly formed ridge that rose like a serpent's spine from the swirling water. The Seer had pivoted the lone surviving beacon, and now used the illumination to observe the column moving in the general direction of Axial.

Except that, to all appearances, that city no longer existed.

Numerous cuts and bruises wrapped his body in a cocoon of pain, but Karkald forced himself to move. He climbed down from the lens of the beacon to find Darann still staring into the distance, as if she willed some glimmer of light to sparkle on the dark horizon. But, as it had been since they observed the city's destruction, there was not a single glint of illumination, or hope.

The watchman turned away, fearing that the heaviness of his heart would reflect in his eyes. Some instinct told him that he had to be very strong now, that he and Darann would need all of his abilities, every ounce of his confidence, in order to have any chance at survival. Despite the agony that ripped his back, that burned in his legs, he could not yield to his weakness.

Even with the departure of so many invaders, Zystyl had left several dozen of his warriors on the island of the watch station, including many waiting on the portico or hiding in the nooks and crannies nearby. Clearly, whatever part of the den hadn't been destroyed remained unattainable to the two Seers.

Again Karkald found himself looking at the departing Delvers, amazed that so many of them had survived such rampant destruction. Several of the Blind Ones bore long, golden trumpets, and periodically raised them to broadcast a blast of sound through the First Circle. This time, a few seconds after they brayed another call, an answering blast rang through from the distant darkness. Moments later still another sounded, making it clear that the Delvers were all around them.

"Is there something strange about the water?" Darann asked softly. She had turned her attention to the Darksea below them. "Should it be so far away?"

Karkald was about to answer that the island's shoreline had expanded, but when he looked again he saw that she was right—the water level was very low. It seemed that a patch of the surface farther out spiraled like a whirlpool. He limped up to realign the beacon, and there was the proof, clear in the light of coolfyre.

"The Darksea," he whispered, awe and caution combining to mute his voice. "It's draining away!"

Over the next half hour more and more of the sea bottom came into view. He passed the beam back and forth, and though the light reflected from many pools and lakes, it was obvious that most of what had once been the Darksea was now dry land. Even more alarming, his beacon had picked up numerous companies of Delvers, all using the trumpets to coordinate a gathering on a low rise a few miles away.

"It's an army," he breathed softly. "This was the start of a full-scale invasion!"

"What are we going to do?" Darann asked. The dwarf-woman's voice was calm, but he supposed that she was still numb from the shock. At least she remembered to speak in a whisper, since many Delvers remained only a hundred feet below them.

"We can't go down there." Karkald stated the obvious.

"Then we go up, right?" she replied.

He nodded. It was, of course, the only option, but at the same time it made for a daunting prospect.

"We'll have to climb for a mile or more," he warned. "But with luck, we'll find some caves overhead, some means of getting"—he realized with a stab of grief that he didn't even know where they were going—"away from here," he concluded, knowing from the pain in her eyes that Darann had experienced the same realization.

"How far?" she asked, her voice even more hushed than her usual whisper.

"I don't know," he admitted, panicked at this failure of knowledge. He tried to think quickly. "The beacons have a range of a few miles, and when they're tilted upward they can illuminate the ceiling . . . That puts it two miles away, perhaps."

"Can you climb that high?"

"It's been done before," Karkald replied, knowing that he was avoiding her question.

"And then what?" Darann asked, her bright eyes shining in the nearly pitch darkness.

He felt rising exasperation and worked hard to stay calm. "There are lots of caves up there, cracks in the ceiling leading up, into the midrock. There'll be fungus there, and bats . . . maybe even pools of fish!" Karkald's mind veered away from the dangers, the savage wyslets that prowled in the darkness and preyed on isolated dwarves, the vast stretches of bare rock with no food or water. Or the most horrible prospect of all: that they would be blocked by a thousand feet of bare, seamless rock. Such a barrier would end their hopes as certainly as any Delver blade or wyslet fang.

"The midrock." Darann blinked, whispering slowly. "How thick is it?"

Karkald almost snorted his irritation. "How should I know?"

By the sight of her eyes he knew she was shaking her head. "You don't understand . . . to Nayve. How far is it to the Fourth Circle?"

"I don't think anyone's ever measured it," he replied, amazed at the audacity implied by her question. "Dwarves have made it that far in the past—though not, perhaps, since we got the coolfyre."

"Well, maybe it's time some dwarves tried to go there again!"

"All the way to Nayve? What makes you think we could do it?"

"What choice do we have?" Darann spat back at him. "Stay here, and starve? Go down there, and get killed by Delvers?"

"We—we won't starve, at least not right away," Karkald said, even as his mind, unwillingly, started to grapple with her suggestion. He gestured along a narrow ledge leading away from their perch, a path toward a barely visible crack in the rocky face. "I stored some supplies in there a half dozen intervals ago, in case I got involved in a project up on the cliff and had to spend a few cycles up here."

"Supplies?" His wife looked hopeful. "Like what?"

In a few minutes he had retrieved the cache, a small backpack that he dropped to the ground between them. "Spare boots—they should fit you," he announced, remembering Darann's bare feet. "A few sacks filled with water, an empty pouch or two. Not much." Karkald felt apologetic as he looked at the meager stash.

"That's good!" The dwarfwoman was already pulling on the boots. "At least enough for us to get started. I can carry this, and you can carry your tools." She stood, lifting the backpack, nodding in satisfaction as she tested the feel of the supple boots.

Karkald, meanwhile, had stopped thinking of objections. He was heartened by his wife's enthusiasm, determined to do what he could to maintain her rising spirits. "Let's go to Nayve, then," he declared. "Are you ready to climb?"

With a resolute motion, she nodded, cinched the straps of the backpack, and looked up the steep cliff overhead. "Can you brighten the first stretch for a minute, so that we can see the best way to go?" she wondered.

"Yes . . . and we can take some flamestone along with us, enough to light our immediate surroundings for a few intervals."

"Good. Then let's go."

Karkald too looked up, running his hands over his tools out of long-trained instinct. "Hammer, chisel . . . I don't have a hatchet!" He almost raised his voice when he encountered the empty loop on his belt.

"It's planted in a Delver's forehead, remember?" Darann said wryly. She pulled something from her own waistline, and he saw that she had one of the cleavers from the kitchen. "Will this do instead?"

"I . . . I guess it will have to," he replied. The cooking implement was neither as heavy nor as well-balanced as his own hatchet, but it had a similar shape and, in the back of his mind, he admitted that it would perform many of the same functions.

"Hammer, chisel, hatchet, file." These were now in order, arrayed in leather loops around his belt. "Knife, pick, rope, spear." And his final tools were also in place, knife and pick in chest pouches, rope around his shoulders, and spear in its tube on his back.

"One more thing," Karkald said, as he led Darann up the ladder beside the beacon. He scooped up some of the flame-stone in his hands, then trickled as much of it as he could into the loose pouches of his tunic. His wife held out a watertight sack, and he filled that as well. Then he turned the gauge on the feeder down to its tightest setting. The beacon faded to to a pale spark, barely brighter than a candle flame.

"It will last for years at this setting," Karkald informed her. "It might let some other Seers know, sometime, that we were here."

She nodded mutely, and he knew she was remembering her family. Could they be alive? Given the utter extinction of Axial's lights, he knew there was very little hope.

But then Darann put her hand on his arm. "Shouldn't we leave a message . . . some kind of note, to let people know what happened—to us, and with the Delvers?"

"You're right," he agreed immediately. "I know where to write it."

He reached into the door of the feeder and pulled out the upper hatch, which was a thin sheet of pure gold. Removing his file, he poised it over the surface. "What should I say?"

"Give the date."

"Year six hundred and seventy of the Tenth Millennium, interval three, cycle thirty-two, right?"

She nodded—Darann had always been better than Karkald at keeping track of dates.

"Attacked by Delvers . . World rocked by tremors . . . saw Axial darken . . ." He murmured as he wrote, painstakingly engraving each letter into the soft gold.

"We are climbing away from here. Signed, Karkald and Darann, Clan Watcher."

"And Clan Silkmaker," added Darann, stating her family's clan. "Put that there, too."

Karkald stifled his urge to object. She had joined his clan with the marriage . . . but still, it was only practical to put as much information here as they could.

"Very well . . . Clan Silkmaker."

He placed the sheaf of gold against the hopper, and stood. "There are stairs leading partway up from here—they'll take us some way toward the roof," he said, indicating the narrow stone steps.

Darann started up, while Karkald's hands moved through the routine.

"Hammer, chisel, hatchet, file. Knife pick rope spear."

And then he, too, started toward the highest reaches of the only world he had ever known.

6

The Tapestry

Threads of life and lovers,
colors bright or gray,
a picture made of human life,
And warriors born to slay.

From the Tapestry of the Worldweaver
Chronicles of a Circle Called Earth

Tamarwind and Ulfgang came to her rooms as Belynda prepared to attend a meeting in the Senate forum.

"Just to say goodbye," Tam explained. Once more he was dressed in his green traveling clothes and boots of soft leather. Ulfgang pranced around, white coat groomed to a cottony fluff. The dog was clearly anxious to go, but the elven scout seemed inclined to linger. "And I wanted to tell you that it was nice to see you again."

"Yes . . ." Again Belynda felt that unusual flush spreading up her neck. "I . . . me, too. May the Goddess watch over your journey." She felt jumpy, unusually worried—which she took to be a lingering reaction to the quake of several days earlier. "Do you know if the road to Argentian suffered any damage?"

"A few rockslides in the hills—that's what the enchantress saw. Even if they're not cleared out, we'll have no trouble getting over them. The elves of the delegation are gathered and waiting for us on the Avenue of Metal. They're anxious to get back home—I think the city has overawed them a bit. In any event, we should get across the causeway by midday.

Ulfang, who had been quivering, tail wagging while he tried to stand still, suddenly uttered a short bark, then hung his head in embarrassment. "Excuse me," he said. "It's just that I haven't traveled in a long time . . . I guess the excitement of departure got to me."

"Well, you have a good trip too," Belynda said, touching the dog's tufted white topknot. "And hurry back."

Tamarwind took her arms in his hands, startling Belynda with the embrace as he stared into her eyes. "I would like to see you again . . . I hope that I can."

"Yes!" she replied, holding absolutely still until he turned and, with an easy wave, ambled away. Ulfang, tail still wagging, trotted ahead, then waited impatiently for the elf. In both of them she perceived—and envied—the eagerness to be starting on the journey that would carry them halfway across Nayve.

Belynda felt a sadly contrasting emotion as she joined several other ambassadors in the slow, dignified procession to the white-columned building that rose in stately majesty beside the College. Here the Senate convened in Grand Forum once every interval of forty days. The sessions were held in the great chamber, and were attended by elven sage-ambassadors as well as at least one spokesperson from the druids Grove. Normally Belynda found the sessions tedious and time-wasting. She had long ago determined that the more people involved in a process, the slower and more frustrating that process became, and there would be very many people indeed in the Grand Forum.

The senators themselves numbered nearly threescore, as every race of Nayve was represented by anywhere from two to twenty senators in that august body. Of course, it was the elves who had the twenty—the next most numerous group were the eight gnomish ambassadors. Some groups, such as the dryads and goblins, were limited to only a pair of senators. In theory, however, the Senate gave voice to every one of the cultures inhabiting Nayve.

As to the sage-ambassadors, there were more than a hundred in attendance. Each represented an elven community in the Fourth Circle—or at least a part of such an entity. Indeed, twelve of the ambassadors represented neighborhoods in Circle at Center, while the others, such as Belynda, were there in the interests of more rural realms like Argentian. The eldest of the local representatives was Rallaphan, a silver-haired patriarch who had held his seat for nine centuries. Belynda dipped her head as he marched past, honoring her with a cool nod. The sage-ambassador, like everyone else, stepped back to allow the regal senator to go by.

On her way toward the great doors she saw Zolaryn, the sage-ambassador of Barantha.

"My lady Sage-Ambassador? Do you have time for a word?" asked her fellow representative. Zolaryn was only a few centuries past the millennium mark, and bowed politely in deference to her elder.

"Of course," Belynda agreed.

Zolaryn's smooth brow creased in concern. "I have recently learned of many elves moving away from Barantha, particularly young males who have not yet bred. And there are similar reports from Kol'sos, too. I was curious to see if the same tendency has been reported in Argentian?"

"That is curious . . . I have heard of the same occurrence in my own land." Belynda couldn't help but be a trifle alarmed at this news. Clan and community were important attributes of elven life, and movement—except for purposes such as studying here in Circle at Center—was quite unusual. "They're not Wayfarers, are they?" she asked, thinking of the small clans that dwelled here and there in Nayve.

The Wayfarers maintained small villages, but were not inclined to belong to any of the major realms.

"If only it was as simple as that. But no, these are elves from good, long-standing families. And even their own clans can't report on why, or where, they're going."

"Perhaps it will be addressed in forum," Belynda suggested. In fact, she would welcome the chance to discuss something meaningful in the upcoming session.

Fortunately for a body that was sluggish almost to the point of utter inaction, the Senate of Nayve had very little work to do. While the elven ambassadors of the College saw to most matters of education, and the druids of the Grove made splendid caretakers for the natural world, the Senators could ponder questions of philosophy and ceremony. Belynda knew that, long ago, the great council had spent the better part of a century debating whether or not to honor the architect who had designed the grand structure housing the Senate offices. In the end, the commendation had passed—though the builder had been deceased for more than a thousand years!

Today, however, as she found her chair in the middle tier of the circular amphitheater, she sensed that there might be some purpose, even some urgency, to the meeting. All the seats were taken, and the two co-speakers on their stools at the center of the ring looked, if not concerned, at least like they were paying attention.

Praxian sat to the left. Short of hair and pinched of features, Speaker Praxian was tall and lanky, perching on the stool like some eccentric construct of sticks covered by a robe of purple and gold. Opposite the lean speaker sat Cannystrius, whose rounded face was capped with a lush head of curling yellow hair. Speaker Cannystrius was as rotund and short as Praxian was tall. Both had held their chairs for centuries, since long before Belynda had arrived in Circle at Center.

Now the two speakers exchanged glances and then stood,

simultaneously. Cannystrius uttered a high, nervous cough, and the arriving senators and ambassadors quickly fell silent. It was Praxian who began, speaking in stentorian tones that resonated through the marble-walled chamber.

"We are honored by the presence of the sage-enchantress Quilene, who has brought herself here from the Lodespikes. Sadly, her news is not cause for rejicing." Praxian indicated an elf, who rose from the front row to join the two speakers on the rostrum.

Belynda knew Quilene, though not as well as she had known Caranor. She was an elven matron with stiffly gilded hair and a stern voice. More significantly, she was a renowned mistress of sorcery, and widely acknowledged as the leader of Nayve's enchantresses. Now she looked across the tiers of the Senate with a grave expression.

"Many of you have learned that one of the enchantress sisterhood, Caranor, has died . . . died by fire." Belynda saw grim nods around the chamber—nearly everyone had already heard the news. Quilene went on to describe the destruction of Caranor's house and belongings, as well as the isolated nature of her abode, and the fact that no one knew who her last visitor had been. She drew a deep breath, allowing the audience to do the same.

"It is my distressing duty to inform you that a second sage-enchantress has also met this awful fate. Allevia of the Lodespikes was slain just in the past tenday, also dying by fire in the midst of her burned abode."

Now the Senate rang with gasps of horror, shouts of consternation. "Who did this?" "Why would she be killed?" The cries came from a few elves, while the rest of the senators fumbled for words.

"These are questions we have not been able to solve. There is a thing that we *do* know, however . . . and I feel it is information that should be shared with the Senate, with all Nayve. Nearly one hundred years ago, another sage-enchantress, an elf named Paronnial, was found slain under similar circumstances." The statement drew more gasps from several of the senators, including a snort of displeasure from the senior giant.

"This is true?" Praxian declared, standing on spindly legs and glaring down at Quilene.

"Of course it's true!" snapped Cannystrius, rising to confront the co-speaker, then turning to the sage-enchantress. "But, dear, why didn't you speak of this then?"

"At the time it was felt that the news would only be upsetting to all of Nayve," Quilene responded coolly. "We couldn't discount the chance that some accident had occurred, and in any event Paronnial was young, known to few outside our ranks."

"Whereas some of us knew Caranor very well," declared Belynda, rising and drawing many startled eyes with her interjection. "And we grieve for the loss of our friend."

"May the Goddess Worldweaver hear you," Quilene said solemnly.

"But we must find out how this is happening!" Praxian blurted. "And take steps to see that it never happens again!"

"As well as the sharing of information, it is to that end that I have come to the Center of Everything," continued the sage-enchantress. "If the death of Caranor was the intent of another, it is an action of brute violence, a threat to all Nayve. As such, it smacks of humankind." She turned to the lone human in the chamber, a druid who sat upon a stool near the rear of the rostrum. "Cillia, we would ask that you consult the Tapestry of the Goddess, to see what information can be divined."

"Is that wise?" Praxian countered, while Cannystrius simply snorted in exasperation. "Wouldn't it be better not to disturb—?"

"Quilene is right," Cillia declared.

The druid rose and strode to the center of the rostrum, where she stood above even the tall Praxian. Belynda knew that Cillia was among the oldest of the druids—she had come to Nayve nearly two thousand years ago. Yet such was the druidic blessing that she remained fit and youthful, her body unstooped and her skin unlined. She had long dark hair that swayed in a cascade down her back and a strong, rounded body, big-bosomed with broad, sturdy hips. She was a commanding presence physically, but was accorded even greater honor because of her long, responsible service to the Goddess.

"Indeed, we shall study the Tapestry and learn what threads are involved. If there is a connection to the Seventh Circle, the pattern will be shown."

"There is more bad news!" cried a high-pitched voice from across the gallery. Belynda saw that the gnomish spokesman, a stout fellow all but concealed by his thick gray beard, had risen to speak. "A giant came to Thickwhistle!"

"Bah!" It was the giant leader, a black-bearded ruffian named Galewn. He stood and shook a fist at the gnome, who jammed his thumbs in his ears and wiggled his fingers back. "The border between Thickwhistle and Granitehome varies with each interval, so far as these gnomes are concerned. More likely it was the town of gnomes come to Granitehome!"

"It was not!" shrieked the gnome. Several of his fellows held him back as he tried to make an impulsive dash toward the giant, who was two tiers below and halfway around the chamber.

"Before we tend to this weighty matter, there is another piece of news I am forced to share," declared Cillia. Belynda wondered if she had used magic to propel her voice—it fairly boomed through the chamber. In any event, the giant and gnome were quickly seated and silent.

"There is a druid who lives beyond the lake, one of the wisest of our number. Her name is Miradel, and she has mastered much magic, and been trusted to read at the Worldweaver's side. I must report, however, that she has gone against the will of the council, and performed the forbidden spell."

Now there were real gasps in the chamber. Rallaphan stood, his face locked in an expression of fury. "Scandal—blasphemy!" he shouted.

"Miradel!" whispered Belynda at the same time, horrified for her friend.

"Why would she do that?" asked Praxian, in a voice like a squeaking donkey.

"She claims that it was her last chance . . . that this human is a warrior of a doomed culture, a realm that faces imminent destruction."

"These . . . these are things that require dutiful discussion!" declared Praxian, with a shake of that gray-cropped head. "I hereby table the matter until we have had time to meditate, to think. . . ."

"And to think some more!" Cannystrius added. "Not tomorrow, certainly!"

"No," agreed the co-speaker. "Nor the day after."

"And I don't think we can . . ." Cannystrius was suggesting reasons for further delay, but by that time Belynda had already run out through the giant marble doors.

"You will start by learning about Earth," Miradel announced after Fallon had whisked away the dishes from Natac's next breakfast.

The warrior merely nodded, his mind still darkened by the lessons of the past few days. He felt an unnatural chill, as if the shadows of the men he had killed were drawing across the sun. The mindless brawling of Owen and Fionn was a fresh memory, as well as Miradel's statement that those two were human warriors, like him. Fluttering around the fringes was the image of Yellow Hummingbird, the knowledge of a daughter's life offered—and horribly claimed—in the name of a god who didn't exist.

And when the burden of this guilt seemed like a crushing weight, he would see Miradel, and be reminded again of the sacrifice she had made in bringing him here. Why did she think him worthy of that gift, the loss of her eternal life? Whatever he did, he knew there was no way he could live up to her expectations—hers would be just another meaningless sacrifice, a life wasted for fruitless purpose.

But so far she had brusquely ignored his brooding, chiding him that self-pity was only a waste of time. Now she led him into a small room, and closed the door behind them both. They were immediately plunged into utter darkness, and Natac knew that extra care must have gone into chocking up every crack and cranny around this chamber. Though it was midday and cloudless, it seemed that absolutely no light could reach them from outside.

He blinked in the light of a flaring match, saw Miradel touch the flame to the wick of a fat candle. Illumination surged into the room, brighter than any candle Natac had ever seen. Miradel held a small glass crystal in one of her hands, and in the fingers of the other she pinched a small tuft of some kind of soft material.

"This is the Wool of Time," she said, following his glance. "Trace threads drawn from the Tapestry of the Worldweaver, and used for the casting of the spell of seeing."

"That spell is what you are doing now?"

"Yes. You should look at the wall, there."

Natac saw that one wall of the room was smooth and whitewashed to a bright finish. It was not marred by any shelves or other features. Abruptly the light flared and then waned, and he saw from the corner of his eye that the druid had dropped the threads into the flame of the candle. Now she held up the crystal, between the candle and the wall, and again Natac's attention turned to that unmarred surface.

He saw a brown swath there, with an appearance of bumps and other irregularities across its surface. In places there were patches of white or large stretches of green, and snaking lines of blue crossed here and there.

"You are looking at the land you called Mexico," Miradel said. "Imagine that you are a bird flying very high . . . Now, picture these places: The bumps here are the hills of Tlaxcala, and this direction is west. The white splotch is the snowy cap of the great volcano, and these are the lakes in the valley of Mexico."

Awestruck, Natac tried to follow her words, and quickly grasped the truth of what she was saying. He pointed to a shadowy notch on the border of his homeland. "There is the pass where we met the Aztecs in ambush, chased them back toward their city."

"And where you were captured."

"You know about that?" he asked, amazed.

"The Tapestry shows all to one who knows how to look," Miradel replied. "I have been following your thread for a long time, so, yes, I took note of your capture, and your place in the ceremony honoring the Aztec gods."

"I . . . yes, I see." He found it disturbing that this woman, and perhaps many others, could have watched all aspects of his life. Yet he shook off that discomfort amid a growing sense of curiosity. "You can see all of Earth through this crystal?"

"Of past and present . . . we can only guess as to the future. Watch." Abruptly the image on the wall began to shrink, as if the watcher were rising upward with dizzying speed. "You see the northern and southern oceans, now?"

"Yes." Natac had heard of these great bodies of water, though he had never set eyes on either of them. Now they were blue splotches on the wall, growing larger as the vast realm of land was shrinking to a small piece of land between great seas. Indeed, he was soon stunned to see that two great continents existed, one north and the other south of his homeland. The place that he had once thought encompassed the whole world was no more than a link in a chain of lands connecting these two land masses.

"One of those lands is the place you called Europe?" he asked.

She shook her head. "Watch."

And then even those continents were reduced, and so much of the image before him was blue water. To the right was a great stretch of ocean, and then more continents, irregular masses of green, brown, and white.

"This is Europe, here," Miradel explained, pointing. "This is the land that will send the warriors who will destroy Tlaxcalans, the Aztecs . . . In time, it seems likely that all the peoples of these two continents will fall under the sway of the men from Europe."

"Have they conquered all the rest of the world?"

"No . . . I will show you."

For an hour Natac gawked at astonishing sights. He saw men like Owen and Fionn, and others who were clad in metal and rode great beasts into battle. He saw huge nations of black-skinned men, and teeming lands farther to the east in a place Miradel called the Orient. Particularly impressive was a massive wall, a battlement running across mountains, valleys, and plains, a structure that Miradel informed him could have wrapped all the realm of the Aztecs within its serpentine length. There were palaces in the Orient too, and sparkling arrows that trailed flame into the sky and then exploded in bursts of bright color. Great boats plied the rivers and coastal waters, and the sheer number of people he saw was overwhelming. Some of these were warriors, and they formed armies that darkened the ground with their numbers.

"They are so many—surely they will conquer all of Earth!" Natac exclaimed.

"There are many reasons why they will not. Here, see." The druid narrowed the picture until he saw two great boats, each draped with white swaths of cloth. Smoke spewed from the flanks of the vessels, inflicting horrible damage upon each craft. He saw men scrambling about the decks, realized that these 'boats' were in fact the size of small palaces, with multiple floors. Quickly he understood that they were propelled by the wind, that the great sheets of cloth were in fact arrayed like vertical wings to catch the force of the blowing gusts.

"These are sea-ships of the Europeans. And see this:"

Miradel showed him a place she called Flanders. A hundred men were mounted on a rank of the pawing, prancing animals Natac had learned were called horses. The great beasts looked terribly fierce, with flaring nostrils and wide, flashing eyes. The men wore shirts of metal, and bore long spears, weapons that were dropped to point forward as the company, in unison, charged. Standing against the riders were hundreds of metal-wearing footmen, and these turned to run as the horses bore down. Natac was appalled by the slaughter as the lancers rode through the broken ranks of the fleeing enemy.

And then there was a line of pathetically feeble-looking men, standing in a row and bearing long, narrow sticks that lacked even the pointed tip of a spear. Nevertheless, these men pointed their weapons at the riders—and then the weapons, in unison, spat a long billow of dark smoke. The attack reached farther than the smoke, dropping a half dozen riders from their saddles, and then the cavalry broke away.

"How . . . how can an army stand up to warriors like that?" Natac asked. "To those riders, and to sticks that spew fire and death?"

"No army on Earth is capable," Miradel said. "Though you should know that the different tribes of Europeans expend most of their energy battling each other. Still, they have good ships now, and thriving populations . . . Already, just twenty years ago, one of their boldest sailors returned from a crossing of the ocean to report the existence of hitherto unknown lands—including the place of your own homeland. The final tie in doom's knot is this: Europeans have a passion for gold above all things, and nowhere else in the world is gold concentrated as it is in the city of the Aztecs."

Next Miradel showed him other facets of life on Earth. He saw small churches and great cathedrals, a multitude of temples, minarets that were narrow spires jutting as high as a great pyramid, and shrines decorated with the rounded image of a plump, boyish god. There were other pyramids too, massive structures of stone that the druid stated were tombs for dead leaders, beings now exalted to godhood. And everywhere Natac saw people of different shapes and sizes, with skin colors ranging from pale to charcoal-black. He found himself looking at Miradel, at the high cheekbones and deep lines of her face outlined in the glow of the magical candlelight.

"Are you a human, too . . . from Earth?" he asked.

"Yes."

"From which part?"

She moved the picture back across the great ocean, but instead of the mountainous country of Mexico and Tlaxcala, she turned the picture south, toward a region of dense forests and flat, endless ground.

"The lands of the Maya," Natac grasped. "I have heard of that place, those people . . . your people?"

She nodded, her violet eyes alight with remembrance— of pain or pleasure, Natac could not discern.

"How did you come here?"

Miradel drew a breath those slender shoulders rising. "I, too, was given to false gods . . . Still a virgin, I was thrown into a well and drowned, in an effort to keep the water from draining away." She laughed sharply, bitterly. "I failed."

"But I know of the magic you used to bring me here. How did . . . ?"

Now she smiled. "I came as all druids came, brought

before the Worldweaver in the Center of Everything. I was birthed before her whole and adult, and granted a life on Nayve in return for . . . things that had happened, that I had done, on Earth."

"What could you have done in such a short life?" he asked, not accusingly, but very curious.

"It was not just one life. Humans live a multitude of times, and each time they are given the chance to be proved worthy of the Goddess's gift. Those she rewards she brings to Nayve as druids."

And some druids bring warriors here, he remembered, completing the cycle in his own thoughts. Yet that still left the gnawing question: Why had she made such a sacrifice, thrown away eternal life, to bring him here?

The candle abruptly sputtered and began to fade. Miradel put the crystal down and once again Natac was looking at a plain white wall, a surface marred by shifting shadow as the wick fizzled away. When the druid pushed the door open, he was startled by the strength of the light, and was forced to squint as he followed her through the kitchen and out onto the terrace. All the while he was thinking, analyzing what he had seen.

"The men riding the horses . . . it's not just the speed of movement that give them a great advantage, but the combined weight of the animal and man in the charge. It must be terrifying to stand in the path of such an attack—and if you did stand, you'd probably die."

"Yes."

"Tell me about the weapons that spew smoke. They must hurl solid objects as well, do they not?"

"You are very perceptive," Miradel said, with a smile of self-satisfaction. "Yes. The large ones are called cannons, and the small ones are arquebuses. Each hurls a projectile, the cannon shooting a large stone or ball of metal that can crush wood and sink ships. The arquebus shoots a small stone, or a pellet made of metal—and that missile is enough to pierce flesh, break bones, and puncture hearts."

"Can cannons be moved without a ship?"

"It is difficult," Miradel allowed, "though—and this is the way of humans—the weapons are getting smaller and more powerful as time goes on. Sometimes a cannon will be loaded with a whole bucketful of small pebbles and bits of metal. When it is fired into a mass of people it can wreak horrible destruction."

"And our warriors, Tlaxcalan, Aztec, *all* of us, fight in tight ranks." Natac felt a growing sense of shock. "Truly, Tlaxcala is doomed—You are right, even the Aztecs are doomed." He looked at her in despair, self-pity tearing at him. He choked out the words, biting back the strength of his own anguish. "It will be the end of my people—and I am condemned to watch it!"

The druid merely shrugged. "It may not be the end of the people in your world—but without a doubt the gods of the Aztecs will be thrown down, and perhaps that is not such a bad thing. The priests who will come with the Europeans have their own foibles, and they, too, will wage war justified by the commands of their god. But they will not rip the hearts out of their captives just to ensure that the sun comes up."

"But those priests, too, worship false gods?"

"All gods are false . . . they are creations of people, stories and beliefs invented because of some human need to claim understanding."

"You yourself talk about a Goddess—the Worldweaver!" Natac challenged. "You said that it was her tapestry we saw! And now you claim that all gods are false!"

Miradel shook her head, undaunted by his accusation. "I meant all gods of Earth. The Worldweaver dwells at the Center of Everything, and she alone is real."

Natac would have argued longer but they were interrupted by the sound of footsteps coming through the villa. "Miradel?" The word was called out in a woman's voice.

"Belynda?" The druid turned away from Natac.

The newcomer, Natac saw, was a woman with hair so blond it was almost white. Her eyes widened at the sight of Miradel, but the rest of her expression remained bland. If she was shocked by the aged appearance of the druid, she did a good job of covering it up.

"I . . . I was going to send you word, after a little more time passed," Miradel said softly.

"Cillia announced the news in the Senate forum," Belynda said bluntly. "I came as soon as I heard."

Natac was conscious of the other woman's eyes on him, cool and appraising. He flushed with shame, sensing that this was a friend of Miradel's—surely she must be blaming him for the doom that had fallen upon the druid. Yet he could discern little emotion in those wide, almond-shaped eyes. Despite his embarrassment, he stared back, realizing that there were other things that were unusual about this woman.

Her ears were pointed in the lobe, he saw, like Fallon's. That cascading array of white-gold hair was bound by a circlet of silver wire, and her face seemed unusually narrow—though she was unquestionably beautiful to behold. Yet, despite the fact that he had now seen humans with faces of fur, and with skin of darkest black or pale white, there was something *different* about this person.

He wondered if it was her lack of emotion, and decided that was it. Miradel's breath had caught in her throat at the sight of Belynda, and Natac saw the trembling of her shoulders, knew the druid was fighting to suppress an expression of her feeling. Belynda was making no such effort—in the frank examination of Miradel's lined face, or her cool appraisal of the warrior whose summoning had thus aged her, she looked as though she might have been examining something of utterly no import.

"Warrior Natac," Miradel said, stepping back to look at him. He saw the emotion in her eyes, was startled to recognize it as pride. She was proud of him! Again he felt that staggering weight of guilt, unworthiness—*why?*

"This is my friend Belynda of Argentian . . . She is a sage-ambassador of the elves."

"I greet you, Belynda of Argentian," Natac said with a bow, even as his mind digested the news. So she wasn't human after all—she was an elf! And Fallon was too, of course. The word had some intrinsic meaning to him, merely because of his familiarity with his new language, but he resolved to ask Miradel many more questions when he had a chance.

"And you, Warrior Natac," Belynda replied, still in that cool, distant tone. "I can only hope my friend has chosen wisely."

"I hope the same thing, lady," he replied sincerely.

"Natac has encountered Fionn and Owen," Miradel said. "In fact, he got them to stop brawling long enough to have a conversation."

"A *brief* conversation" Natac amended.

"I think this warrior may be different from the others," the druid said, again with that sense of pride that made him squirm.

"I see." Belynda looked into Miradel's eyes. "Why did you do it, my friend? When you knew the costs, and the risks . . . and you know the spell has been forbidden by your own council?" It was as if Natac weren't there as she sought for an answer. Yet he listened intently, at least as anxious for the answer as was the elfwoman who asked the question.

"I will tell you," the druid said. "Tell you both . . . but before I do, there is something that I would like to discuss with you."

"What is it?"

"We all felt the world shake a few days ago. I am convinced that was just a symptom of much greater disturbances. And so I ask you, my friend: What have you heard of unusual trouble in the Fourth Circle?"

It seemed to Natac as if Belynda's pale skin got a touch whiter. "The sage-enchantress Caranor . . . she died by fire in her home. And then an interval later the sage-enchantress Allevia was killed the same way!"

Miradel gasped. "Allevia dwelled in the Lodespikes, did she not?"

"On the fringe of the mountains, yes . . . in a high valley overlooking the Greens."

"The Greens," the druid repeated seriously. "It is there I feel the danger lies."

"There are a lot of people there," Belynda countered, though she didn't speak with a great deal of conviction. "Surely we would have heard something in Circle at Center about trouble? Or you druids . . . Can't you look there with your viewing glass?"

"That's part of the problem," Miradel said. "For a long time, now, the Greens have been masked to our magic. Druids have gone there, talked to centaurs and giants and faeries . . . and though they haven't learned anything suspicious, it is not uncommon for them to encounter unusual secrecy. And that was before Debyra's visit, just last year."

"What did she learn?" Belynda asked.

"Nobody knows . . . she was never heard from again."

"That is bad enough—but can you be certain?"

"Not yet . . . not about everything. But Cillia has been watching, and she has told me what she's learned." Miradel looked at Belynda curiously. "Did you know that there are now many elves living in the Greens?"

"No!" The sage-ambassador blinked, for her a dramatic expression of surprise. "I always knew of a few renegades, restless souls who never seemed to fit in. But there are no realms there!"

The druid shrugged. "There are more than a few, and perhaps it is right to call them renegades. They seem to be content to live in the wilderness, away from the sanctity of borders and councils."

"Perhaps that's where they're going," Belynda mused softly.

"Who?" probed Miradel.

"It's just . . . for some years now, an unusual number of elves have been leaving Argentian. And no one seems to know where they go. Just this morning I learned that the same thing is happening in Barantha and Kel'sos."

"All realms within a hundred miles of the Greens," the druid observed.

"And such migration is unquestionably a change . . . an unusual one, in the annals of Nayve. But even so . . . what harm is done? Where is the trouble?"

"I believe that there is something dangerous there," Miradel informed her friend, and took in Natac's eyes with a brief glance.

"Dangerous *elves*?"

"Elves . . . and others. Centaurs and giants, I'm certain. But there is something holding them together, driving them . . . and it is a force that resists even detection by druid magic."

"But stay—I admit that you are making me think," declared the elfwoman, her hand trembling slightly as she raised it before Miradel's aged face. "Now explain something: You were going to tell me why you brought this warrior here."

The druid took a deep breath and exhaled slowly. "I did it for your people," she said to Belynda.

"For the elves? Why in the name of the Goddess would you do that?"

"Because," Miradel said, and now her dark eyes turned to Natac, "you are needed to train the elves in the ways of battle . . . to teach them how to fight a war."

●　　●　　●

Flames rose high around him and he saw Satan writhing against a desperate onslaught. The demon twisted and shrieked, helplessly suffering the torture of his righteous punishment. Slowly, inexorably, the valiant knight pressed forward with sword and staff . . . victory was there! And then that triumph slipped away from him in a gust of wind and a waft of smoke. The fiend had made his escape, and the knight was left alone, facing the enemy horde. . . .

The dream had its own form, and it followed the pattern each time it tormented his sleep. Constructed from the events of Sir Christopher's past, centuries distant, it wove a tale of temptation and failure, and it left alive the hope of redemption and triumph.

It always began with the same disaster: The Saracens attacked from ambush, striking from both ridges above a parched, arid valley. They caught twelve Knights Templar by surprise, slaughtering many of Sir Christopher's companions with their short, lethal arrows. Only three of the twelve reached the great portals, the gates to sacred Jerusalem herself.

But the Saracens cut them off before they could enter the safety of the great fortress-city. Finally Sir Christopher stood alone, hacking to right and left, slaughtering his enemies for the glory of God. He prayed aloud, calling the names of his slain comrades, praising the bravery of his loyal, perished horse. Thirst was a claw at his swollen tongue, talons of fire ripping at his parched throat. His shield, emblazoned with the red cross of the Templars, was torn and broken under the onslaught of a hundred weapons.

His red blade was knocked from his hands. A Syrian lance pierced his flesh, slicing into his heart and lungs. In that instant he knew he was dying, and he commended his soul and his being to Heavenly Paradise. His life flowed away, spattered in crimson blood across the rocks of the Holy Land. In the last glimmer of awareness, he reached upward, sought and anticipated the welcoming embrace of God.

Instead, he found himself in the arms of Hell's Harlot, a beautiful temptress who touched him shamelessly, bringing arousal from his traitorous flesh. At first he fought against her obscene advances, twisting and kicking fruitlessly in an attempt to escape her tender fingers, her soft lips. But his blows passed through her without effect, while her own gentle touch produced a pronounced reaction in the knight. His soul weakened, his flesh yielded, and the witch used him for her obscene pleasure.

And he, in that foggy weakness, he enjoyed the same carnal gratification. He ravished her as if she were the whore of Babylon, and he relished each salacious convulsion of his loins. Only when at last he lay exhausted, and she fell sound asleep, did he realize that he had been tested by God.

It was a test he had failed.

In his surging grief he strangled the harlot, but he knew that his vengeance was too late to cleanse his soul of sin. He staggered from her lair and found himself in a world of blasphemy . . . a world in which he had struggled and labored for more than three centuries.

And once again he awakened, and God's work lay before him.

But now he had a tool, a talisman that would make that work so much more effective. As he did every morning, he reached to his breast, found the stone there, still suspended on its golden chain. He looked at the pearl, at its crimson cross, and understood again that he had been chosen for an important task. The red sigil on the stone was not a perfect cross, since all four of the lines were the same length. Even so, his discovery of the talisman in the possession of the heretical witch Caranor had convinced him anew that his work was here.

And so he emerged from his tent, ignored the stirring of

his small army, and raised the stone toward the already bright sun.

"Come to me, Children of God," he whispered, his fingers clenched around the pearl. "Come to me, and join my new crusade."

7

The Road to Argentian

Coat of metal,
Silver crest,
Sweetwater stream
and glade eternal.
Towers tall
gardens blessed—
Argentian!
A home, a source
a nest.

From the Tapestry of the Worldweaver
Atlas of Elvenkind

Despite the planned early departure, the homebound Argentian delegates needed most of the afternoon to cross the long causeway from Circle at Center to the lakeshore. Tamarwind wasn't surprised that the homesick elves of his pastoral realm were ultimately reluctant to take leave of the city's splendors. Indeed, the scout surprised himself with his own regrets, wistful thoughts centered on the woman with the delicate frame and the strong face. He had known her for centuries, had given her the seed that had created offspring, and yet during the last tenday she had made him feel like a giddy youth. The emotions were strong and unusual, but he liked them.

After the long causeway ended at the shore of the lake, the Avenue of Metal became the Metal Highway. Here Wiytstar, the chief delegate, suggested that the party find rooms in the splendid lakeshore inn. Though a long time remained until the Hour of Darken, the other Argentians quickly agreed. Ulfang, similarly being in no particular hurry, was content to swim in the pond among the birds that had given the hostelry its name.

The Blue Swan Inn rose above its own harbor. The place was a sprawling building of rough-hewn wood, with many lofty towers and beautiful gardens of blossoms and sculpted trees. Though of course it was run by elves, it was popular with druids, many of whom maintained boats in the anchorage. Just before the Hour of Darken Tamarwind enjoyed the sight of a dozen of these craft, each propelled by magical wind gusts, racing toward the lighthouse at the mouth of the harbor.

The next day they had a leisurely breakfast and started out by midmorning. The road quickly entered a large, straight tunnel, and the lake—with its island of green trees, marble buildings, and the Worldweaver's Loom—slowly vanished into a small circle of daylight behind them.

Not that the tunnel was dark, of course. Globes of white light, enchanted balls created by sage-enchantresses a thousand years ago, floated just below the peak of the tunnel's arched roof. These balls were spaced about once every hundred paces, but a full dozen of them seemed to attach themselves to the elven party and float overhead as they walked along.

"This tunnel was carved by goblins, two millennia ago or longer," Tam explained to Ulf, who had commented on the generally smooth walls and straight pathway.

"Goblins?" Wiytstar overheard. "Aren't they terribly dangerous when you get a large group of them together?"

"Not really," Tamarwind replied. "They're clannish, of course, but they can be very hard workers. Give them enough to eat and drink, and goblins have done some of the best building in all of Nayve."

"I see they have drains in many places," Ulfgang noted, sniffing at a metal grate in the ground. "They could carry off a lot of water."

Tamarwind smiled. "In fact, there are tales that some of those drains connect to huge tunnels underneath Nayve. Who knows—maybe the water would drain all the way to the Underworld!"

"Well, I know I'm grateful for the lights," sniffed another of the delegates, shivering and looking sideways as she stepped past the drain set in the roadway's gutter.

"How did one get to Circle at Center before the tunnel was built?" asked Ulf.

"Well, there's always been the Highway of Wood," Tam replied. "And before this route was opened that was really the only way to get from the city to the rest of Nayve."

The travelers proceeded at a measured pace, meeting several groups of elves who invariably wished the Argentians an unchanging life and then walked on past. There was no way to tell how rapidly time was passing, but even Tam was beginning to feel tired when they noticed an unusually bright glow suffusing the tunnel before them. At the same time the air became tinged with a mingled flavor of spice, smoke, and grease.

A half hour later they reached Garlack's Underground Inn. The proprietor was an obese goblin, and if he was surly he was also fair. He offered food, drink, and lodgings in exchange for a few simple tasks. Wiytstar Sharand was no master enchanter, but he easily wove simple spells to clean the bedrooms, wash dishes, and refill the water cistern. In return the goblin and his workers produced heaps of fried fish, strangely spiced but quite savory to the elven palates. The floating globes dimmed enough to let them sleep, then brightened as they started out again. Tamarwind, as always when he traveled here, felt the darkness of the tunnel pressing heavily around them, and he set as brisk a pace as the elders could manage.

Even so, it was late in the day when they spotted sunlight before them, and finally hastened out of the tunnel to stand beneath an open sky. The lofty crests around them were hidden behind rugged shoulders of lower ground. As the enchantress had predicted, patches of rubble tumbled by the earthquake blocked the road here and there, but the druids had already done a good job of moving much of the detritus back onto the slopes and crests of the hills where it belonged.

Tam and Ulf found that they naturally walked a little faster than the other seven delegates. With a laugh the scout abruptly realized that he preferred the dog's company to that of his countrymen.

"I'm glad to have you strolling along the road with me," he declared. "Doesn't it seem as if we're embarking on an adventure of sorts?"

"Anytime I can get out of the city it's an adventure. And as to me strolling along the road . . . well, it's age," the dog admitted. "A century ago I would have bounded up each of these hills—just for the view!"

"I can't say I've ever had that kind of ambition," Tam acknowledged, eyeing the steep heights bordering the broad highway.

The range of rugged elevation surrounded Circle at Center. Barren of trees, with hunched brows of gray slate and here and there a glowering, wind-swept peak jutting far above the surrounding summits, they formed a barrier around the great lake and its precious island city. The route climbed and curved gently as it followed a valley that became the only easy pass through the rough terrain.

"These dry hills seem so barren—it's not until we've passed the Snakesea that I really feel like we're on the way home," Wiytstar confessed when they stopped at a small inn for their next night's rest.

"But there's no hurry, is there?" Tam asked, still enjoying the sensation of freedom and adventure. "The hills are nice to look at—and as to the sea crossing, I've always felt the trip was its own reward."

The elder delegate shook his head. "Personally, I like to stand on ground that's not moving—I should think that tremor in Circle at Center would have been enough to convince anyone of that!"

Nevertheless, it was only a few days later that the party reached the shore of the Snakesea and had a chance to observe firsthand the magic that made a secure crossing possible. The elves gathered in respectful silence. There were a few others who would make the crossing with the Argentian delegates—a half dozen elves traveling in pairs, and a giant with a large, ox-drawn cart.

The druid ferrytender strode to the edge of the sea. The human was a tall man, broad-shouldered and long of hair and beard. His body was corded with sinew. He was naked, and carried only a stout staff of wood.

The shore here was a fringe of smooth rocks, scuffed by the steady drive of waves. These were not thundering boomers such as were hurled by the Worldsea against the shores of Nayve, but even so they crashed with some force, occasionally sending showers of spray cascading across the rocks and onto the grassy soil beyond. The elves were arrayed beyond the reach of these showers, but the druid stood atop a seashore rock and spread his arms wide, as if welcoming the salty splashes. He held the staff, gripped in both hands, horizontally before his chest, and then slowly raised his arms, bringing the shaft of wood to a position high above his head.

A surging wave exploded against the rocks and for a moment the human figure was lost in the cascading mist. In moments Tam could see that he still stood there, as firm as the stone upon which his feet were planted. And then the elf's eyes were drawn to the surface of the water itself, as the bedrock of the Fourth Circle answered the pull of druid magic. No matter how many times he saw it, he was still entranced by the sight:

More waves pounded the shore, and a great shelf of seawater, rising above the level of the observers on shore, flowed to the right and left. Here and there a smooth rock jutted through the flowing seawater, and moments later the expanse was more solid than water. Blue-green brine spilled from a broad rocky raft, a surface that was mostly smooth, though marred by enough irregularities to prove its natural origin. The druid remained rigid for more minutes, and water continued to drain off the sides of the raft.

It was some time before the surface was dry, with the exception of a few standing puddles. Then the human slammed the butt of the staff to the ground, and the rock raft advanced, sliding smoothly through the short distance between itself and the shore. Finally it nestled against the rocks of the coast, and the druid gestured to the elves, signaling that they should advance. The Argentian delegates came forward hesitantly, but Ulfgang showed no reluctance. Indeed, the dog bounded onto one of the shore rocks, then sprang through the air to land on the raft. As the elves stepped cautiously aboard, the dog was already racing back and forth, sniffing at the puddles, splashing through, then shaking himself in the midst of a shimmering cascade of spray.

The druid made no acknowledgment of his passengers as he stalked regally from the shore across the surface of his raft. Tam knew this was not because of rudeness. Rather, the human needed to maintain his full concentration on the magic—a focus that he would maintain throughout the twenty hours required to cross the strait.

The other elves maintained a proper separation, each party finding a vantage somewhere around the edge of the great raft. The giant, however, didn't seemed to understand the propriety of this, for as soon as he had tended and hobbled his ox, he strode around the flat surface of rock, his bearded head thrown back, his great bucket of a mouth wide open as if to gulp down the sea breeze. He spoke to one of the silent elf couples, but neither slender, yellow-haired figure made any response. Apparently undaunted, he ambled toward Tamarwind and Ulfgang, who were watching the sea just a few steps away from the huddle Argentian elves.

" 'Tis a great day for travelin', or my name's not Rawknuckle Barefist!" the giant declared, his booming voice thundering in sensitive elven ears.

Still, after the refined and dignified company of the elves, Tamarwind was surprised to find that he welcomed the garrulous approach of this fellow traveler. He looked up at the giant, smiling as he saw that he—a tall elf—came only to the middle of the big fellow's chest.

"Yes, it is, good sir," the elf replied, as Wiytstar pointedly looked away. "Do you, too, follow the Metal Highway from Circle at Center?"

"Aye, but only for a few days from the far landing." He tilted his chin in the direction of metal, toward the stately raft's destination. "My lodge, 'tis in the Greens."

"A good road through there," Tam remarked, remembering the smooth highway flanked for unending miles by tall trees. In places, great leafy branches arched over the broad road.

The giant scowled, apparently at some private memory. "Y'know, 'tis not the same as it used to be," he suggested, with the gravity that flavored any talk of change in Nayve.

"How so?" inquired Tamarwind. He thought back to his own recent trip, on the way to Circle at Center from Argentian. The only unusual feature had been an inn that was closed down, which forced them to walk an extra few miles one day.

"Well, this:" the giant replied. "On my outbound leg I found meself a nice clearing for my bed. Wouldn't you know but that a lot of elves—fellows like you, only scruffier . . . like they lived outside—came out from the trees and told me to move on. Said the clearing was theirs—in the Greens, it was!"

"And so you left?" Tam asked, startled by news of the confrontation.

The big traveler shrugged. "There were twelve of them—and I wasn't in a mood for a fight."

"I'm glad," answered the elf, with an appraising look at the brawny shoulders and tree-trunk legs.

"But it was a vexation, for all that. And who ever said anyone could own a part o' the Greens?"

"I never imagined," Ulf put in.

"Whoops, there—did ye speak, dog?" Rawknuckle scowled suspiciously.

"Well, yes," replied Ulfgang.

The giant nodded. "Well, and yer right, too. Who ever imagined such a thing?"

The giant appeared to have worked out his irritation, and for the next few hours engaged in pleasant conversation with Tam and Ulfgang. He even offered the dog a swig from the firebrew that he finally dug out of his pack. Ulfgang declined—wisely, it turned out, as Tamarwind instantly regretted the friendly impulse that caused him to take a drink of the burning, stomach-churning draught.

Rawknuckle showed no discomfort, and finished the bottle himself. He spent the rest of the crossing snoring prodigiously, a rumble that at its peak drowned out the sounds of the wind and the water spilling away from the majestic raft. Most of the elves, accustomed to silk sheets and fine inns, spent an uncomfortable night on the wet rock of the raft—though Tam, for his part, found that he enjoyed this night spent under the stars. For hours he watched the shifting patterns of the dazzling lights, and finally, with his knapsack for a pillow, drifted off to a few hours' sleep.

By the Lighten Hour the far shore was a fringe of green

on the watery horizon. A few hours later the raft lodged itself against a bank that was dense with forest. Birds and monkeys chattered in the treetops, and a fringe of undergrowth choked the ground along the shore. A traveler's inn called the Hooting Squirrel stood at the landing, and from here the Metal Highway scored a straight line into the woods.

Given the early hour, most of the Argentian elves felt like continuing on, and the party immediately resumed the trek along the road. Rawknuckle, too, announced that he would be off immediately, and Tam hoped to enjoy the giant's company for a few days. However, the big fellow set a rigorous pace for himself and his oxcart, and soon disappeared down the tree-shaded road.

The elves maintained their more deliberate progression, and Tam found himself increasingly irritated with their lack of speed. It wasn't that he was particularly anxious to get to Argentian. More to the point, it was the company of these stultifying traveling mates that was grating on his nerves. Once he understood that, he made it a point to swallow his impatience, and face the routine of the trip with at least the outward appearance of serenity.

Ulfgang was little help. Now that they had reached the Greens, he seemed to come alive. He dashed through the brush, occasionally returning to the road so that Tam could remove burrs and brambles from his fluffy coat.

"You know, the woods are really much more open once you get past the fringe along the road," Ulf said. "You could come with me—we'll explore!"

Tam only laughed at the preposterous notion. Though his feet were tough and his muscles hardened by the recent weeks of travel, he had no inclinations to make himself extra tired. And the journey through the Greens passed without further incident, except that the elves were somewhat flustered to discover *three* inns that had closed, instead of the one that had been shut down the previous cycle.

Each of these was boarded up, and the party hurried past the vaguely forbidding façades.

The innkeepers they met at other establishments were as mystified by the closures as were the travelers. "They just closed up one day and vanished into the woods—no word on where they went," was the routine comment, before the host invariably steered the conversation around to more mundane matters.

This lack of information didn't surprise Tamarwind. He knew that all these wayside inns, as well as the occasional smithies, farms, and orchards they passed, were the holdings of Wayfarer elves, and they naturally tended to be somewhat clannish. These were people who claimed none of the elven realms as a homeland, but instead drew their heritage from the long lineage of a particular, and large, family. Each displayed its family tree, a detailed chart going back ten or twelve generations—all the way to the Dawning, in most cases—on the wall of their inn's greatroom.

At last, a tenday after the ferry landing, the road broke from the canopy of the trees, and the elves cheered up at the sight of the Lodespikes rising snow-capped and jagged on the horizon. A few days later the lower ridge known as the Silver Crest came into view, and they knew they had almost reached Argentian.

"Ah—you can smell the Sweetwater in the air," Ulfgang said with a delighted sniff.

Tamarwind, too, noticed the fresh air that was the harbinger of Argentian's great river.

"About time," Wiytstar sniffed. "I was beginning to think this journey would never end!"

Tamarwind was no longer irritated by his companions' complaining. Instead, he cheerfully led the way in booking them passage on the *Balloon Fender*. They boarded the riverboat, relieved that the arduous part of the journey was over.

This was a vessel of wood, though, like the druid raft, it was powered by magic. Several elves took turns at the helm, a pair always playing flute and harp. The music flowed into the single sail, and eased the craft down the cool, clear water. After the Darken Hour magical lanterns sparkled into light along the rail, and Tam found himself relaxing into a mood of serene contentment. Ulfgang curled up near the flautist, and barely moved for the three days of the voyage. Trees, somehow softer and brighter than the looming trunks of the Greens, flanked each bank, and the river swept through many curves, always providing a new vista.

The city of Silvercove, Argentian's great capital, came upon them suddenly, towers of marble and silver rising among the trees to form a network of balconies and houses swaying above the top of the forest. Songs from a variety of gardens and plazas wafted over the water, somehow mingling with the music of the flute and harp into a mellow symphony. Massive arkwood trees rose far above the oaks and pines that carpeted most of the verdant city. Vines drooped from the numerous arching branches, some of the tendrils extending nearly to the water along one bank or the other. Flowers of many colors brightened the vines, and lined the boughs of many smaller trees.

The riverboat passed under an arched span of colored glass draped in ferns, one of the two bridges spanning the Sweetwater. Shortly thereafter, the *Balloon Fender* nudged into a small harbor, poking between several other blunt-prowed craft to nestle in a dock formed of gnarled roots. The twisting branches perfectly matched the gunwale of the ship, and like the missing piece of a puzzle the riverboat came to rest against the shore of Silvercove.

Beyond the dock stretched a broad, sunlit garden of hedges, fountains, and flower beds. Nearby, fish were arrayed on a linen cloth. Taken by the fishers, the catches were placed here for any hungry elf desiring to take one.

All around there were cafes and inns, each with its own musicians, each playing its own song. Tamarwind was struck by a sense of familiarity, knowing he'd been hearing the same songs from the same places for hundreds of years.

At ground level the city was a maze of tree trunks and the bases of the high towers, so, after debarking from the riverboat, Tam's companions disappeared from view in a matter of moments. Ulf was trotting back and forth along the docks, and the scout was in no particular hurry to start for his own solitary residence. Instead, he ambled along with the dog, taking in some of the sights.

A dozen boats were anchored here, and an equal number of slips were empty. Elves puttered here and there, some mending sails and scrubbing decks with mundane means, others patching hulls or weaving rope with the use of simple craft spells. Such magic, Tam knew, was the special province of elves, the reason his people could make the greatest creations, the most beautiful artworks, in all the Seven Circles. It was an ability in stark contrast to the crude natural power of druid magic, the kind of incantation that could raise a raft from the sea bottom, control the wind, or repair the damage wrought by a landslide.

"Back from the Big City, I see." The friendly voice drew Tam's attention to the door of a cozy inn, a single-room tavern that occupied the base of one of the city's lofty towers.

"Deltan Columbine . . . good to see you, my friend. I trust your life is unchanging?" Tam couldn't resist a laugh as he said the words, for if there was any elf likely to explore new avenues, to experiment, to create, it was this one.

"I have enough to keep me busy," the poet and teacher replied. "Come have a cup with me, and share the story of your journey," Deltan continued, inviting Tam into the inn. "I need some diversion."

Tamarwind remembered with a flash of guilt the way

several of the delegates had complained about this young teacher. Even if his methods were a trifle unorthodox, the scout could find no fault with him—Deltan was a genial and talented elf, and his students were undoubtedly the better for having studied under him.

"I didn't realize you traveled with a dog," Deltan said as Ulfgang followed Tamarwind toward the light, airy tavern.

"This is Ulfgang. Lady Belynda has asked him to help out with a local problem."

"That name!" Deltan's eyes sparkled. "You saw her, then?"

Tamarwind nodded, blushing, and thrilling to his own memories.

"Well, greetings to you, Ulfgang—and come in, both of you," offered Deltan. "I must hear more."

Ulfgang was willing enough to experience another inn. They settled at a small table outside with a good view of the water, the elves ordering mugs of wine and the dog a dish of fresh milk.

"So what's this desire for distraction?" Tamarwind asked curiously. "Are you getting tired of the monotony of Silvercove life?"

"Actually, I'm at work on a new epic . . . and it's not going very well."

"Did you finish your last project, about the adventure to Loamar across the Worldsea?"

Deltan shook his head. "No . . . I started a fresh work. It's an adventure about a crossing of the Worldsea—to Lignia, this time. But I got a hundred lines into it and feel as though I'm writing the same thing I wrote last year."

"Maybe you need a bit of travel," Tam suggested.

Deltan shrugged. "Perhaps . . . It's been too long since I've spent time out of the city. I envy you, my friend—journeys to the Center, and back."

"And we're off again tomorrow, at least I am," Ulfgang

said, turning to Tam. "Though I'd rather hoped you would come along."

"Certainly," Tamarwind said. "The fields of the hill country are some of the prettiest lands I've ever seen." Noting the curiosity on Deltan's face, he explained. "We're going to see about the shepherds—the dogs that are supposed to be watching the cattle and sheep. It seems that they've been negligent about doing their jobs lately."

"It's more than myself and some dogs that are getting restless, I must say," Deltan observed. "If you'll note, there are more boats starting up the river . . . all of them carrying young elves, and some of them never intending to return." He used his chin to point out the window.

Tam saw that two riverboats were even now departing, and each was crowded with passengers—perhaps thrice the number that his own boat had carried on the return trip to Argentian. "Where are they going?"

The teacher shook his head. "I don't know . . . toward the Greens, for the most part. But I can't imagine that so many are joining the clans of the Wayfarers. In truth, it's a trend that's become pronounced over the last several years."

"I haven't noticed," Tam admitted. "Though perhaps because I spend most of my time in the countryside."

"None of Argentian has—at least, so far as anyone wants to admit," Deltan countered. "You know how it is: We want things to stay the same as they've always been. Perhaps it's just because I've worked with so many of these youngsters that it's come to my attention. But they're leaving even before they reach the breeding age."

"They don't say why?"

"I don't think they even know themselves. It would make for a tale, I imagine."

For some reason the news caused Tamarwind an unseemly agitation. He and Ulfgang departed the inn after their single drink, and he looked at the elves he saw meandering along the streets or tending their hedges and gardens. There seemed to be as many people here as ever, but he couldn't dismiss the bright teacher's suspicions so lightly.

Ulfgang seemed to take a great interest in the elven city, prancing along with ears perked and head held high. Several of the fox-faced wolfish dogs favored by the elves barked or sniffed at him, but Ulf remained aloof, the long white plume of his tail waving proudly in the air.

They reached the massive arkwood tree which included Tam's house in its many apartments, and rather than using the central lift, climbed the long outer stairway toward his rooms. The wooden steps were comfortingly solid, and circled the tree trunk in an ascending spiral. As the ground fell away, they were dazzled by the hanging gardens of the middle terrace, and finally climbed out of the foliage to the balcony of the upper trunk. Here they were higher than most of the trees and buildings of Silvercove—only a few dozen arkwood trees and several ivory and glass towers jutted above the forest canopy. Long bridges of rope, beribboned with flowers and frequently supported by small balloons, connected some of the lofty realms into a giant spiderweb of walkways.

Tamarwind maintained his apartment just above treetop height, and soon they had reached the door. They found the rooms musty, since they had been closed up for several cycles, but otherwise clean and . . . lifeless. The scout was surprised by the realization. He had his artworks, numerous paintings and sculpture, his crystal and silver and soft furniture, with little gardens beside the windows and a small fountain in the water room. Yet somehow, after the splendor of Circle at Center and the changing scenery of the road, he found his walls stifling, his possessions gaudy and irrelevant. As he walked from room to room, or gazed listlessly at the magnificent vista from his balcony, his mind kept returning to Belynda. Odd how that recent visit had reawakened long dormant emotions. Their time of coupling together was long past, hundreds of years away now . . . yet he found himself wishing that she was here with him. Her presence would have brightened the view of towers and trees, added luster to the burnished gold decorating his walls.

Perhaps she would even have quickened the beating of his old, old heart.

E very day Natac learned more about Earth, and about Nayve. He was frequently surprised to realize that facts about his own world seemed far more amazing than details he absorbed about this place to which Miradel had brought him. The Seventh Circle was a wild and untamed place, and he remained horribly fascinated by the inexorable energy of great nations. He knew from Miradel's displays of the tapestry that these powerful states were on courses of inevitable collision, and he spent fascinating hours watching the intrigues in the courts of England, France, and especially Spain. He followed the ships of the exploration, the surging outward that was carrying the influence of Europe into all corners of the globe.

He was also impressed and awed by the variety of combat techniques that had been developed on his world. Diligently he studied these every chance he got, observing wrestling and boxing, watching other men fight with whirling hands and lashing feet. The steel swords of the Europeans struck him as the deadliest of all weapons, though the booming arquebuses showed the potential for great lethality as well.

But despite the sessions in the darkened room, with the candle flaring and the Wool of Time transformed into magical pictures, Natac spent most of his time learning about the place that was his new home. There were times when, amid the activity and new experiences, he almost forgot about the life of blood and sacrifice that had been his previous existence.

Then he would lie in bed at night, well after the Hour of Darken, and he remembered the hearts, the captives. He relived the sensation, an awareness in sinew and nerve and perception, of driving his obsidian blade through soft flesh and brittle bone. And always, when at last he slept, his dreams were haunted by the image of Yellow Hummingbird.

All he could do was apply even more energy to the next day's activities, and it was in this fashion that he drove through the tendays and amassed an increasing body of knowledge about this place called Nayve.

Much of his time was spent in exploration, starting with the view from Miradel's hilltop villa. He learned that the city and island in the middle of the great lake was called Circle at Center, and that the metal spire rising from the island was at the Center of Everything. There were two great causeways connecting the city to the lakeshore—one in the direction of metal, the other running in the direction of wood. He saw many splendid structures in Circle at Center, but when he speculated that these must be temples and palaces, Miradel informed him that they were simply the houses and halls of the city's elves, as well as museums and galleries displaying a host of wonders. The place seemed vibrant and compelling, but for the time being he resisted the urge to go there.

On the inland side of the villa rose a range of rugged highlands. This ring of hills encircled the great lake and its teeming island. Many trails coursed through the hills, and he hiked and trotted along numerous different paths, alternately skirting the lofty, snowcapped peaks that formed the spine of the range, or winding his way down to the innumerable little coves and fjords along the shore of the lake.

Though the heights were rocky, covered only with sparse brush and scrawny trees, many of the valleys were well-watered, home to lush groves and fertile meadows. He encountered animals that he knew, such as deer, turtles, and birds, and others that he had never imagined. There were herds of massive, shaggy beasts that grazed upon the grass, and tall, spotted creatures that stretched long necks far upward to munch on the leaves in the treetops. He saw monkeys in more varieties than he had ever imagined, and once caught a glimpse of a lumbering, sharp-toothed animal slashing fish out of a stream with blows from a huge, taloned paw. The latter beast was a bear, Miradel said, as she gave him the name to add to his list of buffaloes, giraffes, and other exotica.

He was especially fascinated by the small herds of horses that seemed ubiquitous in the nicest pastures. The animals were wild, and quick to spook, but he was reminded of the visions he'd seen in the Tapestry, the spectacle of these animals trained by humans, ridden with a speed like the wind. Miradel told him that several druids had learned how to tame horses, and he resolved to eventually seek them out, to learn the secret of that wonderful skill.

Several times the two of them walked down into the valley for an evening with Fionn, Owen, and the band of druidesses who dwelled with them. These young women, all of whom were stunning beauties, cured the two warriors of their many wounds, shared in their bouts of drinking, and—to Natac's surprise and embarrassment—coupled delightedly with either of the big men.

As to the pair of burly warriors, Natac observed that Owen and Fionn seemed ready to fight for virtually any cause *except* over the women. It was at their third dinner together, while two druidesses worked healing magic on Owen's badly burned back, that Natac finally broached the question to Fionn.

"Why should we fight over women . . . there are plenty for each of us!" declared the Celt, though he cleared his throat and looked awkwardly at the floor.

Owen shrieked in pain as Juliay gently lifted off a sheet of blistered skin. "You'll pay for this, you lout!" he growled as Fionn chuckled merrily.

"You deserved to get knocked into the fire!" retorted the Irishman. "Takin' that piece of cowsteak I had my own eye on—Imagine!"

The Viking clenched his teeth and drew in a hiss of breath as the druid finished the spell. "Thanks, lover," he said, patting her on the cheek before returning to the dining table.

Natac pointed to the platter, which was still piled high with grilled meat. "That's what I mean—there's plenty of cowsteak for both of you, and yet you brawled over who would get the choicest morsel. But you never do that with women. I admit, that surprises me. In my world, it would seem that there is no more touchy subject between two men than who was to receive the favors of a mutually cherished female."

He was surprised to see both warriors look at each other with expressions that were decidedly sheepish. While the pair studied the floor, he turned to Miradel for help. "What's going on?"

She merely nodded to the men, who drew deep breaths and raised their heads.

"They won't let us fight over them," Owen admitted. "Every time we did, they went away . . . and wouldn't come back."

"Not for years," Fionn said lugubriously.

"And we missed them," Owen continued, placing an affectionate, if bearlike, arm around Juliay's shoulders. "So we made to stop brawlin' over them, and now they stay here all the time."

Natac was also curious as to the attraction that the women found in these two rough men, but he decided this was not the time to broach that topic. The night proceeded toward the consumption of a fresh keg of wine, but, having learned that a few glasses made his head spin unpleasantly, Natac quietly substituted water in his own mug.

When the five women and the two men labored their way toward blissful sleep, Natac and Miradel climbed back to the villa. Over the steepest parts of the hill the warrior hoisted the frail body of his teacher into his arms, and as she slept against his chest he felt a sweeping sense of wonder, still awed by the sacrifice she had made to bring him here. Why had she chosen him? And what made her believe that he could prepare the elves of Nayve to fight a war? So far, he knew very little of elves. Aside from the quiet, unobtrusive presence of the servant Fallon, there had been just that single, brief visit from the ambassador called Belynda, who had regarded him so strangely. But with each breath Miradel took, he was careful not to jostle her awake, and he vowed that he would make her proud.

"I need to make a bow . . . I would like to hunt," he told her the next day.

She nodded. "There are trees of ash and yew in the valley. Either will give you splendid wood."

The warrior nodded. He had already harvested several suitable limbs. "But in all my walks, even high in the mountains, I have seen no sign of obsidian. Of course, I can take birds and monkeys with arrowheads of hardened wood, but I have a mind to seek out larger game. For that I need an edge of sharp stone."

"Or steel," Miradel suggested quietly.

"Yes." Natac's eyes narrowed. "I have seen your pans and knives in the kitchen. Can you make things of metal, of this steel?"

"No," the old woman replied. "But there is a druid who is very skilled at the working of metal. He has studied through the Tapestry, and mastered the art as it is practiced by mankind. I will take you to him tomorrow."

Darryn Forgemaster was the man's name, and he had built a smithy on the fjord beyond Owen's house. Miradel and Natac followed the same steep trail that led to the valley of the two warriors, but since they traveled in the morning there was no sign of activity at either man's lodge. Thus, the teacher and student ambled past, and took the last sharp incline down toward the shore.

Natac saw that the waters of the lake, trapped here between two steep, forested ridges, were as pure a blue as any turquoise stone. There were several houses arrayed around a small clearing beside the water, and a wooden dock provided anchorage for a watercraft that was much larger even than a great canoe.

"That's the work of Roland Boatwright," Miradel explained, when Natac remarked about the vessel. "He's another druid who has studied the ways of humankind. But, where Darryn has mastered metalworking, Roland has learned to make the watercraft that have been developed by the men of Earth."

The druids may have been skilled craftsmen, but they were also apparently men of sublime leisure. At least, this was Natac's first impression as he and Miradel made their way through a gate into the little compound of houses.

"That's Roland," she said, pointing to a lanky man who was apparently slumbering on a bench at the dock. He had a floppy hat pulled over his face, and held a fishing pole in his hands. A line, connected to a sodden cork, trailed in the water. "He'll spend most of the day there, though I'm sure he'll meet you later. And this, in here, is where we'll find Darryn Forgemaster."

She pointed toward a sturdy wooden building with an open, arched doorway. Her white hair was pulled tightly against her scalp, and he noticed the way wrinkles radiated outward from her eyes and mouth. Following her point, Natac immediately noted the acrid smell, like soot and ashes but somehow sweeter and more bitter at the same time.

"Darryn?" she called, leading Natac past a great iron box.

The warrior saw the door on the front, and the pipe leading upward from the box, and deduced that this was a fireplace or oven. Beside it was a pile of something black like charcoal, but hard and shiny like smooth rock.

They heard a snort of surprise from across the room, and then a thin, wiry man twisted out of the hammock where he had been napping. He stood and tried to dust himself off, though he remained pretty thoroughly layered in black soot.

"Miradel?" His voice was hushed. "I got your message, but I never expected . . . I mean, it's a pleasure to see you again, old friend." Darryn shook his head. "Not *old*, I mean—except that we've known each other for so long—"

"Yes, *old*," Miradel said, stepping forward to hug the smith. "You needn't be afraid to say it, or to see it."

"Yes . . . of course," said Darryn. "And it is good to see you again," he added with true sincerity. The smith blinked at Natac, who was a few steps behind Miradel. When Darryn squinted, the warrior realized that the other man could barely see him, and so he took a few steps forward.

The metalworking druid stared at the newcomer in frank, and somewhat hostile, appraisal. His rheumy eyes were bright, and didn't seem to blink.

"This is Natac. I am teaching him the ways of Nayve, and of his own world."

"Oh? He was of the folks didn't have iron yet, wasn't he? I believe you told me about him."

Natac was struck by a sudden knowledge: These two had been lovers in the past. He was startled by the jealousy that flashed through his veins. Suddenly he was ready to fight this fellow, to prove that he, Natac, was the better man.

And then, almost as quickly as it had arisen, his anger faded. He found himself imagining Darryn's anguish if, indeed, he loved Miradel. Now she was gone to him,

sentenced to a fate that was utterly horrid in this land of
eternal youth, immortal beauty.

Gone because of Natac.

"I am pleased to meet you, Darryn Forgemaster," he said
politely. "Miradel has told me of your surpassing skill in
the working of metal. That seems to me to be a most wondrous, even magical, ability."

Darryn snorted, but was obviously pleased by the praise.
"Well, it has taken me centuries of study . . . long hours
sifting the Wool of Time, examining the practices of humankind. But I believe that I have mastered the trade, yes."

"Natac expressed a desire to go hunting," Miradel said.
"I was hoping you could help him with his arrows."

"I can do that," agreed the blacksmith.

"And a sword," Miradel declared suddenly. "I would like
for you to make him a sword."

"Why?" Natac asked. "I don't want a sword."

"You should have one," she insisted.

Darryn narrowed his eyes again and peered at Natac.
Miradel reached out a thin hand to touch the smith on the
arm. "Yes . . . he will need a sword. Can you do that?"

With a grudging nod, the smith assented. "I have a dozen
arrowheads I can give you now, but it will take time—a
tenday at least—for me to make the sword."

"Thank you. I will pay, of course," Natac replied.

"Pay me?" Now the smith seemed angry. "I do this work
because I am the one who does this work. Do not insult
me with talk of reward!"

"He is learning fast, but Natac does not know all the
ways of Nayve, yet," Miradel explained. "Where he comes
from, the offer of payment is a way to honor the work of
a skilled craftsman."

Stiffly careful, the two men made their farewells. Miradel
gave the smith a wistful hug, then followed the warrior into
the bright daylight of the courtyard.

"Hey, friends," called a voice from the docks. Natac saw

that the boatwright-fisherman, Roland, was now kneeling over the water, and gesturing them over. "Have you ever seen a more beautiful whitefish?"

He held up a sparkling shape, a fish as long as his arm. The creature wriggled, sunlight gleaming off wet scales that were pale and silvery. "Aye, he's a master of the bay, that's what."

Smiling broadly, the man turned and slipped the big fish back into the lake. With an angry slash of its tail the creature flashed away, vanishing into the indigo depths.

"Welcome back, Lady Miradel," Roland said, standing so that he could bow and take the druid's hand. "And welcome to your young friend, as well."

Once again Natac was introduced to a human denizen of Nayve. Roland turned out to be a druid who, for the past thousand years, had studied all manner of human ships and boats. Natac learned that he had built many of the sailboats plying the waters of the great lake—and that he had taught a dozen or so elven boat builders who had constructed the rest of the watercraft.

"This is my personal favorite, the *Osprey*," he said, indicating the sleek vessel now lashed to the dock.

Natac saw that the boat was long and slender, like a canoe. The prow and stern rose higher into the air, and a single tall mast—a device, with its corresponding sail, as yet unknown in his homeland—lofted from the center of the hull. The sail was furled along a top rail far overhead.

"I can rig two more sails," the boat builder explained as he saw Natac studying the mast. "She'll curl about through just about any kind of wind, she will."

"I'd like to see that someday," replied the warrior.

"When the interval of winds comes around, you will," promised the boatman with an easy laugh.

8

Pillars of the Underworld

Stone forest,
trunks of cosmic girth,
honeycomb maze.
Carved by water,
web of air
in rock
mere stairway
to the dauntless dwarf

From the Tapestry of the Worldweaver
Lore of the Underworld

"Ready?" Karkald called.

"Yes!" Darann hissed, her voice tight with tension. In the outline of coolglow he saw that she was well-braced, rope around her waist and feet propped against a solid rock.

Karkald reached for the handhold, conscious of his ribs aching where the rope had just tightened about his chest. He had already fallen twice on this attempt, with only the rope and his wife's strong belay saving his life. But he had to try again, for if they couldn't pass this small overhang, their long climb faced a grim conclusion here, high above the shallow sea of the First Circle.

For twenty or thirty cycles the two dwarves had lived in a vertical world. Each cycle was measured by the distance climbed, every respite calculated by the size of the flat space they found to make a precarious camp. Rare indeed was the sleep where Karkald and Darann lay side by side. More often than not, he found a narrow ledge a dozen feet over her head and secured himself in place with his rope, while she curled into a narrow niche where surrounding walls gave some security against a fall. Of course, the same walls inevitably cramped her torso and limbs, or forced her to rest in an uncomfortable sitting position.

Sometimes they climbed only fifty feet in a single cycle. Each upward inch came at a cost in fear and pain, in loneliness and the smothering presence of the vast, surrounding dark. Karkald used every ounce of his strength, every scrap of his skill. His tools were always in his hands, pick and hammer shaping the rock, the rope that was, so often, life itself. Occasionally he wedged his spear crossways into a narrow crack and used that as a support, and there were other times when his chisel came into play, either to chip away at a surface of rock or to serve as a makeshift piton.

In fact, it was only his tools that gave him the confidence even to attempt this insane escape. Those eight items were solid, strong, trustworthy . . . he knew their capabilities, understood that he could count on them, and on his knowledge of their use.

But beyond that, he had so many questions about his strength and his skill. Did he really have a chance to make it all the way to the roof of the Underworld? Of not just reaching that lofty goal, but of bringing Darann with him? And even if he did attain the solid barrier at the top of their world, would he ever be able to find one of the legendary caverns penetrating that rocky dome? Or would he and Darann simply be trapped at the summit of the First Circle, too exhausted and hungry even to try and climb down?

Sustenance during the ascent was crude, but at least they were able to find the necessities of life. Water trickled in many places through the column, and every interval or two

they found a clear pool deep enough that they could fill
up the two waterskins they had brought along. By using
only tiny pinches of flamestone, they were able to maintain
a dim presence of coolglow—not bright like the beacons'
light, but sufficient illumination for them to perceive each
other and the route before them.

Food was more problematic. They were able to harvest
bits of fungus and lichen here and there, but they were
beyond reach of any fishing. Furthermore, the bats dwelling
throughout the First Circle—a favored delicacy of Seer
dwarves—seemed disinclined to visit the region of the lofty
pillar.

And even when they could fill the gnawing emptiness of
their bellies, and when a negotiable chimney rose above to
promise another hundred feet of ascent, Karkald wondered
if his strength was equal to the task. Every muscle in his
body ached constantly. His fingers and toes, even his back
and shoulders, were raw with blisters where he had re-
peatedly scraped his skin against unforgiving rock. His
knees and buttocks were bruised from several short falls.
Fortunately, none of these tumbles had broken any bones,
but each added another measure of soreness to the pain that
was his constant companion.

There were times when he felt that he could barely lift his
arms . . . and still he forced himself upward, carrying not just
himself but his tools and supplies, and then he fashioned a
belay so that Darann could follow in relative safety. More
than once they were forced to turn from a sheer rising face, a
seamless cliff that was beyond Karkald's skill. Yet perhaps
the Goddess was favoring them, for each time this happened
they were able to find an alternate route, a place where he
could jam his pick or his fingers into some tiny crack and,
once more, haul himself upward.

Until this shelf of overhang, a slab of rock jutting two
feet into space, threatened to bring the long ascent to an
end. Twice he had tried to climb past, but his arms hadn't
been long enough. Leaning outward to reach the next hand-

hold, he'd lost his grip and fallen—until the rope snapped taut and a gasping, grunting Darann arrested his plunge even as she was pulled hard against the pick that anchored her. Yet there was no alternative except to try the difficult move again.

This time he'd made it just a bit higher in the crack beneath the overhang. Anchoring himself by a fist jammed in that gap, he leaned outward and reached. Karkald clenched his teeth, stretching his long arms to their maximum span. The fingers of his left hand curled around the bottom of the overhang, and he, just barely, touched the lip of a handhold. He winced, anticipating the slip, the plunge, the sharp arrest as the rope would tighten around him. But he had no choice.

He let go with his right hand and started to topple outward. Clenching his left hand, he clung perilously by his fingertips as his body swung sickeningly outward. But this time he was able to get the fingers of his other hand onto the ledge. He hear Darann gasp as he hung suspended, thousands of feet over the lightless water.

Then, with a concentration of effort that ruled out every other thought, he slowly began to lift himself up. By the time his chin had reached the level of the handhold, he had spotted another niche, a foot higher up, with a deeper, much more solid edge. He lunged, teetered again at the brink of falling, and then his hand clutched a solid ledge. He swung his feet up, thankful as Darann continued to pay out just enough rope to allow him to climb. With his boot lodged in a precarious toehold, he pressed higher, and in a few more minutes reached a reasonably wide ledge.

Now it was his turn to belay, as Darann swung free below. He held the line tightly, with a coil wrapped around his waist as she slowly, painstakingly, climbed the narrow line. Only after a long, frightening hour did she join him on his lofty perch. But here, at last, they had reached a broad ledge that angled gently upward across the face of the column. They could actually walk, and at the end of an interval as fatigue dragged them down, they slept on a flat shelf big enough for them to curl up side by side.

When they awakened they continued up, pleased to find that the ledge followed around the curve of the column's face, but still maintained its steady, ascending angle.

"How much farther to the top?" Darann asked, leaning back to stare into the lightless vault overhead.

"I have to figure we're getting close," Karkald replied. "Do you think it's safe to try for an echo?"

"Why not?" his wife answered with a shrug. "The only thing we could attract are bats—and I'd welcome a chance for a nibble of meat. Unless—" Daran suddenly shuddered. "You don't think there'd be any wyslets around here, do you?"

"No—they like narrow caves, rat holes to sneak around in," Karkald declared with certainty. He tilted back and cupped his hands to his mouth to funnel the sound of his voice as much as possible. Uttering a short "Hey!" he was gratified when, two seconds later, the echo came back loud and clear.

"Five hundred feet, maybe a little more," he said encouragingly. "And if this ledge continues . . ." He didn't finish the statement, not wanting to jinx their chances.

He also left unspoken the question on both of their minds: Would they find a cave when they reached the summit? Or would they be faced with an impermeable expanse of rock, a barrier that would end their quest as effectively, if not as quickly, as death on the points of Delver weapons? The query remained in the back of his mind as they continued upward, now moving with long strides, following the natural footpath in a climbing spiral around the face of the massive pillar.

And then that question became irrelevant as they came around a curve to see the sloping ledge abruptly narrow to a thin lip. Adding a little flamestone to the coolglow in his palm, Karkald saw that a few feet beyond, the shelf of rock vanished altogether. He touched off more flamestone, and saw that the cliff overhead veered into a steep overhang, a leaning shelf continuing outward and up to merge with the horizontal slab that formed the upper reach of the Underworld. Even as he listlessly looked for cracks or imperfections in the surface, he knew that he was beaten. There was no way he could support himself from the flaring face, much less find a route to continue the climb.

He slumped to the ground, feeling the weight of his defeat on his shoulders. A soft rustle and the radiance of her warmth told him that Darann had settled beside him. Fatigue and despair overwhelmed, choked him. For a long time they slept there, blissfully unaware of the cruel end to their road.

When Karkald awakened, the full measure of hopelessness immediately resurfaced, but that was followed a second later by the realization that his wife was not at his side.

"Darann!" he whispered, suddenly, irrationally panicked.

"Here," she replied. "I think I've found something!"

Blinking his eyes clear, he saw the spark of fire a dozen paces down the ledge, realized that she was examining the face of the pillar. Quickly he trotted down to her side, and she dropped a little more flamestone into her palm.

"Look!"

She cupped the brightness, shading the light from Karkald's eyes, using her fingers to reflect it onto the dark stone. He discerned a crack there, a vertical line that was considerably longer than his own height. Yet it was no more than a finger's thickness in width.

He snorted in exasperation and she glared at him sternly. "Look again—inside the crack."

This time he leaned closer and saw what she meant. The gap scored a thin shell of rock. Barely a few inches beyond, it widened into a much larger space. How large was impossible to tell, for within the gap the thin rays of light

dissipated into a swath of darkness Still, it looked like there
was space for a dwarf, and he couldn't see a far end to the
cave.

He examined the narrow aperture with a critical eye. "I
could knock it into a wide hole . . . might take me an interval or two." He chuckled sourly. "It's not like we've got
anything else to do."

So he set to work with his hammer and chisel. He tapped
the stone, listening for the hollow sound that marked the
thinnest part of the shell. When he had located this, he
started by chopping at the edges, knocking chips of rock
free. The sound of each blow resonated into the Underworld, and he winced at the knowledge that he was broad-
casting their position far and wide. Still, it was hard to
envision any kind of threat that could reach them here. And
besides, they really had no other choice.

After a full cycle of pounding, thousands of blows that
left his shoulder flaming, his arm numb, and his fingers
cramped into a seemingly permanent curl, he had chiseled
only a few inches of rock out of the way. The next cycle
he shifted the work, swinging with his left arm and poising
the chisel in his right hand. He accomplished less, but by
the third cycle he could use his strongest arm for swinging
again.

While Karkald worked, Darann explored the nearby
ledges. She quickly located a steady stream trickling down
a little rivulet, and subsequently she began each cycle by
bringing them fresh drinking water. Searching farther, she
found bits of fungus and the occasional mushroom, enough
food to hold the pangs of hunger at bay and to keep Karkald's strength up. He suspected that she was giving him
most of the food, and though the thought caused him chagrin he accepted her generosity as necessary to their survival.

They slept on the wide ledge near the site of the exca-
vation, and as the cycles passed, the entry into the rock

grew wider and wider. When they burned a small pile of precious flamestone, they were heartened to see that the cavern beyond the notch continued to the limits of their vision.

As soon as the illumination faded Karkald stood, stretched the kinks out of his muscles, and knocked another knob of rock out of the way. As usual, he worked in darkness, since they didn't use their flamestone for routine activity. Finally he stood back to gauge the distance with his hands.

"I think it might be wide enough for you to fit," he suggested to his wife. "It needs a few more inches before my shoulders are passing."

"I'll see what I can find, then," Darann agreed nervously. Neither of them wanted to acknowledge that this could easily prove to be a short, dark, dead end.

She leaned sideways and slid, head first, through the widened crack. Quickly she stood up and touched off a pinch of flamestone.

"The floor's good—fairly smooth," she said. "A lot of stalactites overhead and some water, still flowing." Her voice and the light grew softer as she moved farther away. Karkald heard her shout, and listened to a volley of echoes returning. Then, for long moments, there was no sound. The dwarf's heart was pounding anxiously by the time she came back, explaining that her flamestone had expired. He had to still the shaking in his hands as he pulled her back through the opening.

"Wh-what did you see?" he demanded.

"It goes for a long way. The water seems to be coming from pretty high overhead. There are some rocks in the way, and I couldn't get over them with one hand holding the light. Still, I could see that the cavern went on far after that, and when I shouted, the echoes lasted a long time."

More hopeful than he had been in a long time, Karkald set to his chiseling with renewed vigor. In another two cy-

cles he had a gap wide enough for even his broad frame.
He passed through and found that there was plenty of room
beyond the crack. Holding hands, hearts pounding, they
departed the ledge that had served as their lofty camp. It
was with a sense of impending adventure that Darann used
a little flamestone to give them a picture of the route before
them, while Karkald checked his tools.

"Hammer, chisel, hatchet, file. Knife, pick, rope, spear.
I'm all set," he declared, and they started into the cave.

The great mountain of rubble completely blocked their
path. Echoes sounded from high and wide, marking the
barrier as almost incomprehensibly vast. Zystyl sensed,
through the location of his many scouts, that the Delver
army would not be advancing any closer toward Axial. Either the city had been buried by the quake, crushed beneath
a mass of stone, or it was masked by this new and apparently impenetrable barrier.

As was so much of his own realm. The Delver commander had recently received word from Nightrock, his
own homeland. Many of the food warrens had been destroyed by the temblor. He knew that if he had taken his
army home, there would have been a critical shortage of
provisions. It was not in his interests to have Delvers eating
other Delvers, and so he had continued on with the campaign, striving to find a way to strike at their hated enemies.

But where could they go from here?

My master. The words came into his mind, the message
from Kerriastyn, the army's other arcane. Though she was
second in command of this mighty horde, he was pleased
that she knew to show proper respect to her leader.

What is it? Where are you?

*I am here, high on the mountain. I have made a discovery
that might prove promising.*

Wait. I will reach you shortly.

Zystyl began to climb, following the rope lines that his scouts had laid earlier. He made his way steadily upward, knowing that Kerriastyn would not have reached out to him if she did not have something truly interesting to report. She was a capable leader in her own right, and would have handled any minor discovery by herself.

It was fully an hour later that the first sensations told him that he was drawing close to her. From a hundred paces away he could smell fresh blood, Delver blood. But the spoor was tainted with another stench, an animal-like odor that seemed to seep from the very rocks themselves. He heard Kerriastyn hiss, the sound a beacon drawing him through the darkness.

When he was within ten paces of Kerriastyn he could sense her excitement in his own mind, and then he could hear the rapid pounding of her heart, the giddiness of her breathing. She was standing between the corpses of two Delvers. From the probing of his mind Zystyl could see that both had been killed violently, and one was partially devoured.

"That smell . . . it is wyslet, is it not?" he asked, finally recognizing the animal stench.

"Yes, master," Kerriastyn replied. "They slayed one of these Delvers and were eating him. They killed the second when he came upon the first, then fled when more of your warriors arrived on the scene." She waited expectantly. His first reaction was to demand further explanation, but his intuition told him that he should know why this was important.

And then he did.

"Which way did the wyslets go?" Zystyl started to see the possibility.

"They ran up the hill, and vanished."

"Indeed." They had disappeared *upward*. Wyslets couldn't fly, he knew . . . so they must have had a path of escape, a route into the ceiling of the First Circle.

Where could that have taken them? Wyslets needed food, and they probably had a route into and through the swath of midrock. Could those caverns take them all the way to the Fourth Circle, to a new world awaiting the cold kiss of Delver steel?

Zystyl remembered another thing that had happened in the last few cycles. He had heard hammering, steel against stone, coming from high up in the world. His best guess had placed that sound near the top of the pillar of the nearest watch station, the place he had been when the quake had rocked the world.

And he remembered the sweet taste of Seer tears, the allure of a woman he had touched, smelled, tasted, and heard. That memory still burned within him, rising into a compulsion, a need that he desperately wanted to slake. Could it be that she had escaped, that she had found a way into the vast canopy overlying their world?

It was enough to fuel his decision.

"Gather to me!" he shouted, a command that would carry for more than a mile through the vast Underworld. He would collect his army, and he would follow the path of the wyslets, knowing that there would be new routes before him, new opportunities for plunder, violence, and war.

Now their progress was encouraging, and Karkald and Darann even felt a few moments of excitement as they were able to stride along, climbing only gradually, making their way through what proved to be an extensive network of rock-walled caverns. After some hours they found a comfortable grotto in which to sleep, and even enjoyed the luxury of a bed of dry sand.

They awakened refreshed, and continued their trek with renewed hope, finding the route steadily advancing before them. Unfortunately, by late the next cycle they had found no sign of animal nor even fungus, and they began to wonder how long they could survive here.

Abruptly they halted, both of them groping for the memory of a sound that had just barked through the darkness, barely rising in volume above the scuffing of their feet.

"What was that?" Darann whispered.

"It sounded like a shout, didn't it?" Karkald's reply was as soft. For a time both dwarves remained immobile and silent, straining to hear. Soon the noise was repeated, a distant cry or howl that bespoke of frustration, despair, and anger. There was something exceptionally plaintive in the sound, a sense of longing that contrasted oddly with the piercing nature of the vocalization.

"Do you think it heard us?" Darann asked.

"It must have," Karkald replied. "We weren't trying to be quiet." Not that they could do much to silence their march, he groused to himself, when they were forced to pick their way over loose rubble, feeling their way.

He was startled out of his private griping by the sound of his mate's shout.

"Hey . . . where are you? Who are you?"

"Are you craz—!" He hissed in outrage, but was startled into silence by the sound of a reply.

"Help! I caught! Help! Help!"

The voice echoed through the cavern, but they could discern a direction. Immediately Darann started out, until Karkald stopped her long enough to get her to touch off a light. She held the coolfyre high over her head and followed along while Karkald took his spear in hand and pointed the weapon aggressively before him.

He quickly realized that they were walking down a smooth, natural pathway. Barely two or three paces wide, it was a seamless surface of rock that twisted through serpentine curves along the floor of a large, natural cavern. Suddenly he came to a stop, as the light revealed a dark hole gaping in the floor before him.

"Who dere? Help! Help, help!" yelped the stranger, in a voice that somehow managed to sound savage and childish at the same time.

And the voice was coming from the hole in the floor. When Darann extended the light over the lip of the pit, they found themselves staring down into a bright-eyed, but exceptionally homely face. The huge eyes blinked against the sudden illumination, and before the figure clapped hands over his face Karkald got an impression of big ears, puffy lips, and large, jutting, teeth. Squinting, the prisoner looked through his long fingers, that mouth spreading into a pathetically hopeful grin.

"Gotta rope?" The question was a chirping squeak.

"We do!" Darann replied, turning to Karkald expectantly.

He shook his head, and stepped back from the edge of the pit.

"That's a goblin!" he hissed quietly.

"I don't care!" she retorted, more loudly, then raised her voice even further. "We'll help you!" she called out, giving Karkald a scornful look and folding her arms across her bosom.

"Tanks! Tanks lotsa much!" cackled the goblin. "Oh, me belly and me feets so sore!"

"How long have you been in there?" asked the dwarf-woman, pointedly turning away from Karkald.

"Lotsa long time. All lone too. Only seed a couple wyslets come by—I howl fierce at 'em, dey go way."

"Wyslets?" Darann's eyes widened in alarm, and Karkald couldn't resist taking a quick glance over his shoulder. Those slimy predators of the Underground were rare, but ravenous and dangerous when encountered. He had never seen one, save in captivity in Axial, but the thought of the fang-toothed killer slinking through these caves was chilling in the extreme.

"Get the rope," Darann directed, and Karkald scowled as he unslung the line from his shoulder.

"Can you climb?" he asked gruffly, curiosity getting the best of him as he threw the end into the pit and automatically wrapped the end around his waist in a sturdy belay.

"Wit' some help . . . Can you pull me too?"

Both dwarves pitched in to lift while the goblin seized the rope in his two hands. Using his flat feet to push off the wall, the creature slowly made his way up the side of the pit. A few moments later he crawled over the edge of the hole and lay gasping on the cavern floor.

Karkald had never seen a goblin, but he was surprised by the wave of revulsion that almost urged him to kick the scrawny creature right back into the pit. Instead, he scowled and took a step back as the goblin climbed to his broad, incongruously large feet.

The fellow stood there, big head bobbing atop a thin neck. His posture was stooped, and his legs were spindly and knock-kneed. The big ears drooped to either side of a round face, a visage dominated by that broad mouth with its array of chaotically arranged teeth, and those bright, watery eyes.

"What's your name?" Darann asked, after extending introductions for the two dwarves.

"Hiyram is me," said the goblin. "And I owe you big tanks."

"That's all right—" the dwarfwoman began, before the goblin cut her off with a disdainful snort.

"But your dwarfy kind is what made dis trap! You two dwarfses big doofuses! I go 'way!"

"Why, you ungrateful cur!" snapped Karkald, snatching up his spear. "You'll change your tone, or I'll pitch you back in that hole—forever!"

Before he could jab the weapon the goblin bounded away, moving in a speedy scuttle that carried it completely around the pit. Hiyram's jaws gaped, baring teeth that suddenly looked dangerous. With a jeering snarl, he raised his head, sniffed loudly and insultingly, then turned to amble into the darkness.

"What a runt!" growled Karkald, who nevertheless restrained his rash impulse to hurl the spear. He had no doubt but that the nimble creature could easily evade the clumsy weapon, and he reminded himself that he would just be giving away one of his tools. Even more, he was surprised to realize that, despite his anger, he really didn't want to kill the wretch.

Still, the encounter had put him in a foul temper, and he glowered at his wife.

"That was a waste of effort and coolfyre. We're lucky he didn't cut the rope."

"Well, *I'm* glad we helped him!" she spat, then drew a ragged gasp of breath.

He was startled to see that she was really upset. Her irritation only soured his own mood and aggravated his hunger. He stomped around the pit and continued through the cave without looking back, though he listened to make sure that Darann was coming behind.

For the rest of that cycle they continued on without speaking. Though they started along the path taken by the goblin, they saw no sign of the creature. Darann periodically touched off a bit of flamestone, and Karkald picked a route through the network of caves and caverns. After making a dozen such choices, he figured that they had safely departed from Hiyram's route, but even so he held his spear at the ready and continued to listen for any sound.

The going was relatively easy, with smooth floors and wide passages that didn't require any steep climbing. They were making good progress, but more and more the question occurred to him: progress toward *what*?

By the time weariness was telling Karkald that it was time for another sleep, his mind had returned to more immediate concerns. Thus far they'd encountered none of the patches of fungus that had provided them with sustenance on the cliffs below, and the emptiness in his belly was a growling, relentless pain. In the deepest reaches of his awareness he admitted to a stark fear, the harsh realization that he had failed his wife in every way possible. Yet it was not a fear he could articulate, for he needed to maintain a façade of hopefulness, to provide some reason for them to keep on trying.

But now, finally, he had no more energy, no more hope, to offer.

With a sullen grunt he sat on a rounded boulder, stretching his weary legs, fighting to keep his fear, his despair, from showing on his face. Darann touched off another pinch of flamestone and they looked around to see the same interminable, winding cavern. They had been following a patch of dry riverbed that boasted a few patches of sand and many jagged rocks.

"You're not planning to sleep here, are you?" she asked.

"Seems as good as any other place," he declared sourly.

"If you don't mind rocks poking your back! No thank you—I'm going on."

"What's the point?" Karkald demanded. "Just to keep on walking till your boots wear out?"

"Maybe the point is to find something to eat . . . or a better place to sleep. Or maybe we'll find a way back to—" Her voice choked off and she turned away from him, standing straight and proud.

"To Axial?" he snapped. He saw her flinch and immediately regretted his tone, and his anger. Still, he was unprepared for the fury in her eyes when she turned to face him.

"Maybe to Axial!" Darann proclaimed. "All we know is that we couldn't see the city's lights anymore. Maybe it's still there—maybe our people are alive, wondering about us! Maybe we can give them warning of the Delvers!"

"And maybe mushrooms will grow around our feet while we're standing here!" shouted Karkald, his own temper slipping away. "Try to understand, we're the only Seer dwarves here! We have no one else to turn to, no city to go back to, nothing!"

"I don't believe you!" she cried.

"Fine. Believe what you want!" he retorted, rising and stomping through a circle in the cave, his body trembling with anger. The force of that rage was a frightening onslaught, a tidal wave of emotion he felt unable to contain.

Rather than unleash that torrent, he clumped away from Darann, marching resolutely along the cavern pathway, backtracking over the route they had taken an hour earlier. He listened, half hoping that she would call out to him, apologize, plead with him to return . . . but she remained grimly, stubbornly silent.

And so he marched out of her sight, and kept going. His feet followed the cavern floor by memory, and his sturdy legs stretched through long strides. Despite his earlier fatigue it now felt good to move, to give release to his contained energy. He drew deep breaths, alternately feeling self-pity, anger, and guilt. Each emotion came with its own level of pain, and the cycle repeated over and over in his mind until he had walked a very long way.

Finally he leaned against a wall, feeling the support in the darkness, realizing that he was in fact incredibly weary. He slumped downward onto a makeshift seat and sighed. The storm of feelings had abated, and in its wake he felt emptiness, a hollow sensation that seemed to have the same effect on his emotions as hunger had upon his gnawing belly. Nothing remained to drive him, to bring him to his feet and to move him toward anything resembling a purpose.

Until the acrid scent wafted past his nostrils and he sat up, rigid with sudden, gripping fear.

Wyslet!

The odor was instantly familiar, a stench every dwarf learned to recognize at an early age. This spoor was faint, but unmistakable—a mixture of urine and carrion that lay across the air, like corpses staining a battlefield. The savage predators had for the most part been driven from the surface of the Underworld, but they were known to lurk in trackless tunnels. They lived in small packs, stalking such prey as they encountered. Primarily this meant that they ate bats, fish . . . and unlucky dwarves.

Terror galvanized Karkald and he sprang to his feet, spear held in his hands. He was afraid not for himself, but for Darann, and he started along the path at a run, searching the air with his nose, hoping that the scent would fade, that the wyslets were far away.

Instead, his fright expanded into panic as the stench only grew stronger. His feet pounded the cavern floor as the odor grew piercing and pervasive. The truth was inescapable—not only were the wyslets between himself and his wife, but they were moving closer to her, at a speed faster than he could hope to run.

W hy did he have to be so damned *stubborn*? Darann shook her head and paced a few steps across the cavern floor. He was an ill-tempered fool, and she really was better off without him! What in the First Circle had ever compelled her to go to that Goddess-forsaken watch station anyway?

And in the next intake of breath she was fighting back tears, feeling the bitter moisture sting her eyes and, against her best efforts, trickle onto her cheeks! Damn her foolishness anyway—she already *missed* him!

Still, she decided with a snort of determination, it would do him good to spend an interval alone in the darkness. He could simmer and stew all he wanted, and in the end he would see that she was right. They had to keep going, had to believe in something at the end of their journey. To give up would be to die, and she was not yet ready to yield that fight. Her face hardened—Karkald *had* to trust her, to see the wisdom of her position.

And he would.

With at least that much resolution she went back to the small bundle of her knapsack, the satchel illuminated softly by coolglow, and allowed herself a few sips of cool water. She was just tucking the waterskin under the flap of leather when the stench wafted past. Immediately she stiffened, then spun to stare into the surrounding darkness.

Of course she knew the smell of a wyslet, but now that odor had a very different character than it had when she'd visited the animal cages in Axial. The thought of the rangy hunters prowling through these caves prickled at the hair on the back of her neck. She wished Karkald was here, and felt a deep pang of regret over the harsh words that had sent him away.

Clenching her teeth, Darann made a small pile of flamestone atop a nearby boulder, a rock with a flat top that rose a little higher than her head. Touching off the coolfyre, she crouched in the shadow at the base of the large block of stone and stared into the cavern that was now brightly lit.

At least four pairs of red eyes glared back at her for a moment until, with snorts of surprise, the wyslets ducked back into the darkness. But in that flashing instant she gained an impression of desperate, unfeeling *hunger*, and the sensation filled her with utter terror. They were soulless, those eyes, and on a visceral level she felt vulnerability reduce her to a living, breathing morsel of food.

An instinctive fury rose in opposition to that revolting fact and she groped around the cavern floor, clawing for loose stones. She pulled up a rock as big as her fist and hurled it in the direction of the nearest wyslet. The missile clattered into the darkness and she heard a startled hiss. A long, lean shape skipped through the swath of her light and vanished into another shadow. Her breaths rushing through short gasps, she snatched up another stone and then whirled at the sound of a rattle behind her.

A slinking shape flickered through the edge of her vision to disappear behind another of the rocks that rose like knobby teeth from the cavern floor. She sensed that the creatures were toying with her—and with that realization she spun back to find one of the wyslets creeping closer. The beast froze, those red eyes bright and unblinking as she deliberately raised the rock to throw.

For the first time she got a good look at one of her tormentors, and it was a sight every bit as revolting as the beast's carrion stench. The ratlike nose was long and pointed, bristling with whiskers. The lower jaw gaped, revealing a black tongue and a ring of jagged teeth. The horrid eyes were set wide apart, far back on a head that terminated with a pair of small, upraised ears. Mangy fur covered the lean, supple body, which was at least as long as she was tall. The wyslet scooted backward with a stuttering of its four short legs, then spat a wet snarl. A naked tail slashed, whiplike, over the creature's arched back.

The only movement was the rhythmic lashing of that tail. The red eyes were bright and hungry, never blinking, never shifting their focus from Darann's face. She sensed that the wyslet was trembling, ready to leap out of the way if she threw the rock. For now it seemed rapt, utterly focused on her, holding her attention. . . .

She pivoted, suddenly remembering that there were more of these things. A wyslet crouched two strides behind her, legs and body coiled to spring. Darann shouted furiously and threw the rock straight into the pointed nose. With an angry yelp the beast tumbled back, then rose to shake its head groggily.

But there were more wyslets, and now her hands were empty. Darann spun again, saw the beast that had been staring at her. It was much closer, racing like an arrow. The last thing she saw before she lifted her arm across her face was the mouth spread wide, obscenely red and bracketed by drooling fangs.

9

A Distant Storm

Purpled high horizon,
yonder rising ground;
tongues of fire flicker,
leaden thunder pounds.

Rocky peaks bedizened,
icy daunting wall;
cliffs of menace llinger
'neath the roaring fall.

From the Tapestry of the Worldweaver
Atlas of Elvenkind

Ulfgang was anxious to look into the matter of the ram-bunctious dogs, so he and Tamarwind decided to head into the country the morning after their arrival in Argentian. The Lighten Hour found them already descending from the lofty arkwood tree to start through the twisting streets of the elven city. Before they'd taken a hundred steps they were hailed by a familiar voice and they saw Deltan Columbine hastening to join them. The poet was dressed in traveling clothes, leather tunic and breeches, with a pack slung over his shoulder. A small harp and a curved silver trumpet were strapped to his back.

"The city's been wearing on me," he admitted. "And,

hearing you talk yesterday, I got to thinking about the hill country. Do you mind if I come along?"

Tam welcomed his friend's company, and Deltan fell comfortably into step with the trio as they passed a pair of towers marking the place where Argentian merged into the vast, surrounding forest. A minute later they were in the thick woods, and dog and elves relished the renewed freedom of the traveler.

"It's been years since I've been outside of Silvercove, at least for more than a few hours," Deltan remarked, drawing a deep breath. "I had forgotten how refreshing the forest can be."

"Our homeland is a wonder," Tam noted, "but I myself am certainly glad to get away now and then."

They swung easily along, and Tam found the faster pace strangely exhilarating after the measured march of the elven delegation. By noon they had reached the first of the pastures, broad, rolling fields where the trees had been shorn away. It was here that the inherently hilly nature of Argentian became visible, with each successive meadow rising higher in the distance. Here and there walls of piled stone crossed the heath, making oddly geometrical patterns. The nearest cows were on a hillside beyond a narrow, sparkling stream.

"But it's not the cows we're looking for—it's field rabble," declared Ulfgang sternly. Tam got the feeling that the dog was reminding himself of his task. Ulf's luminous brown eyes lingered lovingly over the cattle, and when the small herd wandered over the horizon and out of sight he uttered an audible sigh.

"No shepherds with the herd," Deltan observed.

"That's the problem, I imagine," suggested Ulf. "The rabble hounds are always going to look for chances to run in the fields—but the shepherds should be keeping them out!"

"How are you going to solve the problem?" Tam wondered.

"We'll have to find some dogs—shepherds or rabble, it doesn't matter—and then we'll learn what's going on," Ulfgang declared grimly.

They decided that the best way to look for unruly dogs, or anything else, was to get a good vantage, so the trio set out through the meadows, climbing from one pasture to the next. Tam and Deltan scrambled up a rock wall while Ulfgang sprang right over the barrier. The grassy loam on the other side formed a soft cushion, gentle on their feet even as they made their way steadily uphill. Here and there they worked through a grove of aspen or pines, and once they circled a small grotto where a tiny waterfall spumed through the clear air.

Deltan was puffing and red-faced but sternly insisted that he could keep up. "Don't wait for me," he said between breaths. "It's just city lungs."

Finally breaking onto a rounded hilltop that domed above the surrounding pastures, dog and elves spotted several small herds of cows and horses, some so distant that they were mere brown spots on the terrain. But they saw no sign of any other dogs. After catching his breath, Deltan took some paper and charcoal from his pack, and sat with his back against a boulder, sketching the rural landscape. Later he played his horn, which he called a flügel, and from which he coaxed some pleasant and melodious tunes.

Tam took a short nap on the soft grass, then reached for the cheese and sausage he had brought, which he shared with his two companions. Finally the Hour of Darken was upon them, and the sun slowly began to recede into the heights. Twilight fringed the woods and fields beyond the hills, and here and there lights sparkled into being, each a glow marking a village or hamlet of Argentian.

And they heard the sound of frantic barking, a harsh echo rising from the valley behind their rounded summit. They crossed the hilltop at a trot, and even in the shadows that darkened the vale Tamarwind could see a gray shape writhing deliriously on the ground. Ulf inhaled, then shook his head violently, as if to clear an odor from his nostrils.

"Horse dung and a silly bitch," he sniffed contemptuously. "I don't know *what* they smell in it."

Tam couldn't detect any odor, but he trusted the dog's superior nose. "Can you ask her about the shepherds?"

"Hey, you down there!" Ulfgang barked. His voice was sharp and piercing, and the other dog immediately ceased her wiggling dance. After a moment she rolled onto her belly and gazed fearfully up the hill.

"You floozy!" shouted the white dog sternly. "Now, I want you to clean yourself off and get up here. I'm going to talk to you."

In a few minutes the bitch, who was a short-haired hound with long, droopy ears, came hesitantly up the hill. As she came into sight of the pair, she dropped to the ground and crawled toward Ulfgang. Her jaws gaped, and she uttered several sharp, plaintive barks.

"No . . . I understand," Ulf replied in a deep woof. "But tell me, where are the shepherds who should be keeping you out of the fields?"

The hound whined something that caused Ulf to sit up straight, ears pricked as he looked at Tam with concern. "That *is* alarming—they've been gone for a long time, and they're chasing deer, she says." The white dog turned back to the bitch. "Where? Where are the shepherds?"

Again she barked, and Ulfgang followed her gaze. "In the direction that is neither metal nor wood," he said slowly. "And far away."

Tam followed the direction of the dog's look, then turned to meet Ulf's eyes. Left unspoken was the understanding that tickled each of them with a tremor of alarm.

For that was the direction of the Greens.

• • •

Natac studied the image on the wall, and moved his body through the exact maneuvers performed by the man he was watching. The subject of his study was a lightly dressed warrior, a man from the place called the Orient who used his feet and his hands as weapons. Now he was training, dancing alone through slashing kicks, lightning punches, and a variety of leaps and spins.

Mirroring every move, Natac kicked his foot into the air, higher than his head. Next he spun on the ball of his other foot. With his back to the moving picture, Natac worked from memory of the precise form, executing a sharp forward kick, switching feet to repeat the thrust with his other foot, then spinning once more with a roundhouse kick that brought him again into view of the man from Earth. As he expected, he matched precisely the cadence and routine of the other warrior.

The man in the image turned, and Natac had the uncanny feeling that the fellow could somehow sense his presence. When the fighter bowed formally, Natac returned the gesture.

Only then did Miradel puff out the candle and gather the scraps of wool into a basket, saved for the next viewing.

Natac's heart was pumping, and a sheen of sweat covered his skin, plastering his thick hair to his scalp. He felt wonderfully vibrant.

"You are learning much from the people of the Seventh Circle," the druid remarked, throwing open the door to a shimmering blast of daylight.

"Yes . . . there is much learning there, on Earth."

And I have come to see myself as a man from somewhere else. The realization was a constant part of his new life, growing stronger every time he viewed images of his birth world.

They heard a shout from the courtyard, and emerged to find Darryn Forgemaster and Fallon. The smith nodded in familiar greeting to Natac, his expression unreadable.

"Studying with the Wool, eh?" he asked. The wiry druid's expression turned wistful. "Many's the hour I've spent in that same room, learning the tricks of metal."

"Yes." Natac was nonplused, once again pierced by the thought that he had claimed this man's immortal lover, had sentenced her to a limited life of agedness and death. Though he had never asked if this was the case, the suspicion raised a mixture of guilt and jealousy within him. And yet, if his guess was correct, why was Darryn not more overtly hostile to him?

"Here," the smith was saying, laying out a bundle on the big table. Natac's heart quickened at the sight of the long, leather-wrapped shape. Despite his protestations about not wanting a sword, he found himself keenly interested in the prospect of picking up the weapon.

When the smith pulled the leather away, he gasped at the shimmering beauty of the steel blade. It was a slender piece of shiny, supple metal, no wider than two of his fingers where it emerged from its sheath, tapering to a point as sharp as the fang of a viper. Edges sharper than any razor of obsidian rang the length of the blade top and bottom. The hilt, too, was a work of art, carved from some kind of very hard wood to form a protective shield for his sword hand.

"It is a stunning weapon," the warrior said quietly. "I thank you from the bottom of my heart, and only hope that I can prove myself worthy of bearing it."

Darryn's chest puffed out and he allowed himself the hint of a smile. "It's the finest piece I've ever made, if I say so myself. And that should make it the finest sword in Nayve." Somehow he said the words with such honest affection for his work that they carried no hint of arrogance.

"And the hilt is a thing of beauty," Natac continued. "What wood did you carve in such a manner?"

"Ask the lady druid," said Darryn, nodding toward Miradel.

"I made the hilt from the tree called the arkwood," she

said. "It grows only in Argentian, and the elves allow only one tree to be harvested every one hundred years—so the wood is quite precious, as you can imagine. And the Goddess Worldweaver herself was kind enough to bestow some of her goodness into the hilt. So long as you hold the sword in your hand and bear it justly, no weapon will be able to penetrate your skin."

Natac had been in Nayve long enough that he didn't marvel at the suggestion of powerful magic. Still, he was awed by the thought that such protection in battle might be offered to *him*. Again he made the vow, this time to himself and to his Yellow Hummingbird—he would be a worthy bearer of this weapon.

He picked the sword up, amazed at its lightness—it had far less mass than any wood-and-obsidian maquahuitl. The blade was like an extension of his hand as he whipped his arm around. When he looked at Miradel he saw that her eyes were shining, alight with that reflection of pride that disturbed him so much. Once more he wondered . . . Why, in a place where there was no war . . . why did she want him to have a sword?

"Listen . . . I hear them baying. I'll bet they're after a deer right now!" Ulfgang woofed in excitement.

"Can we catch them?" Tam asked. He felt a keen buzz of excitement—after a week of arduous trekking, at last they had caught the spoor of the trouble that had drawn them to the Greens. This was different, unknown—and that very mystery seemed to cause a peculiar thrill. The song of the hounds was distant, yet piercingly eerie. As the chorus of wails rose and ululated he felt a distinct shiver run down his spine.

Deltan Columbine, too, looked flushed and excited. His eyes were bright, and there was no sign of the fatigue that had slowed him down on the first few days of their trek.

"I think they're coming this way—Come on!" urged the dog, breaking into a trot.

Tam loped along behind. His body moving with natural grace, and it seemed that his mind was as clear, as keen and ready, as it had ever been in his life. In one hand he hoisted a stout stick, a shaft as big around as his wrist and slightly longer than his own height. He had carved it a couple of days earlier, when the pair had first entered the lofty forest and Ulfgang had casually mentioned that a pack of deer-mad dogs might not respond immediately to cool logic. Since then the staff had seemed to become a part of him, and now he set it on his shoulder as comfortably as if it were another limb.

Deltan, following just behind, carried a homemade bow and a cluster of arrows tipped with fire-hardened points of wood. Already he had shown a keen eye, enhancing their evening camps with dinners of rabbit, squirrel, and even a plump pheasant. Privately, however, Tamarwind doubted that the light missiles would prove much of a deterrent against anything larger.

Now they ran between huge tree trunks over a forest floor that was for the most part free of brush. They leaped a long, mossy log, then skirted a small pond, and now the sounds of the baying pack rang all around them like a bizarre, demented chorus. The music of the chase soared and swelled with the dogs' frenzy.

Abruptly Ulfgang skidded to a halt. Tam and Deltan came to rest beside him, leaning against the trunk of a huge tree. They heard crashing footsteps, and then a wide-eyed stag leapt by, tongue flopping loosely as it hurled itself through desperate, lunging bounds.

"Now!" cried Ulf, leaping out from behind the tree. The white dog crouched, facing the deer's pursuers, upper lip curled into a very forbidding snarl. Tam, his broad staff upraised, stepped to his companion's side—and immediately felt a searing jab of fear.

At least a dozen large, snarling dogs came to an outraged halt. They bristled and snapped, infuriated at the interruption of their chase. The elf raised his staff as three of the dogs impetuously rushed forward. Deltan Columbine, next to the tree, shot an arrow that grazed a hairy flank, sending one of the animals darting back to the pack. Another veered away as Tamarwind swung the stout weapon, and the third, a large male, yelped in surprise as Ulf feinted a lunge to the left and then drove against the dog's right. Tam saw a flash of white fangs, and then Ulfgang had buried his teeth in the loose wattle of the big dog's throat.

The snarl turned to a yelp and the big dog twisted and fell while Ulf maintained his ferocious grip. Tam swung the staff and Deltan nocked another arrow as several other canines lunged. The animals backed off, and again the male yelped through the pressure of Ulf's teeth.

Spitting in contempt, Ulf released the dog to slink back to its mates.

"Shame—shame on you all! You are shepherds!" Ulfgang bellowed, his voice a formidable roar. Aggressive tails lowered across the group, and Tam noticed several dogs of the pack exchanging clearly sheepish glances. But one of the other animals blustered, hair bristling on its neck as it growled and snapped. This was another big male, larger than Ulf by two or three hands, and it swaggered forward belligerently. Both eyes were bright, almost bloodshot with the intensity of the creature's agitation.

"Don't be a fool," scolded the white dog. "Even if you bite, my friend will smash your brains in with his pole!"

Tam brandished the staff as the big dog eyed him appraisingly. Deltan Columbine drew back his bow and many of the other dogs gaped and huffed, nervously backing away. The leader barked several times, hackles raised, but then Tam detected a note of reluctant compliance as the creature lowered its head and bared its fangs in a drooling grin.

"What brings you here? Why have you abandoned the fields, left your responsibilities to chase deer?" demanded the white dog, clearly in command now.

The dogs started barking, all of them contributing to the din, and Ulfgang shouted for silence. Even so, the baying, howling, and yipping continued, until Tam was getting a headache from the noise. Finally the pack settled down, and the white dog turned to the big male. "You tell me, alone."

The shepherd, voice already hoarse from the hunt, barked roughly for several minutes. When he concluded, panting, Ulfgang nodded his head grimly and turned to his elven companions.

"I couldn't understand much," he admitted. "But they claim there is something that drew them here to the Greens . . . that they were pulled to the chase by a force strange and compelling."

"What thing is that?" Tam demanded, still trembling with the excitement of the confrontation.

"Magic, I fear," Ulf replied. "Of what type, I don't know. But more significantly, that big one—Red Eye—says that he can show us where we can find this power in the flesh."

Two days later Ulfgang, Deltan, and Tamarwind crouched on the lip of a ravine overlooking a small valley, a gorge twisting through the trackless depths of the Greens. The travelers lay in a fringe of brush, silent and unmoving. Their position commanded a clear view of the ground below. In a clearing on the valley floor hundreds of people—mostly elves, but with a few giants, goblins, and centaurs among them—had gathered.

The shepherd called Red Eye had led them close to this place, though an hour earlier the big dog had slunk away without explanation. Nor had Ulf asked for one—he told Tam that he, too, could sense the wrongness in this place, an invisible corruption that marred the trees, the ground, the very air itself.

Tamarwind still carried his staff, and he was disturbed to realize that he was very much afraid. Deltan Columbine was silent, clutching his bow and looking wide-eyed at the mob below them. Ulfgang seemed purposeful and grim. As he searched for this place, the white dog had trotted along with head and nose low, sniffing constantly, seeking some improper spoor, some signal of the magic that had so disrupted life in unchanging Argentian. The warning of the pack had stricken the white dog with visible force, and the change in Ulf's mood had provided a sobering warning to Tam and Deltan.

And now they had come upon this bizarre gathering. Significantly, many of those gathered in the little clearing bore weapons—spears and staffs, a few with the bows and arrows such as an elven hunter might carry. In the center of the gathering a tall, bare stake jutted upward from a pile of kindling. Nearby was a canvas tent, and before that shelter dangled a white banner emblazoned with a red cross. The crowd was mostly silent and attentive, though they were joined by more and more people coming from the trails leading up and down the valley. Abruptly an audible gasp sounded from the assemblage, and all eyes went to the canvas shelter.

A human came out of the tent. His chest was covered by a stiff, silvery shirt. He was bearded, with long brown hair, and he carried a stout staff that was capped with the head of a hooded snake. When he raised his arms and the final murmurings in the assemblage stilled, it seemed to Tamarwind that even the birds and monkeys grew quiet, waiting, tense, afraid.

A scream echoed, startling and eerie. Tam saw a woman, a human druid to judge from her long black hair, dragged forward by two giants. She screamed again, and one of the brutes cuffed her across the face. The crowd murmured and shifted like a hungry being, awakened and thrilled by the prisoner's suffering.

Stunned by the violence, Tamarwind watched in horror as the druid was tied to the post. She struggled in vain, moaning and sobbing as ropes were pulled tight against her flesh. A pair of goblins, cackling excitedly, carried torches forward and thrust the flaming brands into the kindling around the stake. Quickly the fire took hold, snapping hungrily through the wood, spewing upward in yellow and orange tongues. The druidess shrieked loudly as her gown caught fire, as black smoke swirled around her and the blaze grew fierce.

Appalled, Tam, Deltan, and Ulfgang watched the flames spark. The scout tried to imagine the pain the woman must be suffering, but his mind couldn't even begin to comprehend. Fire consumed her garment and blackened her skin. Her shouts and cries climbed beyond the scale of anguish, a dolorous wail of pure agony as her flesh was consumed by the blaze. The unforgettable stench, like charred meat and offal, reached even to the nostrils of the three watchers above the valley. Tamarwind clenched his teeth, fighting against a surging wave of nausea.

And then the woman was no longer screaming. Her cries were muted moans, swiftly overwhelmed by the crackling fury of the conflagration.

The crowd remained rapt, eyes alight. The fire roared eagerly around the writhing body. Her limbs thrashed, and it took a long time before her cries faded into croaks. At last the only sounds came from the flames, crackling, hungry and exultant.

When the druid had been reduced to a blackened shell amid a mound of glowing coals the bearded man spoke.

"Again we have claimed a witch, my valiant Crusaders . . . and again God is pleased with our efforts!" Cheers and whoops rang out from the crowd, a response that chilled Tam nearly as much as had the gruesome death. "See!" The speaker, his voice sharp, raised a hand in a violent, triumphant gesture. A gold chain dangled from his wrist, and the elf caught a glimpse of a small white stone held in the man's fingers. He swung his hand back and forth, and the eyes and heads of the crowd followed the talisman in rapt attention.

Something flared redly in that stone, an X-shaped vibration of crimson light that sent a jolt of pleasure through Tamarwind. Stunned, he looked to the side, saw that Deltan had dropped his bow, that he gazed longingly toward the object in the man's hand. When the hand came down, the stone disappeared from view, and the people in the valley—and the two elves watching from above—sighed in unison.

"But it is time that we did more, labored harder in the name of our Holy Savior. And so I tell you: There is a temple of evil in this wretched swath of purgatory. The place is a monument to heresy. It rises upon an island, forms a minaret of metal that is an abomination, an affront to God. And so I will lead you there, my crusaders . . . and we will see this temple and we will tear it down!"

"The Loom of the Worldweaver!" Tamarwind gasped. Deltan Columbine simply shook his head, pulling back from his vantage to sit, stunned, on the forest floor.

The frightening message was still ringing in the clearing when Ulf leapt up on all fours with a startled snort. The dog and the elves spun in unison, Tam leaping to his feet and then freezing in shock.

A giant with a bristling black beard held a stone-tipped spear leveled straight at Tam's chest. The fellow loomed high overhead, and his body seemed as broad as a wall. Thick cords of muscle knotted his thighs and calves, and each of his arms was as big around as a human man's leg.

"Come, witch . . . you can talk to Sir Christopher." The giant's voice was a growl like thunder. Tam felt the rumble in the pit of his stomach. "There's enough kindling left for a double burning."

Tamarwind's blood ran cold. The staff was still on his shoulder, but seemed like an impotent twig in the face of that deadly spearhead. He tried to think of something, anything, to say.

Turning his head, he saw that Deltan hadn't even picked up his bow. Instead, the poet looked back at Tam, a desperate appeal for help written in his terrified expression, his wildly staring eyes. The scout clenched his hand around the staff, but when the giant lifted his spear toward his throat he took a short step backward, unable to make himself attack.

Ulf, on the other hand, didn't hesitate. He pranced forward, tail wagging as he gazed fawnishly up at the giant.

"Some watchdog," snorted the elf's captor.

Ulf suddenly lunged upward, snapping his jaws hard beneath the giant's shaggy tunic. The fellow left out a pinched scream and doubled over. Somehow Tam's instincts took over, and he swung the heavy staff. The pole whistled through the air, landing with a resounding *crack* against the giant's skull. The shaft of wood shattered but the giant fell on his face with a thud. Groaning once, he kicked, then lay still.

"Come on!" panted Ulf, already starting through the woods.

An impulse penetrated Tam's fear and he reached down to snatch up the giant's heavy spear. Then he was off, racing after Ulfgang and Deltan, the wind of his speed drawing tears from his still-horrified eyes.

10

A Girding of Elves

Poem,
painting,
sculpture;
song and prose
and play.
Girders of serenity,
frame of night and day

Violent shadows shiver,
pain and bloodshed wax
warfare, plunder, murder
are the artwork of the axe.

From *The Ballad of the First Warrior*
Deltan Columbine

Belynda lay awake, fidgeting restlessly. The Lighten Hour was still a long time away, but she felt no need to sleep. She didn't know what subconscious anxiety triggered her unease, but she finally, reluctantly, gave up the attempt at repose. She whispered on the light and found that she didn't even blink against the soft illumination.

Swinging her feet to the floor, she stood, and then paced across her sleeping chamber for the simple reason that she needed to move. She walked past the reading table without pause. The door to her garden glided open as she murmured the word of command, and then she was under the night sky with its fulgent, gracefully shifting patterns of stars. Sitting on a marble bench, she leaned back to watch the stately wheel of the night overhead. The stars spiraled around the axis of the distant sun—the celestial body that was now no more than the brightest star in the twinkling vista of the sky. Each speck of light seemed to move at its own speed. At times thousands of them formed tendrils of blurry illumination, while shortly thereafter those twisting limbs broke apart, dissolving into their individual, lonely components. And thus they wandered until the pattern brought them again into concentration.

All but hypnotized, Belynda stared into the vastness overhead. As she had done countless times before, she tried to sift some kind of design from the cosmic quilt . . . but just when she began to perceive a face, a horizon, an animal or leaf, the twinkling display would distort and realign. Inevitably she was left with a sense of randomness that she found troubling, resonant of a vague sense of insecurity.

But tonight even the spectacle of the skies could not distract her from the agitation that ruined her sleep and lifted her from her bed. She still could not identify a precise source of unease. Rather it was as if too many little changes were occurring in the world, niggling things that combined to portend something different, some dire interruption in the stately pace of Nayve.

For, of course, change was bad. In any kind of alteration there was a potential for violence, and perhaps it was this awareness that caused her to think about pain, and killing, and war. Not that she had seen any examples during her lifetime . . . rather she had learned from tales of the Seventh Circle, stories told by druids who had witnessed the World-weaver's Tapestry. In her lifetime there had been many advances in the way humans made war, and she tried to imagine where they could go in the future. Such a frenetic, furious race they were—even, truth be told, the druids, who were supposed to represent the wisest and most serene of the lot.

But in this past year Caranor and Allevia had died violently. She had just learned from Nistel that *more* giants had come to Thickwhistle, this time rousting a whole clan of gnomes out of a cherished cavern. She missed having Ulfgang to talk to . . . and even more, she wished Tamarwind was here.

She stood up and stretched, and it was then that she heard the rustling in the shrubbery surrounding her garden. In another moment a canine body, white against the darkness, trotted into view. Ulfgang was followed by Tamarwind Trak, who was breathing hard from exertion, and another, similarly exhausted elf. Both wore clothes that were in tatters, and Belynda gasped at the sight of the scout's face, haggard and thin, streaked with sweat and dirt.

"Are you hurt?" she asked, rushing to embrace Tam by his shoulders. She stared into eyes that were hooded and dark, and contained the gleam of burning anger.

"No . . . just tired," he said. Despite the emotion that seethed almost visibly beneath his skin, his voice was soft and calm.

"We came here without rest," Ulf explained. "From the Greens, running nearly all the way. Tam even mounted a horse for the last leg of the trip."

"What's wrong?" asked the sage-ambassador, shaken by the explanation, by the implication of bad news. "And who . . . Deltan Columbine!" She recognized the other elf then.

"My lady Sage-Ambassador," he said with a bow. "I regret that I see you again on an occasion of such dire portent."

"Tell me!" she said, sitting on the bench and forcing herself to be calm. The two men joined her, apparently soothed somewhat by her example. "What is this dire portent?"

"It is death—murder and war come to Nayve!" Tam blurted.

"In the person of a warrior, a human," added Deltan. "One who dwells in the Greens, and gathers others to his cause."

"It is he who has lured the shepherds from their duties," Ulfgang put in.

Belylnda listened in growing shock as the dog and elves continued to describe the band they had observed, and the burning of the druid who had been called a "witch."

"Elves, giants . . . centaurs? And they are all armed?" she echoed in growing fear. "That's enough for a whole army, right here in the Fourth Circle!"

"And there's more," Tam said. He told her about the human warrior with his great staff and his shirt of silver. "He was urging his army into a frenzy. He held aloft a small white talisman on a chain and charged them to come here, to Circle at Center. They intend to tear down the Worldweaver's Loom!"

Belynda felt as though she had been punched in the stomach. It was hard to draw a breath, or to wrap her mind around the idea of an attack against this sacred place.

"How . . ." She let the question trail off, not even knowing what to ask. "We can't let them!"

Tamarwind drew a deep breath. "I know . . . we need to gather against them—to—to fight!" He looked stunned, even sickened, by his own words.

"I have sent word to Argentian," Deltan Columbine said. "There are many of my students there who will join us, I'm certain. I asked them to travel here, to Circle at Center. From them we can form a company."

"A company . . ." With a jolt Belynda suddenly remembered Miradel, and the warrior the druid had summoned at such cost. "To train the elves for war," she murmured wonderingly.

"What?" asked the scout.

"It's . . . there's someone who saw the danger before I did," the sage-ambassador said quietly. "She gave up her future, her whole life, because she perceived this menace and sacrificed herself so that the rest of us might be prepared."

"What do you mean?"

"There is a human warrior called Natac. He lives in a villa in the hills, not far from the end of the causeway. He will take Deltan Columbine's company of elves and teach them to be warriors. And we will get more elves, from here in the city, and from Barantha, and all the other realms."

Now Belynda felt a focus, a direction for the energy and agitation that had disrupted her sleep and brought her, awake and alert, into the garden. She looked fondly at Tam, gently caressed Ulf's head and ears. She smiled at Deltan Columbine, saw that he stood taller, looked sturdier, than she remembered him. "You are very brave . . . all three of you. You must have been in terrible danger."

"Actually, we did face down a giant," Tam admitted, huffing slightly in embarrassment. With a shy grin he reached behind a bush to bring forth a stout spear, the weapon a good deal longer than Belynda's height. "Ulf bit him, and I bopped him over the head—and then I took this away from him."

The sage-ambassador was appalled at the tale, and she squeezed her hand tightly around Tamarwind's arm. "Please—you must try to be careful!" she declared.

"I will. In any event, there won't be any giants around this warrior's villa."

"Actually, it's my friend's house. Miradel is her name, and she will know where your company can make camp."

"Can you show us the way to Miradel's?" Tam asked, again smiling bashfully.

Belynda was strangely touched. "I will take you there in two days—there's something I have to do, first."

•   •   •

Natac and Miradel sat on the veranda, watching the lake turn purple as the sun receded overhead. They had eaten a splendid meal of cowsteak and beans, which Miradel had cooked together in a mixture of spices that still tickled about the warrior's palate. With a few whispered words of magic, Fallon had cleaned up after the meal and retired to his own apartment. Now the elf strummed his lute there, and the gentle chords swirled and soothed through the growing night.

The druid and Natac had just spent long hours in the dark room, where she had displayed for him many pictures of humans using swords—for contests and combat alike. As he had been doing for many days, Natac practiced the moves he had seen, whipping his own blade around with speed and grace. Their session had closed with an hour spent watching the unarmed warrior who had unknowingly taught Natac so much. This man of the Orient was adept at the use of his hands and feet, and by now the Tlaxcalan had learned to exactly mimic his remote teacher's movements.

Tired from the exercise, with his full belly seeming like an anchor as he sat in a comfortable wicker chair, Natac felt his eyelids start to droop. He sighed, and leaned back, watching as more and more stars came into view.

"The time is coming, very soon," Miradel said suddenly.

His tiredness vanished in that instant, for he knew exactly what she meant.

"I will be ready," he promised. He looked across the starlit vista, the sparkling lights of the city across the lake, the placid evening lying still and comforting about them. The promise welled up, and he thought of a yellow hummingbird. Unbidden, the vow came again to his lips.

"I will be ready."

• • •

Belynda strode to the rostrum with every appearance of confidence, though inwardly she suddenly quailed at the prospect before her. The reality suddenly struck her like a blow: How could she expect to get this hidebound body to accept her warnings and, even more difficult, to actually take *action* in the face of danger?

For better or worse, the Grand Forum of the Senate was half empty. Belynda was not surprised, for despite an announcement of this special session having been sent to all the delegates, any break in Nayve's routine was not likely to stir up a great deal of interest. She saw one friendly face and smiled at Nistel, who had done a good job of gathering the most influential gnomes. It had been her faithful assistant, too, who had helped her spread word among the other delegations in Nayve's ruling body. She looked for Cillia, but the statuesque druid was nowhere to be seen.

At the last minute Quilene, mistress of the enchantresses, arrived in a soft twinkle of light. The elves accepted her teleportation with typical aplomb, but the gnomes on the nearby benches stared, goggle-eyed, at this evidence of powerful magic.

Only one giant, the rangy Galewn, had bothered to attend. And she saw that the goblins and faeries had not sent even a single delegate. Most distressing, however, was the sparse attendance of her own people. Barely half the members were here, and of these only one—the venerable Rallaphan, who all but dozed on his stool—came from the districts within Circle at Center.

Tall Praxian and rotund Cannystrius had taken their stations, and now both of the speakers of the Senate looked at Belynda. Each had a nervous expression, despite valiant—and obvious—attempts to appear aloof and unconcerned.

"Peoples of Nayve," began the sage-ambassador, allowing her eyes to scan the entire chamber. Curiosity about the impromptu session, if nothing else, drew all eyes to her. She knew that she would have to startle them in order to make any headway toward persuasion, so she forced herself to speak very loudly.

"The Fourth Circle is entering a period of dramatic change. We face unprecedented dangers, threats of violence and destruction such as our world has not known in ten thousand years. I come to you now with a plea for action— we must organize, and prepare to defend ourselves against a horrible foe!"

Audible gasps and murmurs of disbelief punctuated her statement. Elves exchanged nervous looks while the gnomes chattered excitedly. Belynda saw that Blinker was holding forth among his comrades, that his companions were looking at him with expressions bordering on awe. Also interesting was the reaction of Galewn, who leaned forward on his stool to scrutinize Belynda skeptically. Quilene surprised her too, as she rose to her feet and raised her hand to her chin in the indication of one who wished to address the Senate.

But she saw more as the elven faces hardened to regard her with frank suspicion, even distrust. Old Rallaphan was glaring in open hostility. Perhaps she had miscalculated . . . perhaps she should have taken more time in describing the threat, before making her plea for action.

Praxian and Cannystrius exchanged nervous glances. After a moment it was the latter who rose, waddled forward, and curtly gestured for Quilene to proceed.

"I am glad my sister sage has brought this matter into the light," the enchantress said. "For she states the conclusion of all among my Order. We have been striving to come to grips with an array of very dire portents, each seemingly more grim than the last. It is time that we take action."

"Portents, dangers, threats!" mocked Galewn, standing and planting his hamlike hands on his hips. "Tell me, old woman . . . *what* are the portents? *Where* are the dangers?"

"In the Greens," Belynda retorted sharply.

She was surprised when the giant bit back the outburst he'd been about to make. "Explain," he demanded.

"A wild human lives there. He has corrupted elves and centaurs, even giants. He bears a powerful talisman that I believe to be the Stone of Command. This stone was held by the sage-enchantress Caranor, one of those who was killed by fire. It is powerful magic, for it can influence and weaken the will of all who behold it, or even sense its presence. I have spoken with witnesses who saw these outlaws burn a druid who was tied to a stake in the ground." The blunt description of violence brought the chamber to a stunned silence. "Her death was painful, and horrifying," Belynda concluded sternly. "And the wild human has declared his intent to bring the same fate right here, into Circle at Center!"

"Who are these witnesses?" demanded Praxian, standing tall and glaring down at Belynda.

She had already decided that she would not mention Ulfgang's involvement—the haughty elves would immediately disdain the report of even the most educated dog. "Tamarwind Trak, a scout from Argentian. And one Deltan Columbine, a teacher and poet, also of my home realm.

"I don't believe it!" Cannystrius huffed. "They must be making it up—such an occurence is utterly unthinkable!"

"Outlander lies!" cried Rallaphan, who had presided over his quarter of Circle at Center for nearly a thousand years. "I have heard of this Columbine—a young radical, looking to stir up trouble!"

"It is the truth!" insisted Belynda.

For some reason she looked first to the giant for support, but was chagrined to see Galewn already making his way out of the chamber. Quilene stood in the midst of shouting elves, looking at the sage-ambassador with an expression of mild exasperation. Belynda could only continue, trying to shout over the commotion. "It's not only true—but we have to *do* something about it!"

"What?" Praxian bleated plaintively.

"We must organize ourselves, prepare to resist any attack. It will require training and discipline, lead to hard and unpleasant work. But it must be done, or we are doomed!"

"No!" shouted someone from among the elves.

"We need more proof—we cannot disrupt our world based on the word of some rural scout," Cannystrius declared, the stout speaker addressing the Senate with rare severity. "I, for one, will not hear of it!"

"Nor shall I!" huffed Praxian.

"Listen to her! Listen to Belynda!" shrieked a new voice, and the sage-ambassador was touched to see Nistel standing on his stool, waving his fist at the elves. But his loyal advocacy had no discernible effect. Instead, the elves milled about, chattering and whispering. Several were crying, or casting cold and hostile looks at the sage-ambassador.

"You tried . . . but what could you expect?" said Quilene, who had somehow whisked herself to Belynda's side.

"I thought they might listen, might understand the urgency . . ."

The enchantress shook her head. "They will need the word of more than one witness before they change the way they think . . . and even then, I don't think half of these elves would acknowledge trouble if it was coming through the front door."

Quilene made her farewells, then vanished as quickly as she had arrived. The other delegates trailed out, some pensive and alone, others in tight groups, hunched in quiet, agitated conversation. Finally only Blinker remained. The little gnome was still indignant, his beard bristling angrily as he glared at the empty stools throughout the chamber.

"Fools and idiots!" he snorted. "I've seen faeries with more sense!"

"She was right," Belynda reflected, still thinking about the words of the enchantress.

"What?"

"We need more witnesses, more testimony before the Senate will admit that anything can be wrong. And I intend to get that proof!"

"Who are you going to send?" asked the gnome suspiciously.

"No one. I intend to go and see for myself. When I bring word back, I can stand before them and tell them what I've seen—and they will *have* to believe me!"

"No!" gasped Nistel. "It'll be too dangerous—you should send someone else!" The gnome gulped and drew a deep breath. "Why, *I'll* go. . . ."

"That's very brave, my friend. But it has to be me. It's not fair to send another in my place. And besides, the Senate needs to hear from me directly."

"But . . . you can't go alone," the gnome insisted. He drew a deep, heavy sigh. "I have to go with you."

Belynda smiled. "I appreciate your loyalty . . . I really do. But your place is here."

"Nonsense!" Blinker sounded very firm. "You need protection, and I'm just the person to protect you!"

The sage-ambassador finally had to laugh, and then touched the gnome's shoulder in gratitude. "Then together we'll go have a look at the Greens," she said. "But I must ask you to say nothing of this to Tamarwind or Miradel . . . I fear that their objections would be as vociferous as yours."

"I can keep a secret!" Nistel pledged, and the matter was decided.

"These are elves of Argentian, come to Circle at Center in response to a summons for help. Will you train them, make them into a company of warriors?"

Belynda asked Natac the question frankly. She had come

to the villa this morning, accompanied by a gnome—the first of these Natac had met—and perhaps a hundred young elves. The pair of leaders, Tamarwind and Deltan, had joined them in the villa while the rest of the group had settled into a shady grotto just below the white-walled house.

"Yes," Natac replied without hesitation. "At least, I will teach them what I knew, and what I have learned since coming here, about the making of war."

"Tamarwind and Deltan can tell you about the enemy—they have seen him, and his force. His warriors include giants, centaurs, and many hundred elves."

"Are there more elves willing to fight against him?" Natac wondered.

"I hope there will be, soon . . . there is a need among some of my people for further proof, which we hope will be forthcoming shortly." The elfwoman glanced quickly at the gnome, who whistled and looked away.

"Very well. I think we should get started right away."

"Will you stay here for a while and observe the training?" Miradel asked Belynda, then smiled shyly. "Also, I would enjoy the pleasure of your company, old friend."

The elfwoman looked strangely uncomfortable. "I would like that but, no. I am afraid there are . . . other matters demanding my attention."

"Of course," Miradel said. "These are becoming busy times in Circle at Center, and across all of Nayve."

The sage-ambassador and gnome departed on foot, and Natac set about getting his recruits organized. He appointed Tamarwind Trak as captain, and Deltan as his lieutenant. The rest of the day was spent getting the elves—who, to Natac's surprise, included perhaps twenty-five females among their number—into a comfortable camp.

Three days later, the Tlaxcalan was surprised and impressed by how much progress the whole assemblage had made. Deltan had organized a group who had made many bows and arrows. For now these missiles were tipped with only wooden heads for practice, but Darryn Forgemaster had pledged to provide many steel arrowheads within the next tenday. Meanwhile, Tam had taken another party in search of stout, straight branches. These had been whittled into sturdy staffs. Thus crudely armed, the elves had begun their drilling.

Natac had designated an archery range on a flat swath of ground beside the lake. Now he and Deltan were there with the archers, while the young elf barked commands, and the bowmen practiced shooting in volleys.

"Now!" cried Deltan, and two dozen strings twanged.

The cluster of arrows soared in tight formation, almost as if the shafts were linked by invisible threads. Slowly that thread drew taut as all the missiles converged on the target. Even a hundred paces away Natac heard the thud made by the simultaneous impact of two dozen wooden arrowheads. The target, a rotten stump, bristled like a porcupine—not a single shaft had flown wide of the mark.

"Good shooting," the warrior said to Deltan Columbine, who scrutinized the array of arrows and then shook his head.

"I told them to hit the *top* of the stump!" complained the elf. He turned with a frown to address the rank of elven archers. "You archers—pull and shoot again. Take that next stump to the left, and I want to see some precision this time!"

Without a murmur of complaint or exasperation, the bowmen did as they had been told—and once more Natac marveled at this aspect of the elven troops. Although the whole concept of military practice, and especially the discipline needed for volley fire and marching, was foreign to the experience of these raw warriors, they put themselves to every task with a sense of purpose that still caused Natac to look on in awe.

This time the top of the stump bristled with arrows, and

Deltan allowed himself a grunt of acknowledgment.

"You're doing well, all of you," Natac declared, pleased at the pride evident on the elven faces. He turned to watch the larger group of Tam's fighters, who were clashing and bashing with their staves, when he was distracted by a loud shout.

"Hey . . . you're wasting time on those silly games!" The booming taunt came from the hillside over the training field. Fionn was striding down the steep incline, with Owen lumbering along behind.

"That's no way to get ready for war!" the Viking chimed in. The two men, cloaked in their furs, bearing stout staffs and full packs, swaggered closer. A half-dozen druidesses came behind them.

"Why don't you show us how to do it?" Natac called back, pleased that the pair had come by.

"Show you? Me own lesson would *kill* you!" snorted Fionn, while Owen merely guffawed.

"Try me, then?" Natac said casually. He stood firmly and planted his hands on his hips as the two burly warriors pulled up short.

"Not to offend, little man . . . but I meant what I said," the Irishman growled. He raised one of his own hamlike fists and faced Natac with a grin that was not at all humorous.

"So did I." The Tlaxcalan took a step forward with unmistakable challenge, though his hands remained at his sides. "But before we grapple, perhaps you'd do me the honor of making a little wager?"

Fionn's bearded face split into a broad grin. "Name yer terms," he said jovially.

"My wager is this: If I can throw you on the ground before you do the same to me, then you'll agree to join my company—and to abide by my orders."

The big man frowned and paused. "Yer serious, aren't ya? Thinking you can actually throw me?"

"Perfectly serious, yes."

"And what about when *I* throw *you?* A wager goes two ways, does it not?"

"What are your stakes?" Natac, having watched Fionn and Owen grapple on countless occasions, was fairly confident of his victory. Still, he couldn't suppress his apprehension when, after a moment's thought, the Celt replied:

"Ye'll do my washing for a full cycle, and clean out my lodge to boot. The place is startin' to smell like a pigsty, anyway."

"I accept." The Tlaxcalan gave his word sincerely, privately vowing to win the fight, and quickly.

Abruptly Fionn charged, a rushing bull. He swept his arms around Natac—but before the Celt closed his grip, the smaller man seized a burly forearm and tossed, using the fulcrum of his own shoulder. The Irishman crashed to the turf with an impact that shook the ground. For a moment he flailed weakly, before drawing in a huge gasp of breath.

Even before Fionn regained his feet, Owen doubled over, howling with glee. "Looks like you've found a new recruit!"

"Would ye . . . like a try . . . at the slippery devil?" Hands on his knees, the Celt still strained to breathe. "That was no fair fight!" he finally gasped, standing upright.

"A fair wager, though," Natac suggested. "And welcome to my company."

"Ye'll not be havin' me work with those faerie bows, will ye?" growled the Irishman.

Natac shook his head and laughed. "I daresay you're not cut out to be an archer. No—perhaps you could go and get your staff—I'm of a mind that you can help with training."

Without a word, Fionn turned to trudge back to his kit. He didn't even acknowledge the sympathetic cooing of Julyia and several other druidesses who gathered around.

"Would you take the same wager?" Natac asked, turning to Owen.

"Surely!" Owen accepted with immense good humor. "And I'll do me best not to hurt you!"

"I appreciate that," Natac replied as the Viking swaggered forward. The Tlaxcalan was wary, certain that the Norseman would not repeat Fionn's mistakes of overconfidence and haste.

And clearly, Owen had learned a lot from Fionn's misstep. The big man skirted through a tight circle, forcing Natac to do the same. The two studied each other, feinting with a swipe of a hand, the dip of a shoulder. When the Viking advanced, he still moved with caution, reaching without lunging, keeping his weight evenly balanced between his feet. Despite Natac's own best efforts, he could not draw his foe into a careless attack—all the while Owen's full concentration remained on Natac's hands and arms.

So the Tlaxcalan decided to change tactics. He feinted an attack with his fists, and Owen spread his arms, ready to embrace Natac's careless advance. Instead, Natac snapped a sharp kick with his right foot, smashing hard into the Viking's left knee. Owen bellowed and stepped back, favoring the injured limb.

"How'd you do that?" the Viking growled ominously. "I'm thinking that magic is disallowed in this duel!"

"No magic," Natac replied, dropping into a crouch. He spun through a full circle, putting all of his strength into a spinning roundhouse kick that smashed, hard, into Owen's right ankle. Owen's leg was swept out from beneath him, and with a roar of frustration and pain he crashed to the ground, landing hard on the flat of his back.

Natac rose and extended his foe a hand, but Owen growled fiercely and kicked at the Tlaxcalan. "No fair—I cry foul!" declared the Viking, pushing himself to his feet. He went over to the bundle of his belongings and pulled forth his large staff. "I meant to wager on a fight with weapons."

"This is what you Norsemen call honor?" demanded Natac. Still, he was not surprised—nor unprepared. He retreated to his own cloak and pulled out the shining sword. "I warn you, Owen . . . you've lost the fight and the wager. If you come after me now, it will not go well for you!"

But the Viking was beyond reason. He let out a blood-curdling roar and charged, swinging the stout shaft before him. His aim was good—Natac could neither duck below nor leap over the weapon.

Instead, the warrior extended his sword in a direct parry, knowing that the weapon's first test would be a real challenge. Holding the hilt with both hands, he winced against the impact—and indeed, the blow sent him staggering to the side, his palms stinging from the vibrations of the attack.

But Owen didn't pursue. Instead, he gaped stupidly at the deep gouge that had scored his oaken staff. When he flexed the weapon sharply, the small piece of wood connecting the pieces creaked ominously. With a flick of his sword, Natac struck the top of the staff, and the weapon snapped in two at the cut.

Instantly the big Viking leaped forward. Instincts from a lifetime of fighting with a maquahutal almost forced Natac to hack with the blade, but he recalled the lessons he'd learned from his studies of Earth. Instead, he brought the point sharply against Owen's leather vest. He pushed hard enough to slice through the cowskin and slightly puncture the skin beyond.

The Viking halted, eyes narrowed. "You could kill me, just like that," he said, shaking his head in wonder.

"But I won't do that. You made a wager, and you lost. Now, go find yourself another staff, and report back here, ready to go to work."

11

Journeys Into a Dark Place

Narrowed forest pathway,
oaken gates ajar,
Shadows lurking halfway
danger near and far.

Lullaby of the Hunted

"The Metal Highway is over there . . . are you sure this is the way to the Greens?" Nistel asked, looking up the dauntingly steep trail. They were only a few miles from Miradel's villa, but the gnome had obviously noticed that the sage-ambassador followed a trail leading farther into the hills.

"Not exactly," Belynda said with a laugh. "Though in our case, it will help us to get there. You didn't think we were going to walk all the way, did you?"

"Oh, well, no. *Oh!*" Blinker said with a gulp. "We're going with m-magic?"

"Don't worry—it won't hurt, and will save plenty of blisters on our feet."

The gnome looked unconvinced, but nevertheless followed her up the rugged path. The route was much as Quilene had described it when she gave Belynda directions: an overgrown pathway with a foundation of solid stone, including steps that had been carved into the hillside during some long-forgotten century.

By the time they neared the summit, both of them were huffing for breath. Nistel fell a dozen steps behind by the time the sage-ambassador stepped between two pillars of gray stone to emerge atop the hill. She found the ruin of an old stone wall, and a flagstone surface that was still smooth and flat. Belynda knew this was the right place—the pattern of monoliths rising around the edge of the circular surface, surely distinct in all Nayve, matched exactly the description Quilene had provided.

In the center of the hilltop plaza was a raised stone basin containing clear water. While Blinker nervously checked behind the monoliths, Belynda touched the water with her fingers, then moved her hand through it in a gentle, swirling motion. In seconds the water in the stone bowl was spiraling lazily, circling in the direction of her movement. Satisfied, Belynda removed her hand. The water continued to whirl as she looked around the open space.

"There!" gasped Nistel.

A halo of lights suddenly sparkled, only a few steps away. More and more spots blinked into view, colors of gold and cream and crimson. Moments later those pieces of brightness had coalesced into the form of a serene elf-woman with hair of gold and a gown of bright red silk.

"Hello, Quilene," Belynda said. She had been confident that the spell would work, but even so, the other woman's appearance was a relief.

"Greetings, Belynda, Nistel," replied the sage-enchantress with a graceful dip of her head. "Are you sure you want to go ahead with this?"

"Yes. I must see these Crusaders for myself—the Senate will not dare to doubt my own word."

"I agree," Quilene said. "And I admire your courage. Very well—Are you ready for the journey?"

"Right now?" Nistel said with a gulp. "Can't we have a

little bite of something to eat, first . . . maybe wait for the Hour of Darken?"

The two sages laughed sympathetically. "Actually, the teleportation spell is easier when your stomach's empty," Quilene suggested. "At least, when you're not used to it."

"It has been long since I've traveled this far," Belynda admitted. "You've found a place to send us?"

"Yes . . . there's a small pool in a grotto near the shore of the Snakesea. It will work quite well as a focus for the two of you."

"Good." Unlike the powerful enchantress—who could teleport either from or to a focal point of water—Belynda and her companion would require a swirl of water to anchor each end of the spell. Quilene had agreed to go ahead and locate such a terminus while Belynda had escorted the company to Natac.

"You will arrive in a very small, sheltered valley," the enchantress was explaining. "There is a small trail, quite steep, leading up the side—you'll have to climb about a hundred feet up to the forest floor. From there the path is obvious, running to the left and right. Take the right fork, and within a few hours you'll arrive at the first village, a place called Tallowglen."

"Tallowglen . . . we'll start our search there," said Belynda with a sense of finality.

Quilene pointed to the water in the stone bowl. "Start stirring, both of you. Be very gentle and steady in your movements."

Blinker's small, chubby hands splashed in the water across the bowl from Belynda's graceful fingers. The gnome and the sage-ambassador began to trace movement through the water, and slowly the liquid commenced a graceful whirling. Quilene paced through a series of measured steps, walking around the basin, and past the two travelers, opposite the direction of the water's swirl. The enchantress made three circuits around them while Belynda pushed the water into a faster and faster spin.

Abruptly Quilene stopped pacing, raising her arms as if she would encircle Belynda, Nistel, and the basin. She closed her eyes and tilted her head skyward, while from her throat came a deep, thrumming noise. The sound built in volume and pitch until it seemed to Belynda that a wind was howling through the nearby trees.

The ground seemed to tilt underfoot and, unconsciously, the sage-ambassador grasped the edge of the basin for support. She saw Blinker's goggle-eyed face staring wildly as he, too, clutched the rim of the stone bowl. Colors brightened around them, a brilliance greater than sunlight, a glowing rainbow wrapping them in an embrace of silky hues.

The humming grew louder, a supernatural sound that went far beyond any noise emerging from Quilene's throat. The ground lurched again, but Belynda was confident now that she wouldn't lose her balance. Nistel's eyes were squeezed shut and his mouth was shaping soundless cries of fear.

Belynda felt a sensation of weightlessness, but had no fear of falling. Instead, she might have been floating, soaring and gliding through time and space. She laughed, a slight and girlish giggle that startled her and caused Blinker to moan in dire fear. Her next sensation was of water that suddenly felt cooler against her skin. The whirling rainbow slowly faded, and she saw that they were in a new place—a grotto, as Quiline had described. The sage-enchantress was nowhere to be seen. Instead, steep, rocky walls draped with trailing greenery rose on three sides. A gap in the surrounding cliff walls revealed a stretch of sunlit sea in the other direction.

The basin of water was here a natural depression atop a rock. Belynda and Nistel now had their hands in this cool liquid, which seemed to bubble up from some sort of spring. Belynda exhaled and stepped back, feeling wide-awake, her body tingling with energy.

"Th-that wasn't so bad," Nistel said, after opening one eye and looking cautiously around. "I guess we came quite a way, didn't we?"

"Through the Ringhills and across the Snakesea," Belynda confirmed. Looking around, she spotted a precipitous route up the steep side of the grotto. Overhead, the limbs of great trees reached into view, indicating that dense forest lay beyond. "And there's the trail up the hill."

Atop the cliff they found the two paths, and started down the right fork. The village of Tallowglen, and all the Greens, lay beyond.

For many days the company of elves practiced drills with the bows and staves. Darryn Forgemaster brought hundreds of arrowheads, and—though the archers still used wooden tips for practice—many missiles were outfitted with the lethal steel blades. Owen and Fionn, meanwhile, took turns demonstrating the uses of the quarterstaff in battle, until most of the elves had become very proficient in the use of that weapon. The Celt and the Viking treated Natac with grudging respect, and had thus far accepted his leadership of the makeshift force. He, on the other hand, had been unfailingly polite to his fellow warriors, showing awareness of their knowledge, allowing them to decide how best to teach their skills to the elves.

Natac wished for a means to outfit his warriors with better weapons, but for now no ready opportunities presented themselves. Darryn was working on several swords, but that work took time—and in any event, even given several intervals or a full year he wouldn't be able to make enough blades to outfit even half of the company.

During the same period the elves built many straw houses to serve as their quarters. These were placed around the large, flat field that served as a drilling and parade ground. Juliay, Nachol, and several other druids also joined the band, though not to serve as warriors. Instead, they contributed their magical talents to the healing of wounds and the management of the weather during the long days of drill.

Another druid, one Baystril, arrived one day on horseback. He brought a dozen of the nimble ponies that Natac had observed in the valleys around Miradel's villa. Within a few hours, Natac, Tam, Deltan, several other elves, and a couple of druids had learned the basics of riding. The Tlaxcalan delighted in the speed and power of the horse, and on subsequent days he rode about the camp as much as he walked. Owen and Fionn, however, preferred to work on foot—which was a good thing, since none of the ponies of Nayve could have easily born the weight of either brawny human.

After a full tenday of working, Natac decided to commence the next part of the elves' preparation.

"The best way to condition yourselves for war is to march, to rapidly cover long distances at good speeds," he announced when the elves gathered for their morning instructions. "Today we begin such a march. It will be several tendays before we return to our valley."

"Tendays?" yelped Owen mournfully. He looked longingly at the keg of ale he had just rolled up to his lodge. "Maybe I should stay back here and guard the camp?"

Natac only laughed. "I have in mind that you'll be leading the way. Didn't you tell me that you Vikings are famous raiders? I don't see how you can do much raiding if you don't know how to march at a good clip."

"We liked to travel in our longships," the Norseman countered. "Never did have much use for a lot of walking."

"Well, it's time you learned to appreciate it," replied the Tlaxcalan. "Because that's how we're going to be getting around."

Although he, too, looked glum at the prospect of a long hike, Fionn didn't make any objection. Nor, of course, did any of the elves—as with everything else, they seemed to accept the wisdom of whatever Natac asked them to do.

Tamarwind Trak led the way. His own staff was marked with a plume of red cloth emblazoned with yellow feathers, and he held it upright at the start of the column. Natac thought it added a splendidly martial touch to their procession.

The Tlaxcalan strode along beside the elven scout for a while, directing the company along the path he had selected for the start of this march. In subsequent days, of course, they would venture into parts of Nayve that he had never before seen—indeed, Natac was looking forward to the chance to explore some more of his new world.

For most of the morning they followed a shallow valley, moving away from the lake and gradually climbing toward the heights of the Ringhills. The higher elevations loomed before them, some of the hills looking like mountain peaks. Snowfields dotted the upper slopes, and lofty crags rose into massive gateposts framing either side of their route.

Deltan Columbine played his flügel, dancing in step while the elves shouted, chanted, and sang in accompaniment. As they crossed a low pass Natac stopped marching, stepping off to the side in order to watch the column march past. The elves were invariably cheerful and happy, waving to their human instructor, or exclaiming to each other over the scenes unfolding around them. To judge from their mood, they might have been on a picnic, but Natac was pleased with this evidence of high morale.

Owen and Fionn trudged at the rear of the file, staff and club, respectively, slung listlessly over brawny shoulders.

"Cheer up, men—let the elves set you an example!" Natac encouraged them. He got only sour grunts in reply, but was content enough with that. Almost whistling himself, he fell into step behind them, and looked around at the new wonders of Nayve unfolding before him.

"Ferngarden seems like a nice enough place," Belynda admitted as she and Nistel stood on the porch of a comfortable inn, preparing to make their morning departure. Around them the little village was coming to life, ovens heating at the baker's, a few cows lowing as they waited for their Lighten Hour milking. Daylight filtered through the trees, though even the clearings were still obscured by mist and fog.

The two travelers had spent the night in comfortable beds, after a dinner of good meat, fresh bread, and—for Nistel—the innkeeper's self-brewed brown ale.

"That it does," the gnome agreed. "It's hard to believe that anything's wrong in *this* part of the Greens."

"But we've got a lot more looking to do," the sage-ambassador noted.

"How much of it do we have to see?" asked the gnome glumly. Belynda didn't exactly stride along, but the little fellow was forced nearly into a jog just to keep up with the elfwoman's sedate pace. He had already gone through two pairs of slippers on the journey.

"I don't know," Belynda admitted. "But I know what Tam and Ulf said, and I'm certain they were telling the truth. We just have to keep looking until we find some proof, something I can take back to the Senate, tell them I've observed with my own eyes. No one would dare challenge such testimony, at least not to my face."

"I hope we see something, soon!"

"Here, my lady." Weathervall, the innkeeper, joined them on the porch and offered a package wrapped in white cloth. "Here's some bread and cheese, also a bit of chicken and some apples. But are you sure you want to go that way?" He gestured along the narrow pathway extending behind the inn. "You'll find plenty of comfortable lodgings, if you were only to go along the main road."

"Thank you, but no," Belynda said. "We've already visited many of those places. I fear our search calls for us to go farther into the woods."

"Well, you have a care then . . . and come back this way, if you want a nice clean bed again."

Once more Belynda conveyed her gratitude, and then she and Nistel set out on the narrow path and walked a ways before crossing a rickety bridge over Ferngarden's small stream. There were a few barns and houses on this side of the water, and then the trees of the forest rose ahead.

"Psst—lady!"

The call came from the door of a small barn at the edge of the village. Nistel hopped along behind Belynda as she stepped up to the little building. "Who's there?"

"It's me, like." A stooped figure, a fellow with big ears and wide, watery eyes, gestured from the darkness.

"A goblin!" gasped the gnome, clutching Belynda's skirt.

"That's your name for us," retorted the fellow. "We like to call ourselves nightcrawlers."

"What do you want?" asked the sage-ambassador, gently pushing the gnome away.

"To warn you—don't be going about with your eyes shut, now. Hear me?"

"Eyes shut . . . of course not. But what do you mean?"

"Just beware, eh?" With that last warning the fellow disappeared, scooting through the barn and vanishing through a crack in the rear wall.

The pair of travelers were left to wonder about the mysterious warning as they made their way along the forest track. The road was barely wide enough for a single cart, though judging from the grass growing under their feet it rarely received even that much traffic. Ditches flanked the track, but these were mostly filled with brush and brambles. From what they had learned in Ferngarden, they would have to go some distance along this route before they came to another village.

"I had no idea that the Greens were so big," Belynda admitted many hours later. Nistel, plodding down the road beside her, was too tired to reply, so he only nodded in mute agreement.

"Perhaps we can find another inn, before too many nights have passed." she added hopefully.

The gnome shook his head. "If we can even find *any* place in the next tenday, I'd be surprised," he grumbled. "The road looks so ill-traveled—like maybe it isn't even a road, just some track into the woods."

Belynda sighed. "At least, it *seems* mostly straight. I don't think an animal trail would run in a line like this."

Nistel looked sideways at the sage-ambassador. "What if we just turned back here? We could . . . that is, you could, tell everyone in Circle at Center that you *saw* what Tamarwind and Ulfgang saw. Like you said, they'd have to believe you."

Belynda smiled wryly. "They'd have to believe me because I'd be telling the truth, old friend. You know that. So I can't make up a story about something I didn't really see."

Nistel sighed. Before he could come up with a suitable reply, they were startled by a rustle in the woods.

"Boo!" The voice was youthful, more enthusiastic than forceful. Judging from the sounds of breaking branches, someone with a very large body pushed forward, but Belynda was startled to look up into a boyish face, currently locked in a petulant frown.

"I said 'Boo!' Aren't you frightened?" The mystery of the tall youth was solved when he stepped all the way out, his equine body emerging from the bushes that had concealed his hooves and broad chest. The young centaur pawed the ground and snorted, then crossed his arms over his human torso. "You *should* be frightened."

"But why?" Belynda asked. "Surely you don't intend us any harm!"

The young centaur sniffed. "Maybe I do. What if I did?"

"Why, then, of course we'd be frightened," Belynda said. "After all, you're quite large . . . and, I should say, there's a rather fearsome aspect to you."

"There is?" The centaur smiled broadly. "Well, that's better."

"I am Belynda Wysterian, and my companion is Nistel, called Blinker."

"Hello Belynda, and Nistelblinker. I am Gallupper, of Clan Blacktail."

"Does your clan dwell in this part of the Greens?" Belynda asked.

Gallupper looked sad. "They did," the centaur said, and he seemed to be on the verge of tears. "But they've gone, now . . . they went with the Crusaders."

"The Crusaders?" Belynda was immediately alert. "Tell me about them."

"They're not at all friendly . . . they know how to frighten you, for sure. It was them that I tried to learn from . . . but they wouldn't teach me how. They—" Abruptly Gallupper was crying, and Belynda reached out to pat his shoulder.

"You don't have to talk about it," she said. "Not unless you want to. But would you like to come along with us?"

"Yes!"

They started along the trail, the young centaur sniffling, then brightening as he fell into step between his new companions. Belynda noticed that the sun had begun its Darken Hour ascent, and she looked with apprehension at the shadows thickening in the woods.

"I have heard of these Crusaders," Belynda noted after a few miles had passed under their feet. "Do you know where they live? Where they can be found?"

"They live everywhere!" Gallupper said grimly. "But you can't find 'em."

"Why not?"

"They hide! They'll find you, soon enough. But when they want to. Like they came and found my Blacktails."

"Well," Nistel said hopefully, "maybe we should just find a nice inn—let them find us there! It would be more comfortable than marching up—"

The gnome never finished, as two large figures burst from the woods to either side of the road. They swaggered forward brandishing large clubs, completely blocking the path.

"Giants!" squeaked Nistel.

"Crusaders!" gasped Gallupper. The centaur whirled on his rear hooves and dashed back along the track, so fast that his black tail streamed straight behind him.

"Who dares to enter the realm of the Holy Cross?" demanded one of the giants, raising his club.

Belynda was stunned into speechlessness. Nistel, meanwhile, turned and sprinted away after the young centaur, and the sage-ambassador belatedly decided to join them. She, too, whirled about, but before she could take a step, another great figure burst from the woods, blocking the gnome's retreat. This was a full-grown centaur, the great horse-body bashing aside small trees as one of his human hands wielded a large club. That weapon came down sharply on Nistel's forehead.

Belynda gasped as her companion tumbled to the ground, blood spurting from a deep gash in his scalp.

"Here, now, witch." The centaur's face was screwed into a ferocious grin that was somehow more frightening for all its apparent good humor. "Let's say you're going to come wi' me, all quiet."

Before Belynda could reply, she felt strong arms wrap around her, knew she had been seized by a giant. Without ceremony, the big creature threw her across the centaur's broad back. Ropes quickly lashed her wrists and ankles, and then they were on the move, pushing into the under-bush, leaving the still and pathetic form of the gnome lying in a spreading pool of blood.

"More witches, lord," declared the centaur Sir Christopher had named Sir Gawain. The messenger paused in the doorway of the tent to bow respectfully to Sir Christopher.

"This hellish place is crawling with them—they're like lice!" declared the knight, rising out of his camp chair with a groan. For a week now his army had been on the march, and he was forced to make do with rudimentary comforts such as his folding chair and small campaign tent. "How many this time?"

"Two of the humans, ones that call themselves druids, captured together. And an elfwoman, lord, caught on the Ferngarden trail," replied the centaur. "She's got that gold hair, that stiff look, of a real witch, she does, lord."

"Prepare them for burning. I shall inspect them, and they will be consumed."

The two druids were, not surprisingly, young and handsome humans who had come to dwell together in the Greens. The knight took little note of the third captive, the elf held off to the side, as he allowed Gawain to fill him in about the humans. They were male and female, each forced to stand upright, suspended by hair held in the firm grasp of a giant. Blood streaked down the chins and chests of each—standard procedure required that their tongues be cut out to prevent the casting of magic.

"They was taken from a house over that last stream we crossed," the centaur explained. "After they came out to find us when we killed their cow in the pasture."

The two humans, battered and barely conscious, gaped

at Sir Christopher with haunted eyes and those bloody, cruelly gashed mouths.

"Your cow will be the feast tonight—and your deaths the entertainment," the knight informed them.

The man tried to flail against the grip of the giant, but Sir Christopher merely laughed and cuffed the insolent wretch.

At that, the female screeched at him, opening the gory well of her mouth, and the knight's eyes crinkled in disgust. He dropped his staff at her feet. Gawain stepped back as the shaft of wood suddenly twisted and coiled. It became a serpent, hood spread wide as the head lifted from the ground. The snake struck, burying sharp fangs deep into the thigh of the female prisoner.

She screamed and thrashed futilely at the serpent. Sir Christopher watched impassively as she gasped for breath. The man's eyes blazed with unspeakable pain as the woman twisted and moaned, kicking reflexively with her visibly swelling leg.

"Throw her on a fire," Christopher decided. "Right now, before the venom has a chance to kill her."

In many respects a dead witch was a dead witch, but insofar as possible the knight preferred to have them slain by fire. It was his strong belief that even the black magic of this satanic cult could be broken by the crackling purity of flame.

"Make him watch her end," he added.

The male druid watched in numb horror as his wife was dragged out of the tent and he was pushed roughly after. Nodding contentedly, Sir Christopher touched the snake, which again hardened into a straight shaft of wood.

"And the elf?" he asked, only then noticing Belynda standing near the tent flap.

"She is over here, lord," said Gawain. "We left her tongue in, in case you wished to interrogate her."

"Yes, perhaps," the knight said. He wasn't worried about a little elf magic—save for the enchantresses, they knew only feeble and showy spells. It was the druids, with their raising of earth, their command of wind and waves, whose powers frightened him.

Now he didn't have the heart for a long conversation with one of these ignorant elves. The routine was becoming predictable: No matter how patiently he explained the nature of Purgatory to them, they persistently refused to understand. The myth of Nayve was nothing if not pervasive.

But, as he narrowed his eyes and studied her, something about this elf caused him to hesitate, made him think of her as more than just an enemy, a tool of Satan deserving only destruction. Her eyes, green and deep and wide-set, stared at him with an expression he allowed himself to believe was awe. They followed him as he walked slowly closer. He was certain that his first impression was correct.

This woman, this elf, was different. Her beauty choked his breath in his throat, sent the blood pulsing through his temples. Her eyes were almost hypnotic, and the gold of her hair was like an angel's halo.

Caution whispered a warning: Was she merely another temptation? Or had God at last sent him a true angel? He would find out, and quickly.

"Your gown," he said, mesmerized by those eyes. "It is like a witch's . . . yet you are no witch."

"No, I am not," she agreed, her voice level and those eyes as intent as ever. "I am a sage-ambassador of Argentian."

"But you are not like the others," Sir Christopher said fervently. "For you know of the glory of God, do you not?"

Her expression was puzzled. She paused, then spoke carefully. "I know of many glories . . . and I know of the Goddess Worldweaver, who dwells at the Center of Everything."

"You must know that is blasphemy!" Christopher growled, shaking his head, clearing away the fog that had been settling over him. Maybe she *was* evil, as wicked and vile as any of the others. Or even worse! He saw it now: The witch had been spellbinding him even as he talked to her. It was the only explanation that made sense. But her eyes . . . they drew him in so.

Abruptly he reached under the throat of his tunic, clasped the stone on its golden chain. He pulled it forward and saw her gasp, an expression of fear that confirmed his suspicion. This woman was not here to test him—she was an angel of purity, a vessel of his reward.

"You know the power of the Holy Cross," he said. "Do you yield to me?"

"What is it you wish of me?" she asked, her eyes never leaving the stone.

"I wish your help in bringing the true word to this pagan place . . . Help me share the joyous news of our Savior's reign! And scour the stain of Satan from every tree, every cursed house of this forsaken land!"

With obvious effort she tore her eyes from the talisman, and when they fixed upon his face they were full of anger and scorn.

"You are the stain on the land!" she retorted with surprising vehemence. "You are the evil that should be scoured!"

He raised the staff, ready to drop the wood to the floor, when something, that glimmer of vitality in her eyes, once more stayed his hand. She was teasing him, taunting him with the illusion of wisdom—as if *she* were the one who understood *him*.

"You think to tempt me . . . to be granted a rapid death. But I tell you now, witch . . . you will suffer—you will suffer as only the chosen few of my captives suffer!" He turned to Gawain, who still loomed just inside the entrance. "Leave us—I will be alone with this captive."

With a flick of his black tail, the big centaur quickly ducked out.

The roaring in Christopher's ears was a thunder as he seized Belynda's small body in both his strong hands. Her beauty taunted him, another magic trick, he knew, as he tore away her gown to reveal the revolting contours of her body.

"You could have been an angel!" he croaked. "Instead you are the serpent, disguised with lips of seduction, eyes of deceit!"

He threw her down. Death was too merciful, a relief from the suffering that a righteous God desired, nay, demanded. She would pay dearly for her deception.

And then his own tunic was off, and he fell on top of her. She screamed and struggled, but she was like a child and he was a powerful man—a man blessed by the strength of a Holy God, given the tasks of an Immortal Avenger. She twisted frantically, but he tore the rest of her garment away, roughly parted her flailing, kicking legs.

He used his weight to hold her down as he penetrated her. His own body was a weapon, a sword and a spear and a knife. He pushed and cut at her, relishing the sounds of her pain, laughing as she shrieked, wailed, and sobbed, cherishing the agony he inflicted upon her. By the time she lost consciousness, he was nearly finished with his punishment, and when the moment of release came he saw the full glory of his righteousness, and he knew that vengeance was his, and would be complete.

The small figure pushed through the underbrush, making a careless racket, moving like a thing that feared nothing—or else was so intensely panicked that all rational caution was overwhelmed by the press of unspeakable dread.

Nistel was alive, though he couldn't quite believe it himself. His head remained sticky with blood—*blood!*—and one eye had swollen shut. The other stared wildly straight ahead, and the terrified gnome gave no thought to anything other than a path to escape the danger certainly lurking behind.

He had been running for only a minute or two, the time since he had awakened in the forest to find himself lying in a pool of his own gore. The shock had spurred him to his feet, and then set those feet into motion. But now, as his lungs strained for air and his bloodshot eye revealed only a tangled expanse of bramble and woods, he stumbled into a walk, then finally halted, sitting on a stump while he very slowly caught his breath.

And only then did he remember Belynda.

"Oh!" he cried. He popped to his feet, and then began to cry. Soon he was sobbing uncontrollably, even his swollen eye leaking big tears.

What could have happened to her? He tried to remember . . . he was pretty sure that she hadn't been anywhere in sight when he woke up. Of course, he remembered with a pang of guilt, it's not like he had thought to look around very much.

He knew then that he had to go back to that awful place, to see if Belynda was there. If she was not, he had to . . . to do what? How could he decide? There was no one to ask, and nothing like this had ever happened before. What could he do?

The gnome decided to worry about that part later.

It was pretty easy to see the path he had taken through the woods. Broken branches, trampled ferns and smashed flowers all left an indication of a gnome-sized tunnel bored through the entangling growth. Nistel retraced his steps, tripping over vines and roots, pushing branches and thorns out of his way, wondering how he had ever been able to run through such a thicket.

Many minutes passed before he saw the glimmer of day-light ahead, and then stepped out of the brush onto the forest road. He shuddered as, once again, he saw the dark pool that was his own blood. Searching up and down the road, he peered into the underbrush, kicked through the tall grass in the ditches flanking the track. He returned again to the place where he had awakened, having seen no sign of Belynda. Despairingly he looked down, saw the black patch of gore on the ground and shook his head.

"I must look a mess." he realized, with a gasp of dismay. He quickly pulled out his handkerchief, but now, the blood coagulated and caked with grime, he couldn't really do much to clean off his face.

Squinting upward, he decided that he could see a little bit with his swollen eye, but only if he was looking directly at the sun. It was then that he realized that full daylight blazed around him.

"How long did I lie here?" he wondered, asking the silent shrubbery. "It was getting dark, but just, when . . ."

And finally his thoughts came hard against the reality of the previous evening. Belynda and he had been attacked, violently, in the Greens of Nayve! He, Nistel, had been nearly killed by a centaur's club. As to the sage-ambassador, he couldn't think *what* had happened to her. He knew that she wouldn't have run away and left him there—though he remembered with a moan of despair that, in his initial panic, he had certainly been ready to run off and do just that to her. That memory triggered fresh sobs, and raised horrible questions in his mind. Where was Belynda? Was she hurt? The possibile fates of his friend were terrible to contemplate, but they all involved her being taken away by the centaur and those two giants.

"I'll rescue her," the little gnome said—or started to say. It seemed that the whole sentence just wouldn't work its way out of his mouth. Probably because he knew it was a foolish fancy. What could he, a pitiful, half-blinded gnome, do against centaurs and giants and who knew what else?

"Then I'll have to go get help!" he declared, and this

time there was force behind his words. He looked up and
down the road. He was pretty sure that he and Belynda had
been going *that* way, so he turned in the opposite direction.
Ferngarden with its comfortable inn was a day's walk away.
At least he could tell someone there what had happened.

Nistel started off at a run, but quickly slowed to a bouncing jog. A minute later he was walking, but still following
the road back to the village. He remembered that inn . . . it
was a nice one. He would certainly cool off with an ale
when he got there. Of course, that didn't make what happened to Belynda any easier to stomach, but still, the innkeeper had known how to brew a nice barrel. . . .

"Nistelblinker?"

The gnome nearly jumped out of his boots at the whisper
coming from the underbrush.

"Ga-Gallupper? Is that you?" he asked, trembling.
"Where did you go?" he demanded more sharply when he
saw the young centaur between the branches of the shrubbery.

Gallupper came forward. "I'm sorry I ran away," he said.
"It's just—those Crusaders are so frightening!"

"I know," Nistel replied. He sniffled at the fresh memories. "And I think they took Belynda! Do you know where
they live, where they might have taken her?"

"No," Gallupper said, shaking his head. "Their lord came
and called to my clan . . . and they went away with him.
But they wouldn't take me, and I don't know where they
went. Are you looking for them?"

Nistel looked down. "No," he admitted. "I didn't think I
could rescue her by myelf. So instead I'm going for help."

"I'll come with you—you can ride on my back, and we'll
travel much faster."

"That's a good idea," the gnome said. "Can you help me
up?"

He stepped toward the centaur's side, but before he could

mount, a big shadow moved beside the road. Nistel turned around with a startled yelp, but he was too slow to run. By the time he saw what was happening, a pair of hard-eyed elves had him by the scruff of the neck.

12

The Eyeless Horde

*Scent of sweetness,
flavors thrilling;
Hark the warming touch
of killing.*

From the Delver Chants
Sensations of Death

Karkald raced through the darkness, stumbling over unseen rocks, scraping against the pillars that rose throughout the vast cavern. Before him he saw faint light, illumination filtered around several bends of the subterranean passage, but unquestionably emanating from a bright source.

He heard Darann's shout, then a sound like a rock clattering across the floor. Brandishing his spear, he sprinted faster, turning a corner, squinting in the brightness of his wife's coolfyre. He saw her throw another rock, striking a target out of his sight.

But there was another beast leaping through the air, striking like a snake toward that face Karkald loved more than any other in all the Seven Circles. This was a wyslet—he saw the bristling whiskers, the narrowed snout and body, the gaping maw with its array of razor-sharp teeth. Darann raised her arm and Karkald, still thirty paces away, could only shout in horror and fury. The proximity of his wife to the target ruled out any casting of his spear, and he could never cross that distance in time to help. Even so, he charged in blind fury and then, in a moment, saw the wyslet thrashing across the floor. Miraculously, his wife was sitting with her back against the rock. Karkald saw no sign of a wound on her face.

"Gotya, rock rat!" The jeering voice came from behind the wyslet, and for the first time Karkald noticed the wiry figure with arms and legs wrapped around the predator's body. Hiyram's hands were locked behind the beast's head, and though the pair thrashed and rolled across the floor, the goblin pressed with impressive strength until the snapping of the wyslet's spine cracked through the cave.

"Kark!" Darann screamed.

He turned to see a wyslet slinking around the rock, red eyes greedily fixed upon the dwarfwoman. Karkald hurled the spear with every fiber of his strength, and the steel head and stout shaft tore right through the skinny body. The beast thrashed and hissed, pinned to the soft rock by the force of the throw.

Two more wyslets rushed in. Karkald met those with the hammer in his right hand, hatchet—or rather, Darann's kitchen cleaver—in his left. One collapsed, slain instantly with a crushed skull, and the other disappeared into the darkness, yowling loudly, bleeding from a gash over its eye.

He looked in mute horror at Darann, but saw that she was unscratched. Drawing a few ragged breaths, she reached for him, and he tumbled into her embrace.

"I'm sorry," he whispered, as she was saying the same words. Finally she cried, and pulled him close, and he held her tightly and breathed the scent of her hair, her neck, herself. His own long arms wrapped his dwarfmaid, and he sighed a long exhalation of relief.

"Hiyram—you came back," he said, after his breathing had steadied enough for him to speak.

"Yup," chortled the goblin contentedly.

"Why?" asked Darann. "I thought you blamed us for the trap that caught you."

Hiyram laughed louder. "Lotsa traps . . . lotsa dwarves. But I'm hungry, so I come here."

"Hungry . . . but—" Darann's voice choked off, and she looked at the bloody, wretched wyslet corpses around them.

"Happy news, that!" smirked Hiyram, swaggering up to the couple and puffing out his scrawny chest. He chucked a thumb at the three slain wyslets. "Good eatin', if ya don't mind stink!"

Karkald woke up with a sensation that he was still dreaming. Darann slept, curled against his lap, her back against his chest. They were both naked, covered by the smooth cloth of their blanket. He smelled her hair, let it mingle with his beard as he gently reached for her breast and allowed himself to sigh contentedly.

For the first time in many intervals, his memories were pleasant. Before sleeping, the two dwarves and the goblin had filled their stomachs with fresh meat. Hiyram had stuffed himself until his belly bulged, then announced that he was going to sleep for a year. The dwarves had practiced more moderation, even though the wyslet flesh had proven surprisingly palatable—after they learned not to breathe through their noses. Then the couple found a small grotto some distance away from the snoring goblin, and here they tenderly reaffirmed their love, each soothing away the other's guilt with kisses touches, reassuring affection.

These memories were especially vivid and sweet, and he pulled Darann close with a powerful burst of longing. Cupping the fullness of her flesh in his hand, he pressed against her, felt her shift and turn slightly as she slowly came awake. He squeezed, found her nipple with his blunt finger. Kissing the back of her neck through the mane of hair, he pushed his loins against her with strong, suggestive force.

When she reached her hand between them, her fingers grazed his flesh with an electric, rousing touch. Soon they were turning, she rolling to her back while he slid on top of her. She took him in, and in a breathtaking, gasping moment they became one. For long minutes they lay nearly still, murmuring sounds of love, moving hands and lips. Gradually the pace of their motion increased, though still they were nearly silent. They shared the moment of release with a deep kiss, clinging desperately to each other, love coursing as hot as the blood running through their veins.

As his breathing returned to normal, Karkald thought what a grand thing it was to be alive.

They took a long time getting up, and by the time they had ambled back to the main cavern they found Hiyram sitting, belching and sniffing the air. His eyes were luminous in the darkness and when Darann touched off a bit of coolfyre he scowled in irritation.

"Why's for dat?' he demanded. "Spose'd be dark round here."

The dwarfwoman just laughed.

"Where goin?" asked the goblin, quickly shifting conversational tacks. "Way from wyselts, yup?"

"Why—are there more of them around here?" Karkald asked worriedly.

The toothy face bounced up and down in an enthusiastic nod. "More and more comin', runnin' from Delvers, yup?"

"Delvers?" Now Karkald felt a real chill of alarm. "They can't be around here, can they? Remember, we're in the midrock, miles above the First Circle now!"

"Delvers climb up, too ... like you two, too." Hiyram hooted gleefully at his wordplay. "Lotsa rocks fall down ... Delvers find a way up."

"How many Delvers?" Karkald was remembering the

size of the force he had seen below his watch station.

"More than I could count . . . or you too, either. Fingers and toes on myself, and on you and you . . . makes not even the start of 'em."

"An army—climbing up here?" Darann asked, staring wide-eyed at Karkald. "But why?"

"Go to Fourth Circle," Hiyram exclaimed with a hearty chuckle. "Elves up there—Delvers eat 'em like maggots!"

Karkald looked at his wife, saw the memory of horror in her eyes. He, too, recalled the visage of that steel-jawed monster, Zystyl, and his eyeless horde. Could the scourge of the First Circle be released against a whole new world?

"The elves know nothing of war, of hatred and killing. They'll be helpless!" Darann whispered, and Karkald knew she was right. Nayve's innocents would be massacred in droves. He could only nod in mute agreement.

"Then we have no choice but to keep climbing," she declared, and he had no argument with her decision. "We have to get all the way to Nayve, to carry to the elves the warning of the Delver invasion."

Belynda awakened to a world that had changed in a profound and unmistakable way. She sensed the alteration in the core of her being, in her ragged memories of the nightmare that had been visited upon her in the darkness. Numbly she groped for her gown, pulled the tattered garment over herself like a blanket. Her body was sore, bruised and scraped where she had been used. But that was not even the worst of it—the violation went deeper, touched at the very heart of her being, and then went further still until it had warped the place that was the Fourth Circle.

The sage-ambassador knew that her life, her world, would never again be the same. She tried to remember who she had been, why she had come to the Greens. But those memories meant nothing, had no relevance to this painful thing that existence had become.

Nistel . . . surely he was dead, killed by that awful blow to his head. Perhaps it was only yesterday that his life had been taken, but even that seemed, from her current vantage, like a very long time ago. It had happened before she was changed into this person she didn't know, couldn't even begin to recognize.

A fire burned within her, a raging conflagration that seemed to destroy her peace, her soul, everything that was good about her. Her hands curled into claws as she remembered the man, remembered what he had done to her. She would have killed him in an instant if he had been standing before her.

But when she tried to move, she realized that vengeance was, for now, an unattainable dream. The injuries to her flesh were real, and crippling. It was only with great difficulty that she could push herself to a sitting position and slip the gown over her shoulders. She ached in her limbs and joints, felt a stinging soreness in her neck. And these hurts were as nothing compared to the ripping fire in her loins, the burning, the sense of pervasive poison that, she feared, must quickly consume her body.

Perhaps it was already too late . . . she had a sense that she was already doomed, fatally wounded, crippled in a way that could never be made whole. The despair was so powerful that, for a moment, she almost yielded to a darkness that would have dragged her back down onto the straw mattress, never to rise again.

But it was the memory of that mattress, the place where *he*—the man who was a monster—had worked his evil, that gave her the strength to stand. She moved away from the bed with a shudder of revulsion, and then, once again, her hopelessness began to give way to a stronger emotion.

"I hate him."

She said the words quietly, and they brought her some

small comfort. Until this moment, hate had been an abstract concept to her, a thing that had no place in Nayve. Now she felt it in her guts, in the fury that tightened her jaw and brought a narrow squint to her eyes. She raised her hands and saw that they were fists, small but rocklike, and for an instant she fixed on the idea of striking the man who had attacked her. She swung her arm, awkwardly she knew, but even that flailing gesture brought a sense of satisfaction.

Then the flap of the tent was pulled aside and Belynda whirled. All of her anger turned to panic as she instinctively took a backward step. By the time she had recovered her resolve, she recognized the intruder not as her attacker, but as the massive centaur called Gawain.

"Come with me," said her captor, stomping his great forehoof for emphasis.

"Why?" she snapped. "Where are you taking me?"

Her objections were ignored as Gawain reached for her with a meaty hand, snatching her arm before she could pull away. She kicked and squirmed but he had no difficulty manhandling her around, clasping her back to his chest and lifting her off the ground. Belynda kicked again, but she couldn't reach the centaur, and each movement sent a jolt of pain through her bruised body. Such was the power of her hatred that she kicked and thrashed with renewed violence, ignoring the agony in her own flesh.

The great centaur pulled her out of the tent and she saw the encampment of her enemies in daylight for the first time. They were in a wide clearing amid the high trees of the Greens. Hundreds of unkempt people, nearly all male, stared at her. There were a few dozen centaurs, mostly at the perimeter of the camp. Closer by, in casual clumps of like kind, she saw numerous goblins and elves, and smaller groups of looming giants. All of them, even the few women present in the army, looked at her with a peculiar, disturbing sense of hunger. She saw burly giants lick their lips, goblins nod their round heads eagerly as she was carried past. Even the elves, her own people, watched with a kind of bemused fascination, though they displayed little emotion at her predicament.

Her destination, she soon perceived, was a large tent of white canvas. Before it stood a pole, and atop that staff was a pennant of white and red. It drooped in the still air, but she remembered Tam's description of the crimson cross. Vaguely she recalled that the man's tunic, hellish in the candlelight the night before, had borne that same image on its breast.

Then she looked beyond the great tent and she saw that another post had been planted in the ground. This one was stout, like a sturdy tree trunk, and around its base was piled a mass of brush and kindling.

She remembered the story of the burning, the tale she had heard from Tamarwind and Deltan, and for the first time considered the possibility that she would die here. The irony was staggering and infuriating: She had gained the concrete evidence that she needed, and in doing so ensured that she would not get to bear witness in the Senate. An insane urge to laugh flickered through her mind. But the tent loomed large now, and her hatred immediately swelled. This time it was tinged with any icy fury that, she vowed, would help her to think, to plan.

"In here." Gawain unceremoniously put her down and then pushed her through the open flap of the tent.

Blinking against the darkness, she saw only a little movement. In a moment she recognized the man coming toward her, saw the black beard and the even darker eyes. He looked at her with an expression of scorn. His hands were planted on his hips. His viper-headed staff was propped against a chest on the other side of the tent.

Belynda attacked. She sprang forward with fingers outstretched, reaching like claws for those wicked eyes. At the last second he threw up an arm, and she raked across his wrist to draw parallel lines of blood. Her foot lashed out, but the folds of her gown prevented the blow from having any force.

"Witch!" cried Christopher. "Aye, thou art Satan's deceiver!"

He punched her in the face and she tumbled backward. He strode forward to stand over her. "I had a mind to offer you God's salvation, but you have chosen the pits of Hell instead!"

"I spit on your salvation!" Belynda tried to twist away, but the man was quick and powerful. Seizing her golden hair, he jerked her upward with a neck-wrenching tug. The elfwoman gasped and choked as he wrapped an arm around her throat, squeezing her windpipe in the crook of his elbow.

She flailed with her feet, kicking on his heavy boots with no effect. Her elbow slammed into his solar plexus and he cursed, then pressed her neck until her vision was tinged with red and ultimately faded to black.

By the time she could see, they had emerged from the tent. The men of Christopher's army were streaming toward the stake, gathering in a thick, churning ring of eagerness.

"This is a witch and a harlot!" he proclaimed, to murmurs of agreement that rumbled from all sides. "She will die in the cleansing power of flame—Pray to God Almighty that her evil is expurgated in that passing!"

Hoarse cheers rang from the lot as they formed a corridor leading from the tent to the stake. The big centaur was there, and plucked her from the knight's grasp. Belynda recoiled from the sight of goblins leering at her, burly giants howling for blood. Other centaurs raced about in a frenzy, and the noise swelled thunderously.

Belynda drew a deep breath, ready to fight again, but now she was pinned in Gawain's muscular grip. Her lungs strained for air, and a tinge of madness rose in her mind . . . she had to fight, to kill! Her purpose was only vengeance and the only fear she felt was the terror that she would die without exacting that retribution.

She knew she was hallucinating then, for she thought she saw Tamarwind Trak among the elves of the company. And there was Deltan Columbine, just on the other side . . . surely a sign that she was losing her mind. Still, she found it curiously comforting that she imagined her friends here, elves she had known for so long who could now be the witnesses to her death.

Her delusions ran deeper than she suspected, for she also caught a glimpse of dusky brown skin and a handsome, unsmiling face. Wasn't that the warrior, Natac, summoned to Nayve by Miradel? Belynda had met him only once . . . Why would she now remember him? Perhaps this was another effect of the madness that presaged death. She hurt for a moment when she remembered Tamarwind, and the serenity that had marked their days together. Now serenity was gone, from her life and from her world.

Suddenly Gawain groaned and tripped forward. Tamarwind—it *was* Tamarwind!—grabbed Belynda's arm before the centaur crushed her. A dozen other elves suddenly whirled on the nearby men of Christopher's army. Heavy clubs knocked aside enemy elves and goblins, and two big men she recognized as humans swung heavy staves, bashing the faces of a pair of giants. Both of these tumbled to the ground.

The centaur, Gawain, was kicking, entangled in a noose that had snared three of his hooves. Natac, wielding a long, slender sword, stabbed quickly at an elf who tried to intervene. The weapon left only a pinhole in the victim's chest, but the elf tumbled backward to kick weakly in a growing pool of blood. The warrior froze, looking in shock from his weapon to the bleeding corpse. By the time Natac shook his head and moved again, Belynda and Tamarwind had stumbled away. Tam used his heavy, stone-tipped spear to drive back several attacking elves.

"Come on!" he hissed. "We have to get to the forest!"

In the swirl of battle Belynda saw that Natac stood before Sir Christopher, who was unarmed. The knight slowly backed away.

"Kill him!" The sage-ambassador's voice was a shriek, a sound she had never imagined, let alone heard, coming from her own throat. She shouted at Natac again, her face taut with hatred. "Kill him right now!"

The knight suddenly backed away, turning to run into his tent, while a pair of enemy elves charged the Tlaxcalan with spears. Natac stabbed, cut one elf down and bluffed the other into a hasty retreat.

"Go after him! Kill him!" cried Belynda.

"That is not the way to make war," Natac declared, shaking his head. Still he looked stunned, unsure.

Belynda suddenly broke away from Tamarwind Trak and made a dash for the knight's tent. Natac managed to seize her wrist as she ran past. With surprising gentleness he pulled her back, until Deltan and Tamarwind had her again.

"We don't have time for that!" the warrior whispered, following her. "We've got to move!"

And then they were running, the three humans and a dozen elves fleeing the camp of many hundreds. A roar quickly rose behind them, and Belynda knew that the battle was far from over.

Karkald looked at Darann, the expression in his eyes urging her to remain utterly silent. She nodded, then looked past him, again staring into the ravine where the rocks themselves seemed to be alive, crawling steadily along the floor.

But those numberless marchers were not rocks, Karkald knew. They were Delvers, an army of the Blind Ones that trailed into a column more than a mile long through winding cavern and trackless vault.

"See—there, they goin' up!"

To Karkald, Hiyram's voice was a blaring trumpet, though actually the goblin spoke in a breathy whisper. In any event, the Delver horde continued its inexorable march, working its way up the steep ravine toward another cave, still higher in the darkness.

Karkald knew it was time to back away from here. His hands outlined in gentle coolglow, he signed that Darann and the goblin should follow him. Only after they had wormed through a hundred feet of passage, leaving the large cavern far behind, did they begin to relax.

And so it had been for a full interval, now. Here, as they had done every few cycles, they had found a vantage from which to spy upon the marching Delvers. Always the Blind Ones had been moving upward, climbing through the complex network of caverns that honeycombed the world over the First Circle.

"See," Hiyram repeated through a drooling, triumphant grin. "Like I tole ya, they always goin' up."

Karkald nodded. "How far away is it now, to Nayve?" he asked Hiyram.

The goblin scratched his bald, wart-covered head. "Let's say climbin' for ten, twenty more cycles. Maybe some more and maybe some less. Maybe then we see."

The dwarf nodded. This was more or less the same response that the goblin had been giving since the couple had made his acquaintance an interval ago. Even so, the goblin's vague predictions had more basis than Karkald's own wonderings, for Hiyram, at least, had seen the world called Nayve and its brilliant sun.

"We have to get there first," Darann said firmly. "The Fourth Circle is a world that has known nothing but peace . . . the elves and their neighbors will have no preparation for a horde like the Delvers."

"We will," Karkald said, his own conviction strong in

his voice. For a long time he had wavered in his own mind, but now he knew they had no choice.

Another truth lurked beneath the surface of his awareness: He felt a profound curiosity about this new world, the Fourth Circle. The whole notion of the "sun" was a compelling idea in its own right. Coupled with a plenitude of food and a great mixture of thriving races, the image in his mind became a goal that pulled him steadily onward. Axial was gone, in his mind if not in Darann's, and Nayve promised the hope of peace and a future, a place they could perhaps even make a permanent home.

After a too-brief rest, they started out again, following paths that diverged from the main cavern followed by the Delver army. Hiyram was a good climber, and seemed content enough to stay with the two dwarves.

Some uncounted number of cycles later they paused for a bite of dried fungus and water. The coolglow had faded so that each of the three companions was a bare ghost in the darkness. And then it was that Karkald noticed the phenomenon before them, a glow of powerful brightness originating beyond a few more twists and turns of the cave. He stood, and Hiyram drew a long, snuffling breath and nodded.

"A breeze," Darann said in wonder. She, too, sniffed the air. "And so many scents."

But Karkald's attention was all on the brightness. He was aware of the others trailing behind, but he made his way as quickly as he could, scrambling over rocks and through a shallow streambed. Rich moss coated the boulders, and he squinted against the steadily growing illumination.

He came around another bend and he saw it, finally. He was looking out of a cave mouth, into the shade of a forest. But everywhere there was dazzling brightness, flowers aglow as if burning, shafts of sunlight sparkling through the thick limbs overhead.

He had found it. He had reached the land of the sun.

•   •   •

Belynda ran beside Tamarwind, but looked over her shoulder as they neared the woods. Her eyes blurred with tears, anger and frustration combining to fill her with anguish. By the Goddess, she wanted him dead! And Natac had refused to kill him!

Vaguely she saw speeding shapes coming closer, realized that the centaurs were galloping toward them from all parts of Sir Christopher's camp. Something flashed across her vision—arrows! Abruptly the galloping centaurs halted, one of them tumbling to the ground and others cursing or grunting in pain.

Then Belynda and her rescuers reached the trees. She saw other elves around them, elves with bows and arrows. These archers fired another volley, and the stinging missiles drove the rest of the centaurs into a hasty retreat, a pair of them dragging their wounded comrade by his human arms.

But more of Sir Christopher's cohorts closed in, sweeping around the centaurs to form a line in the clearing. They brandished clubs wildly, and many waved crude, stone-tipped spears. The Knight Templar, now carrying his great staff, was in the lead.

"There they are!" shouted the knight, his voice a thundering roar. "Tools of Satan, minions of the she-witch. I compel you, Crusaders, in the name of God—kill them!"

Immediately five hundred throats echoed their leader's cry, the wave of sound hitting Belynda like a physical blow. Her anger still burned, but for the first time a new possibility intruded into her mind: She had her proof now. She should carry testimony to the Senate, should alert Circle at Center to this very real threat.

"Go!" cried Natac, shouting to Tamarwind and Belynda. "Get away from here—we'll hold them off!"

"No!" roared a fresh voice. *"We'll* hold them!"

The sage-ambassador was stunned by the sight of a burly

giant swaggering through the woods. Her first thought was that they were trapped, attacked from behind before they could make their escape. She was stunned when Tamarwind let out a whoop of recognition.

"Rawknuckle! Rawknuckle Barefist of the Greens!"

The black-bearded giant grinned darkly, greeting the elf with a gentle tap on the shoulder—a tap that sent the laughing Tamarwind stumbling to the side.

"What's going on?" Natac demanded, sword drawn, his eyes on the looming newcomer.

"We're friends o' yours, and enemies o' that lot!" snorted Rawknuckle, gesturing to the Crusaders, who were rushing closer. "Now, let us through!"

"My pleasure," Natac replied, standing back as fully two dozen or more giants lumbered out of the woods after Rawknuckle Barefist. They bellowed fearsomely, and the mob of startled Crusaders hesitated as they were confronted by this new threat.

"Now—hit 'em while they're mixed up!" shouted Owen. "Rout 'em with a Viking charge!"

"Yes!" Natac agreed instantly. "Stay here with the sage-ambassador!" he barked to Tam, as Owen and Fionn rallied the elves.

They swept from the woods in a quick rush, following the giants into the clearing. Belynda saw that there were many more elves here than the dozen or so who had rescued her from the camp. The two big, shaggy men and Natac led them in the attack, while others—following Deltan Columbine's instructions—drew back long bows and launched steel-headed arrows into the mass of the Crusaders.

"Take the fight to them!" roared the Viking.

"For Ireland!" shouted the other human, his voice a bellow cutting through the chaos.

Those two brawny humans were clearly bold warriors. One bore a club, the other a staff—and with these weapons they cracked the heads of the elves and goblins who had skidded to a surprised stop in the face of the charge. The giants, too, kicked through Sir Christopher's warriors. Rawknuckle swung his club and landed a crushing blow to the face of an enemy giant. Other elves rushed forward, wielding staves and a few stone-headed spears.

The shocking attack was too much for the disorganized Crusaders, and the mob turned as one and raced away. Under Natac's shouted order, the giants, humans, and elves on their side halted almost immediately, then quickly started falling back toward the woods. Before they reached the trees, Belynda, Tamarwind, and the elven archers had already started away from the camp.

They moved in single file, along a trail. Though the sage-ambassador gasped for breath in her effort to keep up, she would allow no slowing of their pace. Deltan Columbine was directly before her, and Natac was right behind.

"Where's Tamarwind?" she asked anxiously, when she couldn't find the scout among the small portion of the column within her view.

"He's picking out the path," Natac said. "He is the captain of this company, and seems to have a good head for directions."

"Tam . . . captain?" Belynda was nonplused. So many changes . . . and then her memory hardened again. Of course the world had changed—she herself had become a key instrument of that transformation just the night before.

And how many more nights would pass before she had her revenge?

Her dark thoughts propelled her, gave strength to her legs and wind to her lungs, as the small band fled through the long day. Finally, as night approached, the column veered to the side. Belynda saw the vague outlines of a bluff rising from the woods, and then she saw a darkness that was surely a cave mouth.

All of those realizations faded away as she saw a familiar figure step into view.

"Nistel!" she cried, rushing forward to sweep the stubby gnome into her arms. She felt a sharp pain in her throat, and then her eyes were spilling tears, her mouth making strange, sobbing noises. The gnome, too, was sniffling, and when finally they stepped apart he blew long and hard into his handkerchief.

"I thought you were slain," she said softly. "I am so glad to see you." She stroked his long white hair, fussed over the spectacular bruise that blackened one cheek and eye. "But how did you escape?"

"I, er—I went to get help for you, and ran into Gallupper first. We were going to look together when we, um, found Tamarwind here. He introduced me to Natac, and I told them what had happened. They went to look for you." Blinker burst into tears again. "Oh, lady—I wanted to go too, but they were too fierce. Gallupper and I waited here for you."

"I understand," Belynda said gently, deeply touched by the gnome's devotion. Such loyalty . . . surely it had lain within him for years. She had sensed it, had come to take it for granted. "There's no doubt that you saved my life," she added, feeling a rush of affection for her assistant of so many years. He was more than that, surely! Belynda laid a hand on Blinker's shoulder and looked into the moist eyes. "My friend."

She saw Gallupper standing shyly just beyond, and looked up at him with fondness. "You, too, young centaur . . . you are the bravest of your clan, for you resisted the summons of evil. The knight has used powerful magic to bring warriors into his ranks—I know, for I felt that power myself. You did the right thing by staying away."

Gallupper embraced her, and she sensed that he was holding back sobs, no doubt tormented by the knowledge that most of his clan, the family and friends of his life, had been thus corrupted.

Having received Natac's permission to build a few small fires, the band of warriors made camp around the mouth of the cave and spread out to gather around the smokeless blazes. Tamarwind and Natac joined the sage-ambassador and Nistel as they shared a loaf of dry bread, washed down with sips of cool water drawn from a nearby stream.

"How far away from the camp did we get?" Belynda wondered.

"Fifteen miles, or more," Tam offered. "Owen and Fionn and the giants are waiting back a mile or two, ready to give warning if they're pursued."

Abruptly the elfwoman turned to Natac. Her emotions had cooled, but the ember of hate still burned in her soul and she confronted him frankly. "You had that knight, Sir Christopher, right before you—and yet you didn't kill him? Why not?"

Tamarwind's eyes widened at the question, and Nistel gasped. Natac, however, lowered his eyes and shook his head. "I hesitated, Lady Ambassador, out of the memory of my own training. In battles such as those waged by Tlax-cala and Mexica, we never tried to kill the enemy com-manders. Of course, we would capture them, if possible, and offer their hearts as sacrifice to the gods—but that was not a battlefield death."

"And now you know that those gods do not exist!" she retorted.

Natac winced. There was some kind of deep sadness in his eyes that made Belynda regret her harshness. "Yes, I do know that. And as I think about it now, it seems that I might have accomplished much good by slaying the knight on the point of my sword. But in that, I failed."

"Forgive me . . . You came to rescue me, to save my life. In that you succeeded, and for that heroism I owe you all. It is churlish of me to—"

"No!" the warrior interrupted. "You are right to speak to me of my errors. I must learn, and you must teach me what you can. We must all be teachers, and students, if the Nayve you love is to have any chance of survival."

Belynda shook her head. "I can teach you nothing of war, except that perhaps now I understand the fury that can drive people to slay others. For in the case of that knight, I want very much to see him dead."

"Why are you so determined?" Tamarwind asked hesitantly. "Did he hurt you?"

Anger surged again and the elfwoman whirled on the scout, ready to spew all the reasons for her hatred. But during her next intake of breath she saw the concern on Tam's face, realized the hurt she would cause him, and Nistel, if they knew the truth of what had happened. Furthermore, she felt a sudden, engulfing shame that choked her throat and froze her tongue. She vowed that she would never reveal what Christopher had done to her, not to Tamarwind or anyone else.

"I . . . I could sense the power of his evil," she began lamely, but then found more conviction as she continued. "He is the root of the violence in the Greens, in all of Nayve. If he didn't kill Caranor and the other enchantresses, then the killers were his minions, operating under his orders."

Even as she spoke, she formed the conviction in her mind: Christopher had certainly been the agent of Caranor's death. She recalled the spark of worry she'd felt when she hadn't been able to contact the enchantress through her seeing globe. Now that spark had grown into a blaze greater than any conflagration she could have imagined. And the knight would die, she vowed—but she would find a way to kill him with her own hand. It was not only a mistake, it was a great wrong, to expect Natac or someone else to do this task for her.

"He bears the Stone of Command, and is using it to bind

the soft-willed among our people—and goblins, centaurs, and giants as well—to him. He tried to use the stone on me . . . I think it is only my long years as a sage that gave me the strength to resist."

The others were still pondering her statement when they heard a soft sound from within the cave.

"Excuse me . . . Are you elves?"

Tam and Natac leaped to their feet, the warrior with his sword extended toward the shadows. Three figures moved slowly forward, to be gradually revealed as they approached the fire.

"Dwarves!" gasped Tamarwind Trak.

"And a goblin!" Nistel added, pointing at the figure that held back from its two companions.

The dwarf in the lead was heavily bearded, and carrying many items of equipment, including a spear that was pointed toward the ground. A thick rope was coiled from his shoulder to his hip, and a hammer and cleaver swung from his belt. Other less readily identifiable implements were slung from various parts of his tunic.

The other dwarf was a female, full-breasted with a pretty face that was quite round by elven standards. She carried a knapsack and several waterskins and strode confidently beside the male. When they paused near the fire, she took his arm in her hand.

The goblin grinned foolishly, at last coming around the dwarves so that he, too, could absorb some of the fire's radiance. He nodded his big head atop its skinny neck, snuffled loudly, and then spoke to the dwarves.

"See. I tole ya. Here we are. Dis Nayve, I'm bettin' fer sure."

"I am Karkald and this is my bride, Darann," said the bearded dwarf. "And this is Hiyram."

"Did you come from the First Circle?" Belynda asked in wonder. There were no dwarves on Nayve, though the inhabitants of the Underworld were known from legend and the teachings of druids, who had observed them through the Tapestry. "How did you get here?"

"We climbed, at least we two dwarves did," said the male. "For more cycles than we could count. Ever since the great quake."

"The quake?" Tamarwind did some mental arithmetic. "We felt that here—that was five intervals, half of a year ago!"

"Intervals . . . ten per year," Karkald mused. "They must be the same thing here as in the First Circle. We have forty cycles per interval . . . is that your pattern, too?"

"Forty days per interval," Tam replied.

"Days are when you see the sun, right?"

Hiyram sighed. "I tole him about the sun, but he don't believe . . . even saw it today, from cave."

"It was terribly bright, even from inside," Darann observed.

Belynda nodded. "Welcome to the Fourth Circle," she said. "Please enjoy the warmth of our fire, and share our food."

The three travelers wasted no time in sitting down, and were clearly famished—they ate as much bread as they were given, and quickly devoured the apples and dried meat that other elves, attracted by the visitors, brought over to the fire to share.

After they had eaten, the dwarves told their story. Karkald began bluntly.

"I regret to tell you that we bring warning of a grave threat to your world, an army on the march from our own circle, bringing the promise of violence and destruction."

"You speak of the Unmirrored Dwarves, the Delvers?" asked Belynda.

"You guess correctly wise elf. We fled the First Circle because of two things," Karkald explained. "The attack of the Delvers, which drove us out of our home, and the destruction of Axial because of the quake."

"Axial . . . gone?" asked Belynda. The great center of the Underworld was known to her only by reputation, but that reputation invariably labeled it as one of the great cities of the Seven Circles.

"At least . . . it looked like it disappeared," Darann said, despair written across her features. "We could see the lights from the watch station, until the earthquake. Then there was just the darkness.

"And the Delvers were already on the march?" asked Natac.

Karkald replied. "They number in the thousands, and I believe their original objective was Axial. But in that they were thwarted by the great quake. Since then they have turned their march upward, through the midrock. We last saw them three or four cycles ago, and they did not have far to go before they reached the surface."

"What are these Delvers like?"

"They wear armor of metal, and carry sharp blades in each hand. They fight shoulder to shoulder, and advance in an unstoppable line. Their master is an arcane called Zystyl."

"What is an arcane?" Natac probed further.

"They are the cruelest, and mightiest, of the Unmirrored," Karkald explained. "Arcanes are chosen for the talents of their senses . . . they are sightless, but possess the ability to *feel* the presence of living beings. There are tales that each arcane is tested at a young age . . . that they immerse their mouths and noses in molten steel. The effect layers the jaws in metal, and burns away the outer portion of the nostrils—presumably to enhance the creature's sense of smell."

"I only know that Zystyl is the most frightening thing I have ever seen," Darann said with a shudder. "I thought of ending my own life when it seemed as though I would be his prisoner."

It was a somber group of travelers that settled down for

a few hours' sleep, knowing that they would be back on the march even before the Lighten Hour. Tamarwind suggested that Belynda have the most comfortable bed they could find, a small, mossy niche between the burls of a great oak's roots. Someone lent her a cloak she could use for a pillow, and Tam offered his poncho as a blanket. Nistel, Tamarwind, and Natac were all nearby.

In the darkness the sage-ambassador could not get warm, despite Tam's heavy poncho. She shivered under the chill import of two grave threats now converging on her world. The future was as dark as the night, and seemingly equally dangerous.

Belynda tried to encourage herself. At least her testimony would force the Senate to confront the reality of the Crusaders. Nayve would have to take action! And the presence of the two dwarves would certainly provide evidence of their own story.

Even so, pain was everywhere in her body as she settled against the ground. And when she slept, too briefly, that pain twisted its way into her dreams, bringing nightmares that jolted her awake and left her trembling, anxiously praying for the sun.

To Zystyl's ear, the army of Delvers moved not so much with a cadence of marching feet as with the soft, scuffing slither made by thousands of leather soles. For this stretch Kerriastyn led the way so that the army commander could stand off to the side and experience the passage of this great horde.

First sense was in the sound, of course. For an hour he had relished the almost liquid noise made by the army's passage. Considering their numbers, the Delvers were in reality very, very quiet. Occasionally a stone would rattle through the cavern, or a warrior would grunt or rasp for breath over a tricky part of the trail, but for the most part there was just that sibilant, dry rasp of moving feet.

And the smell of the army was a profound pleasure. The arcane absorbed every spoor, of sweat and grime, of urine and feces and blood and the hundred other taints that marked individuals and groups within the great mass of dwarves. If the sounds of his army established its vastness for the commander, then the smells individualized his men, brought them closer to him. Of course, he often reached out to touch the Unmirrored warriors as they passed—a pat on a shoulder, fingers stroked over an eyeless face, an arm firmly squeezed. Each contact provoked a shiver of pleasure in the dwarf so honored, and it reassured the leader that his role was secure.

Beyond the physical sense, Zystyl also perceived his men through the power of his arcane being. He felt the powerful hunger in all of them. Most pronounced, of course, was the yearning for food, for warm meat that would fill bellies and slake the gnawing aches that had thus far characterized this campaign. But he sensed a hunger for war, as well, and for violence and torture and plunder. He knew that once they reached Nayve and found enough food for a few good meals, his army would be once again ready for war.

No other Delver leader could have engineered such a march, Zystyl knew with pride. Kerriastyn was a skilled enough arcane—she had proven adept at finding a good, wide route through the caverns of the Interworld. But the female had no sense of the grand plan, and she lacked the power to bend a thousand wills to her own desires. In truth, she was content to let Zystyl lead, and as long as she remained that way, he would be content to let her live, and to use her skills in whatever way he desired.

Lost in his musings, Zystel's attention snapped back to the present as a soft murmur of noise whispered along the line. The column slowed to a halt, and the captain was already making his way beside the file of men. By the time he reached the head of the line he knew why they had halted, though Kerriastyn told him, anyway.

"Smell the air . . . and feel its movement against your face. There are living things before us."

"Nayve!" hissed the captain.

"I think you are right," Kerriastyn said, a remark bordering on impudence. Still, in his excitement Zystyl would let it pass.

"Advance with caution!"

Now the two arcanes led the way. The cavern widened around them, and myriad new odors were carried on the gentle breeze. A number of scents were tantalizing, promises of food and nourishment. Others were strange, rich and unusual but not unpleasant. The cavern opened still wider, the Delvers pushing through a curtain of ropy strands that were clearly some kind of vegetation.

Abruptly Zystyl's sensations were overwhelmed with heat, searing pain that scorched his skin and drew an involuntary scream from his throat. He heard Kerriastyn, beside him, similarly groan. Together the two arcanes tumbled backward, through the screen of vegetation into the tolerable coolness of the cave.

"The sun!" hissed the captain, making the word into a curse. "Who would have thought it could be so vicious?" For a moment he felt a glimmer of panic—could it be that this whole expedition was a mad dream, doomed to failure by the presence of unbearable brightness and heat?

It was Kerriastyn who offered him some comfort. "Remember the legends—the sun is bright for half of each cycle. Then the Fourth Circle grows dark. We must wait until then before we venture out."

Her suggestion made sense, and Zystyl was, grudgingly, about to agree, when they were distracted by a noise from outside.

"Who's there?" It was a youthful voice, soft and mellifluous. "Are you hurt?"

Immediately Zystyl tensed, drawing a breath through his wide, moist nostrils. A new scent greeted him, rich and meaty and sweet in a way that no dwarf had ever been.

"Yes," he replied, his voice a rasping croak as he affected great weakness. At the same time he touched Kerriastyn, signaling her to fall back against one side of the cave while he pressed against the opposite wall.

"Where are you?" The voice was closer now. "I can't see through the creepers . . . I say! A cave! Matty, come here and help."

"Yes . . . please help!" gasped Zystyl.

They heard hands clawing at the vegetation. "Here . . . let's just pull this out of the way." The speaker was very close now. Zystyl's arcane senses could sense the living spark of a person barely a step away from him. Tall, slender . . . clearly an elf.

"There you—" The elf's statement ended in a startled gasp.

Zystyl and Kerriastyn came forward at the same time and snatched the elves. Zystyl seized one by the forearms and pulled him unceremoniously into the cave, latching steel-taloned fingers into his victim so harshly that the elf screamed shrilly. The one called Matty, a female, was taken by Kerriastyn. In a few seconds dozens of Delvers had gathered around the two sobbing, terrified elves.

"This one," Zystyl said, indicating the male. "Butcher him now, so that the horde may eat. You." He turned to the female, who had sucked in a dry gasp of air at his words. "You may live, so long as you provide us with information."

The male elf tried to squirm away, but a dagger sliced his neck and he fell without further sound. Matty shrieked so loudly that Zystyl bashed her across the face; the blow was powerful enough to knock her out. As a consequence, the captain was forced to wait, sulking, until she groaned and recovered consciousness.

And then she sobbed so hysterically that Zystyl was on the verge of slicing her throat, too, just for some peace and quiet. He restrained himself only because he so desperately needed knowledge about this world.

Instead, he contented himself by partaking of the feast that was already rejuvenating his army. The male elf was not plump, and the pickings were slim, but the very thought that the Delvers were in a region where there was fresh meat for the taking improved morale many times over.

Finally, they were able to get some pieces of information from the elfwoman. They would have to wait only a few hours before the Hour of Darken, as she called it. Zystyl judged that the Blind Ones would be able to tolerate the world then, at least until the Lighten Hour.

"We need to go to a place where there is a great cave," he said, clacking his metal jaws in anticipation. "You will lead us to that place—or we will eat you."

"I-I will show you the way," the woman agreed. "There is a tunnel through the Ringhills, just such a great cave where you can hide from the sun."

She described the tunnel, a long corridor of darkness that carried a road toward the city. Zystyl determined that the Delvers could reach that tunnel in one night of marching, so he settled his army to rest. When it was dark, they would commence the advance on the Metal Highway and its long, dark tunnel.

13

Battle of the Blue Swan

From hill they came,
and miner's deep
to slay with axe and sword

And bold stood he
the line to keep
before the murd'rous horde

From *The Ballad of the First Warrior*
Deltan Columbine

"We will stay here, on the lakeshore—but you must take word to the city," declared Tamarwind.

Belynda nodded. For nearly twenty days she had accompanied Natac's band on a grueling march through the hills. Now they had come to the edge of the lake, at the Blue Swan Inn, with the Silver Loom rising from its island across the causeway. The Lighten Hour was just past, and the spire gleamed with argent brilliance. The city structures, the manors and museums of so many hues of marble, stood impassive. In their eternal majesty Belynda could almost make herself believe that nothing had changed.

But in truth, everything had changed.

She was more tired than she had ever been in her life. After the first few days, during which she had ridden on the back of the centaur Gallupper, she had forced herself to walk on her own. Her shoes had tattered, been replaced by deerskin moccasins of Tamarwind's making, as the company had fled from the Greens. They had skirted the edge of the Snakesea, knowing that the Crusaders had marched in pursuit. Then, though the tunnel of the Metal Highway had beckoned as an easy route back to the city, Natac had led his little force on a grueling trek through the Ringhills. The elves had not questioned his orders, and the objections of the two men—Owen and Fionn—had been overcome with a sharp rebuke from Miradel's warrior.

Along the way Belynda had learned that Natac had a company of about a hundred elves, and that they had been joined by some twenty-five giants. During the long march back to Circle at Center the fighters had been in high spirits, encouraged by their success in bringing the sage-ambassador out of the enemy camp. Still, they were badly outnumbered by that foe, and their only battle experience was the brief skirmish that had freed Belynda. Led by their captain, the warrior from Earth, they had marched swiftly through the hills.

But they knew that Sir Christopher's army had been on the move as well. Gallupper, Owen, and Fionn had held back from the main body and provided them with detailed reports of the knight's progress. The human warriors had harassed the enemy column, bringing supplies and stealing horses at every opportunity. The young centaur, meanwhile, had served as messenger, carrying regular reports of the Crusader movements back to Natac and the elves. The Knight Templar had been following the same trail as the elves, and at last word he was no more than ten or twelve miles away from the lakeshore.

Now Natac had drawn up his little band beside that shore, at the start of the causeway. They occupied a small rise of dry ground. Before them was a stretch of marsh to the left, then a shallow stream linking to the lake. A small stone bridge crossed that stream. In order to attack, an enemy would have to come across the bridge, wade the stream, or slog through the marsh. Or, as Owen had pointed out, the attack could come from the lake, but the Viking had admitted that it was unlikely the Crusaders were bringing boats along the highway. The Blue Swan Inn, with its lofty verandas and sheltered harbor, was outside of Natac's position. So was the great tunnel leading to the Metal Highway.

"Do you expect that he will try to attack you here?" the sage-ambassador asked Tam.

"Yes . . . and we will fight him," Tamarwind said, trying bravely to sound casual about the whole notion of a battle. "Natac says that we must stop him here, for if we give him the causeway, we give him entrance to the city."

"I think I can see that," Belynda said. She had been paying attention as Natac continuously instructed his elves and giants, and she had begun to understand some aspects of strategy and tactics. "As soon as the Crusaders come down the hill, they will take the Blue Swan. But if you tried to fight at the inn, the enemy could come through the tunnel and attack you from behind."

"Not to mention that we don't have enough fighters to hold the inn," said Tamarwind. "I hope they leave it alone."

"They won't," Natac said grimly, joining the pair. He came up to Belynda and took her hand in his powerful fingers. "Now, Lady Elf, you must do as Tamarwind suggests—hasten to the city and raise the alarm. We will hold here for a time, but you must send reinforcements, as quickly as possible."

"I will try," she promised.

With only a few backward glances, she and Nistel made their way across the causeway. Thoughts of her enemy, of the hatred that blazed within her and of the violence that the Crusaders could wreak upon her beloved city, lent speed to her flight and urgency to her mission.

• • •

"It is a good tunnel, my lord," reported one of the Crusader elves. "I myself have traveled it to Circle at Center. If we take it, we will be at the lakeshore in a day."

"We will follow the tunnel," Sir Christopher decided, looking at the wide roadway as it disappeared into the darkness. His black horse pranced nervously sideways in the face of the shadowy entrance, while the knight considered his tactical situation. "I want my centaurs and giants to follow them across the high trails. I want that witch, one way or the other!"

Indeed, when the knight remembered the way the elf-woman had seduced him, then escaped from his righteous vengeance, he could think of nothing except taking her again—with a culmination in the devil's fire she so richly deserved. His hatred was a strange mixture of longing and revulsion, a memory of harsh pleasure and urgent desire that kept him awake for long hours in the night.

The Crusaders split into two parties, the goblins and elves forming a column for the march into the tunnel while the centaurs and giants took up the hilltop trail, following the tracks of the raiders who had so boldly attacked their camp. The knight rode behind the first company of a hundred goblins, urging speed as they entered the tunnel to find that it was very well lighted by floating globes of magical fire.

The clash of weaponry startled him, as the head of the column suddenly stumbled to a halt. Sir Christopher rode up alongside the goblins, who were armed with bronze-tipped spears. He was shocked to find a group of small warriors hurling themselves at the goblins. These dwarves had face-plates of smooth metal, without even slots for their eyes—and each bore two wicked daggers, steel blades that slashed through the air before them.

The dwarves formed a solid barrier, blocking the Crusaders' progress into the tunnel. Perhaps a dozen goblins were howling, gashed by the daggers, while two or three lay still in the midst of spreading pools of blood. While many of the goblins had jabbed with their stone-tipped spears, the knight could see no sign of any injured dwarf.

Reining his horse a few steps away from this solid, but so far immobile, foe, Christopher considered his options. Nayve was reputedly a place of eternal peace, yet here he was confronting a rank of armored fighters. He was not afraid, not for himself nor his army. While it would be difficult to break this tight rank in an attack, he was certain his goblins and elves could easily evade these short-legged warriors, and eventually he could win a battle by maneuver.

"Ho, small knights!" he called. "Who is your captain?"

"That is I, Zystyl!"

The voice came from the rear of the rank. Sir Christopher stared into the shadows there, and quickly saw the speaker. Now the knight frowned in distaste. Differing from the masked men of the ranks, much of the speaker's face was visible, and grotesque: a gory, moist gap of snuffling, flaring nostrils spread above jaws of shiny metal, a sharp-fanged maw that spread wide to reveal a blood-red tongue.

"Are you warriors of this place called Nayve?" asked Christopher.

"We are the conquerors of Nayve, here to take prizes and treasure!" declared Zystyl. "Do not think you can defeat us!"

"My lord Zystyl," said the knight with oily sincerity. "I should not do you that disservice. But rather still, should you not consider how, together, we might both achieve our same ends?"

Belynda took time only to clean up and change clothes while word was carried by runners to each of the senators and ambassadors in Circle at Center, announcing an emergency meeting of the Senate. With her hair combed and her tattered gown replaced by a fresh robe of gold, she tried to maintain her confidence as she made her way to the forum.

But when she rose to address the body of the Senate, all her old doubts came sailing back.

There hadn't been time to gather many of the delegates. She saw a few goblins and many elves, but there were no giants or gnomes present—even Nistel hadn't made it yet.

Karkald and Darann were there. The dwarves sat near the front of the assemblage, and though a few goblins and fairies looked at them curiously, the elves studiously ignored these visitors who so clearly did not belong here. One faerie, a little creature called Kaycee, buzzed sleepily to her seat near the top of the chamber.

At the rostrum, Belynda made a valiant effort. She told, firsthand, of the deaths she had witnessed, cruel poisonings inflicted by Sir Christopher's serpent staff. She described the stake, and the firewood that was to have been the instrument of her own death. And she noted the threat, in the form of the advancing army, that was even now approaching the lakeshore beyond their precious city.

Naturally, her remarks caused a great deal of consternation, especially among the elves. Both Praxian and Cannystrius shouted for order, but it was several minutes before the assembly quieted down.

More excitement was caused, then, when she invited Karkald to speak. In blunt, plain-spoken language, the dwarf described the army of Delvers that had embarked on an invasion of Nayve. By the time he was finished, goblins were jabbering, but the elves remained stony-faced and aloof.

"I tell you, peoples of Nayve—we must act, and quickly!" Belynda declared, once again stepping to the fore. "Come by the tens, by the hundreds—have them rally at the Blue Swan Inn!"

A few of the elves were nodding in agreement. Several of the goblins were grinning with excitement, all but bouncing up and down, ready to move.

"A point of order." It was old Rallaphan, raising his hand and rising from his stool. The assembly grew silent.

"These are alarming tales, extraordinary occurrences," declared the elder senator. "Perhaps they do call for action. But I would observe that a casual count shows no more than half the delegates are present, here and now. We are clearly lacking the quorum needed for a vote."

"We don't *need* to vote!" Belynda retorted. "We need to act!"

"Ahem." It was tall Praxian, glaring down at her sternly. "Need I remind the sage-ambassador that this is not a body that acts. This is a body that votes—and that only after proper and decorous debate!"

"Quite, quite," chimed in Cannystrius, while Rallaphan snorted in agreement.

The doors to the Senate chamber burst open with a shocking clang.

"We are prepared to fight!" It was Nistel, leading perhaps a hundred gnomes into the suddenly stirring chamber. "We offer ourselves as warriors, ready to lay down our lives to protect Circle at Center."

"And I will fight, too!" cried the lone faerie, Kaycee.

"You are out of order!" cried Rallaphan. "I object to this disruption."

"You're good at that, aren't you?" snapped Karkald, rising to his feet so abruptly that his stool toppled over behind him. He fixed Rallaphan with a contemptuous glare, then let his scornful eyes blaze across the whole gallery of elves. "Objections! Out of Order! Talk, vote, you do everything but act!" He drew a deep breath, and to Belynda it was obvious that he struggled to control a volatile temper. She doubted whether any of the other elves sensed the emotion simmering beneath the dwarf's gruff countenance.

"I've tried to explain to you about these Delvers," he declared. "They'd be delighted to hear you talk like this, because before you make up your minds they would destroy you! I have no doubt that Zystyl, their captain, would personally eat the hearts of a dozen elves in celebration of his victory!"

That graphic suggestion, at least, caused the blood to drain from many an elven face. And Karkald didn't seem inclined to let up. "Can you imagine what it would be like, a hundred faceless dwarves, protected in black steel from head to toe, each carrying two wicked knives. They whirl them, and advance shoulder to shoulder. Some of you might try to stand and fight—and you'd be cut to pieces. The rest, those who run, would have to keep running, and hiding. And even then the Delvers would smell you, and they'd come for you, and your children, and your world!"

"Enough!" shrieked Rallaphan, his face taut, veins bulging on forehead and neck. "You have no voice here—you are an outsider, and you have no right to defile our chambers!"

"You think *this* is defilement?" the dwarf replied with a snort. "Just wait—I know you can do that. I can see you're damned good at doing nothing. As for me, I'll stand with the gnomes and anyone else who wants to be a warrior. I will fight, in this world, against the enemy of my own homeland."

"Then you must go to the Blue Swan Inn," Belynda said to Karkald and the gnomes. The elven delegates hissed and murmured in soft objection, but even Rallaphan refrained from raising his voice. The sage-ambassador raised her voice, sweeping her eyes across the chamber to include everyone present in her response.

"And pray to the Goddess Worldweaver that we are not too late!"

• • •

"Good sir, can I speak with you, please?"

This humble elf was the innkeeper, Natac knew—the fellow had been pointed out by Tamarwind as soon as the company had reached the Blue Swan Inn. Jared Innkeeper was his name, and despite his nondescript appearance and slight size, the scout had identified him as a very influential citizen of Nayve.

"I have only a minute—what do you want?" the warrior asked ungraciously. He begrudged even this tiny shift of his focus, but in truth he knew there was little else he could do now. His warriors were deployed, and they could only wait for the enemy to appear.

"We hear that there's an army on the way—coming here!" stated the elf, his words tumbling out in a rush.

"Yes . . . it was my order that you be told. Have you evacuated the inn?"

"Well, no. It's just that . . . you see, we've never done anything like this before." The frail elf strove to stand straight, to meet Natac's eyes. "And, well . . . there are many families living here, the elves who maintain the inn. Not to mention guests. And we really don't want to leave."

Natac looked toward the ridge crest, the horizon where the highway came over the hill. There was still no sign of the Crusaders, nor of the scouts he had placed up there to bring early warning. He tried to contain his exasperation, reminding himself that war was an utterly foreign concept to the people of Nayve.

"I understand how you feel. In fact, neither myself nor these elves and giants who are with me would choose to be here now, if given a choice. But the matter has been taken out of our hands by the actions of an enemy, one who comes here with the intent to destroy and to kill."

"I am trying to grasp this," said the elf with obvious sincerity. Natac felt a flash of sympathy. Naturally, the fellow's age wasn't apparent, but the warrior assumed he was the patriarch of a sizable clan. Perhaps they had operated this inn for a thousand years, or more. "And you are here to resist that enemy, correct?"

"Yes . . . we will fight them if they try to come onto the causeway."

"Then . . . can you not fight them before they come into the Blue Swan?"

Natac drew a deep breath. How could he briefly explain about tactics? About hanging flanks and untenable positions? Before he spoke, Deltan Columbine came up.

"I think Jared Innkeeper makes a strong point," said the elven poet. "We intend to fight. Why don't we fight for this inn? It's beautiful . . . it has a history that goes back further than two generations of elves. And it is visible from Circle at Center—a very symbol of Nayve."

"If we put our warriors in the inn, then the Crusaders can simply go around us and get on the causeway," Natac argued. "The whole city is open to them."

"What if we try to hold the bridge *and* the inn?" Deltan suggested. "Owen and the giants can stand at the bridge, and the elves can hold the inn."

Natac shook his head. "The giants are not enough to hold the bridge—not if the enemy comes through the stream."

"Perhaps we can prevent that."

Miradel's voice from behind him sent a jolt of happiness through Natac. He turned to embrace his teacher, saw that she had come across the causeway with Juliay and several other druids. "How can you prevent a crossing of the stream?" asked the warrior. Beyond the druids, another column of recruits—short, bearded figures bearing a variety of implements as weapons—marched resolutely toward the bridge.

"It is the same magic that raises the Snakesea raft," explained a tall male human, a man with a flowing beard and long, bronze-colored hair. "We can fill the stream with so much water that anyone trying to cross will be swept out to the lake."

"Oh, brave warrior—is it possible?" asked Jared Innkeeper. "Can you block the causeway, and save the inn?"

With a scowl, Natac glowered at his companions. "What if Sir Christopher sends some of his men through the tunnel? They'll come out right between the inn and the bridge. We'll be trapped."

"Not with us to watch your back."

Natac saw that the dwarf Karkald had arrived with the next group of reinforcements. Karkald and his wife had led a column of gnomes, a hundred or more strong, across the causeway from the city. The stubby little people were armed with big knives, pitchforks, staffs, and clubs. A few of them had crossbows and quivers of small, metal-tipped darts.

"Can you position yourselves across the gap?" asked the Tlaxcalan, knowing that the dwarf—out of everyone present—had some grasp of combat tactics.

"Yes—we'll keep an eye on the tunnel," declared Karkald, while Nistel nodded eagerly at his side.

Natac looked for Belynda and didn't see her. "Any hope of more reinforcements, some elves from the city, perhaps?"

Karkald growled and spat. It was Nistel who answered. "They . . . I think they're too frightened. Anyway, it didn't seem like any of them were in a hurry to help."

Natac looked at the ridge again . . . no sign of alarm there. He looked at the inn, trying to see its defensive strengths, if any. There was a high balcony encircling the upper stories. From there, the archers could shoot unimpeded in every direction. But there were too many doors, and the building was made entirely of wood. If Sir Christopher attacked with fire, the results could be disastrous.

Yet Natac knew the value of a strong symbol, and suspected that value would only be enhanced in the eyes of young, untested warriors. And the inn stood visible even from Circle at Center . . . Perhaps it might prove a rallying point, if they could just withstand the first onslaught. Critically he eyed the ground. The archers could do some damage from the inn, harassing any Crusaders who tried to bypass the position to attack the bridge. If they were forced out, they could possibly fall back to the boats in the harbor, or else try and battle their way to the causeway. It was worth a try.

"Very well," he said. "Deltan, move your archers onto the balcony up there. The rest should take up positions inside, behind the doors and windows." He looked at Jared Innkeeper. "Get your strongest elves. Grab weapons—knives, garden tools, axes. And get ready to defend your home."

The slight elf gulped nervously, but then pledged his agreement and hastened to the inn to start preparations.

In a few minutes, the archers were in position. Natac strode through the ground floor of the building, seeing that the main gates were well-barred, that every door and window was barricaded and reinforced. After a quick circuit he climbed to the balcony, and then to a lone tower which rose above the rest of the sprawling structure.

He looked in the direction of metal and saw movement atop the ridge. A lone figure raced down the road, a centaur who was waving a piece of red cloth clutched in one hand. It was Gallupper, giving the signal that an attack was imminent.

"They come!" cried Natac, and the alarm was taken up throughout the ranks of the defenders.

By the time Natac had descended to the balcony, the vanguard of the Crusaders had come into view: two dozen centaurs who rumbled along the road, shouting and cursing at Gallupper. The youngster held a good lead, however, and as he neared the inn the pursuers pulled up.

"Obviously they remember the sting of our arrows," Deltan observed.

"Good thing—for you'll need to conserve them, now,"

Natac replied. "Tell your men to make every shot count."

The rest of the enemy fighters gradually came into view, a long, dark file, closely packed ranks plodding relentlessly down the hill. Menacing giants loomed over companies of goblins and long columns of elves. The centaurs circled back, raising clouds of dust with their heavy hooves as they flanked the marching army and fell into an easy walk through the fields beside the track.

Sir Christopher was clearly visible in his silver shirt, riding a black horse and cantering back and forth along the formation. He halted near the top of the hill, and spent several minutes eyeing the inn, the bridge, and the mouth of the tunnel—where the gnomes were already forming up a line. Even in the distance Natac could hear the human warrior barking orders, and he saw several centaurs take off running, no doubt bearing their leader's commands to the various units on the road.

When the lead giants were a half mile away they left the road, and the rest of the column followed. For ten minutes they marched into a line perpendicular to the highway. Their discipline was unimpressive, compared to the precise formations followed by a Tlaxcalan or Aztec army, but soon the Crusaders had formed a formidable front, standing shoulder to shoulder, facing the Blue Swan.

Then, with a yell that began as a rumble and swelled to a ringing cry, the giants, elves, centaurs, and goblins surged forward. The sound swelled into a wave of noise, a roar that might have emerged from a single, monstrous throat. Feet and hooves pounded the ground, adding to the din, and as the attackers swept closer the sound rose to a thrumming crescendo.

The first arrows streaked out to vanish in the mob. In moments the attackers were closing around the inn, and racing toward the bridge, where Owen, Rawknuckle, and the other giants stood waiting.

With a quick glance from his post on the balcony, Natac saw that the placid stream guarding the causeway had swelled to a raging torrent. Whitecaps churned through the roiling river, and water surged over the banks and rushed to spill in great waves across the lake. The druids, tall and serene in their brown robes, stood in a line about one every twenty paces along the stream's course. Natac nodded in satisfaction—the bridge would be the only crossing.

Three of the Crusader giants led the charge, pounding onto the bridge with clubs upraised. Owen roared a battle cry—it sounded something like "Odin" to Natac—and met the leading giant with a slash of his great club. The giant howled and fell back, blood spraying onto the cobblestones. Rawknuckle and his comrades met their foes with staffs made from whole trees, bracing the poles against the bridge and lowering the ends into the charging enemies.

And then Fionn and three more giants rushed forward, wading into the confused front rank, the Irishman bashing with his staff while these giants laid about with heavy clubs. Within seconds the impetus of the Crusaders' charge was broken, and the attackers fell back with shouts and curses.

Meanwhile, a few centaurs had tried to wade the raging stream, but the nearest druid chanted and swept her hands through an elaborate circle. Abruptly, white water churned upward, surging over the bank, sweeping around the legs of the rapidly retreating centaurs. One of the horse-men tumbled and slipped into the stream, and despite the best efforts of his comrades the hapless creature tumbled down the stream, rolling and bobbing as the water carried it into the lake.

Natac couldn't wait to see if the centaur swam back to shore—the Crusaders were milling about outside the inn now, and he heard crashing and pounding below as they battered at the barricaded entrances. Clutching his sword, the warrior raced downstairs, just in time to see two elves tumble back as the front door gave way.

Five leering goblins clawed and scratched at each other, each trying to be the first through the opening. Natac rushed forward and, reminding himself to stab, not chop, thrust his blade into the packed bodies. The goblins howled and kicked, recoiling in a tangled mass. Natac stabbed again and four of the creatures scampered back from the broken door. One was bleeding, dragging a limp leg. The fifth lay motionless, pierced through the heart.

Natac felt the same chill he'd experienced when he slew an elf in the Crusaders' camp. Never in all his years of warring had he killed so easily—this keen weapon cut flesh in a way that went far beyond the capabilities of the stone blades of his homeland. He had no time for further reflection, as giants and wild-faced elves lunged toward the opening.

"Get this door back up!" shouted the warrior to his own elves, several of whom gaped, horrified, at the breach. Natac stabbed again, puncturing a giant's belly, then slashed his sword back and forth across the opening until the door was pushed back into place. Other elves were ready with beams and a great table, which they used to prop the barrier in its frame.

A clatter of hard blows mixed with shrieks of pain drew Natac to a room in the back—a private dining room. Here a window had been pushed in, and a dozen Crusader elves had forced their way into the chamber. Already several defenders—mostly cooks, to judge from their greasy, flour-stained garments—had been cut down. One crawled toward the door, while two more lay in pools of fresh blood.

Natac attacked like a madman, shouting a challenge as he rushed into the enemy's midst. He struck left and right— killing blows to neck and chest, crippling slashes to hamstring or calf. Within seconds half the elves were down and the others were diving back out the window.

Then a cheer rang from the ramparts. Natac looked outside, saw that Sir Christopher was ordering his men back, regrouping on the slope of the ridge. A glance toward the bridge showed the same—the Crusaders were backing away, and the giants and elves of Natac's company were shouting in joy.

Natac looked up, saw that the sun had already begun to recede. It looked as though his warriors had carried the first day.

The giant was covered with blood, sprawled across a two-wheeled oxcart that had been violently tipped onto its side. The leather traces were sliced to ribbons, and there was no sign of the great bovine that, Karkald deduced, must have been pulling the wagon. The whole gory tableau lay at the mouth of the tunnel carrying the Metal Highway away from Nayve.

The dwarf felt a dull sense of hopelessness. This world was so different from the First Circle . . . how could he manage? He was in command of a hundred gnomes, but none of the little fellows had ever even delivered a blow in anger before. And he couldn't even keep Darann safe— she had insisted on marching here with him. She had been cursedly stubborn about the matter, too—he had only acquiesced because they needed to get on the march, and she had been unwilling to yield to his authority.

Now this giant lay here, clear proof that the danger was greater than just that offered by the Crusaders—for in the cruel, slicing cuts Karkald felt certain he was looking at the work of Delvers.

"In here!"

It was the faerie called Kaycee, who had flown along as the gnomes and the two dwarves had marched out of the city. Now she called from inside the tunnel, and moments later came flying woozily out. She plopped into the ditch and retched noisily.

"It's the ox . . . what's left of it," offered Nistel, who had gone ahead to investigate. "Mostly bones, I should say." The gnome, too, looked a little queasy as he emerged into the fading light.

"What could have done this?" Darann asked, moving closer to the motionless giant. She leaned toward his face, brushed away the blood with a tentative hand. "He's alive!"

"Bring him over here, to the grass," Karkald directed the gnomes. The little fellows, who seemed to welcome his assumption of authority, hastened to obey. In a few minutes the giant was stretched out, compresses laid against his many wounds. Most of these, fortunately, proved shallow. As Darann gave him some water, and washed his face, his eyelids flickered and then, with a start, he sat up.

"Little murderers!" he howled, raising his fists as gnomes scampered in all directions.

"Wait!" declared Karkald, his sternness matching the giant's outrage. "We are not the people who did this to you!"

The giant scowled and squinted, rubbing one of the wounds on his scalp. "No," he admitted. "They were ugly runts, no eyes in their faces! And one of them had jaws of metal—'twas his bite did this." The fellow displayed a nasty wound in his forearm. "There was hundreds of 'em, teeming like rats, they were."

"Did you fight them off?" Karkald asked, amazed.

The giant shook his head ruefully. "Not the like. It seemed like there was no hope. We'd fought our way out of the tunnel, just before the Lighten Hour . . . must have been this morn. But the little wretches came after, pulled Bess out of her traces." The fellow's voice caught, a mixture of pain and rage, and his great hands clenched into fists. "They were eatin' her while she was still kickin'! She bellowed for me, and I tried to get to her. But they was too many."

"You fought bravely," Karkald said. "Your wounds show that."

"And then they just left me . . . like the sun was getting brighter, and then run back into the tunnel."

"They are Delvers, blind dwarves of the First Circle who live for killing and cruelty. They have indeed come to Nayve," Karkald declared grimly. He looked up, saw that the sun had receded far into the heavens. "Probably they wait only for nightfall before attacking."

"And here they come!" squeaked Kaycee, buzzing out of the tunnel where she had ventured to keep watch. "Get ready!"

"Gnomes—form a line here, across the tunnel mouth!" shouted Karkald. The little people hastened to obey, but the dwarf's heart sank at the prospect of these untrained troops facing a Delver assault. Still, there was nothing left to do.

Or perhaps one thing. He shouted to Darann, who was moving into the gnome line. "Take word back to the inn— tell Natac that the Delvers are coming! He's got to be ready on his flank!"

"Send one of the gnomes!" she objected, with a meaningful nod into the tunnel. She had armed herself with a wooden shaft sharpened to a keen point, and she rose head and shoulders above their doughty comrades.

Karkald didn't have time to argue. "Kaycee—get to the inn and warn them about the Delvers!"

With a nod the faerie buzzed off. By the time she disappeared, the tromp of marching feet formed a cadence coming from the tunnel. The Delvers emerged from the inky darkness into the twilight in a whirling front of slashing swords and cutting axes. Each of the Unmirrored was clad in metal armor and stood shoulder to shoulder with his mates. A few of the gnomes poked with their pitchforks or whacked with their staves, but the weapons bounced off steel-plated shoulders and heads.

And then the Delver weapons met flesh. Gnomes shrieked

and screamed as dozens of wounds were scored along the line. Some were cut down in the first contact. Others dropped their weapons and turned to flee. Still more fell slowly back from that inexorable crush.

As soon as the Unmirrored had emerged from the cave they began to spread out, rear ranks moving to the right or left of the first row. Soon the mass was a hundred paces wide, and advancing into the open. The rest of the gnomes could do nothing but turn to flee, running into the night.

And the Blind Ones followed.

S he was near!

Zystyl's wide nostrils quivered in anticipation. More than a scent, the arcane perceived a presence on a visceral level, in a place that superseded the keen depths of his four senses. There was a sweet aura, proof that he had found the same Seer female who had eluded him in the First Circle.

Now she was running with the gnomes, the runts who had offered such pathetic resistance. Still, the victory had been a delight—the Delvers had immersed themselves in the stench of a real bloodletting. The taste of gnomish flesh still lingered in Zystyl's mouth, an oily residue which, after the long intervals on march rations, he found vaguely sickening.

But that was forgotten as the arcane now led his warriors after the retreating gnomes. The dwarves followed the sounds of their retreating foes, the Blind Ones rolling easily over the ground.

And somewhere before him was that Seer called Darann. He remembered the taste of her sweat when his tongue had stroked her cheek, the softness of her warm flesh in the grip of his strong fingers.

He had followed her to a new world, and here at last he would have her.

• • •

Sir Christopher launched his next attack under the full cover of darkness, once more sending waves of elves and goblins against the inn, while most of his giants again pressed the onslaught against the bridge. Natac watched the first maneuvers from the balcony of the Blue Swan, and saw a small group of enemy giants rushing out of the night. They carried a heavy tree trunk, and raced toward the front doors of the inn.

The warrior raced down to the ground floor, hurrying to the entrance, where he watched through the crack in the broken front door. As the horde emerged from the darkness, another volley of arrows lanced out from the Blue Swan's high parapet. Now Deltan directed his missiles with lethal accuracy, and they found targets in centaur chests, giants' throats, and the bodies of goblins and elves. A dozen or more of the attackers fell. But still the Crusaders rushed forward, and Natac threw his own shoulder against the door just in time to meet the shock of the onslaught.

The barrier shuddered and broke under the impact of a heavy ram. The Tlaxcalan tumbled out of the way, struggling to draw his sword and climb to his feet. The first giant, with the end of a big log under his arm, plunged through the doorway and spotted Natac. With a bellow that almost deafened the warrior, the hulking creature lashed out with a huge fist. Natac's sword snicked outward and up, slicing across three knuckles. When the brute recoiled, the blade lashed out again as Natac stabbed the giant right in the heart.

By then another burly Crusader had entered the room, this one bearing a club. An elf charged forward, jabbing with a wooden staff, but the giant brought his club down on his victim's skull, killing him in an instant. Natac turned, but he was too far away to intervene as the giant started toward the next room. But then another elf stood in his path, this one—like Natac—stabbing with a deadly steel longsword. The giant fell back, bright red blood spurting from his gashed thigh. By the time his comrades pulled him out of the room, the elves had lifted the door and once again barricaded it in place.

"Where did you get that sword?" Natac asked, recognizing Tamarwind Trak as the elf wiped and sheathed his blade.

"From me." It was Darryn Forgemaster. The blacksmith druid stood with Miradel in a hallway. "I brought four more weapons over . . . thought they might be of some use. I gave two to those big humans, the Irish and Vikingman. One went to Tamarwind, and I have the other."

"Good—and thank you!" Natac replied. Before he could say more, shouts of alarm rang through the hall.

"The inn is on fire! We're burning!" The alarm spread quickly, and by the time Natac raced through the several connecting halls he found one wing of the Blue Swan nearly engulfed by flames. Elves frantically poured buckets of water onto the blaze, but the fire continued to consume the wooden structure. Interior walls glowed red, and smoke belched into the hallway from the open doors of several rooms.

Jared Innkeeper was there, sooty and gasping. The elf directed the firefighting efforts, even lending his slight body to the task of hauling buckets. But a quick glance showed the courageous elves forced to fall back, retreating in the face of intense heat.

"You—all of you! Help fight the fire!" Natac shouted, mustering a dozen elves who were milling about, wide-eyed and near panic, at the top of the wide stairway. They hastened to obey as the warrior rushed onto the outer balcony to get a view of the damage.

He saw that the roof was ablaze over the entire wing, with cheering Crusaders gathered around to watch. Turning back to the door, Natac was startled to find that Miradel had followed him onto the balcony. "Go back inside!" he ordered, but immediately saw that she was paying no attention to him. Instead, her eyes were fixed upon the sky.

She raised her hands and shouted. The voice that boomed from that frail and elderly form was a shocking pulse of pure power, and when she lowered her voice, the cry sank to a rumble that reminded the warrior of distant thunder. He stared in wonder, awed by her power, her calm majesty.

And then real thunder crackled through the night, exploding from dark clouds that were just now churned into being. Abruptly rain pummeled Natac, the inn, and the ground in a torrential deluge. Miradel wove the magic with her hands, threads pulled from fingers to palm in delicate motions. And while she worked her spell, the rain poured into the flames, sizzling and hissing into steam, dousing the fire wherever a finger of flame dared to rise—at least, on the outside of the great building.

However, when he went back inside, Natac saw by the smoke-filled halls that the conflagration continued to spread. He encouraged Jared's efforts with a report of Miradel's spell, then started for the stairs to check on the battle at the ground floor.

"Natac!" Tamarwind met him on the steps. The elf's eyes were wild, and there was an edge of panic in his voice.

"What is it?"

"Over there—at the bridge. You have to see!"

Natac followed the elf back to the balcony and looked toward the other part of the battle. Torches flared in the darkness, and it looked to him as though the bridge still held. But there was churning movement beyond, dark forms coming from the mouth of the great tunnel.

Abruptly the night was split by a brilliant light, a glow of whiteness that seemed somehow even brighter than the sun. At the same time, it was a cold sort of illumination, suggestive more of a bright star than any kind of fire. Natac saw that the dwarf Karkald was holding his spear over his head, and it was the point of the spear that was aglow.

In the light the warrior could see that the gnomes were in full flight, running from the Metal Highway tunnel. Behind them came other figures, dark and crablike in the way they moved. They rushed after the routed gnomes in what was clearly an aggressive pursuit.

And Natac saw the grim truth in an instant: With this new attack, the whole defense of the causeway was outflanked.

"Fall back!" he shouted. He seized Tamarwind by the shoulder. "Go through the inn—get word to the far wings first. We'll retreat to the courtyard, then make a rush from the gates—we have to reach the causeway, and soon. Now, move!"

The elf raced away, while Natac found Deltan Columbine. "Give them a few quick volleys—then get down to the courtyard!"

The poet nodded in understanding, then turned to shout orders to his archers. "You elves—go for the kill, now! Shoot three!"

Arrows whispered outward, but Natac was already down the stairs. He found Jared Innkeeper still leading the valiant, but failing, battle against the fire.

"The inn is lost," the warrior said bluntly. "Gather your clan in the courtyard—we're going to fight our way to the causeway while we still have a chance."

With a gasp of utter despair, quickly contained, the elven patrician nodded and threw down his bucket. His eyes, rimmed with soot, were moist but his voice was strong. "All you of the Blue Swan—this way! Follow the warrior!"

In moments they had gathered before the main gates, which still stood intact. Miradel was there, and Darryn Forgemaster, as well as nearly all the elves of the company. Tamarwind arrived with the defenders of the far wing, and they gathered in the courtyard, waiting for word.

"Go to the stream!" Miradel shouted to him. "The druids will let us pass!"

The warrior nodded in understanding. "Open the gates and charge for the causeway!" shouted Natac. "Don't stop for anything."

The gates parted swiftly to reveal a few startled goblins. These wretched Crusaders hastily scampered away, as Natac led the elves out. Here and there a giant or centaur moved to intercept, but the sheer number of elves allowed them to brush these obstacles aside. However, as Natac looked ahead, he saw that the attackers still pressed against the bridge. Remembering Miradel's instructions, he led the elves not toward the bridge, but toward the high, roiling stream.

Before the defenders reached the water's edge the druids across the stream abruptly dropped their hands, ceasing the weaving motions they had maintained for so long. Immediately the roiling waters spilled away, leaving a shallow and placid waterway no more than a foot or two deep.

Swiftly the elves pushed across, the stronger helping the weaker. Churning over the muddy bottom, they climbed up the far bank, then turned to pull their comrades out behind them. Natac stood on the bank, watching as several centaurs galloped toward them.

"Get your bowmen ready to shoot!" he cried to Deltan Columbine. In the confusion of the retreat, however, the archer was able to assemble only a half dozen of his men. "Take aim—make each shot count!"

Most of the elves were across. Where was Miradel?

The warrior was shocked to see her just moving down to the stream, aided by Darryn Forgemaster. Natac went to her other side, but then Christopher's centaurs galloped up, undeterred by the few arrows launched by Deltan's archers. The warrior slashed back and forth, holding the first of the hoofed attackers at bay, but others circled around, out of range of his steel.

"Away with you!" cried Darryn, stabbing with his sword.

"Damned tooth!" cried a centaur, as the tip gouged his flank. Another of the big creatures reached down, seized the blacksmith by the wrist and pulled him out of the stream. Natac, holding Miradel with one arm, dragged her across the waterway and into the grasp of their comrades. Darryn tried to break free, to come after, but the centaur's big hand was too strong. The smith raised his sword, but another centaur lunged at him to snatch the weapon away.

"Fine weapon!" roared Darryn's captor, lifting the blacksmith off the ground and flicking his black tail. "You can tell our lord knight where you got it!"

More centaurs and several giants charged into the stream, and the druids hastily churned the water high, driving the aggressive Crusaders back to their shore. But Natac could only watch in helpless dismay as Darryn Forgemaster was lashed to the back of a big centaur. The blacksmith was hauled away even as the magic torrent churned through the streambed with renewed force.

The elves from the battle at the inn, battered, sooty, and defeated, streamed onto the causeway in the wake of the fleeing gnomes. Owen, Fionn, and the giants fell back from the bridge as Natac, too, joined the rearguard. A minute later they formed a living barrier across the terminus of the causeway, the Tlaxcalan standing with Rawknuckle Barefist and two other giants, as well as the other two human warriors, and Karkald and Tamarwind.

The Crusaders milled about at the bridge, hesitating to follow, and quickly Natac saw why. Churning out of the darkness came a solid front of black armor and swirling, vicious blades. The eyeless dwarves attacked like an unthinking, unfeeling machine. Sensing where the lake waters blocked them, directed by the shouts of their leader, the Delvers intuitively formed a wedge and drove down the road straight onto the causeway. They advanced shoulder to shoulder, a wall of steel breastplates and helmets. Every dwarf clutched a blade in each hand, and these deadly short swords whipped back and forth in front of the line like so many slashing scythes.

Natac stabbed and parried, with a lunge driving his blade through the breastplate of a Delver's armor. Any further thoughts of aggression were curbed as he saw his companions forced back to either side, with the Unmirrored continuing their advance unimpeded. It quickly became clear that the only thing they could do was retreat faster than the Delvers could follow.

And so the warriors of the rearguard withdrew toward the city, staying just out of reach of those deadly swords. Around midnight, near the middle of the causeway, the eyeless dwarves finally abandoned the pursuit—to be safely underground by the Lighten Hour, Karkald speculated. Exhausted and wounded, the battered defenders could only look across the lake, where the flames still consumed the Blue Swan, and smoke and fire seemed to rise into the sky as a funeral pyre for the world.

PART TWO

14

War Years

*Rely not on the likelihood of the enemy's not coming,
but on our own readiness to receive him;
Not on the chance of his not attacking,
but on the fact that we have made our position
unassailable.*

From *The Art of War*
by Sun Tzu, warrior scribe of the Seventh Circle

Natac stood in the prow as Roland guided the *Osprey* into the sheltered cove. The stars sparkled above them, and the night was so still that the sailor had used a wind of his own casting to glide them silently, quickly across the lake. By following a circuitous route, tacking far in the direction that was neither metal nor wood, then approaching this anchorage along the lakeshore, the *Osprey* had avoided the heavy Crusader galleys that controlled so much of the water.

"That's half of the job," Roland said in a hoarse whisper as the boat glided to a halt within a few paces of the grassy shore. "And if we can get out of here before dawn, I can outrun those hulks back to the harbor."

"I'll be back before then," Natac promised. "I hope she'll come with me. . . ." He sighed and shook his head.

"I know," Roland said sympathetically. "But she's al-

ways lived here . . . and who knows how much longer—"
He stopped, but the question lingered in Natac's mind as
he slipped into the shallow water and waded ashore. He
heard a splash behind him as Ulfang, too, sprang from the
deck. The white dog swam to the shore and then, consci-
entiously turning away so that the warrior didn't get
sprayed, shook himself vigorously until he was nearly dry.

Roland whispered encouragement and then, with the aid
of his small crew, pushed off. Natac knew he would keep
the *Osprey* waiting in concealment against the Tlaxcalan's
pre-Lighten Hour return.

Natac and Ulf climbed the hill to Miradel's villa. Still
the night yawned around them, vast and utterly still. Far
away the lights of Circle at Center blinked across the city's
expanse. Great houses and fabulous museums stood outlined in yellow illumination, while the fortified towers at
the ends of the causeway were surrounded by the bright,
white light of coolfyre. Even at this distance the Metal
Highway stood outlined in clear relief—and Natac knew
that, on the other side of the city, the causeway on the
Wood Highway was similarly protected.

The camps of the enemy armies were for the most part
invisible from this vantage, but he knew that within the
valleys and lowlands along the shore there were ten thousand or more fires burning. The blazes marked the great
city-camp of Delvers and Crusaders, the two armies that,
in uneasy alliance, had worked so ceaselessly to breach the
defenses of Circle at Center. The sprawling encampment
had, through the years, grown to include the shoreline ends
of both causeways, effectively cutting the city off from the
rest of Nayve. Preventing those attackers from gaining a
foothold on the island had become a life's work for the
Tlaxcalan, and it was a task that had no foreseeable end.

But now Natac's thoughts turned inward, a mixture of
melancholy and delight as he and Ulf approached the white-
walled villa. Candles and torches glowed around the outer

walls. Halting just beyond the periphery of brightness, Natac knelt down and looked into Ulfgang's bright, intelligent eyes.

"You'll keep an eye out here?" the human asked.

"All night," promised the dog. "I'll be a ghost on the hillside." And just like that he was gone, vanishing into the shadows to commence a circuit of the slopes below the villa.

Natac climbed into the corona of light surrounding Miradel's house, following the path toward the wide front stairway. He was not surprised when Fallon met him at the top. The elf, as always, had been keeping watch—indeed, Natac wondered if he ever slept. Now Fallon spoke very quietly.

"Warrior Natac . . . I thought it would be you. She is waiting."

"Thanks, old friend. How is she?"

"The same." The elf's eyes were sad, and Natac touched him on the shoulder, then crossed the veranda to enter the house.

He saw her immediately, sitting upon a wooden chair near the fireplace. A blanket, a weave of many bright colors, was pulled over her thin legs. Her face was a relief map of wrinkles, creases radiating until they met the scalp of snowy white hair.

But the smile that brightened her face was as familiar to Natac as his own skin. And her eyes of violet, still as bright and colorful as they had been on the night so long ago, when she had sacrificed her own future to bring him life here in Nayve, pierced his heart with that mixture of joy and sorrow that seemed always to mark his visits to the villa.

"Hello," she said, almost shyly.

"Hello." His voice was thick, and he leaned down to kiss her on each cheek. "You're as beautiful as ever."

"And you're as big of a liar," she said with a tart laugh. "The Goddess knows, I can barely lift myself out of bed on these chill Lightens. But come, let's eat—and talk."

He helped her up, let her lean on his arm as they walked, very slowly, toward the large wooden table. As he did upon each of his visits, he noticed now that her steps seemed shorter, her stance more frail and halting, than ever before. Her hands trembled slightly, an effect he had witnessed in the elders of his birth world, but something that seemed monstrously out of place in Nayve.

"It has been a long time since you visited," she said, and though there was no accusation in her tone, he felt a stab of guilt.

"Yes . . . three intervals now," he said. "The war—"

"Of course, the war." She cut him off, gave him a quizzical look. "How long has it lasted now, that war?"

"It was twenty-five years ago, just last seventh interval, that we fought the battle at the Blue Swan," he reminded her.

"Twenty-five years," she mused. "It seems only yesterday—you were a naif from the Seventh Circle, and I—I was so much younger."

Natac knew that she was right. In the time since she had begun to teach Natac the ways of Nayve, Miradel had continued to grow older at a shockingly rapid rate. It was probably nothing more than the ordinary mortality faced by every person of Earth, but in this eternal place it seemed to the warrior as though she were withering before his eyes.

"Of course, many things besides myself have changed over those years," the druid said pointedly, in her oddly disturbing way of responding directly to Natac's thoughts. She looked at him with that same sense of pride she had shown from the beginning. "You are the general of ten thousand warriors—a whole army answers your command, and a city depends upon your skill for its survival."

"I play my part—but there are so many others. Rawknuckle, Tamarwind, Karkald—"

"Of course. But I don't want to talk about them. You

must return to the war before the dawn, yes?"

Natac nodded, and drew a breath. "This time, *please* come with me! You will be comfortable in the city—you know Belynda has offered you rooms. And more importantly, you'll be safe. You don't know how many times we've seen Crusader patrols coming along this shore of the lake. It's only a matter of time before they come here."

"Nonsense. I've seen some of those patrols—my eyes are quite good, you know. They stay miles away from here."

"That's no guarantee that they'll always stay away." In fact, Natac too had noticed that the enemy troops had so far assiduously avoided the stretch of shore below Miradel's villa. He drew little consolation from this observation, since it was something beyond his control, and a fact that could change at any time.

"This has been my home for hundreds of years," the druidess declared. "Ever since I came here from the Seventh Circle . . . from our birth-world." She looked at him directly and he nodded.

"I have plucked the Wool of Time. I am ready for the casting, if you want to see," she said quietly.

"Is it finished yet?" he asked, looking at the door into the darkened viewing chamber.

"Soon . . . soon it will be over."

It had become a place of horror for him, that room. Natac knew that he would have to go in there, to watch the final scene in a terrible story of violence and treachery, of theft on an incomprehensible scale, and of the end of the world that had been his home. But each time now, that watching, that remote observation, was a brutally agonizing affair.

Through the past few years, the warrior had observed the tragedy unfolding as an inexorable progression. He had insisted that Miradel show him every moment, each step in the destruction of everything he had left behind. The story held an intense, if horrifying, fascination. Unlike the people of his native land, he had some awareness of the power of European weapons, and he had at least a vague understanding of the invaders' passion for gold. Furthermore, he had witnessed the power of European religion, in the belief in one god, in whose name works both good and evil were consecrated.

But he had been awed and enraged by the audacity of the man called Cortez. Natac had watched the captain general of conquistadores sink his own ships on the coast of Mexico so that his tiny army would have no means of retreat. Even as Natac hated them, he admired the Spaniards' discipline in battle, felt the courage of a small force facing overwhelming numbers. The efficacy of metal armor against weapons of stone was proved and proved again, and he saw the sweeping power of a cavalry charge against men who, though they were bold warriors, had never seen horses.

His own Tlaxcalans, the bravest fighters in all the world, had waged a frenzied battle, a full day of fighting against the small band of invaders. Hundreds of warriors, including one of Natac's sons, had perished during the savage fray. Cannons had roared fire and iron, and whole swaths of brave fighters fell. And at the end of that long and bloody day, only three of the conquistadores had been wounded— *wounded*—by the full might of the armies of Tlaxcala.

So his homeland had surrendered to Cortez, and now Tlaxcalan warriors fought under the command of Spanish masters, slowly choking a ring of death around the heart of the Aztec realm. In that army they had been part of the Aztecs' destruction, but to Natac it was a hollow victory for, at the same time, they were helping to obliterate their own world. Now Moctezuma was dead, and a terrible pox— another gruesome weapon of the insurmountable invaders— had decimated the ranks of the surviving Mexicans.

Miradel lit her candle and once again the pictures played across the wall. The great temples and pyramids, structures

that had risen like mountains into the sky above the Aztec
capital, were already gone, razed by the deliberate pounding
of Spanish guns. Most of the city was a ruin, and in the
rest the defenders fought like madmen, and were slaugh-
tered like dogs. Lancers charged on horseback, picking off
any Aztec who showed himself. Arquebuses blasted lethal
volleys, and each fortified building was simply smashed to
rubble by thundering artillery. It would be a matter of days,
Natac saw, before the world of the Aztecs and Tlaxcalans
was gone, replaced by something he couldn't imagine.

The picture began to fade, and he noticed that Miradel
had drifted off to sleep, her head resting on her frail-looking
hand. Gently the warrior lifted her up and carried her to
her bed. He thought for a long time of simply carrying her
away, taking her to the boat, but in the end he carried her
to the same sleeping chamber—the room that held his first
memories of Nayve—and laid her gently on the bed.

Fallon escorted him back to the stairway. Natac clasped
the elf by the arm, then looked upward to see that the sun
had just barely begun its descent toward daylight. It glowed
as a star bright enough to cast a faint illumination on the
flagstones of the courtyard, but the hillside below was still
cloaked in shadow.

"Take good care of her," said the warrior.

"Of course—now, make haste," Fallon encouraged, and
Natac nodded.

He trotted down the path, and quickly found the white
dog sitting in a clump of underbrush. "Let's go," the warrior whispered.

"You go," Ulf replied. "I think I'll stay over here for a
while, to keep an eye on things."

Natac was touched. "Thanks, friend. I'll feel better
knowing that you're here."

"I've already spoken to Fallon about it—he's quite a

good cook, you know. He said he'd be delighted to keep me fed."

Laughing quietly, Natac ruffled the dog's fur with an affectionate pat. "You'll eat better than most of us, I wager," he said, before starting down the trail, directing his footsteps toward the *Osprey,* Circle at Center, and the war.

"Come up here, where we can get a good view," Karkald urged Tamarwind, gesturing toward the tall stone tower that flanked the end of the causeway. The dwarf had found his elven comrade on the harbor dock, where Tamarwind was inspecting the modifications to his caravel, the *Swallow.* Though the Lighten Hour already brightened the sky, the lakeshore and causeway were still illuminated by the coolfyre globes mounted on tall poles all across the area.

"I'll come too," said Deltan Columbine. The two elves followed the dwarf off the dock, to the base of the tower, then up the steep stairway ascending to the upper parapet. Finally they reached the top, Karkald pushing through the trapdoor to the upper rampart. From here the trio looked across the lake.

The detritus of war was all around. Masts jutted from the water where the last naval skirmish had carried the enemy almost to the shores of Circle at Center. These were like ghostly trunks in the growing light of day. Karkald looked at the steel-springed battery atop the tower, feeling a flush of pride. In the most recent fight, it had been the fireballs launched from here that had destroyed Sir Christopher's lead galleys only two hundred yards from the harbor.

Both attacking armies were visible in their encampments across the lake. Sir Christopher's Crusaders, now numbering some twenty thousand elves, centaurs, goblins, and giants, occupied more than a mile of the lakeshore. The surroundings, once pastoral forest, were now a barren landscape of muddy hills. Crude barracks huts dotted the slopes above the flat ground. A hulking structure of sooty stone crouched beside a muddy stream, black smoke billowing from its tall chimney.

Beyond, near the mouth of the Metal Tunnel, they saw the bristling barricade of the Delvers' camp. During the hours of daylight, most Delvers remained in the darkness of the tunnel while others moved about only with elaborate precautions to ensure constant shade. At night, however, the Nayvian warriors had learned that there were no more savage fighters than the Unmirrored.

When the blind dwarves and the savage crusaders had first encountered each other twenty-five years earlier, it had taken only a few days before it became obvious to those in Circle at Center that Zystyl and Sir Christopher had formed an alliance. The two forces had linked in dire purpose, both dedicating themselves to the capture and destruction of the city, the island, and the Center of Everything. In a series of ensuing campaigns the attackers had closed the ends of both causeways, and destroyed many of the villages, harbors, and settlements on the shore of the lake. Though they had never made it onto the island for more than a quick raid, the enemy had developed a fleet of large, powerful galleys. The great ships were slow and cumbersome, but conversely they had proven virtually unstoppable in the attack. For at least a dozen years they had patrolled the waters of the lake with virtual immunity.

It had only been an interval ago when the fleet of Crusader galleys, fifteen ships strong, had attempted to land the largest raiding party of the war right on the shores of Circle at Center. Karkald's batteries, completed only during the last year, had seen their first action, launching balls of incinerating shot into the massed galleys from the two closest towers. Five of the ships had burned completely, while the survivors had beat a hasty retreat.

"That bastard blacksmith's forge is roaring," Karkald grunted, pointing to the plume.

Tamarwind nodded, not surprised. For all the years since his capture, Darryn Forgemaster had apparently labored nonstop to provide the Crusaders with metal weapons. The druid had been scorned as a traitor by Karkald and many others, but the elven scout suspected that Darryn's apparent betrayal had a deeper explanation. Still, it galled him to know that without the smith's weapons and armor, the Crusaders would be less deadly foes.

"Of all the enemies who deserve to die," spat Karkald, "that bastard blacksmith would be at the top of my list. If not for him, they'd have no swords, no steel heads on their spears and arrows. I suppose the scum is making himself rich on this!" It was an opinion the dwarf had expressed many times, but he still managed to work up a good measure of vehemence.

"You might be right. But I still can't help wondering why . . . why he works so hard for our enemies." Darryn Forgemaster was not the only person changed by this war, far from it. Tam remembered the changes in Belynda since she had been a captive of Sir Christopher, so long ago. The elfwoman he had known for many centuries had seemingly vanished in that instant, to be replaced by someone who was as dark and bitter in her own way as any warrior accustomed to death and destruction.

But now their attention was directed across the lake, where the long galleys of the Crusaders could be seen gliding along the shore.

"They're up to something," the dwarf grunted, squinting across the sun-brightened waters. "Natac's not far away from there."

"They're still a mile or more from Miradel's cove," said Tamarwind, trying to sound more optimistic than he felt. He knew that Natac and Roland would be trapped if the galleys continued on their current course.

Deltan gestured to the ships in the harbor below, a dozen three-masted caravels currently riding at anchor. In the prow of several of the ships gleamed a silver contraption, a miniature version of the great weapon atop this tower. "Perhaps it's time to give your nautical battery a test."

Karkald grimaced. "You know Natac wanted to wait until we had all of the ships outfitted. To get the most out of the surprise."

The elf nodded. "I know—but he couldn't have foreseen this! And it's not just the *Swallow* that's ready—we can shoot from the *Nighthawk* and the *Falcon*, too! Besides, we'll probably get out there, and the galleys'll turn after us and we can get away without firing a shot. That'll give the *Osprey* time enough to race for safety."

"I can't argue with that," the dwarf agreed. Tamarwind nodded decisively.

"Ahoy—crew of the *Swallow*!" Deltan shouted down from the tower. "Prepare to sail—we're coming down!"

Instantly the deck of the ship became a beehive of activity. Elven crewmen started to hoist the sails, while others cleared away the clutter of routine sail-mending and rope work, or made ready to cast off the lines. In moments the two elves and Karkald had scrambled down the stairs and were running along the dock. By the time they boarded the caravel, the ship's druid, Juliay, had brought out her bowl and windspoons.

"Cast off!" cried Deltan, as magical wind swirled upward and began to billow the sails.

"Look." Karkald said the word quietly, but his blood chilled as he looked across the lake. "There's the *Osprey*."

Roland Boatwright's ship had broken from its cove, twin sails full of wind. But the big war galleys were close now, and with their prey in plain sight they wheeled majestically, turning into position for an attack.

●   ●   ●

Natac stood with his hand on the line, leaning out to add his slim weight to the digging of the sailboat's keel. The war galley loomed huge off the port bow, and Roland was rapidly spinning the spoon in his wooden bowl, casting every bit of wind he could muster into the taut canvas.

In a rush of wake the *Osprey* scooted past the first of the big ships. Several giants roared and hooted, then hurled big rocks. With some trepidation Natac watched the boulders soar close, but Roland twisted the tiller at the last minute. The crushing missiles landed to either side of the racing boat, raising tall cascades beside the gunwales, showering the deck with water. Swiftly the little sailboat raced away, and the next volley of stones fell just short of the stern.

But now they saw the other two galleys, big ships waiting farther away from shore. Those vessels had been screened by the first of the Crusader vessels, and were perfectly positioned to block the *Osprey*'s escape either to the right or the left. Giants loomed in the prows and sterns of both galleys, while the banks of oars, powered by rowing goblins, pushed the massive hulls through the water with churning speed. Natac could hear the drumming, the cadence of pounding feet and rhythmic chants made by the laboring rowers. The pair of galleys seemed to leap forward, closing the gap with startling quickness.

Beyond the enemy ships, far away across the lake, Natac caught a glimpse of white sails and felt a momentary chagrin. The caravels had sortied! His disciplined plan, to wait until all of his ships could be outfitted with Karkald's new weapon, had been thrown into disorder by the need to rescue him. Still, the fleet's presence at least raised the hope of escape. The warrior turned back to Roland, ready to announce his observation..

"I see 'em," the druid declared from his position at the tiller.

"We need to buy some time!" Natac urged, knowing the

caravels would not reach them for many minutes.

"I can do a little something about that—but it's a risk!" Roland said.

"This whole war's a risk," Natac replied. He held the line and watched, his heart pounding with that precious excitement raised by a contest in which the prize was survival.

Roland pulled the tiller again, adjusting the force of his magical wind so that it still roared against his boat from the stern quarter. The little craft cut a tight half circle through the water, slicing through the gentle waves, now racing directly away from the two galleys—and straight back to the shore, only a few miles away.

Tamarwind stood at the helm of his ship. A stiff wind filled the sails, pushing him on a course of interception. The other caravels of the little flotilla fanned out to either side, a line of white canvas and sleek hulls. He had not ordered them to follow, but he was gratified to see that the Nayvian fleet had taken to the lake with alacrity.

Beside him, Deltan Columbine grinned, white teeth flashing. His hair streamed in the wind, and his face, bronzed by years of sun and weather, glowed with a golden sheen of vitality. Just for the joy of it, the poet-warrior raised his flügel, sent brash notes ringing across the water. Just beyond Deltan, Karkald leaned over his battery, fiddling with the sights, checking the ammunition in the compact breech. He, too, was weathered and browned, his full beard flowing to either side of his broad chest.

How much we've changed, reflected Tamarwind. He looked at his own hands, browned, muscular, and calloused in a manner that he never would have imagined. Years of warfare had hardened his fingers and his palms, just as those same years had hardened him all over. Life had become a constant fight to protect the city. Matters of life and death were faced every day. Tamarwind himself had made mistakes that had sent brave elves to their deaths. And yet, in a secret part of his mind, he admitted to a bizarre vitality to this life, an appreciation of each day that he had never before imagined.

For the most part, it had been Natac and Karkald who had instructed the elves in matters of defense. The human warrior had studied many ways of making war, Miradel frequently utilizing the Wool of Time to teach him more about his birth-world. And Natac had put that knowledge to good use. When the attackers sent a wave of centaurs advancing rapidly down the causeway, the Nayvians had quickly formed a barrier of giants armed with massive pikes, an array of sharpened steel that had effectively thwarted the thundering charge. Sir Christopher sent legions of bowmen to shower the giants with arrows, and Natac had overpowered them with volleys from Deltan Columbine's deadly longbows. And when the huge war galleys had been launched, more than ten years ago, Natac had enlisted Roland Boatwright to build the caravels. The little sailing ships, while unable to significantly damage the galleys, were—with the aid of druid-cast winds—always able to escape the lumbering Crusader vessels. The contrast had resulted in a situation where each side could still send ships across the lake, but neither could attain full control.

During the same time, the Seer dwarf from the First Circle had shared many secrets of technology with the druids and elves of the Nayvian army. Karkald's skill at stone-working had, with the aid of goblin labor, erected the towers on the island's shoreline. His recent discovery of a large quarry of flamestone, existing right in the city, had allowed coolfyre to be developed, and the bright lights had proven invaluable in night battles. It had been the dwarf's knowledge of metals—since the capture of Darryn Forgemaster—that enabled the defenders to make steel weapons and armor for much of the army, as well as to craft the mighty springs that powered the newest weapon. When Karkald's great batteries had been mounted in the towers, the galleys were at last held at bay.

Now, with the smaller versions of those weapons placed in three of the caravels, the war was entering another period of change, Tamarwind reflected. Once again, he raced toward battle, hoping for the key victory, the triumph that would change the war forever.

But then his attention was drawn to the drama on the lake before them. He gasped as the *Osprey* turned, then vanished behind the closing shapes of two massive galleys. More rocks flew, and splashes rose from the water beyond the great ships, but finally Roland's sailboat darted into view, racing toward the shore.

"Come and get us, you bastards!" Karkald growled, and Tam silently repeated the prayer. He could sense the indecision in the enemy captains—the small prize of the sailboat, almost certainly doomed if the galleys turned and followed it toward the shallows. But here came the much larger prize of the caravels, the vexing little ships that so often before had darted away from the galleys rather than face the larger ships in battle.

Now the galleys were turning, oars pulsing, great hulls slicing the water as they veered toward the elven fleet.

"They're taking the bait!" Deltan shouted, as Tamarwind called for more wind. Juliay spun her spoons with intense concentration, the wooden utensils a blur in the large, empty bowl. Somehow she managed to avoid clicking against the sides, and freshening wind surged in the sails.

The enemy galleys came at them in a line of three abreast, several giants at the ready in the prow of each vessel. Tam knew that they would have plenty of rocks on hand, ready to unleash a devastating barrage as soon as they got close enough.

"Now—make ready to shoot!" he shouted.

Immediately sails slackened on the elven ships, though

the sharp bows remained pointed directly toward the advancing Crusaders.

"Remember—aim low," Tamarwind urged, speaking quietly to Karkald as if he were worried that the enemy, still five hundred yards away, would overhear.

"I'll remember," said the dwarf, with a wry smile. "After all, I made the damned thing!"

Already he was squinting along the grooved sights, lining the massive barrel onto the prow of the nearest Crusader galley. Juliay slowed the stirring of her windspoons, and the *Swallow* settled into a gentle roll. Soon all the elven vessels bobbed gently on the placid waters while the three galleys swept closer.

Tamarwind gave the signal, a sharp downward chop of his hand. Deltan had been waiting and watching from the rigging, and at the gesture he gave a single, loud blast of his flügel horn.

Immediately Karkald pulled the release.

The caravel lurched backward as the spring whipped free to fling the silvery balls through the air. On each side another elven ship shuddered, and the air rang with the whining sounds of bending springs and swiftly flying missiles.

Karkald's aim was good. Tamarwind saw the spreading cloud of shot streak outward, arcing high above the waves before settling back toward the water. Many of the balls struck the Crusader ship, scattering across the deck near the bow, instantly blossoming into flames. Screams of fear and pain echoed across the water as, within moments, the entire wooden vessel was engulfed by roaring fire. The wounded ship shuddered like a living thing as orange tongues of fire crackled along the hull, devouring the oars and spindly mast. Anguished cries rent the air as elves, giants, and goblins hurled themselves from the flaming deck. Some of these hapless victims were themselves ablaze, their flesh hissing as they struck the water. Quickly the hull was obscured by smoke and steam, but still came the insatiable roar of the flames and the horrible sounds of the dying ship.

To either side the other galleys were also afire, though neither had been hit so solidly as the middle vessel. Water splashed across the decks as many goblins fought the flames. Others manned the oars, slowly backing the two surviving vessels away from the caravels and the death pyre of the third ship. A column of black smoke rose into the sky as the doomed vessel was gradually consumed right down to the water line.

"Look—we've knocked all of them out of the fight!" cried a crewman on the *Swallow*.

Whoops and shouts swept from the elven ships as the fleet of caravels wheeled away. Druids cast their magic, and as wind again filled the sails it was a triumphant fleet, with pennants flying and crews cheering, that sailed back to the anchorage below the Mercury Terrace.

Zystyl clumped across the encampment and nodded to the two guards, giants who stood outside Sir Christopher's palisade. He couldn't see them, of course, but their auras—of scent, sound, and vitality—clearly marked them in the Delver's mind. The first was full of lust, he sensed, yearning for a giantess he hadn't seen in a long time. The second was a dullard, head fogged by too much firebrew consumed the previous night.

Numerous adaptations allowed the Unmirrored commander to move about under the light of Nayve's sun, which had at first been almost unbearably painful to all his senses. A shield of silver was now attached to his helmet, deflecting the horrible light and providing him with an area of permanent shadow. His body was cloaked in a silk of fine weave and bright white color, a covering that extended right down to his fingertips. Only his sensitive nostrils were bared—as always, those moist apertures sniffed and sucked at the air, drawing in sensations that were far deeper than mere odors.

Leaving the giants behind, Zystyl relished the cool shade of the knight's great stone-walled house. Shrugging the silken cloak from his shoulders, he allowed the sensations of warmth and chill against his skin to locate the walls and arched doorways surrounding him. With unerring accuracy he started toward the knight's audience room.

And then, hearing the sound of a harsh voice, he halted, listening.

". . . a time when I would have had you killed . . . burned at the stake." It was the knight, Sir Christopher, speaking patiently, as if to a recalcitrant child. "You should be grateful that you have lived all these years, have been granted the chance to serve me."

Zystyl listened and smelled, ensuring that he was alone in the great hall. Soundlessly he sidled closer to the closed door of the audience chamber.

"You are a fool—a blind fool," snapped another voice, which then dropped into a register of bleak despair. "Or perhaps it's myself who's the fool . . . laboring in your name for all these years. How do I know you don't hold me with an empty threat?"

Christopher laughed. "The druid crone is allowed to live at my sufferance . . . and my sufferance depends upon your steady labors. Do not think to change our arrangement now, or I assure you that your precious Miradel will pay the price. Take a look at her villa tonight, blacksmith . . . look long and hard, for it is only your labors on my behalf that keeps your precious druidess alive."

A door slammed in the distance, and the Delver knew that someone had just left the audience room by a different exit. And he knew who that person was.

After a moment Zystyl cleared his throat and stomped noisily toward the room. He heard Sir Christopher rise out of his chair when he entered. The dwarf could smell the anxiety in the man, hear the tension in the rapidity of his breathing. Beneath his gauze mask the Delver's metal mouth twisted into a smile—he had his ally at a disadvantage, and he would make use of the opportuntity presented to him.

"Your galleys have been driven from the lake, those that survive," said Zystyl bluntly.

"We were met by a new weapon," snapped the human. Frustration and fury thrummed beneath the surface of his voice, and the Delver relished the knight's agitation. "Something we have never seen before. Globes of metal flung through the air from the deck of the enemy's caravels . . . they shattered, and burned like the fires of the devil on my ships."

"I heard the springs," Zystyl replied. "It is a mobile battery, much like the weapons that the Seers used in the First Circle. Quite deadly, I imagine, to thin-hulled wooden ships. They have a command of metal technology, in Circle at Center—it is no surprise that they are putting it to such good use."

"These are the uses of Satan!" Sir Christopher retorted. "Not the forging of good, honest steel—in the manner God intended for His warriors of virtue."

"Ah . . . the forging of metal. You continue to get many tools—all your swords and armor, yes—from the druid prisoner?"

"As I have for all these years, yes."

"It was a fortunate thing for you that you captured the man who, among all druids, is the one who knows the forging of steel."

"It was the will of God."

"Then let us use that will for more constructive purposes."

"What do you propose we do?"

"What I have suggested for years. Now, perhaps, you will listen to me?"

"You may speak. But remember, the man who shapes steel is mine . . . he answers to my commands, and only I know the secret of his bondage."

Zystyl nodded, knowing the human would observe the gesture, accept it as a positive response. In the heart of his mask, the metal jaws twisted into a cruel smile.

15

Scar Tissue

Skin healed
bone mends;
flesh restored,
body tends.

Spirit's gouge
torture's deeds;
wounded spirit
ever bleeds.

From the *Lore of the Healers*
Tapestry of the Worldweaver

Belynda tried to take some encouragement from the columns of figures on the pages before her, the tallies of recruits and armaments that should have been good news. She saw the proof of a growing army, a force that steadily gained might, confidence, and experience. Every cycle, more elves made the decision to join the Nayvian forces— seventy-four of them in the last forty days alone, most drawn from right here in Circle at Center. When added to the goblins recruited by the loquacious "Captin" Hiyram, the giants who steadily emigrated from the Greens and crossed the lake by raft in the dark of the night, and the young centaurs who rallied in answer to Gallupper's entreaties, Natac's army had gained another two hundred souls in this, the third interval of the twenty-fifth year of the war.

But then there were pages with other columns, different figures, such as the dolorous list of thirty-two brave elves who drowned when their caravel had been shattered by giant-thrown boulders, the four giants who had perished in recent skirmishes on the causeway, and the dozens of goblins who were killed during the routine brawls that rocked their camp with inevitable frequency. Always the gains were balanced against the losses, as they had been since the Battle of the Blue Swan. Even if that balance showed that the army defending the city was continuing to grow, as it had in nearly every interval of every year of the war, it amazed her that she could muster even the pretense of dispassion as she pondered such matters of life and death.

And to what purpose?

It had fallen to her to be the organizer, to gather the mortal fodder that Natac, and his lieutenants such as Tamarwind, Karkald, and Rawknuckle Barefist, sent into battle. Often they won, and sometimes they lost. Always warriors died, and others were recruited to take their places.

The sage-ambassador sighed, and rose from her writing table. She went to the window, looked across the Center of Everything, saw the great loom rising from its base in the shallow valley. Her colorful songbirds regarded her from their branches, still and silent. Beyond the garden and the valley she was aware of the teeming city, for the most part still going through the days as though nothing had changed. Music reached her ears, the tune wafting from some idle street-corner concert within a nearby elven neighborhood.

Even farther beyond, past the outskirts of the city and the once-placid lake, Belynda felt—though she could not see—the presence of the Knight of the Crimson Cross. Her hatred flared unbidden as the awareness seeped through her mind, burning in her breast and surging with all the force

of that brutal night so long ago. She caressed that malice
with her thoughts, holding it close, breathing the fetid smell
of his sweaty flesh, remembering the anguish that had
pierced her when he pressed home his brutal assault. Sometimes it seemed to be all that kept her going, that hatred,
and so in her own way she cherished it, recalled it willingly,
knowing that amid the inaction and apathy of Circle at Center she, at least, had a powerful cause, a reason for waging
this war.

The knock at her door startled Belynda. She drew a
breath and tried to stem the trembling in her hands, the
tremors that arose, unbidden, every time she was surprised
or frightened. Only after several deep breaths was she able
to control her voice enough to speak calmly.

"Enter." She turned as the opening door revealed the
worried face of her assistant and friend. "Oh hello, Nistel."

"Hello, my lady," the gnome said, rising from a deep
bow. His eyes wrinkled in concern as he surreptitiously
studied the sage-ambassador. "How are you feeling?" he
asked nervously.

She laughed—or tried to laugh. The sound that emerged
was more of a bark, she realized. Short, nervous, warning.
"As good as ever, I guess," she admitted. "What about
you . . . any word from Thickwhistle?"

Nistel's face fell. "Thickwhistle is no more—there are
only giants there, and so what was once Thickwhistle is
just Granitehome now."

Belynda knew that the gnomes of Thickwhistle had simply moved to a different part of the hill country, and she
found it hard to share the gnome's palpable sadness. Instead, she made vague noises of sympathy and turned back
to the window.

"Did you see the war today?" Blinker asked.

"No . . . for once I stayed inside. thinking, trying to rest.
I know the war will be there tomorrow—that's one thing
that doesn't seem to change."

"It changed a little today," offered the gnome, advancing into the room, chattering enthusiastically. "Tamarwind went out there with a new weapon—and the caravels burned up a big galley, and sent the others packing back to port!"

Belynda sighed. "There's *always* a new weapon. One side or the other burns up, or is torn to pieces. How is that a change?"

"The war has changed Circle at Center a lot," Nistel continued. "I can remember when we didn't have fortress towers by the causeways, didn't have any warships on the lake."

"But we still have concerts on every corner, people laughing and going about their lives like there's no danger, like nothing's wrong!" she retorted bitterly.

Now it was Nistel's turn to slump his shoulders and hang his head. "You're right—in so many respects the war hasn't changed anything at all."

Belynda spoke harshly, determined to prove her point. "The Senate meets once every interval, and during those forty days most of the city's leaders seem to work very hard to ignore the danger. If it was up to them, we'd have simply let the Crusaders march in here, invited the Delvers to dig their tunnels under the Center of Everything."

Indeed, many elves still hosted fabulous parties, and every day there were celebrations and festivals throughout the city. Some foods, and especially wines from the outlying realms of elvenkind, had been scarce or nonexistent, but most of the elves had preferred to make do with substitutes rather than make any changes in their lives that might acknowledge the difficulties raised by the war.

Of course, Belynda admitted, there had been some awakening. Many individual elves had rejected their clans' complacency and joined Natac's army. These included outlander companies from Barantha, Kol'sos, and other realms, as well as a number of recruits from Circle at Center. And still no elven land had sent as many companies as Argentian, the sage-ambassador thought with a touch of pride—pride tinged with sadness, for by the same token no realm had given as many lives to the war as her own.

Another knock sounded at the door, and Nistel hopped up to answer. He came back to speak to Belynda.

"Tamarwind is here to see you . . . maybe he wants to tell you about the battle. It was his ship, you know, that burned up that galley!"

Belynda shook her head, suddenly irritated. "I told you . . . I wasn't paying attention."

"Can he come in?"

The elven warrior was standing behind the gnome, and Belynda saw the eagerness, the high spirits in his expression. Tiredly, she nodded.

"It was a great day!" the warrior exclaimed, rushing into the room with un-elflike haste and taking the chair nearest to Belynda. She saw again how he was dark, weathered, hardened in ways that centuries of his earlier travels could never have done.

"What happened?" she forced herself to ask.

"Another weapon of Karkald's," Tam explained. "Like the tower battery, only mounted in the bow of a caravel. We burned three Crusader galleys!"

Belynda's eyes narrowed, and her teeth clenched at the image of suffering and death. "Was *he* there?"

Tamarwind looked crestfallen. "Sir Christopher . . . no, of course not. He hasn't gone out on the lake in years . . . but tell me, Belynda. Why do you always ask?"

For an instant the fires of hate welled up so strongly within her that she couldn't speak, afraid the blaze would flash its awful truth from her eyes. But she kept her expression blank, saw that Tam was looking at her with sincere curiosity. And she knew, she had *convinced* herself, that solid logic lay behind her question.

"You should understand by now: If we can kill him, we

will win the war. The Crusaders will fall apart . . . go home. Nayve will be as it was!"

Tamarwind shook his head, apparently oblivious as Belynda's temper began to mount. "They still have that arcane Delver, Zystyl. Karkald claims he's more dangerous than any *ten* human warriors could be."

"That's right—there are still the Delvers," Nistel declared, his beard bobbing sternly. "I don't think they would cease the war even if the Crusaders gave up."

"The Delvers are not going to destroy us by themselves, whereas I fear, sometimes, that the Crusaders might do just that," Belynda replied. "He keeps them in thrall with the Stone of Command, molds them to his will by ancient magic." She fixed Tam with a direct stare. "Why can't you just *kill* him, take the stone away, and be done with it! Natac had the chance twenty-five years ago, and he failed. Someone has to do it!"

"I-I have tried!" the elf declared, shaking his head in frustration. "We all have—but the knight no longer leads his troops in battle. He doesn't expose himself to our weapons! But please, my dear lady, have faith and patience! We will find his weakness, and we will bring this war to a victorious end!"

Abruptly she felt monstrously tired, unwilling and unable to face up to Tam's enthusiasm, or his attention.

"I'm sorry," she said firmly. "I've been hit with a terrible headache . . . can you come back tomorrow?"

She felt a twinge of guilt as Tam's shoulders slumped. Naturally, he agreed to see her the next day, and made the appropriate noises of concern before rising to depart.

"I will go, too," Nistel said, bouncing to his feet. "Please, my lady, try to get some rest . . . and do not let your hatred sicken your soul."

She wanted to snap at him—Who was he to tell her what to do? But she let him depart without another word. In her silent apartment she tried to go back to work, and had even made some progress when Darann came to see her an hour later. Belynda admitted the dwarfwoman with no pretense of headache or other discomfort. Moments later the two females were seated at her conversation table.

"Have you thought about my idea?" asked the sage-ambassador.

"Yes," Darann replied quickly. "I'm thinking about discussing it with Karkald, but I'm not sure he'll be ready to listen."

"That's not surprising," Belynda said. "It seems counter to the way men think about war."

"Still, *I* know you're right." The dwarfwoman met the elf's eyes squarely. "And I'm ready to help you try."

"Good," Belynda said. "You know that if we succeed, we might be able to end this war."

Darann nodded. Both of them knew, though neither of them put it into words, what their fate would be if they failed.

Ulfgang loped through the night, following the network of trails around the slopes below Miradel's villa. He had maintained his post here for many days, ever since Natac had left him following the warrior's last visit. Familiar by scent, by sight, and by sound with every inch of the ground, the white dog patrolled tirelessly, seeking any sign of something out of the ordinary.

During this time, the elf Fallon had cared for the dog well, providing a spread of meats, bread, cheese, eggs, and milk with each Lighten. During the day Ulf generally rested, finding comfort in one of the shady grottoes or cool, stream-washed ravines that dotted the rough landscape around the great white house. Even then he slept just below the surface of consciousness, every chirping bird or rustle of wind bringing his head up, ears pricked and clear eyes open, searching. But it was at night that the dog went to work, constantly circling the hill, ensuring that nothing approached unnoticed. He moved quickly, endlessly roving around the elevation of rough, isolated ground.

He padded through a shallow stream and shook himself quickly on the far bank, then raised his nose and sniffed at the air. The wind was behind him, unfortunately, pushing his own scent into the stretch of hill he had yet to explore—and at the same time, carrying the spoor of any possible intruder away from him.

But this was inevitable, on every windy night—when he searched through a circular path, there was always going to be one part of the patrol where the breeze worked against him. Ulf didn't hesitate. Springing up the rocks flanking the stream's narrow ravine, he emerged on the brush-covered hillside and trotted along a low trail he had worn here over the last tenday. The cloaking branches formed a roof over his head, allowing the dog to move through a tunnel of vegetation. Even if he couldn't smell what lay in front of him, at least he knew he was invisible to observers who might be looking at the hillside from overhead.

Ulfgang moved steadily along the trail, panting slightly as he quickly covered a long uphill stretch. He broke from the brush near the top of a ridge and stopped on a shoulder of rock. From here he could look down to the lakeshore, follow the course of two adjacent ravines, and look all the way up the slope to where Miradel's torchlit house beckoned so brightly in the night.

He heard a sudden sound that immediately caused him to stop panting, to lift up his ears and listen intently. Something scuffled across smooth stone, and then he heard a thud, as of a heavy body falling. The sounds came from above, from a source either at or very near the villa. He sniffed, mentally cursing the wind that still continued to blow from behind him, and then leaped upward. Ulfgang ran as fast as he could, streaking toward the top of the hill, racing along the crest of the ridge in long, bounding strides.

The white body was a ghostly shape in the night, slashing quickly toward the grand stairway below the villa.

At last he could smell the wrong smells, proof that danger was abroad in this dark night. His nose brought to him traces of metal and sweat, the acrid smell of unwashed dwarves. Shapes moved on that stairway, and Ulf wondered if he should shout a warning. But he was so close now—instead, he opted to charge in silence, to maximize the confusion his sudden arrival would have on the intruders.

Racing up the stairs, he smelled the ferrous stench of fresh blood, a great deal of blood to judge from the intensity of the odor. Atop the steps he almost groaned audibly at the sight of a crumpled form lying motionless on the flagstones, pouring lifeblood in a crimson-black flowage down the smooth white stairs.

"Fallon!" he whispered, gently nudging the faithful servant with his nose. The elf's eyes were open wide, but they saw nothing, and no faint breath rasped through a throat that had been cruelly sliced.

Ulfgang heard a heavy blow, a splintering of wood in the villa, and he raced across the plaza toward the shadowy alcove leading into the house. He saw an eyeless dwarf there, suppressed the instinctive growl that tried to rumble from his chest. Racing toward the enemy, he leapt.

But he did not see the second dwarf, the Delver crouching against the wall of the house. Nor did Ulfgang see the blunt-ended club of metal that whistled toward the sound of his approach.

His skull met the weapon with full force, and the white dog smashed into the ground. Once again metal struck downward, and Ulfgang knew nothing more.

They came from the darkness, moving in almost perfect silence. Still, the aged druid continued to listen to their approach. She had been admiring the sprouting plants in her small spice garden when she heard Fallon's gasp of alarm, and then the shocking, gurgling sound of air bubbling through his slashed throat. Instantly knowing her faithful assistant was dead, Miradel had forced herself to put off her grieving, to think, to make a plan so that she might not meet the same fate.

But she was so *old*. It was work just to lift her arms, to weave her fingers through remembered patterns of magic. She heard the splintering of her door, a violent sound of crude power and arrogant destruction. The intruders were in the garden, pounding at the front entrance. How could she resist?

She moved toward the garden, following the connecting corridor behind the kitchen. Some remembered sense of power drove her motions, guided her crooked digits through the incantation. Hoping to conceal her location until the last minute, she whispered the words of power under her breath, virtually silent.

Even so, she sensed the intruders halt in their surreptitious movement, knew they were locating her by the faint noise of her breathy speech. But she had reached the garden, saw her objective glimmering in the starlight. She didn't hesitate—instead, she spoke with growing force, tightened her hands into fists, pulled the threads of magic together until, in another instant, the spell was done. Advancing into the garden, she brought the power with her.

Immediately a roar like the pounding of a waterfall thundered from the basin in the midst of the garden. A figure rose there, a foaming, gray-limbed creature of liquid power. Water compacted into solid form, dropping one wave-tipped foot onto the ground, then another. The being rose far above the frail druid's head, with two arms of ice-like silver and a face capped by white, frothy hair, marked by a whirlpool mouth and eyes as black as the limitless depths of the Worldsea. Looming like a mountain before her, the watery guardian turned toward the front door.

A moment later Miradel saw small, dark figures rushing around the garden. She backed away, conscious of her frail legs, the tenuous balance of her retreat. The intruders were fanning out to come at her from both sides, wicked metallic warriors with helmets covering their entire faces. Immediately, she knew these were the deadly Unmirrored Dwarves.

The water-creature lashed out, a clublike fist crushing a Delver to the floor, shattering the metal helmet and the skull beneath with a deadly hammer blow. More dwarves attacked, and the great foot kicked brutally, denting metal and crushing flesh and bone. She heard groans, sensed the fear as her attackers shrank back, hesitating.

"Go—drive them back!" Miradel ordered, her voice strong and commanding. The water creature took a step toward the door, and another, reaching to smash another dwarf to the floor.

But then sparks flashed through the darkness, stuttering and trailing to the floor. In the sudden brightness Miradel saw a stout female dwarf, her grotesque face revealed by a partially open helmet, raise a metal club. Red nostrils flared on this Delver, and magic pulsed through her arms and into the coppery shaft. The end of the weapon touched the water-creature, and abruptly the room flared into fiery brilliance. The guardian threw back its head, gurgling a sound of unmistakable pain. A second later, the being dissipated, cold water sloshing chaotically across the floor, running over limp Delvers, splashing past Miradel's feet.

Quickly, she backed into the main room of the villa. Next she drew on deeper magic, igniting a tuft of tinder by snapping her fingers. Immediately every candle in the house burst into bright flame, and a crackling fire rose from the logs in the hearth. With another whispered word, she pulled the blazing logs out of the fireplace by the power of her magic. Trailing sparks and embers, they rolled into the Delvers, sent several of the invaders shrieking from the villa. Others flailed and thrashed at the flames running hungrily up their leggings.

Falling back to her kitchen, the druid snatched up a knife and slashed, but somehow the nearest dwarf sensed her intentions and dodged out of the way, the blade deflecting off his steel helmet. Others were drawn to the clatter, hands outstretched, wielding cruel hooks that the dwarves hacked into Miradel's clothes, her hair, even her skin. With a gasp of pain the druid was pulled off her feet. She grunted, trying to scramble away even as she fell to the floor. For a moment she lay stunned, fearing that a brittle bone had broken, watching as two dwarves advanced with a net of black silk. They raised the lattice of thin cord, ready to throw it over her.

From somewhere she found the strength and speed to rise, leaning to the side as the Delvers cast the net. It swept past Miradel and she lashed out, slicing threads, then driving her blade into the neck of the closest dwarf. With a mortal hiss the creature whipped around, slashing with a curved dagger even as his life sluiced from a ripped artery.

But that dwarven blade, wielded in a dying frenzy, found its way between frail ribs. Miradel gasped as her heart was pierced, as strong arms seized her. She kicked, but there was little speed or strength in her struggles. Before she thought to scream, her blood spilled in a circle across the floor, her mind grew dull, and she died.

Natac turned with a start, his eyes narrowing as he stared across the dark, still swath of lake. The lights of Miradel's villa were barely visible in the distance, twinkling on the hilltop, flaring with routine brilliance. Yet it seemed to him as though some shadow darkened the fires, masked the vitality of that distant place.

"What is it?" Karkald asked in alarm, joining the army commander at the parapet of the defensive tower.

"She's sad about something . . . I can feel it," he said. *I wish I was there with you.* He lingered over the private thought, knowing it was a luxury he could not afford.

Shaking his head, he tried to return his attention to the command problem facing them: what to do about the increasingly rambunctious goblins. He knew that the problem was real, that the unruly recruits in their great regiments were running wild in sections of Circle at Center, rendering many neighborhoods uninhabitable by the elves who had once lived there.

"We could break up the regiment into companies," Owen suggested. The Viking, who had been commanding the goblins for more than twenty years, was as frustrated as Natac himself with his unruly charges. "I can tan the hides of those that still get out of line, and Hiyram can keep tabs on some of the others."

Natac shook his head. "I want to avoid that if at all possible. We have, what, four thousand or more of them? That makes them our biggest single force, and if we need them in the fight, I'd like to use them together."

"I would, too," Owen agreed, relief written across his bearded visage. "So let's keep 'em in camp, and I'll *still* find some hides to tan!"

"Good . . . for now, anyway." Natac tried to move on, to think about the next problem facing his large army. But despite his best intentions, the warrior found that he couldn't concentrate. Over and over his mind wandered across the water, to the white villa on the lakeside hill.

"I tell you—it's our best chance. You have to let me try!" Darann hissed, her face darkening as she made the effort to keep her voice down. She confronted her husband in the plain barracks room that had been their living quarters for more than two decades.

"Are you mad?" roared Karkald, uncaring of the elves

who lived in neighboring rooms and were undoubtedly shocked by his outburst. "You'd be killed—or worse!" His rage was fueled by stark, raw fear, emotions howling through his veins.

"But listen to me! I might be able to distract him—"

"I forbid it! I utterly, absolutely forbid you from acting on this craziness—in fact, you are not even to *think* about it!" He struggled to regain his breath, to lower his voice. "Why—you're talking about the most powerful, unpredictable kind of magic there is! And you'd put yourself in terrible danger!" It was all so logical, such an obvious decision. Surely she could see that?

When his wife didn't answer, Karkald grunted in acknowledgment, sorry that he had shouted so loudly. And he made the mistake of thinking that her silence indicated that she had accepted his mandate.

16

The Marching Acres

*Fear is a capricious weapon
effective only as a credible threat.
When no such threat exists
terror and dread are fruitless,
as transient,
as wind on wave.*

From *The Ballad of the First Warrior*
Detan Columbine

Everything was a dim, gray haze . . . a haze punctuated by pain, agony that speared through his skull, stabbed his mind with relentless, fiery force . . . until again the murk would rise, granting him the only relief from his constant hurting.

Sometime later he smelled blood, and came awake with a start. Once again that pain rushed through every nerve end, but he forced his head up, off the hard stone floor. Drawing a breath, he felt more pain searing through his ribs, but he fought against it, pushed himself through a slow, awkward roll onto his belly. Still he held his head up, though his vision was blurry and his head still pounded.

With an effort, he thumped his tail against the ground once, and again. And then he knew he was whole. Grunting from the agony, he pushed his shoulders up until he was sitting. His head throbbed with an agonizing cadence of pain, and one ear was crusted with dried blood, but stiffly, slowly, he forced himself to stand. Sunlight flooded the garden, the villa, the landscape. The blood he smelled came from very nearby, where Fallon's corpse lay stiff and drained, with a dried, brownish swath extending in a ghastly spill down the stairs from the elf's body.

Shaking his head, seeing and smelling better with each passing second, Ulf started into the big house. And then he froze.

Miradel lay on the floor in a pool of her own blood, a smear of darkening crimson across her belly staining her gown. Nearby was the corner of a black silk net, apparently sliced with ragged force from its parent. Whimpering unconsciously, Ulf slowly approached the motionless figure. He lowered his head, sniffed hopefully, knowing that those hopes were futile. The druid was utterly, irrevocably dead.

The stench of Delvers was everywhere, so he had no doubts as to who had killed her. Growling almost inaudibly, he padded back onto the patio and blinked in the bright sunlight. The lake was an azure blanket below, cut by the thin white line of the causeway.

Ulfgang knew that Natac needed to be told about Miradel, and that road was his only route back to Circle at Center. Taking several deep breaths, then lapping up a good drink of water from the druid's garden pool, the dog ignored the pounding in his head as he started down the hill.

Kerriastyn cowered before her master. Zystyl could sense her fear, reveled in it as his rage flexed through his nostrils like an odor, touching the cringing female, stroking her senses like the disingenuous kiss of a hungry vampire. She stood on her feet, but leaned forward abjectly, with her face turned up to him in mute acceptance of whatever justice he would deliver.

You failed me. The phrase was a whip, used against her thoughts, striking with a lash that drew a moan of agony from her silver-plated jaws. She dropped her face, unable to meet his punishment directly.

You disappointed me.

Again he struck her with the power of his mind, and again he thrilled to the sound of her pain as she took a step backward. Kerriastyn was crying now, a pathetic murmur of sound that echoed through the tunnel in dolorous solitude. Doubtless there were Delvers who could hear, but they remained utterly silent lest the weight of their general's displeasure should fall upon them.

You have cost me a precious opportunity.

His final rebuke whipped through her being, dropped her to her knees, sent her writhing across the floor. He observed her convulsions with keen pleasure—the sounds of her pain, the raw stink of uncontained terror, the keen awareness of her utter subjugation, all bathed his senses in sublime ecstasy. She expected to die—he could sense her anticipation of his judgment—but it gave him cold pleasure to defer his retribution.

"But it is my decision that you shall live, shall continue to serve." He began to speak aloud, letting his mercy be known to all witnesses within earshot. "For even with your failure, the elven city will fall, and a world of treasures will become mine."

The white dog crouched at the top of a hill, looking at the scene spread along the muddy lakeshore. The mouth of the Metal Tunnel yawned at the base of the opposite elevation. The Hour of Darken approached, so the shadowed entryway teemed with Delvers, hundreds of the Blind Ones milling like ants, waiting for full darkness to release them to raid. Ulf knew that Zystyl's warriors had created a city for themselves, a virtual hive of sunless caverns, dens, and warrens, within the massive subterranean passageway.

Closer by, the ruins of the Blue Swan Inn lay scattered across the shore, a monument of charred stone walls, blackened timbers, and soot-covered ground that the invaders had left undisturbed, in full view of Circle at Center. Ulfgang noticed again how even now, twenty-five years after the destruction, not so much as a blade of grass had sprouted from the blackened and bloodstained ground. To the right and left of the ruins, however, the Crusaders had erected massive, log-walled barracks buildings. Muddy streams flowed from valleys denuded of timber, while companies of Sir Christopher's warriors gathered, marching along the lakeshore and out of the hills to converge here, at the place that now held Ulfgang's considerable interest.

It's like . . . a floating island, he realized, studying the massive expanse of solid ground filling the place that had once been the harbor of the Blue Swan. But it was ground made out of wood and metal, he finally saw, and it had many gridded openings where he could see the water sloshing just below the deck.

Surrounded by sheets of metal armor and several tall, wooden walls, with a surface as broad as a hundred palatial courtyards, the great raft completely filled the harbor that had once served as an anchorage for the Blue Swan Inn. Thousands of Crusaders and Delvers were assembling on the massive deck, and they didn't yet come close to taking up all the space. Ulf saw columns of giants and goblins, companies of centaurs, huge regiments numbering a thousand elves apiece, all march down the ramps leading to the flat surface. Still more of these troops were assembled on the shore, waiting for their turns to board.

Beyond, even more of the enemy troops were in the camp—and only past these, past tens of thousands of deadly enemies, Ulf could see the causeway, his route to the city, starting across the lake. As the Hour of Darken closed around him, he saw the Delvers start to file out of the cavern. Soon the column would form a barrier across the road, blocking his retreat.

Drawing a deep breath. Ulfgang rose and started to trot down the hill. He stopped to sniff a pile of fresh horse dung, took a long detour to urinate on the only tree trunk on this part of the slope. Taking great care to appear nonchalant, he started past a company of goblins, keeping a wary eye on the hungry-looking warriors. When one of them tossed a spear, the dog sprinted away, ears trailing from the wind of his speed.

Trotting around a group of bored giants, he finally saw the paved roadway of the Metal Highway. The wide avenue started across the lake on its raised causeway, a straight line leading to Circle at Center. Ulf flopped to the ground, tongue drooping lazily, as a rank of elves marched past. When they were gone, he rose and slowly padded forward, crossing in front of the advancing column of Delvers while the Blind Ones were still some distance away.

Now he was near the lakeshore. A pair of centaurs paced back and forth at the terminus of the causeway. Each was armed with a stout cudgel, and their attention was directed mainly along the road extending into the lake, where they remained alert for any sortie from the city.

Ulf trotted down to the shore and lapped up some water. At the same time, he watched the reflections of the centaurs, saw that one glanced at him, then turned his attention back to the road. Still wandering slowly, the dog paced along the shore, up onto the road. Nose down, he padded past the nearest centaur, as if he had no purpose before him other than the next exciting sniff.

"Hey!" The growl came from the second centaur. "Stop that dog."

Instantly Ulf flew into a wild sprint, belly low, feet pounding the pavement in urgent, rhythmic strides down the straight road. He heard one centaur thundering in pursuit, heavy hooves clattering on the pavement, but by then the streaking Ulfgang was two dozen paces ahead. Without looking back, he stretched further, running faster than a strong wind. The guard kept up the chase for a half mile, but by then the dog was far along the causeway.

And even when he wasn't pursued, his legs reached, stretched, hurled him along the pavement. His lungs strained for breath, and his long tongue dangled, flopping loosely as he streaked above the water toward the sparkling city. Halfway across the lake he passed a company of giants, the first line of the city's defense. They made no move to stop him, and Ulf did not slow down. Lights, coolfyre beacons, blinked into life along the upcoming shore as night thickened. Even as the pain of exhaustion rose through his chest and throat he held his speed, swerving around the elven guards that moved to intercept him as he darted onto the island.

Racing across the Mercury Terrace, he ignored the protestations and surprised stares of the few elves who were out at this dark hour. Now his claws clicked along the paving stones of the Avenue of Metal. Ulfgang knew that he could find Natac at his headquarters building, formerly a gallery of iron across from the College. It was still a long run from here, but the road was straight and wide.

A minute later Ulfgang came over a low rise to find that the entire street was blocked by a riotous crowd. He smelled the bittersweet stink of goblins, heard their whoops and shouts as they danced on the pavement and quaffed great mugs of stale-smelling beer. Partners whirled each other in a frenzy, sending drunken goblins careening into each other, provoking insults, kicks, and punches.

"Hoo—hoo! A doggie!" cried one wild-eyed fellow, reaching out as if to smear Ulfgang's nose with a slobbery kiss. White jaws snapped, and the goblin lurched backward, howling and pressing hands to his bleeding lip.

"You lot!" The bellow was Owen's voice, roaring above

the din. Ulf couldn't see the Viking, but as the crowd grew suddenly quiet he sensed that the human warrior had waded into the celebration. Goblins yelped in dismay, and several abruptly flew through the air, tossed by blows of Owen's hamlike fists. "Stop this commotion right now! Or I'll have yer heads on pikes over the lakefront wall!"

"What for you make ruckus?" demanded another voice, and Ulfgang saw Hiyram swagger through his fellow goblins, jabbing his finger at a chest here, meeting a belligerent eye there. "We's gotta fight Delverdwarfs—not you too each other!"

Sheepishly, the carousing goblins shuffled from the street, filing into the large manors that had been given them as barracks. But by then Ulf was already moving, pushing through the goblins until he caught up to Owen and Hiyram.

"I've got to get to Natac!" He barked frantically, trying to get the goblin's attention.

"We'll take you to'm—I'm wantin' to tell about this mess, anyway," Hiyram said disgustedly. He looked as though he wanted to take off after the retreating goblins, but Owen, at least, seemed to sense the dog's urgency. Moving at a trot, they started up the Avenue of Metal.

Natac tried to deny the truth of the message, but deep in his heart he felt the reality of Miradel's loss. He listened in dull horror to Ulfgang's dispassionate report. For a long time the warrior couldn't seem to speak, couldn't make his mouth shape the words he wanted, needed to say.

"*Why?*" he croaked, finally. "Why kill her?"

"I think they wanted to capture her, really," suggested the white dog. "I saw a piece of net there. And water, and marks of fire. It seems she put up a fight."

"And she will be avenged," Natac said, though the phrase, the very intention, seemed a hollow mockery.

"We'll start by figuring out how to face this raft, this 'floating island' that you spotted."

He looked around the table in his headquarters chamber. Natac's subordinate captains watched him warily. Deltan and Galewn, the giants representative of Nayve's Senate, were there. That pair were responsible for the two forces who had held the causeway against every attack over the last twenty-five years. Karkald, too, was present, as were Tamarwind and Roland Boatwright. Owen and Fionn stood on the other side of the table, Owen with Hiyram and the Irishman with Nistel. They were gathered in a room of metal, with an iron floor and vaulted ceiling of bronze. At the door stood a guard, a giant armed with a massive, hook-bladed halberd and wearing a cap of shiny steel.

The general was acutely conscious of the meeting that had been in progress prior to Ulf's arrival. It had been a routine affair, a report from the garrison on the Metal Causeway, the awareness that the enemy's heavy galleys had stayed off the lake since the ships had been destroyed by Karkald's seaborne batteries.

The training of the gnomes and goblins was proceeding slowly, and Natac fervently hoped that he could continue to spare both big regiments the shock of mortal combat. For years they had been part of the army, of course, but they had been spared many of the ravages suffered by the giants and elves. He admitted to a quiet affection for the diligent gnomes, typically pudgy, bespectacled, and squinting, yet so earnestly intent on becoming warriors, on redeeming the disgrace of their flight during the Battle of the Blue Swan. But in truth they weren't warriors, and Natac had done everything he could to keep them out of harm's way.

And the goblins, too, he found strangely likable. Rude and disorganized to the core, they still possessed the exuberance of healthy, fast-growing children—even if they should have decided to grow up long ago. Still, he couldn't bear the thought of putting them into battle, any more than he could have accepted sending his own ten- or twelve-year-old sons into a mortal fight.

So instead, the defense of Circle at Center had fallen to the elves and the giants. So far they had done an effective job, but Natac admitted private concern at the reports of this great raft. How would it be used? And if it came toward the city, how could they hope to stop it?

"The caravels will sortie at the first sign of this raft," he said, indicating the map spread out before them. "We can't let them get on the flank or rear of the causeway. We have to assume it's got a wooden structure, and if it's wood it can be burned."

As the others nodded in agreement at his sage pronouncement, Natac felt a stab of guilt. He could only hope that he was right.

"What in the Seven Circles is that?" growled Raw-knuckle Barefist. He held a great axe against his chest, caressing the smooth handle, taking comfort in the keen steel blade that Karkald had given him twenty years before. The giant squinted across the lake, staring at movement he perceived through the mists of the Lighten Hour. Around him, the forty others of his company, hulking and bearded warriors to a man, stirred from their rest, a few picking up their weapons to join their chieftain.

Theirs was a lonely outpost, a wide spot on the middle of the causeway amid the generally placid waters of the lake. The small island boasted flat ground, a few trees, and benches and shelters for travelers' rests. The smooth causeway departed from the islet in two directions, in the direction of metal toward the lakeshore, and in the opposite bearing toward the city, and the Center of Everything. In that direction the company of Deltan Columbine's archers was rousing itself, cooking fires ignited and lookouts joining the giants in staring across the lake.

Now, just past Lighten, mist shrouded the water in gauzy curtains, visibility closed in enough that the giant chieftain knew he couldn't be looking at the far shore. And yet something solid stretched across his view, more suggested than substantial in the vaporous air—but far, far closer than any land should be.

"Looks like the lakeshore is moving," suggested his comrade Broadnose, with a noisy snuffle. He went back to the haunch of mutton that served as his breakfast.

"Well, I know what it *looks* like," snapped Rawknuckle. "I want to know what it *is*!"

A great wall seemed to emerge from the mist, pushing through the water so slowly that it raised barely a ripple on the smooth surface. Far to the right the barrier seemed to curve away, and it was there that he caught a hint of a wake—long, rolling ripples coursing across the still water, confirming that the vast shape was in fact moving closer.

"It's gotta be that raft we was warned about. Give a rise on the horn," Rawknuckle decided. Young Crookknee, the bugler, hefted the instrument and placed his lips against the mouthpiece. Once, twice, and again he boomed long, lowing notes. The sound resonated across the water, many seconds later echoing back from the heights of Circle at Center.

"'Eh, chief. They're coming the same old way, as well," muttered Broadnose, lifting his bearded chin to point down the causeway in the direction of the enemy camp.

"No centaurs in front, this time," said Rawknuckle regretfully. "I guess we'll have to save the pikes for later." He was disappointed. The last time this position had been attacked, the Crusaders had come at them with a rushing mob of centaurs. The giants had blocked the causeway with a bristling array of long-hafted spears, and dozens of centaurs had spilled blood and guts when they collided with the immobile line. The attack had been brutally shattered, without a giant suffering a serious wound, so in practicality Rawknuckle knew that the enemy tactic was unlikely to be repeated. Instead, it would be cast upon the growing pile of ideas that had been discarded by one side as the other found an effective countermeasure.

This time, the front rank of the attackers was a line of giants. Each bore a large wooden shield, and a club, hammer, or axe. By advancing in shoulder-to-shoulder formation with shields held high, they left little target for the elven archers who were forming to back up the giants.

"Where do you want us?" asked Deltan Columbine. The famed archer and poet stood ready with two hundred of his deadly bowmen. In past engagements they had formed on the city side of the little islet, shooting over Rawknuckle's company to shower the attackers forced to concentrate on the causeway.

"I don't like the look of that," Rawknuckle declared, indicating the massive raft. "Why don't you give us some room to fall back—say a few hundred yards? We could use your covering fire if that big thing floats in on our flank. And it's just possible we'll have to get out of here in a hurry."

"You got it, Chief," Deltan agreed. He crossed to his men and started them filing onto the causeway toward the city, while the giant turned around and watched nervously as the raft, and the rank of Crusaders on the causeway, moved steadily closer.

Natac and Karkald stood atop one of the towers flanking the end of the causeway. From here they could get only a vague sense of the true vastness of the raft.

"They must have taken the breakwater out of the harbor," the warrior observed. "Just pushed the damned thing right into the lake!"

"Are we ready for a two-pronged attack?" Karkald asked, looking along the miles of exposed shoreline on the city's fringe.

Natac frowned. There were elven companies placed throughout the city, and a small, mobile force of Gallupper's centaurs and the few dozen elven riders who had mastered the art of horsemanship. But these forces were spread thin, and the only sizable reserves he had were the huge regiments of goblins and gnomes. These were deployed to either side of the base of the causeway, with the goblins on the Mercury Terrace and the gnomes on the other side of the road. If the raft could not be stopped, those untested troops would have to bear the brunt of the first attack.

"The caravels are ready," the general observed, gestured to the ships that sat, sails limp, in the protected anchorage beside the terrace. "Best send them out, now."

The signaler, a young elfwoman who had trained herself to anticipate her commander's orders, quickly pulled out a blue banner scored with lines of white to represent billowing sails. With a crisp command of magic she sent the standard fluttering aloft, where it attached itself to the top of the flagstaff and streamed outward.

The reaction in the harbor below was instantaneous. Immediately the druids in the stern of each caravel started their casting, and wind puffed into the limp sails. Slowly, but with steadily increasing speed, the little ships scuttled past the breakwater and turned onto the lake. They made a brave display as they deployed into line abreast, steel batteries gleaming from the prows of no less than half of the dozen ships.

"But I still don't like the size of that thing," Natac confided, as the racing ships, even spreading into a wide fan, did not make as wide a formation as the flat prow of the great raft.

"And trouble on the road, too," remarked Karkald. The enemy phalanx of giants attacking down the causeway had almost advanced to Rawknuckle's islet, and that massive raft—apparently propelled by hundreds of polers in the stern—had nearly reached as far into the lake. The metal and wooden walls protecting the floating platform were clearly visible, while the fore and both flanking faces bristled with weapons.

"They're going to get around behind Rawknuckle," Natac said. He shouted to one of his signalmen. "Run up the green flag—I want the giants to withdraw!"

The banner swiftly soared up the long shaft, supplanting the sailing orders to the caravels, streaming into the gentle breeze. But when he looked down the causeway, Natac wondered if they weren't already too late.

From the main battle tower he could see the whole causeway of the Metal Highway, as well as the great stretches of lake to either side of the smooth, wide road. Rawknuckle Barefist's company of giants were forming an orderly line on their islet in the middle of the causeway.

A cloud of dust billowed into the air, marking a swath along the Avenue of Wood.

"Here comes that centaur again," Karkald noted with a frown. "Maybe we'd be better off just to let him charge and be done with it."

Natac shook his head, though he shared his comrade's frustration. Gallupper came into view as he and his company cantered across a wide market. The young centaur led a band of perhaps fifty hoofed, thundering chargers. Half the number were centaurs, disowned youngsters of the Blacktail, Craterhoof, and other clans, while the rest were elves mounted on horseback. Natac had to admire the speed of the racing advance, even as he recognized its futility in the tangled streets and buildings of the city. "Sometime we'll find a use for them . . . until then, we'll just have to keep talking to him."

"Can we charge yet?" hailed the young centaur, shading

his eyes with his hand as he looked up from the base of the tower.

"Not yet! Just wait there a minute," barked Karkald. He turned to Natac. "I've been working on another invention, a little device I'm about ready to try—I'd like to give it to the young fella. It's something that could use a speedy wielder."

"Give it a try," Natac said, immediately curious. Still, Karkald, as always, tended toward secrecy while his inventions were being developed—he very much relished revealing them with a flourish. So the warrior turned his attention to the enemy's progress while the dwarf went down and spoke with the centaurs for some time.

Rawknuckle roared a challenge, allowing the by-now familiar joy of battle to suffuse his body and inflame his temper. He and his giants straddled the road, retreating slowly against the press of their kinfolk who had been corrupted by the Crusader knight. With a flexing of corded sinew, he brought his axe through a vicious overhand swing, cleanly splitting the wooden shield of the nearest attacker. The deadly blade continued unabated, cleaving the enemy giant from chin to belly. As the dying Crusader tumbled into the steaming heap of his own guts, Rawknuckle was already striking a different target, wielding the axe in great back and forth swipes that felled another attacker and halted the rest in a respectful arc around the huge chieftain.

Tremendous noise surrounded him, the cries of grievously wounded giants, the crushing blows of steel and stone against wood and metal—and, sometimes, flesh and bone. Giants pressed back and forth, limbs tangling, brutal blows landing against both sides. A heavy body fell against Rawknuckle, and as he pushed it away he recognized Broadnose. His companion grasped at his shoulder, mouth working soundlessly, until a gush of blood gurgled forth, smearing the chieftain's side as the dying giant sprawled onto the road.

His sturdy legs planted like tree trunks, Rawknuckle sliced at the attackers with renewed fury, grimly exacting vengeance for his slain friend. The steel axe carved into a thick neck, nearly decapitating one attacker, then swept back to take the arm off another. But even in the press of his deadly blows he was forced back, sensing the weight of the massive column of attackers as an inexorable tide. Comrades to either side fell or retreated, and Rawknuckle was forced to go along—else he would have quickly been surrounded and cut down.

Even so, he stepped back slowly, begrudging each bloody, precious pace. Gore spilled from his axe, and many a bold Crusader quailed from the slash of his deadly weapon. Others of the attackers, those in the rear ranks, howled and cursed as arrows showered onto them. Shields were raised, and many of the steel-tipped shafts thunked harmlessly into the wooden barriers. But more fell through the gaps to strike deep into shoulders, thighs, necks, and chests.

The shower of arrows grew thicker, and now many of the missiles were falling among Rawknuckle's own company. He trusted the aim of Deltan's elves, but with a quick look to the side he saw that the great raft was creeping slowly past his position. Another volley of arrows darkened the sky, scattering indiscriminately among both the attackers and the defenders, as Crusader archers sprayed the causeway with their dangerous missiles.

The big warrior cursed as he plucked a missile from his hamstring, then snorted in disgust as another pricked his cheek, nearly taking his eye. Beside him Forestcap, a rugged specimen who had joined the company at its inception twenty-five years before, howled in rage as a volley of deadly barbs rendered his arms and shoulders into an approximation of a porcupine. Rawknuckle offered his old comrade a brawny arm and aided him limping backward, crossing the islet as the Crusaders rushed forward.

"The green flag is up—Natac is calling us back!" shouted a giant. The chieftain took the time to glance toward the city, ensuring that his comrade's eyes were not being deceived, and he, too, saw the signal to retreat.

Bellowing for the rest of his giants to follow, seeing that Deltan's company was already hastening toward Circle at Center, Rawknuckle Barefist led his bloodied company in a hasty withdrawal along the causeway.

Darann went to Belynda's chambers and was surprised to find that the outer door was closed and locked. Still, the dwarfwoman knocked without hesitation. She was startled when, without perceptible sound, the portal glided open to reveal an empty antechamber.

"Come in, Darann." Belynda's voice flowed from the main room, and the dwarf followed the sound down the short hallway. She found the sage-ambassador and another elf she recognized by her silver robe as a sage-enchantress. There was a third chair, currently empty, beside them.

"This is Quilene," Belynda said. "She is the greatest of our enchantresses."

"And you'll help us?" Darann asked, taking the elf-woman's hand.

"I will," Quilene replied.

"We were expecting you," said Belynda, gesturing to the extra chair.

"But how did you know I was coming tonight?" asked Darann as she joined them.

"Because we share your purpose . . . and we all sense that time is growing short," the sage-ambassador said, looking directly into the dwarfwoman's eyes. Darann felt as though she were laid naked, bared even beyond her skin. She settled into her seat with a sense of warmth and belonging, a lightening of the lowering cloud that had been hanging over her.

"So tell me," she began, relieved enough to speak bluntly. "How are we going to save Circle at Center?"

"The battles that rage with such endless repetition are fruitless," Quilene began. "At best they are short-term exercises in courage that, perhaps, will win us a little more time. At worst, they are a waste of lives—the lives of bold defenders, and the lives of misguided attackers who, all unwitting, have become the tools of evil. And no matter how many of those attackers are killed, they are only nettlesome pinpricks, tiny blows against the body of a beast that must be killed by a strike to that brain."

"And that brain is in two parts—Sir Christopher, and Zystyl," Darann said grimly.

"Two parts linked by a single soul. I don't know if either of you realize it," Quilene said, "but the real key to the enemy's destruction lies in the Stone of Command."

17

Heartblood in the Center

*Violence spreads
a stain across the world.
Mayhem's surge,
and grieving holds
for no border.*

From *Tales of the Time Before*
from the First Tapestry

"There's the blue flag—make sail!" cried Tamarwind, who had been watching Natac's command post as the mist-shrouded Lighten began to grow into full daylight.

Within seconds wind gusted into the sails of each caravel. Tam felt the deck shift slightly underfoot as the vessel quickly, smoothly gained speed. Juliay whirled her spoons, her brow furrowed in concentration. Her skill was proved again as the *Swallow*, by a nose, pulled out in the lead of her sister ships.

The other eleven caravels raced to either side, white wakes frothing back from the narrow prows. Tamarwind stood next to the battery, peering across the lake at the vast expanse of the enemy raft. He tilted his head back, spotted his lookout perched high in the rigging.

"What can you see?" the elf shouted.

"They're falling back on the causeway—that raft must have a thousand archers on it!"

"Let's burn 'em out of there!" retorted Tamarwind with a fierce grin. He turned and hollered along the line of ships. "We're taking the war to them!"

Druids worked at their posts below the after masts of each of the caravels. Elven sailors worked their lines, climbed into the rigging with bows and arrows, or lined the gunwales with weapons drawn while the humans continued their magical casting, windspoons stirring the wooden bowls, local gusts of air filling out the sails, propelling the nimble ships across the lake.

All around Tamarwind sails strained as the twelve valiant caravels surged toward the battle. A smaller hull streaked just to starboard, and Tam grinned at Roland, seeing that the steel-prowed *Osprey* accompanied the fleet. "Just stay out of the way!" the elf shouted cheerfully.

Roland waved back with a quick gesture of his wooden spoon, then returned his full attention to sailing. Unlike the captains of the larger caravels—who employed a helmsman at the wheel in addition to the wind-caster—the druid ship-builder raised his wind with one hand, whirling the spoon through the bowl with swift precision, while he held the tiller of the sailboat clenched in the fist of the other. Even so, the nimble *Osprey* bobbed and glided amid the larger craft, keeping pace with no difficulty.

For the first time, Tam turned his attention to their enemy. He felt a momentary puzzlement as he looked across the lake, for he had been told the raft was quite big and yet he could see no sign of their enemy—there was just a stretch of shoreline before him. And then he realized that the shore was *moving*.

"It's huge!" breathed a crewman, coming to the same realization.

"Let's trim it down to size, then," Tamarwind declared, suppressing his own misgivings. In truth, he had to wonder how much damage they could inflict on the massive raft. He felt like one of a few mosquitoes who had been sent to sting an elephant to death.

Nevertheless, each ship, with wind filling the sails and a white wake frothing from the hull, turned toward the attack. Tamarwind's *Swallow* soared in the lead as the whole fleet swept in from the direction of metal.

"Fire the batteries—now!" cried the elven commander, his order underscored by the trumpeter's blare.

Springs snapped and the ships lurched from the force of the launch. Sunlight glinted on orbs of steel as all the caravel batteries lobbed their shot toward the enemy. Most of the globes clattered onto the raft, and Tam immediately saw columns of smoke churning into the air. At least a dozen fires sprang into life across the deck and the elven captain felt a simultaneous flaring of his own hopes. If they could destroy that raft, sink it into the lake, they would annihilate a great portion of the enemy forces. Could it be that the knight had given them this opportunity?

But as quickly as his hopes ignited they were doused, like the splashing waves that spilled through great slots in the deck of the raft. Here and there Delvers and Crusaders shrieked and died, burned by the caustic flare of Karkald's missiles. But the flames that might have ignited the deck quickly fizzled away. Some of the crewmen took up buckets or manned huge, bellows-driven pumps, directing sprays of water on every budding conflagration and thoroughly dousing the larger fires. Other Crusaders flocked to the gunwales of the raft. Volleys of arrows darkened the sky, the missiles tearing into the sails, thunking into the decks and hulls of the valiant caravels, here and there piercing elven crewmen.

Tamarwind remained undaunted. He signaled his helmsman to make a hard turn to port, and braced himself as the deck heeled and the caravel carved a tight arc into the water's surface. Following his lead, the other captains mirrored the *Swallow*'s maneuver, sweeping in unison away from the huge raft. Meanwhile, the elven gunners worked hard to crank back the springs and load another salvo of ammunition, readying the batteries for another shot.

A few minutes later the caravels wheeled around again, reversing course to once more close rapidly with the enemy platform. Tam was encouraged to see plumes of smoke rising from the raft, a series of smoldering fires apparently burning behind a wall of iron encircling the central portion of the vast deck. Perhaps the first volley had done some lasting damage after all. The little fleet of sailing ships pressed in, ready to launch another salvo of blazing missiles, while splashes rose before the caravels as giants hurled great rocks. The range was great, even for the iron-thewed giants, and nearly all of the boulders fell short. Tamarwind saw two caravels lurch as a sail or mast came down, and both of these turned from the attack, limping away from the menacing platform.

"Fire!" called Tamarwind, and once more the trumpet echoed his command. The *Swallow* lurched again as the great spring compressed, flinging the load of shot up and out, sending the incendiary globes bouncing across the deck of the raft. A great volley of silver spheres rained onto the raft, the balls slicing through tightly packed Crusaders along the rail. Flames erupted here and there, and some of the enemy warriors, engulfed by fire, hurled themselves into the lake. But the slain and injured warriors were merely pushed overboard by the press of their comrades advancing to take their places.

Again volleys of enemy arrows arced outward, stuttering along the caravel decks, tearing through the sails with soft rips. The caravels veered again, beginning their turn. More boulders flew through the air, but these too splashed well short of the speeding attackers, and Tamarwind allowed his hopes to flare.

But then the wall of iron on the enemy raft fell flat, and

Tam saw that he had led his ships into a trap. Smoke flared into orange flames as a hundred catapults snapped forward, and balls of oily fire soared into the sky, tumbling in lazy parabolas toward the elven fleet.

Sir Christopher stood atop the tower that had been erected on the raft's foredeck. From here he could see across the teeming surface of the platform, had watched the caravels wheel gracefully into a line abreast, and had seen his ambush work to utter perfection.

The caravels had raced close, and then went into a turn across the broadside of the massive raft, unaware of the imminent and lethal barrage. The catapults were a total surprise, launching a volley when the enemy was in easy range. The knight cheered as many of the catapult loads spattered into the water among the elven ships to form bobbing, burning slicks of oil-soaked wreckage. Black smoke blotted the air, swirling crazily as it was caught in the gusts of the druid-spawned wind.

A few of the missiles struck with even greater effect. Christopher shouted a hurrah as a white sail caught a fire-ball and quickly erupted into flames. At the same time, rivers of fire trickled down the mast, and immediately the planks of the main deck began to burn. Another caravel wheeled out of line, flames streaking the port gunwale, engulfing the helmsman and half the crew within an inferno. And at the far end of the elven line, fire crackled in the prow of a wildly steering caravel. White flames suddenly shot skyward, and Crusaders cheered at the knowledge that one of the hated batteries was now turned upon its owner. More explosions rocked the hapless vessel, blasting away the mast, tearing at the planks of the hull. Within a few heartbeats, the ship was gone, the grave marked by a smear of crackling flame and hissing steam boiling upward from the surface.

"Give it back to the heathens!" Christopher shouted, delighting in the results of the lethal ambush. Already his elves and goblins were hastening to pull the great baskets backward, to ready the next load of flaming doom.

"Hurry, bold Crusaders!" shouted the knight, voice shrill. His hand went to the Stone of Command and he clenched it. "Make haste, and smite the enemy again!"

With a frenzy the last of the baskets was loaded, crewmen diving to get out of the paths of the coiled weapons.

"We're ready, lord!" shouted his elven gunners' chief.

The knight looked down, watching with satisfaction as the caravels reeled through the smoking chaos on the water. The catapults were fully revealed now, the wall that had once concealed them having dropped to lie flat on the deck. And even the undamaged caravels were still in easy range, veering and swerving on the water now marred with a hundred crackling, oily blazes. Christopher knew the time had come for the killing strike.

"Let fly!" he cried, and one hundred supple weapons snapped forward. Bundles of oily rags soared through the air, trailing smoke and fire, plunging toward the wooden hulls of the slender elven ships.

"Fire!" cried a crewman, flinging himself to the rail as the *Swallow* swerved past a flaming swath of floating debris. Tamarwind got a quick glimpse of broken staves, greasy rags, and oil burning into a column of thick, black smoke. Thankfully the caravel slipped past without damage—though they clearly remained in grave danger, as another series of smoking fireballs burst upward from the stunning array of catapults.

"Another volley!" Tam shouted. "Get out of range!"

But he saw that it was too late for at least half the fleet. He watched in horror as caravel after caravel caught fire, sometimes losing masts and sails, with all too often decks and hulls succumbing immediately after.

"They got the *Robin*—and the *Goshawk* is burning too!"

Tamarwind tried to follow the reports of his lookouts, tried to think, to decide what to do. The surviving caravels were curling around to port and starboard, frantically maneuvering to avoid the rain of smoldering missiles. Another volley smudged the sky, and still another elven ship was suddenly immersed in fire.

"Come about—fall back!" Tam shouted in anguish, knowing that to run away was to yield the lake to the invaders.

But what else could he do?

Only four of the caravels were sailing away from the raft, these ships—including the *Swallow*—having suffered only minimal damage. Of the other eight, two were already gone—destroyed by the explosive combustion of their battery ammunition. Tamarwind watched, horrified, as a third—the beleaguered *Goshawk*—abruptly vanished in a thunderous explosion of white fire and roiling smoke.

Five more of the valiant ships struggled to make headway, often with only a jib or stern sail. Broken masts were cut away and tattered sails tried to corral the slippery wind. The crews seemed to be bringing the fires under control, and now at least the surviving ships were safely out of range of the lethal catapults. Two of the caravels, apparently the *Robin* and the *Cardinal*, were still burning savagely, and it was clear that they would never make it back to port.

"Pull up!" Tamarwind shouted to Juliay and his helmsman. "Let's get over there and see if we can take off survivors." The other captains apparently had the same thought, for the caravels were slowing, gathering together like frightened sheep.

But the next piece of bad news suddenly became apparent, as the last of the Crusaders' galleys came into view,

moving out from behind the great raft, oars driving it steadily toward the elven ships. In that lofty, metal-jacketed
prow Tamarwind saw utter disaster. The caravels were
bunched together, half of them dismasted or lofting only
tattered ashes of sails. The *Swallow* was the only elven
vessel with a battery, and it was badly out of position, too
far away to shoot without endangering allied ships.

A streak of white moved across the lake, coming terribly
fast from the shores near Circle at Center. Sails bulged, and
the ship raced like a soaring bird, skimming over the surface of the water.

"It's the *Osprey*!" The shout came from his lookout, and
Tamarwind watched with a sense of sick horror. What was
Roland Boatwright trying to do? His ship skipped across
the lake with stupendous speed, surely traveling faster than
any craft could sail. The druid was visible as a distant figure
standing in the helm. There were no other sailors in sight,
and Tam understood intuitively that Roland had sent his
crew off the ship.

The course was set, the speed fantastic, as the little sailboat—with its sharp metal prow—angled toward the hull
of the massive galley. The wind in the distance was a moaning howl, and whitecaps lashed the lake around the *Osprey*,
swelling the sails with powerful pressure. The captain of
the galley obviously recognized the danger, as the big ship
started a slow turn, wheeling in an attempt to meet the
audacious attack head-on. But the galley was too slow,
barely starting to swerve as the *Osprey*, like some deadly
missile, raced into the inevitable collision.

The impact against the hull of the galley was a thunderous crunch, accompanied by a flash of fire and an explosive
concussion. Timbers flew, and the *Osprey* vanished in the
instant of destruction. A moment later the galley, fatally
holed, was settling into the water, sinking quickly by the
bow.

• • •

By the time Karkald climbed to the top of the tower the sun was receding. He found Natac staring expressionlessly across the lake, where smoke still smudged the water. The dwarf's first reaction was that the raft was horribly close, already through the patch of lake where so many elven ships had died. The surviving caravels were limping back to port, several of the damaged ships being towed by their full-masted comrades.

"I've given Gallupper a few instructions," Karkald said. "I don't want to use him unless we have to, but this new invention might work."

"I'll leave that to you, then," Natac said. The dwarf was surprised—he had expected the army commander to make some inquiry, probe a bit to find out about the new device. Instead, the human warrior stared into the growing darkness.

"How many died out there?" Natac asked after a moment's silence. "Roland, for certain . . . and brave captains, and young sailors . . . sons and daughters. And still they come. Are we doomed, like Mexico?"

Karkald cleared his throat. He knew the tale of the conquest—Natac frequently used it as a lesson for all of his lieutenants. But he couldn't think of an encouraging reply.

"Or like my Yellow Hummingbird . . . is there no point to any of this?" the warrior continued. Karkald didn't understand the question, but he wasn't going to ask for an explanation.

As darkness thickened, the two veterans looked at each other. "The war still comes, closer every minute," Natac noted.

"And we're drawing close to the Delver Hour," Karkald said grimly.

"Are you ready?" the human asked.

"Almost," Karkald replied. "I'm going to go up the street

and talk to Darann for a moment—make sure she's safe, let her know what's happening. I'll be back here before those bastards touch ground."

The great raft moved with stately, implacable force. Zystyl felt the progress with his feet, and with every other sense, just as he could feel the full darkness of Nayve's night. The lightless air was a cool embrace, wonderfully soothing against his skin. He rode near the center of the flat surface, under a metal roof that protected him from the rays of the sun, and from the flaming missiles that the city's defenders hurled with such vexing persistence. Awnings had covered the Delvers during the day, but now these had been taken down as, with the Hour of Darken past, the Unmirrored were ready to go into battle.

Zystyl tried to get a sense for the location of the enemy ships, the causeway, and the city, but in the chaos of battle noise it was too confusing to try and determine ranges by sounds. And any echo he cast would have been instantly swallowed in the clamor.

"How far to the shore?" demanded the Delver of a nearby giant.

"Five hundred paces."

"And the causeway?"

"The same distance to the side, Lord Blind One."

Zystyl stiffened, hearing the insolence in this Crusader's tone. Yet this was not the time for a confrontation.

"Make ready to attack. I will have this city ablaze before Lighten."

Rawknuckle plucked another arrow from his shoulder and bellowed in anger as he snapped the missile like a twig and tossed the pieces into the lake. The shower of arrows from the raft had pelted his company the whole grueling march back to the city. Every one of the giants was bleeding from dozens of wounds, and several had been blinded, or had collapsed from loss of blood.

The Crusader giants were pursuing them steadily, but seemed content to hold back a few dozen paces, just far enough to ensure that they didn't fall into the scatter range of the massive volleys launched from the raft.

The elven archers had already made it back to the city, Rawknuckle was relieved to see. The surviving giants broke into a lumbering run, hurrying along the causeway toward the welcoming shelter of the two great towers erected on the island's shore. Many elves had fallen, and their bodies remained on the causeway, but the gruesome obstacles didn't slow the retreating giants.

And then the giant chieftain stumbled to a halt, staring down at the road in shock. A body lay before him, face down. It was one of many elves who had perished on this retreat, but this one was marked by a broken harp jutting upward from his pack. Slowly, reluctantly, Rawknuckle turned the body over.

It was Deltan Columbine. The archer and poet lay on the road, pierced by a dozen arrows. His blood formed a circle around him, a great pool of drained life that seemed too red, too rich, to have flowed from this lifeless form.

18

Fulcrum

Seven circles;
balanced,
poised,
and centered.

Tilting pivot,
center misaligns,
and seven worlds fall.

From the *Tablets of Inception*

"Where's Darann?" Karkald pushed his way through the rank of gnomes, shouting his question, roughly shoving several of the rotund warriors aside. Ignoring their howls of protest, he made his way to Fionn, grabbing the Irishman by his arm and pulling him roughly around. "Have you seen Darann?"

"Your wife?" Fionn scowled, and gestured to the raft gliding inexorably closer, the armored prow separated from the shore by a steadily narrowing gap of water. "Shouldn't you be thinkin' about them, right now?"

Karkald turned around in anguish, then looked down at the note in his hand.

*I'm sorry—if I fail, you will not see me again.
But if I succeed, our lives have hope of a new, bright
future.*

He had found the paper in their apartment, when he had
gone there earlier in the day. She could not have been expecting him, would have left the message thinking that he
wouldn't discover it at least until after the imminent battle.

Now she was gone, but *where*? And she spoke of success
or failure, but he didn't even know what task she had un-
dertaken. How could she influence the future, change the
course of history? She was only one person—his wife, of
course, but she was not even a warrior.

His eyes turned to the lake, which he could clearly see
across the plaza. The raft was surging closer—in minutes
the fight would reach the very shores of the city. He imagined the teeming ranks of Unmirrored and Crusaders, their
twin captains of evil. Karkald had seen the Knight Templar
in battle, knew his fearsome powers of command. Furthermore, he vividly remembered Zystyl, with terrifying memories of the two instances where he had come so close to
capturing Darann.

And with that memory he understood what his wife was
trying to do. By the Goddess, she had suggested the thing
to him a few days before! Instead of listening, he had re-
buked her, forbidden her to discuss it, only to have her
ignore him.

Pretty much as he had ignored her, he realized. He stared
at the raft, knew that Zystyl was there, that somehow Darann was going to try to reach him, attack him. Of course
she would fail—the villainous Delver was too well protected, both by his allies and by the power of his own arcane senses. Her courage awed him, even as the futility and
waste of her actions infuriated him.

Again he was aware of movement around him. Trumpets
blared and signals dipped. Several elven companies filed

out of side streets and courtyards, forming lines of spears across the routes from the waterfront. A small unit of giants, many of them bandaged and limping, took up arms at the very fringe of the Mercury Terrace, which looked to be in the center of the raft's landing frontage. Great gaps in the line yawned to the right and left of the giants, extending along the shore toward the causeway, and opening across much of the terrace.

Around Karkald the gnomes whispered nervously, pulling together into a knot of bristling beards and wide-eyed stares. "We'll be ready for 'em, you bet!" Nistel declared cheerfully, his voice cracking on the last word.

Then, even more amazing, the dwarf saw the command flag dip, knew immediately what Natac had ordered. Fionn and Nistel recognized the signal at the same time. The human uttered a whoop, while Blinker raised his voice to shout orders to his fellow warriors.

And the Gnome Regiment started forward.

Natac trotted across the Mercury Terrace, a hundred paces back from the lakeshore. He was making his way from unit to unit, checking readiness for the battle, knowing there was little time left. The raft surged closer with an almost animal eagerness, pushing ripples of water out of the way, forcing wavelets against the rocky shore. The front of the craft was a wooden wall high enough to conceal any Delvers behind it, as well as most of the Crusaders except for the giants. Some of those hulking warriors hurled boulders at the plaza, sending big stones clattering through the Nayvians who stood ready to meet the attack. But those companies bore the bombardment stoically, and even the skittish gnomes avoided panic when a rock tore through the tight ranks and scattered the diminutive warriors like tenpins. Druids tended those who were injured, while other gnomes hastened to fill the gap left in the line.

A howling sound rose along the waterfront, and abruptly lake water surged against the raft, splashing and foaming, driven by a sudden and unnatural wind. Dozens of druids stood amid the defenders, and in unison they called upon their power to raise a small gale. The raft staggered to a halt as larger and larger waves churned against the blunt prow, rising in cascades of spray to wash over the troops huddled behind the walls.

At the same time black clouds roiled overhead, gathering in the center of the defensive position. Natac could see Cillia, mistress of druids, handmaiden to the Goddess Worldweaver herself, holding a wooden staff over her head and chanting sounds of deep magic. The dark mass of cloud churned and billowed upon her command, and suddenly tongues of orange fire blasted from the tenebrous belly of the stratus, gouging and crackling along the face of the raft.

Natac halted in his tracks, watching awestruck as lightning bolts exploded, one after the other, against the face of the raft. Each time the druid gestured with her staff another blast erupted from the cloud, smashing against the wall and tearing away great chunks of the wooden barrier, forcing the huge craft, by inches, away from the shore. Bolts of lethal energy sizzled into the packed troops, burning and searing, killing in great swaths. But still the raft pushed, rising and surging with that almost sentient eagerness to reach land. For a long interval the two forces battled, with countless attackers charred and blasted by lightning, great pieces of the raft exploding away or burning furiously. The warrior allowed himself to hope that magic alone might hold the enemy at bay.

But no human could sustain such an outpouring of strength, and finally Cillia lowered her arms, dropped the staff from numb fingers. She swayed weakly and was caught by a nearby giant before she fell to the ground.

And in the absence of the lightning strikes, the raft surged forward with renewed speed. Despite the gusting winds, the craft floated into the shallows, the blunt prow crushing through the marshy fringe of shore, shuddering slightly as the massive transport was firmly grounded. Volleys of arrows, launched by unseen archers in the center of the raft, showered the defenders. The wooden wall at the front of the attackers' vessel—except where it had been blasted away by lightning—suddenly toppled forward, dropping into the shallow water to form a ramp leading from the deck of the raft to the shoreline of Circle at Center. Immediately, roars and shouts emerged from thousands of throats, and the Crusaders and Delvers rushed into the attack.

The enemy giants were the first to charge ashore, followed immediately by swarms of Crusader elves, and then the masses of goblins, centaurs, and Unmirrored Dwarves who spilled into the attack. Howling madly, smashing weapons against their shields to increase the level of the din, the whole army surged toward the Nayvian defense. Giants strode through the shallows, knocking aside brave elves who tried to stand at the water's edge.

"Bring your left up!" Natac shouted to Hiyram, who tried to yelp orders to thousands of goblins organized into three long ranks.

On the other end of the line Owen roared his commands. Hundreds of goblin voices yodeled agreement, though an equal number of the flop-eared warriors looked askance at each other, and at the swarm of attackers.

"Stand here!" cried Natac, waving his sword and turning his back to the approaching enemy. He tried to meet the goblins' eyes, to force them to acknowledge his presence and his authority. He was somewhat surprised to see the big regiment stabilize, fists clutching weapons, faces marked now by determined snarls.

The Nayvian warriors formed a line at the shore, but there were too few of them to stem the tide. Natac rushed to help, charging into a gap and standing alone with his steel sword flashing back and forth in the direction of suddenly hesitant giants. One of the huge Crusaders swung a big club, but the human ducked under the blow and then stabbed upward, piercing his enemy's guts with the razor of steel. But moments later he saw that the giants had ruptured the defensive line in several places. Centaurs raced through the gaps, charging toward the companies of brave elves who tried to resist.

A quick glance showed that the Gnome Regiment was in place, a rank of the short warriors forming a solid wall of shields, bristling with big knives. As the attackers rushed forward the gnomes stood firm, meeting the weight of the heavier enemy troops with sturdy stances and a rank packed so tightly it proved to be all but immobile. As the elves and goblins reeled back, a few giants tried to create a breach, and Natac watched in astonishment as each of the brawny warriors toppled like felled trees, hulking bodies vanishing into the melee.

A look in the other direction, however, showed him that more and more of the goblins were backing away. One turned on his heel, big ears flapping as he started to sprint away.

"You there—Ratlock!"

Owen's voice cut through the fight and froze the cowardly warrior in his tracks. "Stay there—be a man, not a worm!" demanded the Viking. He strode along the rank, glaring at the scruffy, pot-bellied troops. One after another the quailing goblins started to swell, to swagger, and make ready for battle.

"All goblins—dress your lines!" Again the Viking shouted, striding back and forth before the line, his back to the enemy. The warriors hastened to obey, apparently more frightened of their captain than of the teeming enemy.

And moments later, when the rush of Crusaders spilled past the gnomes and smashed up against the goblin wall, that regiment, too, stood firm.

The Tlaxcalan raised his sword and led a contingent of elves forward. He slashed to the right, cutting a giant's hamstring, then plunged forward to disembowel a rearing centaur. Beside him Tamarwind Trak thrust with his own steel, dropping a goblin by piercing his heart. Everywhere fighters cut and slashed, banged, bled, and died, and across the whole breadth of the plaza the Nayvian defenders held firm and the attackers milled about in a packed mass of confusion.

More lightning crackled, a bolt of brightness that slashed across the front. Blinking his eyes against the residual glare, Natac saw that Cillia had again unleashed her elemental magic, this time scoring a bloody swath through no less than a hundred Crusaders. But as quickly as she cast the spell, she fell back and was again carried off by her assisting giant. Natac could only imagine the debilitating effect of this explosive enchantment, knew that they would have to win the battle with courage, sinew, and blood.

A band of fanatical enemy elves hurled themselves at the juncture between the gnome and goblin regiments. Owen stepped in to hold the breach, his great war hammer smashing back and forth, driving back the Crusaders in a tangle of broken limbs and bruised flesh. Natac cheered the human warrior, awed at the display of skill—until a spear snaked out from the elves to bury itself in the Viking's brawny chest.

By the time Natac reached the scene, Owen lay in a pool of bloody gore and Fionn stood over his body, sobbing like a baby. Around the Irishman lay a scattering of Crusader corpses—obviously Fionn had already avenged his friend.

Gasping for breath, the Tlaxcalan looked for another enemy, an elf or a giant, any of Sir Christopher's lackeys upon whom to exact his own vengeance.

But gradually he noticed that there was a strange respite to the battle. The Crusaders were not pressing the attack along the line, instead drawing back to regroup, tighten their ranks, regard the defenders from a short distance away.

And they were waiting.

You must break through in the center—be the tip of the blade, and slice into our enemy's flesh!

Zystyl's groping thoughts found Kerriastyn, entered her mind in the midst of the fray, and now he sent her his command.

Master, I shall.

His own senses absorbed the violent urges of a thousand dwarves, felt the will of his lieutenant as she summoned the Delvers to her side. Zystyl remained safely in the rear, vicariously relishing the sensations of battle. The Blind Ones formed a tight wedge, as the companies of their allies fell away to either side. The enemy was a hot image of blood and the promise of glory, a sensation etched in the awareness of every one of the Unmirrored.

In moments a phalanx of steel had formed around Kerriastyn, and Zystyl felt its weight, its power in his own mind. Tightly packed, with shields and weapons ready, they waited for the command.

Go. Kill. Win.

He felt the rush of anticipation as Kerriastyn commenced the advance, sensing that she drove into the joint between the goblins and gnomes. Beyond, straight as an arrow piercing directly into the city's guts, the Avenue of Wood offered easy access to the Center of Everything.

For a moment, Natac thought that the lull indicated a real halt to the enemy onslaught. He momentarily considered ordering a sudden counterattack, but quickly saw that his troops were too fatigued, too shocked and frightened and plainly exhausted, to make more than a token effort.

Better to let them breathe, drink water, recover spirit and morale while they pondered the knowledge that they had checked the enemy's most vigorous attack ever.

Yet even before this fact could sink in, Natac saw the Delvers gathering in the center of the enemy rank. Great dark files of armored dwarves moved through the night, gathering in a mass directly before him. They formed with precision and discipline so that within a few minutes a huge rank of sturdy fighters faced the center of the Nayvian line. As if in response to some unspoken command, they started forward, black breastplates and blank face masks arrayed in a wall of steel. Each Delver carried two knives, and these blades were extended forward, whirling back and forth in rhythmic cycles. Natac was forced to admire the way that the dwarves in the middle advanced, outer ranks joining in until the formation marched like a great spearhead, a triangle with the tip pointed directly between the gnomes and goblins.

Where Natac stood. He took comfort from knowing that Fionn stood at his left and Tamarwind at his right. Nistel and Hiyram shouted encouragement to their troops, and Natac was further heartened as those great formations stood firm in the face of the deliberate, measured attack.

Some innate sense of discipline guided the blind fighters toward the defenders, and rank after rank of savage, armored dwarves rushed forward. Their weapons whirled like scythes, and they came at the Nayvians like a deadly and purposeful killing machine.

Natac knocked away the blades of a pair of eyeless dwarves, slicing through their metal shirts with the point of his own deadly sword. Daggers slashed toward him and he knocked them away, cutting into hands and arms, hacking and stabbing with a quickness that he'd never guessed he possessed. One after another of the Unmirrored fell, bodies lying in a heap around his feet. He heard gnomes and goblins shrieking, crying out in pain and fear—but then he was aware of others, led by Hiyram and Nistel, who raced to take the places of those who fled or fell.

But there were too few weapons, and too few warriors with the skill and courage to wield them. More and more tightly packed Delvers pushed ahead, driving their wedge inexorably deeper into the slowly widening gap.

Fionn and another group of elves attacked from the left, but there the blind dwarves formed an impenetrable front. Clashing weapons echoed from all sides, while cries of glee and terror mingled in a rising cacophony.

"Flee, or die here!"

"We're doomed!"

The shouts of panic rose from more and more of the horrified Nayvians. Goblins and gnomes began edging backward, and Natac sensed the line behind him wavering. His sword trickled blood onto the street, but he couldn't take the time to wipe the weapon clean. Instead he lifted the blade and chopped again into the mass of attackers, feeling the keen steel slice through metal and flesh.

And then he saw something different. In the midst of the Delver phalanx was a being of grotesque aspect, a face of red, pulpy flesh framed by steel jaws, sharpened teeth, and a helmet that dropped down to conceal a forehead and eyeless brow. A swelling breastplate suggested that this thing was female, and the slender metal rod in her hand looked like a lethal weapon. Sparks trailed from that rod, and she lashed back and forth with a ritualistic frenzy—a frenzy Natac could see translate directly into the passion of the warriors immediately surrounding this arcane leader.

The Tlaxcalan charged, propelled by a single, desperate idea. He hacked to the right and left, grateful as Fionn and Tamarwind rushed beside him, guarding his flanks. The steel blade cut down a Delver immediately in front of the dwarven female, and then he lunged at her, sword thrusting for a killing stab.

But somehow sensing his attack, she parried with the

metal rod. The two weapons met in a loud, sparking clash. Natac gasped as searing pain shot through his weapon hand, and he quickly darted back, ducking away from her savage swipe. She swung past his face, a gesture powerful and quick, but wild.

In that attack she left herself open, and Natac slashed again, driving the edge of his sword into the pulpy flesh of her flaring nostrils. The Delver shrieked and tumbled backward, and the human followed up with a lethal thrust, twisting the weapon in his hand until he saw the convincing proof of black blood gurgling upward, spreading across the horrible face, the dark armor, and the paving stones in a growing sheen.

Zystyl reeled backward, gasping for breath, staggering to retain his balance on ground that seemed to tilt crazily beneath him. But it was not the ground that shifted—it was his own reality.

Kerriastyn was dead—he himself had felt the pain of the slicing blade, had choked on the blood that seemed to well in his throat, filling his lungs and darkening his senses. Finally he dropped to his knees, ignoring the concerned murmurs of the elves—cursed Seers!—who stood near his command post.

How could she have fallen? What fighters had the capability, the audacity, to break a Delver phalanx? Human, he knew, had sensed in Kerriastyn's last thoughts, final sensations.

Even more surprising was the sense of loss twisting and growing within him. Kerriastyn had been merely a tool, a useful and attractive tool, but nothing more. She had served him well, but that was no more and no less than he deserved. The fact that she had given her life in that service was only appropriate, since it now seemed clear that she had been incapable of attaining immediate victory—the only other outcome Zystyl would have accepted.

Still, she had been precious to him in her own way, and now she was gone. The Delver arcane vowed, very solemnly, that she would be avenged.

19

Cold as Fire

*Frantic thoughts
of a night in pain
storm through my mind.*

*I have to hurt someone,
and I wish
it could be you.*

Creed of the Hunted

"We will build a palace here," Sir Christopher said, sweeping his hands around the broad, flat expanse of the Mercury Terrace. At his side was Darryn Forgemaster, though the blacksmith seemed to take little note of the knight's expansive gesture. The Nayvian night still loomed dark and starlit above them, and the sounds of battle marked skirmishing a half mile or more away.

"I tell you this," Christopher went on, turning to address the smith, "because you will be doing much of the work. Our troops are well-armed now, and the war is nearly concluded. With our ultimate victory I will raise an edifice that will be a monument to God!"

"You need carpenters and stonemasons, then—not a blacksmith," retorted Darryn.

But the knight was not paying attention. Instead, his eyes

narrowed as he watched his ally approach from the darkness. Zystyl, accompanied by a dozen of his faceless Delvers, strode up to Christopher with that disquieting directness, confirming for the knight that the blind dwarf knew exactly where the human was standing. The knight put his hand upon his chest, feeling the comforting Stone of Command under his tunic. He let the power of his talisman infuse him, renewing and readying him for the meeting with his horrible partner.

"We need to erect shelters, awnings across this terrace, before the Lighten," declared Zystyl. "A pavilion that will protect my warriors from the murderous sun. We can use the tarpaulins from the raft."

"Of course, yes," Christopher said irritably. "But beyond that, we need to create something lofty, permanent, glorious. Your troops are skilled with stone, are they not?"

The dwarf nodded, sniffing with those grotesque nostrils as if he sought the spoor of the knight's thoughts. Christopher shuddered, squeezed the stone more tightly, and tried to keep the revulsion out of his voice.

"And our goblins work well with wood. I shall assign a thousand of them to the building task. The blacksmith shall make himself available as he may be needed."

"Don't you think we should complete the conquest, first?" snapped Zystyl. "And perhaps there will be a better place for your palace—in the Center of Everything, I suggest."

"That land is blasphemed by the presence of the demon's loom," retorted the knight. "No, this shall be the place. When that foul temple is destroyed, I intend to salt the grounds and make the land around it a waste."

"Very well." The dwarf shrugged. "But before we move on with your plans, let's get some shade up. My troops can use a day of rest—so tomorrow night we shall take the rest of the city."

• • •

The captains of Natac's army met their general on the Avenue of Metal, a hundred paces from the place where it emerged from the Mercury Terrace. The Nayvians had withdrawn to the edges of the great plaza, but thus far the attackers hadn't broken into any of the city streets.

"How are we holding?" Natac asked. He addressed his question to Fionn. "You first."

"We've got gnomes and the rest of the goblins dug in on Marble Hill," the Irishman reported. "The only way they're comin' over the top is when the last of us has died."

Natac looked into his fellow warrior's eyes and knew he was being truthful. At the same time, both men were aware that the suggested eventuality was a real possibility. So many were already gone . . . Miradel, Owen, Deltan Columbine, Roland . . . the names could roll on and on. How many more would fall before they were done?

Tamarwind spoke next. "I've found enough elves to block off the Avenue of Metal and the surrounding streets. We've garrisoned the walls and fortified the roofs of the Hall of Granite and the Gallery of Crimson—they're big, stone buildings rising to either side of the road. The Crusaders and Delvers might push through on the avenue, but we'll make it pretty bloody for them. We've got arrows and stones, even oil-bombs, ready to throw down from above."

"Good."

"And I've got a little surprise for the bastards," Karkald announced. "Gallupper and his centaurs have it now—they can make a good mobile reserve."

"Now can you tell us what the new invention is?" Natac pressed.

The dwarf nodded smugly. "It's a mobile battery—three guns, on wheels, that can be pulled around by centaurs or horses. They're smaller even than the batteries on the caravels, of course, but they can still toss some nasty fireballs into the enemy ranks. And the centaurs have had a little practice now—they seem pretty good at lining them up, aiming, and reloading."

"Let's get them into place in the rear, then," Natac said. He looked at the sky, which remained fully dark, many hours away from Lighten. "I have a feeling that our respite is just about over."

Three women—two of them elves, their companion a dwarf—sat in the darkened chamber, their faces illuminated only by the pearly light of Belynda's scrying orb. The image in the glass globe was faint, a poor source of light, but even so, the sage-ambassador and the others could follow each movement, study the people and locations thus revealed.

Sir Christopher stood at the center of the image. His hand was held at his throat, and Belynda sensed that he clutched the Stone of Command there, while his eyes followed the form of the hideous dwarf, the one called Zystyl. So intent was her hatred of the knight that, for a time, Belynda had paid little attention to the dwarf. Instead she watched Sir Christopher, saw the outline of the great rooms he would make his headquarters, scrutinized his mannerisms and his defenses as he stalked from one part of the plaza to the next.

Much of the stronghold was formed from buildings already existing at the edge of the plaza, including the two towers at the end of the causeway, and several great warehouses and gathering halls that had housed numerous elven functions during the last centuries. Outside, great tarps were being pulled across the spaces between the buildings, awnings that would create shade by the time of Lighten. Darann had reminded them that the Delvers, all except the few who had the bright, mirrored armor such as worn by Zystyl, would have to spend the day sheltered from the rays of the sun.

Sage-enchantress Quilene touched the globe, and in response to her magic the image pulled back, until the figures were small, even antlike, and the view encompassed the whole of what would be the invaders' makeshift palace.

"By Lighten, that whole enclosure will be packed with the Blind Ones," Darann noted. "I reckon that we have perhaps three hours to go."

"Do you know where you want to arrive?" Quilene inquired.

"There," Belynda said, indicating a small alcove where a basin held a steadily dripping birdbath. Once part of a small garden, it had become an enclosed room as the awning was pulled overhead. "With luck we won't be noticed, and will be able to move into position to . . ." She couldn't quite finish the statement, wasn't ready to articulate the fact that she fully intended to kill a man before the Lighten Hour.

The enchantress didn't have any such hesitation. "Remember, whether or not the knight lives or dies, you *must* get the Stone of Command from him. That is the only way to break the thrall in which he holds his Crusaders."

"I know," Belynda replied.

"Now is the time," Quilene said. "If you are ready."

"I am," Belynda declared. She touched her waist, where she had a long, slender dagger concealed beneath her golden robe. The weapon was in a protective sheath, but she had already practiced, knew that she could draw it in an eye blink.

"Me, too," Darann, who was similarly armed, added.

"Then come to the other table, and place your fingers in the bowl of water. I will begin the spell."

Belynda thought that the water was pleasantly warm. She remembered the last time she had traveled by teleportation, and tried to prepare herself for the sudden disorientation as

Quilene took up position and began to weave the words and gestures of her spell. Darann put her own fingers in the water, and met the eyes of her elven companion.

And then the magic crackled into life.

"Wait!" Ulfgang barked, rearing to scratch at the door to Belynda's chambers. He yipped in agitation, and dropped to all fours again, shaking his head. His fur stood on end, and he could sense the aura of powerful magic—the same sensation that had lifted him from his slumber in the garden.

The white dog paced through a tight circle, then reared to paw at the door again. To his utter astonishment, it opened.

He recognized the sage-enchantress Quilene as he rushed past her to look anxiously around the main chamber. His claws skidded on the marble floor as he raced from room to room, finally coming back to Quilene, who still stood placidly by the door.

"It's too late . . . they've gone," she said gently.

Ulf sat with a heavy sigh, shaking his head. "She's crazy . . . she'll be killed," he moaned, his words twanging into a sorrowful whine.

"Perhaps," Quirene admitted. "But she's brave enough to try."

Suddenly Ulf hopped to his feet. He saw that the door was slightly ajar, and he pushed it wide with his nose. In a second he was outside, racing through the darkness. He could find Natac, or Tamarwind . . . perhaps they could help.

Or perhaps Belynda and Darann were already doomed.

The magic took Belynda's breath away. She staggered, gasping, as she felt a floor solidify under her feet. Her hands were in water, cooler than before, and vaguely she recognized the birdbath she had observed in her crystal. Darann, looking wide-eyed and a little queasy, clung to the opposite rim of the basin. Both of them held on for several moments, and at last Belynda's sensations returned to normal.

"Are you all right?" asked the dwarf, in a barely audible whisper.

Belynda nodded, then raised her eyebrows in similar query. Darann, too, nodded, though she scooped up some water from the basin and touched it to her forehead. They saw that, just as it had appeared in the globe, a canvas tarp was draped across the entrance to the alcove. They heard the sound of footsteps from beyond the screen, listened as those sounds slowly faded away.

Touching the dagger, reassuring herself that it was still resting at her waist, Belynda reached for the tarp to pull it out of the way. Before she could grip it, however, the canvas was torn down, and sturdy hands grasped her waist and legs. She kicked, and tried to twist away, but more arms went around her, pinching painfully.

Only then did she notice that there were many Delvers in the room—small figures cloaked in dark steel, reaching for her with groping hands. Darann was somewhere behind her, and Belynda had a sense of things gone terribly wrong as she saw the warriors close in from all sides.

Three seconds later Darann had disappeared, but Belynda squirmed futilely in the grip of the Unmirrored Dwarves.

"Why aren't they attacking?" Natac wondered aloud. Karkald and Tamarwind, flanking him on the hilltop overlooking the Mercury Terrace, had no answer.

"If they don't attack, can *I*?" Gallupper asked.

Natac shook his head. He had seen the batteries, the short, wheeled carriages that Gallupper and his small company had readied for battle, but he was determined to wait until the proper time to release what might prove to be a devastatingly effective weapon.

"No . . . for now, we'll wait, and see what happens."

And as the night moved into its final hours, the Nayvian warriors, the place that was the Center of Everything, and all of the Seven Circles waited, countless fates and futures in the balance.

Sir Christopher stalked into the chamber. His eyes narrowed as he recognized Belynda. "You—witch!" he hissed.

The elfwoman stared back at him, the full memory of his villainy flooding through her mind. She bit back her first instinct, which was to spit her hatred. Instead, she drew a breath, and forced her thoughts into order. A Delver held each of her arms, and their grip tightened as if the eyeless dwarves sensed her agitation. Zystyl was a few steps away—he had just taken her dagger, and was starting to question her as to her purpose and intentions.

Darryn Forgemaster came behind the knight, and his eyes widened in surprise as he spotted the elfwoman. He halted, flustered, looking at her, at the Delvers, at the knight who had become his master. For her part Belynda ignored the smith, forced herself against her revulsion to lean close to Sir Christopher.

"Be careful, my lover," she said in a barely audible whisper. "We do not want this blind oaf to learn too much about us."

Zystyl's head whipped around, the gaping red nostrils flaring in suspicion. "What does she say, warrior?" he demanded. "Do you seek to betray me?"

"Of course not," snapped the knight, irked.

"Caution!" whispered Belynda.

"I suspected you all along, traitor!" hissed the Delver arcane. "And now here is the proof!"

"Don't be a fool!" The knight shook his head in irritation, and Belynda saw that he did not yet perceive the extent of his danger.

The sage-ambassador looked at Darryn Forgemaster, saw the anguish, the guilt and suffering written across the man's face. He was looking into her eyes, searching for something—forgiveness, perhaps. Again she looked at the knight, but then her thoughts returned to the smith. Why did he feel such anguish? Was he not the rank traitor that everyone assumed—was there a different reason for his years of treachery, his steady labors in the name of Circle at Center's enemies? He had been a loyal druid, a favorite friend of Miradel's for centuries, and his work was known throughout Nayve.

With a flash she understood, and knew how to turn that knowledge to her own use.

"You had her killed, didn't you?" she said conspiratorially to Christopher.

"Had who killed, witch? Who?" demanded the knight.

"Miradel. You knew she was murdered in her villa a few nights ago, didn't you?" She saw instantly that one part of her guess was correct. Darryn staggered, face blanching, hate-filled eyes turned upon the knight. She was surprised, however, to see that the Knight Templar was equally shocked.

"No!" gasped Christopher. "She . . . she lives! She must!"

It was the Delver arcane who laughed. "The druid *is* dead . . . I would have made her my prisoner, but she fought too well. And so she died."

The knight was obviously stunned, trying to understand the implications of new developments. He stood before the sage-ambassador, glaring at her, then shifted his accusing stare to the arcane. Belynda gently twisted an arm, and the dwarf holding her on that side released his grip, apparently content to let his comrade restrain the prisoner. Still pinioned by the other limb, she reached out a hand and stroked her fingertips along Christopher's arm with just the tiniest rasp of sound.

"Proof!" repeated Zystyl, his voice rising hysterically. "You touch in my presence."

"It was the witch!" cried Christopher. He backed away, reaching under his shirt to pull out the white stone on its golden chain. He clutched it in his hand, eyes wild as he regarded his ally with growing fear.

"Do not think you can flee!" declared Zystyl. He uttered no other words or sounds that Belynda could tell, but several other Delvers advanced, apparently summoned by some unseen, unheard command.

"Halt!" cried Sir Christopher. "All of you dwarves—stay where you are!"

Surprisingly, the Blind Ones ceased their advance, several twisting in place as if their feet had been glued to the floor.

"You will stay here," Christopher shouted, clutching the stone with a white-knuckled grip. "Leave me in peace—"

A sudden, violent blow interrupted the knight as Darryn Forgemaster struck him from behind. Christopher twisted and fell, trying to strike back at the enraged blacksmith. The smith clawed at the knight, reaching for his throat, grunting inarticulately. The white stone, held by its chain, slipped from Christopher's fingers as he drew a dagger and drove the blade again and again into the chest of the smith.

A second later Darryn collapsed onto the floor, swaying weakly on his hands and knees as crimson lifeblood spurted from a wound in his breast. Sir Christopher, still wielding the bloody dagger, scrambled to his feet, stood over the man who had served him so well, raising the blade for a killing strike. The stone on its golden chain swung loosely against him, tangled in the strands of his beard, apparently forgotten.

But now the Delvers were moving, a half dozen of the blind dwarves rushing in, grabbing the knight by his legs and arms, dragging him down. In seconds the man's limbs were bound, and his fear-maddened attention had returned to the hideous dwarf who had once been his ally.

"I tell you—the witch is lying!" shrieked Sir Christopher, struggling vainly against Zystyl's bonds.

Darryn Forgemaster lay dead, his blood already congealing on the slick paving stones. His eyes were open, staring sightlessly, and the sage-ambassador wished she could close them, could bring the man, at long last, some peace. But she was still held by another Delver.

Belynda turned to look at Christopher, watching coldly. This was her moment, her triumph—and though it would be the last thing she saw in her life, she would bear witness to the death of this monstrous creature who had so unspeakably violated her.

Yet why, then, could she take no pleasure in the victory?

20

Seers in the Sun

What care has the ant
if his temple takes a hundred generations
to build?

And what matter to the tree
if her roots make home
in the rotted pulp of her forebears?

But to the mortal person
in midst of frantic life,
the desperate present
forms the purpose of eternity.

From the Tapestry of the Worldweaver
Lore of the Underworld

The sky over the Mercury Terrace was an angry red, fiery and full of smoke, unlike any sky Natac had ever seen on Nayve. He watched from the balcony of the old Iron Gallery, the building that had served as his headquarters. Tamarwind and Karkald were here with him, not talking for now, just watching the growing daylight illuminate the scene. Rawknuckle Barefist and Fionn had just departed, and Natac could see them making their way forward along the crowded street, moving among the waiting troops, encouraging and steadying by their very presence.

Around the lakeshore terrace teemed tens of thousands of Crusaders and Delvers, the latter gathering in the shadows below buildings and trees as the sun descended toward full Lighten. Vast, tentlike shelters had been raised, casting much of the terrace into protective shade for the blind dwarves. Below Natac's position he could see the massive blocks of his own warriors, gnomes and goblins waiting restively in the city's streets. After their valiant stand on the terrace he knew that, when the enemy attacked, the big regiments would again be ready to fight.

On the flanks of the gnomes and goblins waited the remnants of his elven and giant forces, while directly below Natac's balcony Gallupper and his small detachment of centaurs and horse-riders waited beside a trio of Karkald's newest weapon. The mobile batteries were each mounted on a carriage between a pair of large wheels. From above they looked like huge crosses, with steel springs coiled back and small magazines full of silver shot waiting for the release of the trigger.

"Natac!" The shout was barked from the street with unmistakable urgency, and the warrior looked down to see a white dog racing toward the building.

"Ulfgang—up here!" he called, and was immediately seized with a sense of terrible apprehension. He tried to shake off the feeling, suggesting that he was only remembering when Ulf had brought him the news of Miradel's death, but found that he was barely breathing as the dog leaped up the outer stairway, arriving on the high balcony after a half dozen long bounds.

Natac met him at the top of the stairs, kneeling. "What is it?" asked the man.

The dog's brown eyes met his, and he saw the sadness there, an emotion that grew to despair as Ulf lifted his head to look at Tamarwind and Karkald. "It's about Darann and Belynda," he said. "They've gone!"

Tamarwind gasped and Karkald grunted a bitter, inarticulate sound. "I knew it!" the dwarf exclaimed. "Did they . . . ?" He couldn't seem to finish the question.

Ulfgang nodded, clearly understanding. "They went by magic into the enemy camp. They will try and kill Zystyl and Sir Christopher, and steal away with the Stone of Command."

B elynda stared into the gaping, gory sockets that had once held Sir Christopher's eyes. There was no movement there, no indication of vitality save for the blood that still seeped slowly onto the floor. At last he was dead.

The killing had taken a very long time. Zystyl had been content to let his whole army stand idle for the rest of the night, while he took his vengeance on his former ally. After taking the Stone of Command from the terrified knight, the arcane had ordered his prisoner secured between two massive pillars. With obvious relish the Unmirrored Dwarf had proceeded to demonstrate the full scope of his fiendish skill. No minute source of pain, no excruciating technique for inflicting agony, had been bypassed in slowly, gradually bringing the human warrior to a quivering, pain-racked end.

The sage-ambassador, her hands now confined behind her by a length of supple chain, had watched it all. Seeing the knight bleed, listening to him scream, beg, whimper through the hours, finally observing the gory, eyeless mess that he became, she had felt strangely detached from the scene, the experience. She knew that this had been her goal, her purpose in life for the past twenty-five years, and yet now she was untouched by the fulfillment of that objective. Her enemy's agony had been like a living thing, some grotesque serpent writhing and dancing for her pleasure, a performance enacted with her as the only seeing member of the audience—and yet she could find no shred of satisfaction in the watching.

The sage-ambassador knew that it would be her turn next, and that knowledge was vaguely depressing, but not terrifying. She was too tired even for dread, too drained to grasp the horror she knew she should be feeling. For some reason she thought, instead, of Tamarwind, regretting the curt way she had sent him off the last time she had seen him. He deserved better, she knew, and she was sad that she hadn't realized it sooner. Ironically, that regret was the strongest emotion she felt right now.

Her thoughts returned to the present, and to her immediate future. It was true at last: Sir Christopher was dead. That was the thing she had wanted, the goal that had risen before her, more important than anything else. She had watched him die, and his passing had been as brutal as any being could have imagined. Why, then, didn't she feel something, *anything*, more than this ennui that so deadened her now? Surely horror, anger, frustration—*some* kind of powerful emotion—should be arising within her.

The room in the great pavilion was filled with Delvers, and she could see from the illumination in the halls beyond that Lighten had come, the sun descended to full brightness. The dwarves were restive, cramped and confined in here. Already the faceless helmets were turning toward her, with silent but ominous attention. Zystyl, meanwhile, stood over Christopher's mangled corpse, pacing a slow circle around the remains of his victim. The arcane was fondling the Stone of Command, swinging it from its golden chain, obviously assessing its power and capabilities.

Suddenly she heard a commotion, shouts of alarm and cries of warning. Trumpets blared outside the pavilion, a brassy, rising sound that was unlike anything Belynda had heard from either the Nayvian army or their enemies. Weapons clashed as fighting erupted in many places, with some of the violent engagements right outside the main hall.

"We're attacked! From the causeway!" Delvers shouted

the warning, scrambling to gather weapons, to garrison the doors of the pavilion. Instinctively, Zystyl seemed to seize control of the situation—the arcane didn't speak, but his flaring nostrils turned this way and that, his hands made curt gestures that were translated into actions by his rushing troops. Despite their blindness, the Unmirrored moved with discipline and precision, forming ranks across the numerous entrances to the makeshift shelter.

Only then did Belynda realize that the Delvers were turning their attention toward the lake, as if a new enemy approached from their rear. She recalled the sounds of alarm—"an attack from the causeway." But an attack by what, by whom? Had the Crusaders turned on their allies? Belynda doubted that—it was not likely, not while Zystyl held the Stone of Command. But who was the new enemy?

The sage-ambassador felt a tug on her hands, which remained bound behind her. Perhaps she would die now— fortunate to be killed quickly at the onset of battle, spared the anguish she had just seen inflicted on the Knight Templar. She froze, waiting for the cut of a knife, the blow of some blunt weapon.

"This way! Quickly!"

The voice in her ear was no Delver. Instead, she recognized the sound of her companion—Darann had found her! Belynda's arms came free as the dwarfwoman somehow unfastened the chain, allowing the freed prisoner to stumble back. Expecting an alarm, the sage-ambassador saw that the Unmirrored seemed fully occupied responding to their leader's commands. Hand in hand, the two women darted away from Zystyl, picking their way past the blind, milling dwarves, making for the escape promised by a nearby doorway.

"We've got to attack!" Karkald said, frenziedly speaking to Natac. "Fight our way into their pavilion, right now! It's the only chance she's got!"

"If you won't lead the charge, I will!" Tamarwind added, his face twisted by anguish and fear.

"That's enough of that!" Natac snapped. "Yes, we will charge—but let's do it right!"

"Hurry!" cried the dwarf, leaping down the stairs. Natac followed him and quickly found Gallupper.

"Yes, Warrior Natac?" said the centaur, with a crisp salute.

"Your mobile batteries—I want you to wheel them to the edge of the terrace, and start shooting. Punch a hole in those Crusaders lined up over there. Rawknuckle!"

"Yes?" The giant was there, with two dozen of his fellows. They were bandaged and battered, but their grim expressions and ready weapons clearly indicated their willingness to attack.

"As soon as the batteries have cleared a path, I want you to charge into the breach. The rest of us will be right behind—but you need to try and get to the pavilion. Belynda and Darann are in there. We're going to try and bring them out!"

"It will be a pleasure," promised the big warrior, his voice an anticipatory growl. "You can count on us."

"General Natac! Look at this! You've got to see!"

The cry came from one of the lookouts still on the balcony overhead. Seeing that his troops were moving into position for the attack, Natac raced up the stairs and looked over the teeming plaza, past the awnings and buildings of the enemy pavilion, to the causeway beyond.

"What is that?" Natac asked, squinting into the distance.

A column of warriors, sunlight glinting off their steel caps and metal breastplates, was marching across the causeway. They seemed to be emerging from the Metal Tunnel, far away on the mainland, and the file was so long that it clearly included many thousands of warriors. His first thought was that the Crusaders were receiving overwhelming reinforcements, but then—seeing the way the enemy troops scrambled to get a line of defense set across the end of the road—he deduced these were not additional allies of the invaders.

"Let us go now!" came the plea from below. He looked down to see Gallupper rearing, pawing the pavement and snorting eagerly.

Natac looked across the front of his army, and knew that the Goddess—or someone—was granting them a unique opportunity. The newcomers were attacking the enemy rear, throwing the large army into utter confusion.

"Bugler—sound the charge!" he cried.

And the Nayvian army surged forward.

Darann and Belynda moved silently through a narrow corridor. The commotion from the rooms beyond was as loud as ever. Delvers and Crusaders hastening to take up defensive positions, to prevent the new attackers from entering the pavilion. Already they could hear the clash of weapons, the shouts of battle as savage melees raged to all sides. A dozen steps later the two women reached a wooden screen which gave them the chance to see into the main hall.

Zystyl's voice rose above the din, shouting orders, calling for reinforcements at the gate. They could see him standing on a table, directing troops this way and that, sometimes calling out his orders, other times conveying commands with those bizarre nonverbal thoughts. Many giants hastened to follow an order in response to the arcane's gesture, and Darann shook her head. "I'm astonished they'll obey him!"

"It's because of the stone," Belynda said in a whisper, pointing to the gem clutched in the arcane's fist. "The power makes his word very difficult to ignore."

"Then we should take that stone!" Darann declared with

a sense of finality. "Do you still have your knife?"

Belynda shook her head. "They took it while I was a prisoner."

"I owe that bastard a good, deep cut," the dwarfwoman said grimly. "When I make my move, try and pull the stone out of his hand."

The sage-ambassador found that she was trembling, but she nodded quick agreement. Darann continued down the corridor until they came to a door leading into the great hall.

Slowly, soundlessly, the dwarfwoman pushed open the portal. Delvers milled around a dozen paces away, but the Unmirrored were focused on Zystyl, apparently ignorant of the intrusion. The arcane climbed down from the table, clomping urgently, ordering his troops to rally. His rolling gait took him within ten feet of the door where the two women were watching.

Darann rushed forward and Belynda came right behind. Zystyl turned, nostrils flaring in alarm, but by then the dwarfwoman's knife was slashing toward his face. He fell back with a shriek, hands flailing, and Belynda saw the gold chain flash. She grabbed it and pulled, and the Stone of Command was in her hand.

The dagger glanced across the arcane's nostrils and he tumbled to the floor and scuttled, crablike, away from the women. Other dwarves moved in, forming a protective circle, instinctively gathering to their injured leader.

"Let's get out of here!" Belynda hissed, as Darann hesitated, obviously ready to pursue the wounded dwarf. But finally, reluctantly, the dwarfwoman turned and accompanied the sage-ambassador toward the wide gate and the bright daylight beyond.

They darted past a Delver who apparently sensed their presence and lashed out with his dagger. The dwarfwoman stabbed with her own blade and, with a groan, the Blind One fell back. A moment later they were outside, facing a long column of warriors marching off the Metal Causeway.

"Who are they?" Belynda asked, as she saw the metal-armored warriors surging onto the plaza.

"They look like . . . no, it's impossible!" Darann gasped, then shouted in delight. "It's my own people, the Seers of Axial—come here from the First Circle!"

Each of the mobile batteries cast a single silvery sphere, the balls bouncing across the paving stones, rolling into the rank of Crusader elves who formed a barrier before the Nayvian onslaught. Knocking some of the elves out of the way, the spheres abruptly ruptured, spilling a spray of white liquid fire across everything within a dozen feet of the erupting missile. The flames were brilliant, difficult to watch even in bright daylight.

"Now—go!" shouted Natac.

Rawknuckle had already anticipated the command, responding instantly by leading his giants in a rush toward the elves who were scattering away from the lethal fires. Wounds and fatigue were forgotten as these veterans attacked with a fury that stunned and terrified their enemies.

Natac came behind, leading his whole army, riding a wave of savage joy, propelled by thousands of voices joining in a ground-shaking roar. Goblins whooped, gnomes cheered, and more fire bombs clattered and burst as the mobile batteries fired again. The warrior's steel sword felt hungry in his hand, and he was ready to kill, braced for the shock of imminent battle.

But instead, the enemy troops scattered, breaking away even before the first shock of combat. Many of the Crusaders threw down their weapons and raised their hands, pleading for mercy. Others simply ran away, vanishing into the pavilion, along the city streets, or even splashing into the lake. Natac stopped before two Crusader elves who were looking around in confusion. They stood numb and

silent as he took away their swords, and even as he ran on
they stayed in place, like heavy sleepers awakening from a
long nightmare.

"Papa!" Darann threw her arms around the shoulders of
a burly, gray-bearded dwarf. Belynda found herself
crying tears of delight as she watched the reunion, saw the
rest of the Seer Dwarves pursuing the Delvers who frantically sought shelter in the tunnels under the Mercury Terrace.

Other Seers were looking around in wonder, or coming
up to greet the woman from the First Circle. "These are
my brothers!" Darann declared, delightedly hugging two
muscular warriors who crushed her in a return embrace.
The sage-ambassador received a rib-cracking hug from her
friend's father, and only barely heard the snatches of rapid
explanation.

"Axial wasn't destroyed—just cut off by a cave-in? I
knew it!"

". . . Delvers, here?"

"And we're here, too! Karkald—Papa, he's a hero! He
brought coolfyre to Nayve, and showed the elves how to
make batteries! We'd have lost the war without him."

"We found the message left by you both," the patriarch
said. His eyes narrowed. "Your husband is well, then . . .
he survived . . . ?"

"He's alive, somewhere over there," Darann exclaimed
breathlessly. Already the Nayvian troops were coming into
view, rushing through the pavilion, rounding up the confused Crusaders who had lost all inclination to fight. "Karkald!"

The dwarf rushed up to them, his eyes frantic. "Darann!
By the Goddess, I was so afraid . . . I thought . . ." He
couldn't complete his thought, instead wrapping his wife in
a long-armed embrace.

"Ahem . . . Darann tells me you're something of a hero." The gray-bearded veteran spoke awkwardly, but his pride was obvious.

"No," Karkald said sincerely. "Not really . . . it's your girl, here. She's the *real* hero!"

Belynda, holding the Stone of Command, uttered a silent prayer to the Goddess, thanking her for the victory. Then she went to look for Tamarwind.

The tunnel led down, and Zystyl led the remnants of his force into the cool blackness. It was a narrow passage, but for now it promised escape.

"There are wells and mineshafts here, lord!" declared one of his underlings. "Routes the sun-lovers would never dare to follow."

"Very well—keep going," declared the arcane. Around him were the remnants of his army, but he could tell from the sounds and smells, and from the deeper auras of fury and despair, that many thousands of the Unmirrored still survived. "We shall seek escape in the tunnels under the Fourth Circle."

And later, he would plan for revenge.

Natac and Karkald watched the Darken Hour settle over the lake. The crest of the distant hills still glowed bright even as the valleys, the streets and byways of the city, fell into thickening shadow. The two old veterans, joined by a shared sense of melancholy and reflection, had climbed to the top of the tallest battle tower, where they could look over Circle at Center and so much of Nayve.

Sounds of revelry reached them from the terrace, where the enemy's pavilion had been torn down and thousands of elves, goblins, dwarves, giants, centaurs, and humans mixed in a frenzied whirl of dancing. Natac had seen Tamarwind and Belynda gliding like soaring birds, while Darann and Karkald had swung each other about with acrobatic enthusiasm.

"I'm thinkin' I might be going back to the Greens," Rawknuckle said after a period of comfortable silence. "I kind of miss the forests, you know . . . and the quiet."

Natac nodded. He looked across the lake, toward the hilltop were he had once found something like a home. That place had no appeal now—it was instead a storehouse of haunting memories, physical reminders of the sorrow and misery that had come to this world with him.

"What about you?" the giant asked softly. "Going anywhere special?"

"No," replied the warrior from Tlaxcala. "I think I'll be here forever."

---⟨∞⟩---

Epilogue

The small village lay on the western shore of a great inland sea. The horizon-spanning lake was full of sweet, fresh water, home to trout and sturgeon, fertile feeding grounds for the two hundred people who dwelled in the long wooden lodges, who survived by the bounty of the lake and forest. They were part of a tribe calling themselves the Winnebago, and they were a clan of the vast nation known as the Algonquin.

Life and death had been experienced by these people, on this lake, for many generations. Mysteries had been pondered, discoveries made, and always fathers and mothers had tried to make the existence of their offspring just a little easier, a little safer and softer, than had been their own. Rites of many kinds had been practiced, and if none could claim to ultimate knowledge of the supernatural, people knew many rituals that made them feel better, and added a sense of continuity to their lives.

Now a man was embarked upon such a celebration. The proud father carried the little bundle of his newborn daughter, walking through the forest night until he came to a high bluff overlooking the water. The babe, a scarce six hours old, slumbered against his chest while he stared out at the freshwater sea, seeing the dark and misty surface slowly lighten, bluing in anticipation of the slowly rising run. For a time he sat and watched rosy dawn pale the sky, relishing the feel of the tiny body against his chest. Hopes and aspirations entered his mind, and he let them float away . . . for now, it was enough that there was new life, and that he could feel joy.

When the rays of the sun sparkled off the treetops above him he stood, waiting patiently for the light to work its way lower. The ritual had a meaning that was lost to him, but he took comfort from the clear skies, from the dazzling sunlight over his head, that would warm and welcome his child.

He raised his daughter high, and allowed the sunlight to illuminate the child before the rays fell upon himself. She yawned sleepily, then opened an eye of pure, bright violet— a shade that darkened to purple in the gleam of daylight. She smiled for a moment, cooed peacefully, and then the eyelid slipped shut. Again she slept.

"Welcome to the world, my little girl," said the father. He held her still for a moment, and then turned back onto the forest trail, to the village, and the tribe and the rich promise of new life.